The Color
of Broken

Praise for *The Color of Broken*

The Color of Broken has reached #1 on Amazon, multiple times, and was *Longlisted for "Adaptable - from book to the screen" (2021)*.

"I just finished reading The Color of Broken. I read it in 2 sittings (only stopping the first because of the onset of a migraine). It was beautiful, and powerful. I lost myself in it, and forgot that I was reading, which only happens with the very best of stories. As a fellow MD sufferer I truly appreciated Fleur's depiction of the illness, but it was Yolande and her PTSD which hooked me from beginning to end. I, too, suffer from anxiety and panic disorders, and your portrayal of Yolande's brokenness and fear was masterful. Thank you for this extraordinary experience!"

"Beautiful story... on so many levels there's a connection there for everyone - a must read!"

"I am 3/4 the way thru it and love/hate it. Love the book and all it stands for, hate the book for all of the bad/sad memories it is bringing back when my Meniere's was really awful. Everyone who has or knows someone with Meniere's should read this book!"

"Yolande and her PTSD struggles were compelling and had me hooked from the start."

"I would single this book out as one of my favorite books, ever!"

"My hubby is reading the book now too! I am so pleased. He got to page 50 and remarked he felt like crying."

"It's a wonderful story, you won't be able to put it down, one of the best books I've ever read (and I've read stacks lol)"

"I am in process of re-writing my will and looking into bequests and since buying your book have put them on my list. Not formalised yet but at least in my papers for people to find."

"I'm at the very end. I'm going to be sad when it's over."

"I finished The Color of Broken. I was crying throughout. Very good."

"I loved my book, I've read it twice! It's now one of my most treasured possessions."

"I just finished The Color of Broken, and I just want to say congratulations on writing one of the best books I have read in a long time. I'm an avid reader so I've read a lot of books , and I could not put it down. I laughed, cried, loved all of the characters. A wonderful storyline, characters which you fall in love with, truly an incredible book - congratulations, you are very very talented x"

"My mother never believed I had MD. She thought I was faking the symptoms. I gave her your book and she came back to me begging for forgiveness. Thank you from the bottom of my heart!"

"Love my book - will keep it for ever!"

"I've nearly finished it Amelia, and it's BLOODY fabulous!! Long time since i enjoyed a book this much. My partner started reading before me the bugger so I had to wait till he had finished(his special way of being supportive). He said (as a non sufferer) that from his outside perspective, the portrayal of MD symptoms was fantastic."

"I loved your book, please do a follow up I'd love to know if Andi & Xander end up together too lol x"

"The story captures you from the first sentence and keeps you entertained with passion and hope for the future. It shares the very real struggles of life with Meniere's and the hope we have for a cure. A must read!"

"Could not put this book down."

"I was hooked from the beginning of this book. I'll be reading it a second time."

Adult Fiction Book
Published in Australia 2018
by Lilly Pilly Publishing
lillypillypublishing@outlook.com

Lilly Pilly
PUBLISHING

NATIONAL
LIBRARY
OF AUSTRALIA

A catalogue record for this book is available from the National Library of Australia

https://www.nla.gov.au/trove

ISBN: 978-0-6480846-6-2 (print book)
ISBN: 978-0-6480846-3-1 (eBook)

2nd Edition, 2021

Cover design by Lilly Pilly Publishing
Cover image: 123rf artlana Image ID: 31489766

Content warning: anxiety, panic attacks, blood, PTSD, physical assault, suicide attempt

Medical disclaimer:
This book is not intended to be a substitute for the medical advice of a licensed physician. The reader should consult with their doctor in any matters relating to his/her health.

Suicide/Crisis Disclaimer:
Suicide is a difficult topic to talk about. The events in this book are fictional.
The number one cause for suicide is untreated depression.
Suicide is never the answer. Getting help is the answer.
Suicide is preventable, and if you are feeling suicidal, you must get help.
Please visit Suicide.org for a list for worldwide numbers to call
http://www.suicide.org/international-suicide-hotlines.html
or 1-800-SUICIDE or 1-800-784-2433
Suicide is never the answer. Getting help is the answer.

*This book has been written with
deep compassion and many tears,
for those who live with the
incurable condition of Meniere's disease.*

A cure will be found, until that time,
take my hand ...

Amelia Grace is the pen name of Julieann Wallace, a bestselling multi-published author whose *#8wordstory* was chosen by the Queensland Writers Center to be featured on the back of their business cards in 2018.

She resides in Australia, and was diagnosed with the incurable (for now) Meniere's disease in 1995. In her quest to defeat the violent unpredictable vertigo, profound hearing loss, and relentless, impossibly loud tinnitus, she chose to have her balance cells destroyed in 2004 to stop the vertigo, relearning to walk again. In 2020, Julieann regained her hearing with the gift of a Cochlear Implant.

Prior to her career as a writer, Julieann was an educator with Education Queensland (Australia) for 25 years, and was nominated twice for the National Excellence in Teaching Awards. She now teaches in the Arts Faculty at a Secondary School, encouraging students to use the Arts to be change-makers, and a voice for others through use of the power of written words and visual art.

Julieann is a self-confessed tea ninja, chocoholic, and papercut survivor, and tries not to scare her cat, Claude Monet, with her terrible cello playing.

The Color
of Broken

Amelia Grace

Lilly Pilly
PUBLISHING

Chapter One

ather, scrub, rinse ... lather, scrub, rinse—and breathe.
My hands moved fast. Obsessively fast.
Lather, scrub ... lather, rinse ... lather, scrub, rinse—
and breathe. Just breathe!

Lather, scrub, rinse ... lather, scrub, rinse—that's better, and
breathe.

Horrific, painful memories exploded around me.

I squeezed my eyes shut. Tight. 'STOP!' I shouted. 'JUST,' my breath hiccuped, 'stop!' I whispered, and turned off the tap.

Emotional turmoil spilled through me. And guilt. Crippling, excruciating guilt. My insides clenched with dread and I leaned over the basin, panting, struggling to fight off the need to vomit.

I lifted my right hand in front of my face and twisted it—over and back, over and back—checking for blood. It was insane. I knew there wasn't any blood. I wasn't even bleeding. But I couldn't get the abhorrent memory out of my head. The one where my blood dribbled down onto my hand before it trailed along my fingers and dropped to the rocks below, where Mia lay, twisted.

I started to shake as anxiety poisoned me, again. I clenched my teeth and turned on the tap once more, my urge to scream fading as I fell into rhythm ...

Lather, scrub, rinse ... lather, scrub, rinse—and breathe.

Lather, scrub, rinse ... lather, scrub, rinse—and breathe.

Lather, scrub, rinse ... lather, scrub, rinse—

'Breathe ...' I told myself, '... in for a count of three ... and out for a count of five. You know how to deal with panic, Yolande. What do you need to say?' I closed my eyes. Gently this time. I wanted to cry but I couldn't.

I slid down the wall of the bathroom, the water still flowing from the tap. Maybe I should take my medication and be buried in the fog of the mind-numbing drugs.

I shook my head. No. I wanted to feel something, not nothing, despite my savage, suffocating flashbacks that penetrated me to the core.

Intense. Emotional. Exhausting.

'STOP!' I finally said.

Chapter Two

'Flowers, tea, coffee ... or books?' The words rolled off my tongue with a melodic sound. It felt like the millionth time I had said it. I sighed inwardly.

The tall, dark-haired man standing before me lifted his chin and looked down at me. He narrowed his green eyes and loosened his tie. My skin prickled, and I stiffened.

'Flowers, and ... chocolates,' he said, his voice like velvet. He blinked once. He was the color of pure red, like a high-performance sports car—fast and dangerous.

I watched him with caution. He was too smooth. 'For an anniversary?' I asked.

'An apology,' he said, blinking on the word apology, and in the moment afterward, blinking multiple times. *Liar ...*

Oh, I mouthed. *Of course it would be an apology for his type.* 'How big an apology?'

He hung his head and smirked. Conflicting words and action. Warning bells rang.

'That bad?' *And good?*

'Worse!' he said.

Had he been unfaithful? 'Do you still love her?'

He narrowed his eyes at me again. 'She's my wife, my life ... I need her,' he choked on his words.

Yes, he'd been unfaithful ... 'Then you need a bouquet of sincere apology. Do you want them delivered?'

'Yes.'

'No!' I said, a little louder than I intended. I gazed around at the people in the flower store, looking at me. I lowered my voice. 'The personal touch is best. Give them to her yourself. It will mean ... *more.*'

He nodded. 'You're right.'

Of course, I'm right. I knew a thousand reasons why men gave flowers to women! 'Would you like coffee while I prepare the best apology you have ever made?'

He pushed his hands into his pockets and looked to his right at the florist café where our barista stood. 'Sure.'

I watched as he walked over to Darcy and ordered.

Do not judge. Everyone makes mistakes ... but was it a mistake? Or had he just been caught?

I went to the workbench of flower imagination, tucked a stray lock of hair behind my ear then busied myself preparing his order—white tulips and soft pink hyacinth with a few green leaves here and there, the green stems wrapped with a gorgeous pale pink ribbon. I added exquisite hand-made chocolates. I placed the bouquet and chocolate into a white-lined gift bag to amplify their magnificence, then inhaled the scent of the hyacinths—floral, light, delicate, old-fashioned, sweet, sensual, fresh—spring-like. I hoped it wasn't more than he deserved.

I leaned over to cut a length of ribbon to tie to the handle of the bag to finish my work of flower art. When I looked up he was standing in front of me, eyes on my chest.

A shiver ran down my spine and I straightened at once. I

pulled the top of my work dress and apron higher. *Bastard.*

I pushed the ribbon to the side. I had done enough for this person with the XY chromosomes. Y, mathematically speaking, is the unknown. And that is why I can *never* trust an unknown male. Y also equaled "why?". The answer is almost entirely explained with the treatment of women as sexual objects, by *some* men, or their need to feel powerful because they are pitiful cowards. *Bastard.*

I picked up his bouquet of apology and walked to the sales desk. He followed behind. Too closely.

'Cash or card?' I raised an unimpressed eyebrow at him.

'Card,' he said. His eyes widened. 'Make that cash. How much?' His words came in a flurry.

Hmmm. An untraceable transaction. What tangled web is he weaving? 'How much do you have?'

He opened his wallet. 'Seventy-five bucks and a few coins.'

I shook my head. 'You'll have to use your card. It's eighty-five bucks for this special, apologetic order, sir. It's imbued with a thousand apologies and a melody of love,' I said, ready to puke on him.

He took a deep breath. 'I'll give you $75.00 now, and bring the remainder later.' He reached forward to pick up the flowers.

I pushed the flowers to the side, away from him. 'Since you're such a lovely man who wants to win over his wife's heart, I'd like to say yes, but store policy won't allow me to. I'm sorry, sir ...' I said, trying to rein in my sarcasm as I held out my hand for the card.

He searched through each of his suit pockets, tapping each one. He paused, then pulled out ten dollars, and smirked at me like he had just won the lottery. He handed over the money.

'Thank you, and ... good luck with your apology.' I tilted my head to the side with a fake, sweet smile, and gave him the flowers and chocolates. My stomach bubbled with nausea filled with repulsive bile.

The moment he stepped out of the shop I let out an exasperated breath. I looked down to the top of my dress that my grandmother had chosen as the florist's store uniform. Part of my chest scar was visible. *Damn!* I repositioned my dress and shook my head, hating that fact that I had been damaged for life—three years ago when I was twenty-two, on that terrible day of the scars. My eyes burned.

The tapping sound of Gram's shoes became louder. I watched her approach me with a spring in her step. She was the color of light pink—love, affection and romance ... full of peace, hence her flower store. When she stopped before me, I plastered a pretend smile on my face. I didn't want her to see my sadness.

'That tulip and hyacinth bouquet was beautiful, Andi. And a nice fifty-dollar sale to end the day!'

'Pity he didn't read the sign.' I pointed to the flower menu behind me that clearly listed personal flower art for $50.00. 'I charged him eighty-five bucks. Fifty for the flowers for him, and thirty-five, revenge for his wife.' I smiled at Gram. This time it was genuine.

'Hmmm. Maybe I can make a florist out of my steel-capped boot wearing granddaughter after all?'

I looked down at my brown steel-capped safety boots. They didn't match any of the floral dresses I had to wear as a uniform for Flowers for Fleur, but they guaranteed me a powerful, painful kick to the groin of any man to protect myself.

I removed my apron and hung it on the hook on the wall behind the sales desk. I kissed Gram's cheek and gave her a warm embrace. 'See you tomorrow when the sun peeks at the new day and whispers, "Good morning!"'

Chapter Three

I stopped at the mulberry-colored , 1950s Cruiser bicycle in front of Gram's flower store, panting. The bike rested against the off-white, bagged brick wall with flowers in the front basket. Today it was roses, in a color I had never seen before— pale pink with a tinge of light orange. The new days' sun rays bathed them in a golden light, accentuating their magical color. Their presence reminded me of two things: Gram was here; and I was late.

I took seven steps forward and leaned into the white French door to push it open. A sharp glint caught my eye. I looked down, and there on the step was a shard of glass. And blood. Bright red blood. *Just like that day ...*

I sucked in a sharp breath through my clenched teeth and tensed. My heart rate spiked as my head began to swirl. I stumbled into the store with a gut full of nausea, feeling like I was going to pass out. I ran to the powder room and leaned over the basin, panting, struggling to fight off the need to vomit.

'Breathe ...' I said to myself, '... in for a count of three ... and out for a count of five. You know how to deal with panic, Yolande. What do you need to say?' I closed my eyes. I wanted to cry but I couldn't. Not here.

'Stop,' I said, 'then what?' Talking to myself was one of my coping mechanisms. It was also a sign of genius, apparently. But I beg to differ. 'Distraction,' I said.

I turned on the tap and started to wash my hands under the water with soap—

Lather, scrub, rinse ... lather, scrub, rinse—and breathe.

Lather, scrub, rinse ... lather, scrub, rinse—and breathe.

Lather, scrub, rinse ... lather, scrub, rinse—

I knew there was no blood on my hands, but I couldn't get the image out of my head: the image of my blood dribbling down onto my hand before it trailed along my fingers and dropped to the rocks below, where Mia lay, twisted.

I turned off the tap and lifted my right hand in front of my eyes. I twisted it; over and back, over and back, time and time again, making sure there wasn't any blood. It was insane. I knew there was no blood. I wasn't even bleeding.

I clenched my teeth and turned on the tap again.

Lather, scrub, rinse ... and breathe.

Lather, scrub, rinse—

A knock sounded on the powder room door and I stilled.

'Andi, are you okay?' It was Darcy's deep voice. Beautiful Darcy. The tall, red-bearded barista who saw all that went on in the store from his café throne. He never missed a beat. He was the color of blue, like a clear sky, giving a sense of peace and calm where the world was indeed a wonderful place.

I turned off the tap, cleared my throat and caught my sob. 'W-whose blood is that?!' I called.

'What blood?' he asked.

'At the front doors. Did you see it?'

'Nope. I came in through the back door, like I always do.'

There was silence between us. I swallowed the contents of my stomach back down to where it belonged.

'Do you want me to clean it up?' he asked.

I took a deep breath. I had to find my courage and step out of my comfort zone and confront my fear.

Step boldly, Yolande!

'Nope. I've got it,' I said, sounding more confident than I felt. I squeezed my eyes shut, turned my head to the side and cussed. I walked into a cubicle and flushed the toilet to cover up my act of obsessively washing my hands. Then I turned on the tap again and washed my hands one last time, like a normal person would.

I stepped outside the powder room and stumbled, almost tripping over Darcy. He lifted his red-bearded chin and looked down at me with concerned eyes. 'Just say the word, and I'll clean it up for you.'

I blew air between my lips, thankful that he didn't say the "b" word. 'What?! And unleash me in your kitchen to bake cupcakes while you clean?' Humor was the best way to deal with it; skirting around the problem.

'You're right. The customers would never come back.' He gave me a whimsical smile.

I raised an eyebrow at him and turned on the heel of my steel-capped work boots. I strolled over to greet Gram at the workbench of flower imagination before I dealt with the crime scene at the front of the store.

'Morning, Gram. You look wonderful today!' My voice was bright as I covered up my panicked state. I didn't want her to know about my anxiety attack.

'Thank you, dear. I left my bed to thwart off a spinning session ... with success, I might add!' Her sparkly blue eyes smiled at me, the color accentuated by the aged-blonde color of her short, wavy hair. They were two things I shared with my grandmother—blue eyes and wavy blonde hair, except, I had dyed my hair dark-brown after that terrible day of the scars.

'Well done,' I said. 'It's good to have you here. Fridays are crazy!' I pressed my lips together. I sounded like I was a permanent fixture of the flower store, not someone who had come to help.

Gram stopped like she was frozen in time and stared wide-eyed at the bench, her body stiff.

'Are you okay, Gram?' I watched her with intent while a sizzle of anxiety ran through me.

'Sure,' she answered with a forced smile and a shaky voice. She kept her eyes focussed on one spot in front of her. She was lying. After a moment she relaxed and continued preparing the long-stemmed roses for delivery.

I frowned, keeping a careful eye on her. 'Did you see the blood outside?' I asked after a moment, and cleared my throat, internally wincing.

'There's blood?' Gram's eyebrows furrowed. She had *always* noticed everything.

'Yes ... and glass ... you're not well are you, Gr—'

'I'm fine!' Her words were curt and thumped me in the chest. This woman before me was not my grandmother! Gram was always kind and considerate. Beautiful. Inside and out. She was always the color of pink, overflowing with love. But she had suddenly changed. She was now red. Dark, irritated red.

I cleared my throat. 'Should we call the police about the blood, and perhaps a possible attempted break and enter?' I cleared my throat again to stop myself from melting into another panic attack at the thought of blood.

'I need to lie down. Do whatever you like?' she said, her voice lacking its usually vibrant energy.

Do whatever I like? No—no—no! My heart ached. Where did my grandmother go? Normally she would have fired off instructions left, right and center and the entire saga would be dealt with in an instant and forgotten.

Gram kept her head still and turned, slowly, her hands splayed out in the air like she was walking on a tight rope. I watched her as she took slow steps across the store, past the sales desk, and turned left, into her office.

My heart cried. How can an active, deliriously happy, loving and flamboyant woman change into a flat, emotionless person in an instant? Something was wrong. Very wrong.

My throat choked up. I looked over at Darcy. He was behind the coffee machine, polishing it. He made eye contact with me, then pressed his lips in a hard line and shook his head. My eyes burned.

'I'll have an Irish Coffee thanks, Darcy,' I called.

'At six in the morning?' He raised a sardonic eyebrow at me.

'You're right. Just give me the whiskey! I'll have the coffee later.' I sighed. I walked over to him and leaned on the counter. He smelled woody and spicy at once, making me feel safe.

'She only speaks to you like that. She puts on a brave performance for the rest of us.' Darcy looked up at me and raised his eyebrows as he poured a whiskey.

'Lucky me,' I said, my voice monotone. I lifted the glass to my lips. I felt the whiskey heat the back of my throat as I swallowed it, then it bloomed in my chest.

I closed my eyes and let out a deep breath. None of this situation was fair. Firstly, Gram was unwell, and secondly, I had to take leave from my career to help keep the blooming flowers alive! *Perhaps I should give them the kiss of death with my blood, just like …*

I brushed my hand over my forehead. 'Hold the fort while I clean up the evidence to who knows what happened out the front.' The liquid courage of the whiskey was warmly welcomed by my highly anxious self. Self-medication.

'Sure,' Darcy said, watching me with cautious eyes.

I turned on the heel of my steel-capped work boots and went to collect the hydrogen peroxide, detergent, and a broom.

The blood led off in a trail. I followed it, looking but not looking, until it stopped at the curb. I pursed my lips and breathed through the nausea, then followed it back to the entrance of the store, looking but not looking. I peered at the closed sign on the door. It was red, like blood. And like the blood that once ran down my body and pooled at my feet. The blood that once dripped off my hand and landed on the side of my best friend's face.

I shuddered, and looked through the glass windows at the flowers to distract my mind to stop another anxiety meltdown. There, on Gram's workbench, were long-stemmed roses. Red. Like blood. Except ... someone was in love. Why did red roses signify love?

I cleared my throat and poured the mixture of cleaning fluids onto the trail of blood, looking but not looking. At least that way I couldn't see the red color anymore. I leaned into the broomstick and scrubbed. Hard.

After fifteen minutes I stopped and wiped the perspiration from my forehead. Not a trace of life-giving bodily fluid remained on the pavement, nor any glass. I hoped no one had died from their injury. I shuddered as the image of my best friend's hand flickered through my mind. It was covered in blood. My blood. I grimaced, picked up the cleaning products and entered the store.

I slowed my step when I saw Darcy standing outside Gram's office door. 'Can I get you anything, Mrs. Lawrence?'

The sound of muffled vomiting slithered under the door of her office. Darcy hung his head and squeezed his eyes shut.

'Please ... call ... Mr. Lawrence.' Gram's broken words came between sobs.

I rushed to the storeroom, off-loaded the cleaning implements, and ran to Gram's office. I touched Darcy's arm, 'Call Grampapa, please. And I've got this now. Thanks.'

Darcy ran his hand through his hair and frowned, then turned and walked to the café serving counter and picked up the phone.

I hesitated before I pushed on the door and entered with caution, leaving it slightly ajar. My heart dropped. Gram was on the floor, lying on her side. Vomit was pooled in front of her.

She stared straight ahead, keeping her body still. Like death. A memory flash tore through me and I held my breath, then I remembered Mia moving her arm, and I breathed again.

I hurried towards Gram and kneeled in front of her. 'Gram,' I whispered, panic seizing me.

'Get out of my line of sight ... NOW!' she yelled.

I gasped and moved as fast as I could.

Gram vomited. Violently.

I put my trembling hand over my mouth. 'I'm sorry,' I whispered.

'Please ... just hold my hand ... *take my hand*,' Gram said, her voice barely audible.

'But I need to clean up the floo—'

'I don't care about the friggin' floor! Please ... just ... *take my hand*.' Gram started sobbing. Deep, gut-wrenching sobs.

I swallowed the lump in my throat. 'Are you spinning, Gram? Is that what's making you sick?'

'Yes ... the room is spinning around me and it won't stop ... it's so fast, Landi, anti-clockwise ... *so* very fast ...' Gram's lips turned pale and she started to perspire. I shut my eyes at the sound she made before she vomited hard, once again.

The door swung open and I looked up. Grampapa stood there, his mouth open. He moved quickly and kneeled behind Gram with a gentleness. 'Fleur, my darling. How long have you been on the floor this time?'

This time? How many times had Grampapa found her like this?

'It feels like forever ... please ... make it stop! I can't do this anymore! I don't want to keep spinning for three hours.' Gram's voice was low and rough, not at all the gentle and warm voice everyone knew.

I looked at Gramps. He stopped his convulsive cry with his hand over his mouth.

I shook my head. This ... this scene ... was heartbreaking. Grampapa was always incredibly strong and calm. Nothing made him cry. Ever. I held my breath while I watched him. He was beyond anguished.

I watched as he took a shaky, deep breath, then started to sing. Perhaps it was his way to soothe Gram when she was in the midst of a vertigo attack. And, I suspected, to soothe his breaking heart. His glorious tenor voice filled the room and the flower store. I looked down as Gram sobbed—loud, ugly sobs that made the world a very dark place.

And I ran. I weaved my way through the store, my heavy steel-capped work boots protesting against the floor, waking the flower buds from their intense sleep of peace.

I rushed out the back door, leaned against the brick wall and squeezed my eyes shut. Watching Gram suffer was unbearable. And I hated it with every fiber of my being. *If she was an animal,* I thought, *they would've euthanised her by now.*

The back door squeaked and Grampapa's singing oozed outside. *Ave Maria.*

I glanced at Darcy as he walked towards me. He stopped before me and winced. 'I'm sorry, Andi, but customers will be here soon. We must keep going ... for your gram.' He reached up and pulled the top of my dress over the scar on my chest.

I sucked in a short breath and pressed my hand over my long, ugly scar. My scar of violence. My forever reminder.

Damn this dress style Gram had chosen as a uniform! I hated it!

My throat tightened. 'Sure. Just give me a moment.' I turned my face away from him. I hated that he knew I had a scar on my chest. Did he know how it came to be? Had Gram told him anything about it? Did he know where it stopped on my chest?

Darcy placed a hand on my shoulder. 'She's lucky to have you.' He turned, opened the back door and walked into the store. The sound of Grampapa's voice flowed out, reminding me of the trauma happening behind the closed office door. Then stopped.

I straightened my back and caught a tear on my eye lashes. I had a mountain of jobs to do, and thanks to the blood on the pavement and my panic attack, I was way behind.

I opened the back door to the sound of Grampapa's classically trained operatic voice, walked to Gram's workbench of flower imagination, and called out to Darcy, 'Tea, if I may ...'

Darcy gave me a crooked smile and a nod. He was a good man. He was now the color of brown instead of sky blue; brown like warm chocolate: delicious, welcoming, calming and satisfying. He was reliability and comfort personified.

I have, what some people would call a peculiarity, except, I don't call it that—I call it a *gift*. I see people as color s. Metaphorically. I have the uncanny ability to assign a color to a person based on my intuition, or observation of their behaviour or words. When I look at a person, I don't just see a body; I see a body with a color, like a mist above and behind their head. That color is never set; it can change, depending on their emotion and mood. I have what they call, synesthesia.

My gift has been my beacon of safety since I was seven. Except once, just once, I was fooled by it, or rather by the effect of alcohol that changed their color, and my life ...

I opened Gram's order book. There were nine orders due to be created and delivered this morning before I processed and cut the new flower arrivals, and arranged fragrant floral bouquets to display outside the store.

I pulled the top of my dress up to cover my chest scar, irritated and unsure of my ability to become an insightful and successful "florist". For Gram.

Darcy placed a teacup and saucer onto the recycled timber workbench. He had added a heart-shaped chocolate. I choked-up, then walked around the workspace and pulled him into a hug. 'Thank you. Your kindness is beautiful.'

He stepped back from me and nodded. He was one of those quiet observative types. A good problem solver. He'd kick the arse of any psych doctor.

With the sound of Grampapa's voice filling the flower store, I smoothed down my apron, checked that my scar was covered, and got on with the pre-opening duties.

At least she had put the flowers into the bicycle basket this morning, I thought when I placed the final bucket of flowers onto the white-washed ladder outside the store. She was fanatical about it. The day wasn't right unless there were flowers in the bicycle basket!

"This is our florist signature, Andi. It's not
Flowers for Fleur without flowers in the bicycle basket!"

I had heard those words one hundred and one times. Probably more. I smiled and looked at her flower choice for today. The new rose colors were exquisite—pale pink with a tinge of light orange. I touched my nose to a rose bud and inhaled with high expectation, but was sorely disappointed. No fragrance. I pulled a sad face, then frowned when I saw a torn-off, folded, brown piece of paper that had been pushed in between the floral arrangement, barely noticeable. I pulled it out and opened it.

Dear Flowers for Fleur,

How much is the bicycle?
I would like to acquire it.

The name and phone number was washed out. I raised my eyebrows. Fat chance the person had of "acquiring" Gram's bicycle. It was a family heirloom. And I was seventh in line to get it. Fat chance I had of "acquiring" Gram's bicycle as well! I tucked the note into my pocket. I would write a reply, on a *nice* piece of floral paper, and leave it in the basket for the person tomorrow.

Grampapa's singing continued. And when the doors opened at 8.30am, he was still singing. My chest ached. For Gram.

I watched the customers as they entered the store. They slowed their walk when they heard Grampapa's operatic voice, listened and then smiled, before they continued. The café was buzzing with people, drawn in from the streets of Tarrin. Pre-made flower bouquets were a hot item, as well as tea and coffee. Was it because of Grampapa's well known tenor voice?

At 10am, the singing stopped. It was a sign that Gram's vertigo had ended. Gramps poked his head out the door. 'Any customers, Andi?' he asked in a voice that was barely audible.

I looked around. There was the lull in customers after the morning rush.

'Only five, in the café,' I said.

'I'm taking Gram home ... I don't want anyone to see her this way.'

I looked around again. 'You're good to go.' I frowned as my heart ached. I didn't want Gram to suffer anymore.

Within a minute, Grampapa opened the door wide. He disappeared and returned with Gram in his arms. Her hand was over her eyes and she looked washed out and ragged, like she had run a marathon. I held my breath while Gramps walked to the rear exit of the store, then rushed over and pushed the door open and followed him to the car.

I opened the passenger door and Gramps placed Gram onto the seat carefully, like she was a delicate piece of fine china—precious and breakable. He secured her seat belt before he took quick steps around to the driver's side of the car.

Gram kept her hand over her eyes. She didn't even acknowledge me. She was crying, softly, and my heart broke at the tragic sound.

Gramps hesitated before sitting in the car. He looked at me. 'I've cleaned Gram's office. Everything is in a rubbish bag. Put it in the bin and place some peonies in the room for when she returns.'

I placed my hand over my weeping heart, and watched as Gramps drove off. Life sucks. Why do bad things happen to good people?

I twisted my fingers together and held back my tears, then returned to the store with my happy-face mask. No one would see the sadness underneath. I had perfected it in the months after that day of the terrible scars.

I stopped mid-step when I saw Charlotte standing behind the sales desk. She always came in at short notice if we needed extra hands on deck. She reached up and retrieved her apron then turned to me. 'Mr. Lawrence called me in.' She shook her head and sadness fell over her beautiful face. 'I'm sorry your gram isn't well.'

'Me too. Whatever it is, she'll recover soon. I'd say it's just an ear thing. Antibiotics will help.'

I walked over to the workbench. I ran my hand over the smooth timber. It was handmade by Gramps from recycled timber forty years ago. This is where Gram collected her creativity and put amazing bouquets of flowers together. Flowers for Fleur was *the* store to go to for blooms. Gram had worked hard to build a remarkable reputation over the last fifty years.

Hmmm ... the township of Tarrin. It was an interesting place. It was also where I was born, twenty-five years ago. It had a country town feel to it, but was a hive of activity like you would find in a metropolitan area. There was nothing but locally owned shops, plus one tallish building that was fifteen storeys high: a grand hotel. Weird.

The township was designed in the shape of a square with a splendid park in the middle, and was central to places that branched out from it—a hospital, a large university, two massive housing estates, a police station, two schools, a creative arts precinct with a massive performance theater , as well as a community hall. Each of those places were fifteen minutes' drive from the town center. And it was always bursting with visitors.

Tarrin was strange in an indefinable way. It seemed to be a little bit "more" of everything—more sunny, more rainy, more hot, more cold. The sky was more blue and the plants were more green, the flowers more colorful. It was like you had stepped inside a bubble of heightened awareness of the space around you.

And it was never dull in Flowers for Fleur. All types of people came in for flowers, frequently, which is odd. Perhaps Gram imbued the flowers with a magical alluring potion ...

I opened Gram's "Orders and Deliveries" book and ran my finger down the list.

Darcy placed a café latte on the workbench for me.

I looked up from the book. 'Grazie,' I said, inhaling the heavenly aroma of the coffee beans. 'But whiskey would've been better ...' I was going to be busy for the entire day. But first, I had to do a crash course in flower arranging.

'Perhaps, but you don't want to look like Gram when she's having one of her attacks.' Darcy inclined his head to me.

I stilled. He was right. Gram did look somewhat drunk *if* she tried to walk while she was spinning, which, most of the time, she often could not walk at all while having a vertigo attack. She was completely debilitated.

My fingertips touched the switch to turn off the lights for the day. I remembered the reply note I had to write to the unknown hopeful purchaser of Gram's bicycle.

I returned to the workbench and cut off a piece of delicate floral paper to write on. I would put the note in the fresh flowers of the bicycle basket early tomorrow morning.

Dear ?

The bicycle is not for sale.

Regards,
Andi

Chapter Four

The mulberry-colored 1950s Cruiser bicycle leaned against the antique white storefront of Flowers for Fleur. The peonies in the front basket beamed their colorful happiness at everyone who ventured past. I leaned towards them to smell their scent—spicy and citrusy.

The bicycle was a good sign. Gram was back. Whatever had made her ill must have gone.

Maybe she had a bad case of food poisoning?

I pushed on the French doors and entered. Grampapa's singing filled the shop. I'm certain his voice made the plants grow better!

'Landi, good morning!' Gram said, her voice as bright as the new day. 'Did you see the Anna's Hummingbird flitting around the blue sage? Such a delightful creation.'

I took quick steps over to her, my work boots thumping on the floor with each step. I gave her a hug. 'Yes. I saw and *heard* the hummingbirds. Plural. Amazing! How are you feeling today?' Gram was the color of fuscia this morning, like helium-filled balloons at a pink birthday party infused with wishes, then released to freedom with happiness and expectation, rising above the hollow dramas of the earth.

'Never better. Help yourself to a cup of tea before you start on your job list.' Gram stopped and stared at me, for more than a moment of stillness. 'I'm so glad you're here.' Her voice had lost its joy and her color changed from fuscia to pale yellow, like butter that had started to melt in the hot sun.

Anxiety shot through me. Before she had a vertigo attack, she stared.

'Me too,' I said, sending up a silent prayer for her.

She moved again, like she had been in a freeze-frame and become unfrozen. 'I'll be fighting fit soon, and then you can go back to your flight simulators.' She smiled at me. Sort of. But not her usual Gram smile that infused the entire store with light that bloomed in your heart until it felt full with love.

'I know ... would you like tea as well?'

There was no reply.

'Gram. Would you like a cup of tea?'

She turned her head. 'Say it again, dear?'

'Would you like one of the many morning teas?'

'Oh no. I haven't had any tears this morning. It's a good day.'

I frowned, then smiled at her. *What an odd reply* ... I put my hand on her shoulder, so she turned and faced me. 'I'll get you a cup of tea, Gram.'

'Lovely, that would be nice.'

I walked over to the florist cafe. 'Morning, Darcy!'

He gave a slight smile through his red manicured beard. 'Tea?'

'Actually, I'm tempted to have coffee. That brew you're working on smells magnificent!' Darcy was back to the color of sky blue today—the color of peace and stability, trustworthiness.

'Thanks, Andi. I call this one the heart-starter. It's a new concoction. I'll make you one when you're struggling with energy this afternoon.' Darcy gave me an amused smile.

'Hmmm. A test subject! Count me in!' I gave him a thumbs

-up. His barista handiwork and baking were becoming famous in the township of Tarrin. The township of "more". Flowers for Fleur was not only *the* place to go to for flowers, but for hot beverages as well. Fortune rained down on Gram when she hired the good-looking, red-haired, hipster-bearded Darcy on that fateful day. 'Tea for Gram as well, please.'

I sat at a table and my tea soon arrived. I looked out the window while I savored the calming brew. It was early morning, and the main street was starting to come to life with shopkeepers opening stores.

When I finished my cup of tea, I collected my apron and commenced with the mundane daily jobs while Gram created bouquets of magnificence. The only consolation was that the time went quickly.

As I watered the plants on the sales desk, I saw the reply note I had written to the person who wanted to buy Gram's bicycle. I picked it up and went outside and placed it into the peonies in the basket on the bicycle, with hope that the note writer would see it.

I waved to the baker up the road before I returned to the store. I glanced over at Gram at the workbench, smiling as she worked on orders while Grampapa's voice filled every nook and cranny.

I looked at my pre-opening job list. I had gift-ware to unpack and price tags to add before they went on display, as well as having to sort through the chocolates and fudges Gram had ordered from Lily's Lollies, the locally owned candy store in Tarrin, as was the town policy.

I opened the double French doors at 8.30am to a multitude of "good mornings" and "hellos", and placed silver buckets of flowers outside for sale. People streamed through the doors and headed to Darcy to feed their morning tea and coffee addiction, while others picked bouquets of flowers ready to purchase.

I stepped behind the sales desk, and pulled the top of my

dress higher over my chest scar. Flowers for Fleur was open for business ...

❦

'Flowers, tea, coffee ... or books?' The words rolled off my tongue for the seventeenth time this morning. I wished I could just say, "Can I help you?", or "Hi!", but Gram insisted I say all five words, each and every time, just like she had from the very first day she opened the store fifty years ago. "It's tradition," she had said.

'Flowers, please.' The middle-aged woman smiled at me. She looked like she was on top of the world. She was the color of bright yellow—happy and triumphant.

'I get the feeling you're celebrating,' I said.

'Yes. My granddaughter was born at 2.13am.' She gave a little squeal. 'She's so perfect ... so adorable.'

My heart melted. There was nothing more precious than the gift of a baby. 'Congratulations! Gram makes the most amazing floral arrangements for new babies. Go over and tell her your good news, then head to Darcy for a celebratory coffee or tea, on the house!'

'Thanks, Andi.'

'You're welcome, and you must visit with your granddaughter to introduce us sometime!'

'Definitely!'

The moment she walked to Gram, I dashed into the cold room to grab more bunches of flowers for outside the flower store.

Flowers were in hot demand today.

Gram would be ecstatic.

After I placed the blooms into the silver buckets, I stepped back to check their placement, then looked over at Gram's bicycle. There, in the flowers, was another note.

I grabbed it and opened it up.

Dear Andi,
You misunderstand me.
I need that bike.
Name the price.

Xander

'What? Does Xander not have manners?' I strolled inside the store, thinking of an apt reply that would shut him down. I placed the note next to the laptop computer to reply to later when I had more time. He'll keep.

I opened the "outside flowers" book to record the flowers I had placed in front of the store. When I looked up, the milkman stood in front of me. He was the color of admiral blue—trust, responsibility, honesty and loyalty. 'Good morning, Mr. Wilson. Just take the milk and cream right over to Darcy.'

'I know. But first I must apologize.'

I frowned. 'Why's that?'

'The blood ... yesterday.'

My eyes widened. I touched each of my fingers on my right hand with my thumb, one by one—the hand that dripped with blood on that terrible day, three years ago ...

A tingle of anxiety shot through me, threatening to grow into a full-blown panic attack. My head started to swim. *Distraction. Move on with the conversation.* 'What happened?' I asked.

'It was dark, and I turned my head towards the noise down the street. I tripped and dropped a bottle. When I put my hand down to stop my fall, I cut myself. Sorry about the blood.'

I swallowed. *Keep talking* ... 'Is your hand okay?'

'Seven stitches. But I'll survive.'

'I hope it heals quickly. I'll organize a light for the front of the store so you can see better.' That was my Workplace Health and Safety brain kicking in from working at the Defence Force Base. I jotted it down on my job list so I wouldn't forget.

'Oh. That's not necessary. I carry a torch, most of the time.'

'It's not a problem, Mr. Wilson. Consider it done.' I turned towards Darcy. He gave me a questioning look. 'Darcy's eager for your milk delivery. Have a lovely day.'

I looked around the store trying to focus on things other than the conversation I just had with the milkman. There was a lull in customers. I stretched my back before I found some floral paper and a pen. It was time to respond to dear Xander's request.

Dear Xander,

You misunderstand me.
The bike cannot be exchanged for $ $ $ $.

Andi

That would do. Short. To the point.

I'll put it in the flowers in the bike basket early tomorrow morning.

Chapter Five

Gram was standing by her bicycle at the front of the store with flowers in her hand. Today it was roses. Three of every color from the cold room. There were fifteen blooms in the bouquet. The perfume swirled through the air, permeating it with a scent of damask with crushed violet leaves and a hint of lemon. I frowned. I was more of a florist than I thought. I looked down at my steel-capped work boots and uttered a silent apology.

'Look at you, Gram ... happiness shining out of you!' I leaned forward and kissed her cheek. She was the color of bumble bee yellow today, exuding cheerfulness. 'I love that song Gramps is singing.' It was muffled by the closed store door, yet easily heard.

Gram looked at me and paused. She frowned, then turned her right ear towards the doors, lowered her head and listened.

A contagious smile spread over her beautiful face. 'Me too. *Una Furtiva Lagrima* from the Italian opera *L'elisir d'amore, Act 2.*'

My smile disappeared as I watched a tear slip down her cheek.

'I remember the first time I heard him sing it ... I sneaked into a rehearsal like a thief in the night and stood behind the side curtains. I closed my eyes and soaked in every note, every word, every nuance. His voice transcended time and place. When he finished, the cast and crew were spellbound, and took a while to snap out of it. A slow clap started, but you could see they were still affected—an attack on the emotions—in the most beautiful way. I still can't believe our life paths collided. God smiled down on us when we first met.' Gram brushed a tear away and placed the roses into the bicycle basket.

I loved listening to her love stories. They gave me hope and a little bit of light in the darkness of the violent male world I had encountered on that terrible day of the scars.

I opened the door of the store and Grampapa's loud singing voice penetrated me. I paused in my step, so thankful Gram and Gramps were my grandparents. I looked over at Darcy. He was polishing cutlery. He gave me a wink.

I skipped over to Grampapa and wrapped my arms around him, inhaling his comforting scent of wood and leather, reminding me of horse-riding lessons when I was young. He was the color of earth brown—a simple life, good friends and happiness.

He stopped singing. 'Yolande, the morning is beautiful, eh?'

'More so with you belting out a tune and Gram smiling!'

'I know. We've decided that she'll have no more vertigo attacks. And that is that!' Gramps smiled at me. His words were convincing, but his eyes betrayed him.

A sadness vibrated through me. I needed to change the subject. 'It looks like a storm is brewing this morning, which is odd, this early in spring.'

'Yes, but not unheard of. I guess you're shielded from the weather conditions while you work inside those gigantic industrial structures at the base.'

'Classified information, sorry. Please keep singing while I get on with my job list.' I stood on my tiptoes and planted a kiss on his cheek.

He smiled at me. 'Thanks for being here for Grams.'

'How could I not, after she got me through ... you know ...' I still couldn't speak about it, about the time when my scars came into being. No one knew of the exact details of the entire incident of what had happened on that terrible day. Except the police and the judge. I closed my eyes for a second and saw Mia's hand gripping mine. Covered in blood. *My blood ...*

I cleared my throat and headed to gather my apron, then went to the sales desk. I glanced at the note from Xander yesterday, and picked it up.

Dear Andi,

You misunderstand me.
I need that bike.
Name the price.

Xander

I folded it and put it away, then reread the reply note I had written.

Dear Xander,

You misunderstand me.
The bike cannot be exchanged for $ $ $.

Andi

Had I been too harsh?

No. I folded the note in half and walked towards the front

doors. Gram passed me on the way. She didn't appear to see me. She kept her head ultra-still and her eyes focussed in front of her. *Odd.*

Outside, I tucked the note into the roses, ensuring enough was sticking out so Xander would see it. I wondered what time he passed by Flowers for Fleur, and whether it was a regular occurrence. I shrugged my shoulders. For a guy like him, coming by Gram's store would purely be to acquire the bike. Otherwise, he wouldn't give the flower store the time of day.

I walked back into the store. It was quiet, for now. Gramps was over at the workbench of flower imagination talking to Gram. He gathered a box full of bouquets and headed out the back door, no doubt to deliver them.

Darcy walked by with a cup of tea for Gram. The aroma of a citrusy blend of tea caught my attention. Then I watched as she waved it away. I frowned. Gram never refused a cup of tea at this time of the morning. In fact, she never waved away anything gifted to her ... ever.

I looked at her with more intent. Some of the incandescent inner light that shone from her face had faded. She was no longer a pink person of warmth and affection, or a bumble bee yellow of cheerfulness. She was a shade of orange like a light amber honey. Fear and anxiety. I had to stay attuned to her.

After scrubbing the fifteenth flower container, I wandered over to the double French doors and opened them for the beginning of the business day. It was 8.30am.

I stepped out onto store frontage and walked closer to the road and looked up at the heavy clouds. I could smell the sweet, pungent zing of a storm. A spot of rain fell onto the center of my forehead. I inhaled sharply at the memory of a red drop of blood that fell onto Mia's forehead, then stiffened when I felt a sharp electrifying shock of anxiety. I let out my breath through pursed lips to calm the feeling and concentrated on being present in the moment—not looking back at the past, nor into the future—but to the here and now. I listened to the sound around me, and at that moment, the rain began to fall.

There was a flash of bright lightning, followed by the vibrating boom of thunder and a heavy downpour. The street became mayhem while people ran about seeking shelter, including under the awning of Flowers for Fleur, where the smell of fresh coffee wafted out and lured people inside.

I looked to my right at the sound of pounding feet and splashing puddles. A dark-haired man in his twenties was taking a direct route towards me for shelter from the deluge. He stopped beside me, puffing, and ran his hand through his drenched dark hair. Three years ago, I would have melted at his sight, and gone all gooey. But not now, not after that terrible day of the scars ...

I looked back at the storm clouds. 'The coffee smells good. We might be here for a while,' I said. I had learnt the power of suggestion was a valuable tool in selling. Invite them into the store, and they were more likely to purchase something.

'If one had time,' he said. He lowered his head for a moment, his eyes on the ground, on my boots, then smirked. He looked back up, pulled his backpack over his head and ran into the rain.

Gram was at the sales desk tending to customers when I returned inside. To the right, Darcy was flat out with a very long line of eager coffee and tea drinkers. I headed over to help Darcy. This was no time for a one-man barista show.

He uttered a thousand thanks as I took over taking the orders. And after thirty minutes, I had a moment to look at Gram. She seemed flustered, and anxious, rubbing her hands together. I had never seen her act that way before. She was always cool, calm and collected.

I put my hand on Darcy's arm. 'Gram needs my help. Sorry to abandon you.'

Darcy looked up at Gram while he was making a latte. He pressed his lips into a hard line. 'Absolutely, and please don't apologize.'

'Thanks, Darcy! You're one in seven billion.'

'No problem.'

I pulled out my cell phone while I walked towards Gram. 'Hi, Charlotte. I need you to come to work as soon as possible. Gram's not well.'

I stopped on Gram's left side. 'I'll take over now, Gram. Darcy has everything under control in the café.'

Gram didn't move. She didn't even look my way. I walked around to her right side. 'I'll take over now, Gram. Darcy has everything under control in the café.'

Gram turned her body towards me like her head was fused in place. It was an odd, robotic type of movement. 'That would be wonderful, Landi. I think I will sit down in the office for a bit.' Her voice was flat, not the cheerful, uplifting voice we were used to.

I watched her walk away. There was no bounce in her step. It was almost a smooth shuffle, and looked like an attempt to walk without making any body movement of any kind. My skin burned. When I heard the office door click, I turned to the next customer.

'I was wondering if you sold umbrellas?' she asked.

What? This is a flower shop with a café! I took a calming breath. 'What a brilliant idea! No umbrellas, but I could probably find you a large sheet of plastic to use, like a poncho?'

'I'll take it, please. I have an important meeting.'

'Sure,' I said, and went to the storeroom. I returned with ten plastic sheets. I gave one to the woman and had some spare to hand out to others requesting umbrellas, then wrote down "order floral print umbrellas" on the to-do list.

I looked up when Charlotte rushed in and grabbed her apron.

'That was quick!' I said. She was the color of yellow, like sunflowers, smiling at the sun as it threw beams of unending joy, life, happiness and vitality.

'I was at The Last Cupcake, the bakery. I'll take over the sales desk. I don't have a flair for creating bouquets of flowers like you and your gram.'

'Thanks. You're a Godsend! I'm going to check on Gram.' I gave Charlotte a quick hug.

I walked around the corner to Gram's office and tapped on the door, twice, before I opened it. I took one step inside and stopped in my tracks. Gram was sitting in her chair, staring at the wall with a look of terror on her face. She neither turned her head towards me, nor moved her eyes to look at me.

'Get me a bucket, now!' Gram's voice was a rough whisper.

I didn't answer. I walked briskly through the shop on light footsteps in my safety boots. I didn't want to alarm any customers, so I added a small smile to my face: a fake small smile. I was good at those. I'd had three years practise at it.

I went to the storeroom and grabbed a bucket then hightailed it back to Gram, closed the door behind me and approached her from the side. I placed it on the desk in front of her, remembering her fury when I stood in her line of vision the last time she had a vertigo episode.

Gram blinked slowly, shaking, then vomited. Violently. Relentlessly.

I covered my mouth with my hand. No one should ever see their grandmother like that. She eased herself back into her sitting position, her eyes still focussed on a spot on the wall.

'Damn this vertigo to hell!' Her voice was angry, low and rough. I had never heard her speak that way.

A chill traveled down my spine and I wanted to look for a place to hide. I started to tremble. 'I'm calling Gramps. You need to go home.'

'No! I can't move! It makes it wor—' She vomited again. Almost choking. 'I can't do this anymore ... I can't do this ... anymore.' Her repeated words were whispered, but they bellowed through me like a freight train and hit me in the stomach, winding me.

'I'll get another bucket,' I said, and swallowed the bile in my throat.

'Do that, Yolande, but don't you dare call Gramps! He doesn't need to know about this.' A tear ran down her face.

I held my breath to stop a sob from escaping from me, and left her office. I went to the storeroom and sat on the floor, and pulled my knees to my chest and rocked to and fro for a moment, then pulled my phone from my pocket and dialed a number. 'Gramps ... it's Gram—'

The call went dead. He had hung up on me.

I looked at my phone then placed it back into my pocket. I hated defying Gram. But the situation was desperate. I slowly stood, pulled myself together and found another bucket. I returned to the office where I replaced her used bucket with a clean one. Gram didn't look at me. She didn't talk.

'Do you want me to hold your hand?' I asked. *That is what she wanted the last time she was spinning ...*

She took a deep, slow breath. 'Not today. I just want to be alone with this beast in this damn nightmare.'

I raised my chin and looked at her, stopping myself from ugly crying. 'Okay ... I'll come and check on you in ten minutes.' I held in my sob, once again.

'Make it thirty.'

I nodded my head, not that she could see me. 'I'll be here.' I took one last look at Gram staring at the wall, then left her office, with burning skin and a churning stomach. I closed the door with a faint click.

In my mind, I saw Gram as the victim of the color of black,

which was like a panther, stalking its prey while it built up its appetite to devour its meal, taunting until the victim was on its knees, begging for mercy.

I released a heavy sigh. Why couldn't the vertigo be stopped? Surely there was a magic pill she could swallow to return her to her normal self? I looked down at my steel-capped boots—my personal protection from a physical attack. But what was there to protect a person from an attack from the inside—from your own body, or your own mind?

I walked to Gram's workbench. I couldn't look at Darcy or Charlotte. That would be my undoing. I opened Gram's order book. There was one more order to create. A bouquet for "Get Well". Apt.

I fumbled as I searched for a foam holder and knocked over a vase. It splintered as it hit the floorboards. I reached for the dustpan and brush and swept up the glass. But not without cutting myself. I stood, and wrapped my fingers around the cut to stop the blood, feeling faint. But I didn't hold my finger tight enough. Blood ran down my finger and dripped onto the workbench. The same hand that once held another's.

I should never have let go of Mia' hand ...

In a mad panic to starve off a major anxiety attack that would send me running to the powder room, I searched for the adhesive bandages in a container. I reached for one and applied it to my finger, tightly—wound covered. Blood stopped. Good.

Nausea swam in my stomach. 'Breathe ...' I whispered, '... in for a count of three, and out for a count of five ... stop,' I said, 'distraction.'

I finished clearing the glass on the floor and wiped the blood from the workbench. I shook my head to stop it swirling with light-headedness. This was not a good day.

Distraction. I flicked through a florist magazine and searched for a recipe of flowers for "Get Well". I found a pink floral arrangement that would be perfect. I headed to the cold room and collected two pink roses that had a strong fruity raspberry scent, two pink lilies that smelled of honey, two pink gerberas and three pink daisies, plus some decorative greenery. I worked with diligence cutting and placing the floral elements into the rounded foam. Then lowered them into a white ceramic container. It was ready to go. I photographed it and called a delivery service.

I startled as Gramps flew in the back door. He stopped and glanced around the store, then made his way to the office in haste. I followed behind, my heart trying to thump through my chest.

He turned the doorknob and pushed the door open with care while I held my breath.

'Where is she, Yolande?' Grampapa's voice was frantic, accusing.

My eyes widened. She was sitting in her office chair when I left her. I looked over Grampapa's shoulder and gasped. Gram was gone. 'She was ... I ... I—'

Gramps turned and walked with large steps towards the powder room. I stepped in front of him and entered first, in case there were any women attending to their needs. All the cubicle doors were open except one. I looked down from the door and gasped at the sight of Gram's legs protruding from under it.

'Gram,' I said, my voice trembling. My heart raced.

Gramps was behind me then. 'How long has she been here— on the toilet floor—of all places!' He was angry, like the color of dark red, ready to infiltrate everything around it.

'Leave me be. I don't want to move,' Gram said. Her voice was weak.

'Go get the screwdriver set, Andi,' Gramps ordered.

I left the powder room and went to the sales desk. I pulled open the draw and picked up the screwdriver set. 'Don't ask,' I whispered to Charlotte, then returned to Gram and Gramps.

I held on to the toilet door while Gramps removed the screws of the hinges. He then lifted the door off and placed it to the side. Gram was sprawled on the tiled floor, staring at one place on the wall.

Gramps ran his hand over his contorted face. 'Fleur ... my darling ...' His voice was tender. He grabbed her hand and kissed it.

'It's nearly finished. I can tell. The spinning's not so furious now. If you leave me alone here for a little while longer ...'

Gramps sat on the floor beside her, still holding her hand. 'Yeah, well ... you're stuck with me now. Yolande has everything under control with the store.' Gramps gestured for two glasses of water.

When I returned with the glasses, he took them, then waved me off. I hung a "cleaning in progress" sign on the door to stop people entering. Gram most definitely would not want people seeing her this way.

I put my hand on my chest. My heart was breaking. Not only for Gram, but for Gramps as well. I hated seeing him distressed. How could my safe, comforting grandparents, who were my pillars of strength, become shattered messes of ruins that left me standing, grappling for something to hang on to that was no longer there?

I held in a cry and touched my scar through the top of my dress, then walked out the front of the store for some much-needed fresh air. The rain had stopped, and the sun had broken through the clouds. I shook my head in disbelief. *What was this monster attacking Gram?*

I lifted my face to the golden sun to absorb every beam of its life-giving energy. I needed it to keep going. I felt so useless. There was nothing I could do to help Gram when she was spinning.

When I turned to enter Flowers for Fleur, a new note in the flowers of the bicycle caught my eye. I detoured from the store entry, picked it up and opened it.

Dear Andi,

It's for a loved one.

Xander

I closed my eyes. Maybe this Xander did have a heart?

Chapter Six

Dear Xander,

It's from a loved one.

Andi

I folded the note I had just written. I didn't get time to reply to Xander's note yesterday after Gram's episode. I glanced over at her. She was back at her workbench of flower imagination with collections of blooms under strict orders to take it easy. A new chair had been placed nearby so she could sit when she needed to, as well vomit buckets under the workbench, in her office and in the powder room.

Happy that Gram was doing okay, I delivered Xander's note to the flowers in the bicycle basket outside. Today it was an arrangement of pink carnations. My nose twitched at the spicy clove-like fragrance. I returned inside the store and stood next to Gram, on her right side, so she could hear me.

'Why is Charlotte here today?' Gram asked.

'To help get on top of the mountain load of work,' I lied. I was scrupulous with my work ethic and never left the store until I had completed every set task, and then some more. Gramps and I had decided Charlotte should be here, so I could float around the shop to keep a closer eye on Gram.

Darcy placed two cups of tea on the workbench, his woody and spicy scent lingering, offering a feeling of protection.

Gram covered her ears at the sound of the bone china teacups clinking, then she stilled. 'Thank you, Darcy. Just what I need. Perfect timing, as always,' Gram said, and gave him a small smile.

Gram was back. She was the color pink again, like the dark pink lipstick kiss of family—warmth, acceptance and unconditional love. My heart warmed.

'You're welcome, Mrs. Lawrence,' Darcy said, before he turned and walked back to the florist café, his woody, spicy scent leaving us.

I picked up my teacup and wrapped my hands around it, inhaling the biscuity smell.

'The storm did wonders for business yesterday,' I said to Gram, watching as she picked up her teacup and sipped it. 'Twelve customers asked me if we sold umbrellas.'

'A valid request considering the unpredicted weather,' Gram commented.

'Yes. I found some lovely floral umbrellas on the Internet and was wond—'

'Great idea, Andi. Floral ones would be a perfect addition to the store.'

'That's what I thought. I ordered a few to check the quality.'

'Wise. I hope they're made here and not overseas.'

'That's one of my conditions.' I finished my cup of tea at a slow pace, savouring the taste and enjoying Gram's light mood. 'Let me know if you need a hand with anything,' I said.

'Shall do, my sweet!' Gram beamed me an infectious smile.

She was back. *Gram* was back.

The rear door buzzed. Deliveries were here. Once they were inside, I placed the fresh flowers into the cold room and the other items into the storeroom.

With eagerness, I found the carton of umbrellas and opened it. Seven floral umbrellas were there, plus two plain oatmeal -cookie-colored ones with a wooden crook handle.

I gathered them in my arms and took them to Gram. We looked over the floral umbrellas for quality, then decided on a suitable price for them.

'What are these ones for, dear?' Gram asked, turning the oatmeal-cookie-colored ones around in her hands.

'I pictured a hanging unopened umbrella with flowers showing at the top of them—pink tulips actually. A bit like a door wreath, I guess. I wanted to fiddle with a flower and ribbon design—if that's okay with you.'

Gram looked at the umbrella and closed her eyes. 'I think I can see it too. Get those work boots moving and fetch us some tulips from the cold room!' Gram smiled, and I disappeared from her.

When I returned to the workbench, there was nothing but the two umbrellas laying there. I looked around and saw Gram walking about the store talking to people. I took the opportunity and worked on my flower vision. After an intense fifteen minutes I gazed over my umbrella wreath, pleased with the final product.

I walked over to Gram and held them up for her to cast her scrupulous florist eye over. 'What do you think?'

'Ah ... beautiful. Hang it on the French door. When it sells, you can make another one.'

'Thanks, Gram.'

I hung the door wreath on the white French door and stood back to admire my handiwork. Pleased with myself, I went back to my list of jobs and added gift tags to the floral umbrellas and took them outside to display. When I walked by Gram's bicycle, there was another note. I removed it from the flowers and opened it.

Dear Andi,

Can I hire the bicycle for a day?

Xander

Hmmm. Persistent wasn't he. I went inside and wrote another message to him.

Dear Xander,

How do I know you'll return it?

Andi

I went outside and placed the note in the flowers. I looked up. Storm clouds were gathering again. I had a funny feeling those umbrellas were going to be a hot selling item.

When I entered the store, a middle-aged woman was considering a bunch of red roses, turning them this way and that, undecided. She was the color of viridian—a green of mixed emotions, melancholy.

'They're beautiful aren't they. For yourself?'

She sighed. 'My daughter.'

'Lovely. How old is she?'

'Twelve.'

'Birthday?'

'No. It's her menarche—the first day of her first period. The flowers are for commiserations. She's got possibly forty frigging years of blood and pain and inconvenience. That's 480 periods if she doesn't have kids ... that's 3, 360 days, or nine years and two months of leaking blood out of her vagina. No wonder we get cranky!'

I burst out laughing. I placed my hand over my mouth, embarrassed by my reaction.

'It's also because I'm sad about it. She's growing up. She won't be my little girl anymore. She'll be all secretive and boys and girlfriends and cranky instead of sugar and spice and all things nice.'

'But that's how you want her to be. She needs to find out who she is and how strong she can be, right?'

'I know. But I wish she could stay my sweet girl for a little while longer ...'

'With uncomplicated lives ...' I sighed. I wished I could go back in time and change my life path. Then Mia and I would still be best friends. 'I think you should celebrate it with a positive bent.'

'I agree, hence the flowers.'

'And most girls love flowers ... although, if it were me, I wouldn't want red flowers.'

'Why not?'

'Red ... blood ... it's a reminder.' A shiver traveled down my spine. Or perhaps it's just a reminder for me. A reminder of the blood that dripped to the rocks below on that terrible day of the scars. I pulled the top of my dress higher over my already covered chest scar.

'She loves red.'

I winced. Memories are powerful. Associations of color with

memories are powerful.

'Red roses are a declaration of love. I wouldn't give a bouquet of red roses—just in case a future boyfriend gives her red roses, and it reminds her of her first period ...' I shrugged. 'How about you bring her in and create whatever takes her fancy, together. It will be fun that way.'

The woman looked at me and tilted her head to the side while she considered my words. 'That sounds like a wonderful idea. Thank you.'

'See you at 4pm then?'

'Yes. Yes, you will.'

I watched as she left the store. I wondered if she would return with her daughter this afternoon. What if the daughter wanted nothing to do with celebrating becoming a woman?

I should have just sold her the flowers.

Red. Like blood.

Chapter Seven

I highlighted day two on my calendar. Day two of Gram being okay. She didn't know I was keeping a record of her health, and she didn't need to. I was looking for a pattern. There must have been some sort of trigger for her vertigo. Or perhaps, maybe it was viral and had run its course. I hoped it was the latter.

I pulled Xander's note out of my pocket. I had found it in the bicycle flowers yesterday afternoon at closing time.

Dear Andi

Cross my heart

Xander

How do I know he has a heart? And, he had no punctuation!!! Uneducated douche! His persistence was starting to irritate me. And I don't do irritated—well ...

I Googled persistent:

persistent

adjective
1. continuing firmly or obstinately in an opinion or course of action in spite of difficulty or opposition.

He was also annoying:

annoying

adjective
1. causing irritation or annoyance.

And pig headed:

pig-headed

adjective
1. stupidly obstinate.

The word obstinate came to mind:

obstinate

adjective
1. stubbornly refusing to change one's opinion or chosen course of action, despite attempts to persuade one to do so.

Yes. He was all of those. He was a persistent, annoying, pig-headed, obstinate human being who wouldn't take no for an answer. I raised an eyebrow. *Had I actually said no?* Literally? Guys are literal creatures, aren't they?

I found the floral writing paper I had been using and replied to his note.

Dear Xander,

No.
I am not in the habit of hiring out
my grandmother's bicycle to strangers.

Andi

There. I had said it. No. Now he would stop. That would be the last of the note exchanges. I folded the piece of paper and took it outside to the flowers in the bicycle basket. Gram had graced the bicycle with mild earthy smelling daisies today. Pure white with a yellow center. Simple. Like my no.

I returned to the buzz of the flower store and a sense of relief washed over me with no more hassling about Gram's bicycle. I looked over at Gram. She was content at the helm of her workbench, creating blooms of beauty.

I looked over at Darcy. He gave me a wink and a killer smile. Everything was in motion, working smoothly as it should. I went to the sales desk in the center of the store and took my place as the chief florist's assistant in magical blooms that changed the perception of the giver, and the mood of the receiver. Giving flowers made anyone look good from the outside. Unless you knew their true heart. And then the flowers could become a source of bitterness ...

'Flowers, tea, coffee or books?' The words rolled off my tongue with a melodic sound like it was inborn, and like Gram had insisted upon. Perhaps I even muttered the words in my sleep by now. The middle-aged woman was dressed in black. *Was she in mourning?* Doubt it. She had black fingernails, lipstick, hair and thick black eyeliner, like a Goth. The color I saw above and behind her head was purple. She was seeking the meaning of life in the future, or perhaps a reconnection.

'Lavender, actually.' Her voice sounded casual.

I raised my eyebrows at her, surprised she didn't ask for black roses, or black tulips, black petunias, black pansies or the black iris, "Before the Storm".

'It's for my cat,' she elaborated.

'For your cat?'

'Yes. He loves it ... or ... I mean, he used to love it. He would smell it and rub his face in it ... until he ... you know ...'

I lowered my head and frowned as my heart grew sad. 'I'm sorry for your loss.'

The woman shrugged and shook her head. 'I buried him in the garden in alkaline soil. I didn't want an acidic soil to decompose him entirely. The lavender's for on top of his grave.'

'He'll love that,' I said, and gave her a small smile.

She nodded and smiled back. 'I'm looking forward to six months' time when the decomposition process has ended. I'm going to dig him up. I have a plan for his skeleton ...'

My stomach churned. 'You do?' I said with wide eyes.

'Yes. I'm going to clean his bones, dry him out and paint his skeleton all sorts of colorful. Because that's how he made me feel. He'll be on display in my study.'

I blinked three times. Then I blinked more than freaking three times again. *Don't judge* ... 'Ahhh, yes. The unconditional love of pets. Have you ever owned a dog?' I kept my voice smooth to conceal my shock.

'Once. Twice. But I prefer the independence of cats. My cat was so affectionate. He loved me. I know he did.' The woman closed her eyes and held her breath.

It was time to change the subject. 'Purple lavender, pink lavender or white lavender?'

'Purple. French lavender ... if you have it.'

'Of course. I'll fetch a fresh bundle of lavender from the cold room. While I do that, I need to know what you think of our fresh catnip, if you don't mind. It's over with the animal friendly flowers.' I pointed to the right corner of the store where terracotta pots of cat grass, lemon grass, catnip and valerian sat on a whitewashed table with wooden cat art.

'Sure,' she said and wandered off.

I scooted to the cold room and collected three bundles of fresh lavender, then returned to the sales counter. Three is a magic number. Three would look better than one. I placed them on the desk and stilled, remembering the time when Mia and I kept lavender in our pockets, stolen from my grandmother's store. We went to a party and had planned on getting kissed by a boy or two. We held the lavender over their heads and told them it was mistletoe. A small smile started to uncurl on my lips—

'Beautiful. I will take all three lavenders, plus the catnip please,' she said.

I blinked away my memory of Mia. 'Are you sure you want all three bundles of lavender?'

'Absolutely,' she said. 'How much do I owe you?'

'Nothing ... it's a gift for your cat. Enjoy.'

She wiped a tear away. 'You're too kind. Thank you.' She picked up her bag of cat gifts and left. She would be back. When you showed heart, they always came back. Compassion was the key.

I tidied the top of the desk and took the opportunity to step out of the store to check the flowers at the storefront. I lifted my face to the sun and closed my eyes. The warmth energized me at once ...

Mia and I loved sunshiny days. We would head to the beach in our summer break. Boys. It was always about boys for her. And there were plenty of them at the beach—with their shirts off, making Mia drool. She would lay beside me and tell me which boy she wanted to marry. I would look at him, peeking over the top of my book, behind my dark sunglass disguise, while she proceeded to tell me how he would propose. Then I would give her my version of the events and add an ugly twist of fate.

I sighed.

I missed her. Terribly. There was no way she would marry now. And I didn't see marriage in my future. We would never be each other's bridesmaids, like we had promised when we were fourteen.

Fractured dreams. Irreparable dreams ...

I gave the flowers a quick misting spray before I returned to the sales desk and jotted down the time of misting in the flower care book.

I saw polished black shoes in my peripheral vision before a man stopped before me.

I looked up. 'Flowers, tea ... coffee ... or ...' The words started to roll off my tongue with a melodic sound from the word flowers, and it was downhill all the way from there. He was not a book type of person. The man standing before me made me feel uneasy. I tensed. His color was black—oppressive black, and sounded like someone had just hit the piano with a clenched fist.

'Flowers ... to make me look good,' he said, and threw me a mega-watt smile that reeked of deceit.

I cringed inwardly but stood straighter, only because I had my steel-capped safety boots on. I tapped my right boot twice on the floor. 'What's your definition of "good"?' I punctuated the air with inverted commas with the word good.

'Oh ... you know ... kind, considerate, puts others first ...'

'And you don't do those "good" things?'

'Two of them *sometimes*, the other ... never.'

'Do you prefer to be known as bad?'

'Yes. I can have more fun if I'm a bad boy!' He puffed up his chest and crossed his muscular arms.

'Then ... why do you want to look good? It's a girl, right?'

'Yes.' He unfolded his arms and put his hands into his pockets.

'Don't you think you're being a phony by pretending to look good? What if she loves the flowers and this "good" act, but discovers the real you underneath?'

He scowled. I had hit a sore spot. I needed to tone down the truth.

'Listen, babe.' His voice was lowered. Threatening.

I narrowed my eyes at him. He was a monster. Just like the men on that terrible day of my scars, except, I could see his true colors from the outset.

'I don't want a lesson on morals. I want flowers. Get me a handful that will make me look good.'

I tapped my work boot on the floor, again. Twice. He would have to choose his own "make me look good" flowers. I started to walk to a pre-made bunch of blooms, then stopped. Gram would be experienced in creating a "special" bouquet for his type.

I turned to him. 'I'll organize a unique bouquet of "make me look good" flowers. It'll work a treat ... please have a drink on us while you wait for me to make a bouquet from scratch for you. Just tell Darcy, our barista, that Andi sent you. I'll let you know when your flowers are ready, Mr. ...'

'John's the name.'

'Go and enjoy, John,' I said, and walked off the to workbench.

I stopped beside Gram, on her right side. 'He's a nasty piece. He wants to look "good". He's such a fake. He deserves the golden rule.'

Gram looked at me and smiled. 'Hmm. Treat others as you shall be treated ... fake for a fake. I have the perfect bunch of flowers in mind—the white candytuft—known for its unpleasant experience if you put your nose close to it. Hmmm ... the girl would have an unappreciative reaction—'

'And his true self will come out in response. Intuition tells me he's violent and abusive when he doesn't get his own way, or if he's exposed to what he really is. It's best that we save his target now ... no woman, or man for that matter, deserves to be treated with disrespect.' Anger boiled inside of me. I wanted to call him out for what he was.

I sighed. A bouquet of revengeful flowers wouldn't be good for business. Better to go about it in a clever way.

I closed my eyes and put my palm to my forehead. 'Gram, what if it ends badly for the girlfriend, or us? What if she gets hurt, or he returns fuelled with anger?'

Gram stopped. 'You're right, Landi. Let's play nice.' Gram went to the cold room and returned with a variety of flowers in various shades of pink. She added sprigs of green and bound them with twine before she wrapped them in natural colored paper and added a bow of lace.

'Perfect.' I took the bouquet of flowers to present to John.

'Winning,' he said when he saw the blooms, then stood and followed me to the counter. He threw money on the desk, took the flowers and left.

I waited until he had walked out the door then followed him. He got into a black sports car. I memorised his number plate, just in case it ended badly for the woman.

When I turned to enter the store the bicycle flowers caught my eye. There was a new note. *Damn.* He really was a persistent, annoying, pig-headed, obstinate human being who wouldn't take no for an answer.

I removed the note and opened it up.

Dear Andi,

What if I become an unstranger?

Unstranger? Is that like being strange and then becoming less strange, though you are still a little strange? Or does he mean known instead of unknown. Because technically he is known via the notes, but not known as we don't have a face to the name. He sounds like a middle-aged businessman trying to make an acquisition.

I folded the note and slipped it into my pocket. I looked down at my work boots. I'm sure people thought I was strange. A girl wearing floral work dresses and steel-capped boots in a flower store ...

I returned to the sales desk and wrote down the license plate of the car before it disappeared from my memory, IMGR8, then turned and looked at Gram. She was deep in her creative zone—imagining, designing, creating. The bicycle belonged to her. She would have the final say about whether Xander could hire her Cruiser bicycle for the day. And I knew for a fact that she would never lend it out to anyone. She would sell the flower store and everything else before she sold her precious bicycle, and then it would only be on her deathbed.

I opened *Word* on the laptop computer and typed the new note. I put the floral note paper into the printer and pressed print:

Dear Xander,

Then you must meet Grandmother Fleur.

Chapter Eight

I turned on the tap.

Lather, scrub, rinse ... lather, scrub, rinse—and breathe.
Lather, scrub, rinse ... lather, scrub, rinse—and breathe.
Lather, scrub, rinse ... lather, scrub, rinse—

I knew there was no blood. I wasn't even bleeding, but I couldn't get the image out of my head of my blood dribbling down onto my hand before it trailed along my fingers and dropped to the rocks below, where Mia lay, twisted.

I turned off the tap and lifted my right hand in front of my face. I turned it over and back, over and back, time and time again, checking to see that there was no blood. It was insane. I clenched my teeth together and turned on the tap again.

Lather, scrub, rinse ... lather, scrub, rinse—and breathe.
Lather, scrub, rinse ... lather, scrub, rinse—and breathe.
Lather, scrub, rinse ... lather, scrub, rinse—

'There you are, Landi.' My saving grace stopped beside me. Gram. I could clearly see her flowing color of pink this morning, like cotton candy at the fair, reminding me of warm summer nights, love, laughter and fireworks. She turned off the tap and dried my hands then grabbed my left hand and led me out of the powder room. She pulled me to a table by the window and called to Darcy, 'Two cups of tea, please.'

Darcy gave Gram a nod. He knew the routine when I was like this, lost in a scene of reality that happened three years ago, one that I couldn't climb out of.

Gram sat opposite me at the reclaimed hardwood timber table. I stared at the fresh flowers that sat between us. We were in a florist store with a café attached, so of course there had to be fresh flowers adorning each of the tables. It was like an advertisement for Flowers for Fleur. I blinked. The white hydrangeas reminded me of a snowball. Anxiety swirled inside me as I remembered when I was fifteen ...

'I will win today, Mia!' I had said.

'No you won't. You never beat me in the snowball vertical tower challenge!' she had said.

I crouched in the snow and made twelve snowballs, then stood. I held one snowball in my hand and balanced another on top. Mia handed me the snowballs, one at a time, while I carefully added them on top of the other, trying to make a snowball tower. I was killing it today. My placement of the balanced freezing spheres was perfect, probably from all those ballet lessons I had from when I was eight. I placed the seventh snowball on top, and was about to add one more to break the record set by Mia—

'Seven snowballs ...' Mia had sung in the tune of the chef who fell down the stairs on Sesame Street, and doubled over in laughter.

I held my breath to stop the onslaught of giggling from being set free from inside me. But it was no use, the giggle monster had been unleashed. I closed my eyes and laughed so hard I fell over, losing my tower of snowballs in the process, all except one.

'Cheat!' I said, and walloped her with my remaining snowball. I

always lost, only because Mia always cheated with the Sesame Street song.

Mia fell into the snow beside me. I looked at my best friend. 'One day I will win. Let's make a bet!'

Mia looked into my eyes; her face lit with excitement. 'Okay!'

'If I win ... you will have to hi-five everyone you see at school at lunch time—no matter who it is.'

Mia raised a single eyebrow at me. 'You're on ...'

A warm hand covered mine and pulled me back to the present. 'Close your eyes, Landi ... breathe in for a count of three ... and out for a count of five. You know how to deal with intrusive thoughts. What do you need to say?'

I closed my eyes. I wanted to cry but I couldn't. Not here.

'Stop,' I said.

'Then what?' Gram pressed. She knew the cognitive behaviour therapy cheats as well as me.

'Distraction.' I opened my eyes as Darcy placed teacups and a teapot between Gram and me.

'Go on, Landi,' Gram said.

I turned the teapot three times to the left, then three times to the right. It was a ritual I had watched Gram and my mother do forever. I poured Gram a cup of tea, then myself, and added milk.

There. My intrusive thought was gone. For now. I shook my head. I knew the repetitive behaviour of trying to wash the imagined blood off my hand was completely stupid and irrational. But it always seemed so real at the time.

'Sorry, Gram,' I whispered.

'It's not me you need to apologize to.'

'I know.' I sipped my tea and looked out the window. The rain poured down casting a muted light outside. A young girl sat on a bench seat and slipped on her yellow rain boots. She beamed up at her mother. The first time I saw Mia she was on a seat just like that, sliding her green rain boots on ...

She stood and buttoned up her raincoat and ran into the rain and jumped in puddles. I wished I could be like her. Not afraid of the mud. My mother hated the mud. And so I hated the mud. The girl stopped jumping and looked at me. I held my breath, frozen.

She walked towards me, her hand outstretched. 'Come and play,' she had said.

I looked down at my pink rain boots, my clean, pink rain boots, and took her hand. She pulled me into the rain and we jumped in puddles and spun around and around and around with our arms outstretched, our faces towards the dark clouds. Rain splattered my face, touching my poked-out tongue. I felt free. For the first time in my life.

I closed my eyes and fell over, dizzy, straight into the mud puddle. The world kept on spinning around me. The girl fell beside me and giggled. I looked at her and giggled too. The type of giggle only eight-year-olds can have.

'Yolande!' My mother's angry voice threaded between the raindrops. I was in trouble.

'I'm Mia,' she said when I stood, and rubbed the mud from her eyes.

'Mia,' I repeated, and ran off.

'Yolande,' Gram said, bringing me back to the present. 'You know you can't change it.'

I put my teacup down. What I would give to go back in time and never to have jumped in the puddles with Mia. To never have met her. To never have become best friends.

'Gram ... do you think we have control of our lives, or has it already been laid out before us, and we're just going through the motions?' I asked. Gram was wise and knowing.

She raised her eyebrows at me. 'Look out the window at the

people, Landi. Are they deciding what to do next? Or are they like robots, and have no choice in the matter?'

I looked out the window and watched. Gram was right. We chose what to do, and you dealt with the consequences of your own choices, or another's choices. Good or bad.

I looked back at Gram. 'If Mia and I weren't friends, do you think it still would have happened to her?'

Gram didn't answer me. Her silence sparked a wave of anxiety inside me and my body tensed.

'Yes,' she finally said. But her words didn't make it any better for me. 'Look forward, Landi, not backward. You ca—'

'Can't change the past,' I finished. I'd heard it a million times.

'Imagine if we could choose one thing to change in the past ...' Gram said.

I gave Gram a sad smile. I knew exactly what I would change. Somehow my heart felt lighter. 'Would the world be better for everyone then, Gram? Or would we keep making the same mistakes?'

Gram placed her cupped hands under her chin. 'Philosophical ponderings will be continued later, my dear. The flowers are in need of a refreshing drink to lure in the people.'

'Right you are, Gram.' I stood and collected the teacups and teapot. I balanced them and took them over to Darcy. 'I owe you. It's true. Tea solves everything.' *And nothing*, I wanted to add, but didn't.

'Aye. For a moment in time,' he said and gave me a small smile.

I sighed. 'A moment in time is all I needed. Thanks.' I bent at my waist and performed an altered ballerina's bow to him.

'I'm only nice to you because I get paid to work here, you know,' Darcy said with smiley eyes.

'Nah ... you would be nice to me even if you didn't get paid. Genuinely nice people can't be bad, even if they tried.' My words were true.

'You should leave now before you see my bad side,' he said, and threw a tea towel at me. I smiled and gathered it in my hands, and threw it back at him, twice as hard. He chuckled, looked down and shook his head, his admiral blue color comforting me.

I walked over to the sales desk and pulled out my to-do list for the day, and the typed note for Xander. It needed to go into the flowers of the bicycle basket. I opened it up and reread it. Surely this would be the note to put an end to the notes. He certainly would not want to meet a bossy old woman who would point and wag her finger at him.

Dear Xander,

Then you must meet Grandmother Fleur.

I didn't sign it for the same reason that I typed it. I wanted to keep him guessing who wrote it, and hopefully scare him away. I walked outside and placed it into the flowers of the bicycle basket. Today it was a living pot of Tumbelina petunias—pinks, white and purples. There was no scent, as they only released their perfume from dusk and into the night. The note looked obtrusive sitting amongst the foliage. I decided I would keep watch for the persistently annoying Xander while I worked. In my mind's eye he was a middle-aged, balding, rotund man dressed in a suit with polished black shoes with beady, greedy dark eyes.

I rearranged some floral blooms for sales near the front entrance to the store, then returned to the sales desk and checked the jobs off my list.

I looked up when the sound of the shoes stopped before me. It was a middle-aged woman. She wore a white layered cotton linen dress. She was the color of indigo, like she was restructuring aspects of her life.

'Flowers, tea, coffee or books?'

'Flowers, dear.'

'Flowers for ...'

'Myself. It's the anniversary of my divorce.'

In an ideal world I would like to have said I'm sorry to hear. But the reality was, there were some men who were pitiful excuses for human beings. And some women as well. 'Good for you,' I said.

'Take my advice. Never marry ...'

I looked into her weary eyes. They were filled with pain.

'Advice taken and considered. Let me create a special gathering of blooms for you with an aromatic infusion that will leave you breathless and fill your house with victory.' I don't know where those flowing words came from. But they sounded astounding. I hoped Gram could create something like that.

I looked down, aware of my scars. No man would ever get past them, even if I did want to marry—which I didn't. Not after that terrible day with Mia ...

'Oh my. That sounds like a celebration!' Her words pulled me back to the present.

'It is indeed. Give me your name for when your gathering of blooms is born.' I twirled my hand in the air, adding a swirl of mystique.

'Maria.'

'Thanks, Maria. Please have a complimentary drink while you wait. Tell Darcy that Andi sent you.'

'Really?'

'Absolutely. I'll bring the flowers to you when Gram finishes the work of natural art.'

'Thank you.'

I inclined my head to her and turned to Gram. She watched me walked towards her with a twinkle in her eye. She had the type of face that lit up a room when she smiled. The type of face you looked at, lingering, floating on the light and happiness she gave, and when you walked away, your heart overflowed with warmth like the golden sunshine on a beautiful spring day.

It was day three without vertigo, and I was glad for her.

'Maria would like a bouquet to celebrate her divorce, Gram,' I said. 'I told her you would create something that was like victory.'

Gram slowed her movement and a sadness fell over her face. 'Granddaughter ... divorce is never a victory. It's the breaking of sacred promises. It's broken dreams and hearts.'

'Grandmother ... divorce is also freedom ... freedom from a toxic relationship ... freedom from betrayal ... freedom from abuse. You don't know her story.'

'You're right, Andi. I'm just a forever romantic. It's easy for me to forget the world is not a nice place for some ... I'll build a victory bouquet and spoil our Maria. She's been through an emotional journey of the heart.'

Sometimes I wished I had rose-colored glasses like Gram, instead of my jade-colored glasses.

Healing takes time, I reminded myself ...

Healing takes time ...

Chapter Nine

'Flowers, tea, coffee ... or books?' I said, according to Gram's script, still looking at my list of jobs and trying to decipher Gram's shaky writing. It was so unlike her meticulous decorative cursive script ...

'None. I'm delivering this letter in person instead of putting it in the flowers of the bicycle.'

I froze, unable to move my sight from the list. Xander was standing before me? His voice sounded so unlike a rotund, balding, middle-aged businessman. I looked up at him and my thoughts scattered. His blue eyes were decadent, his dark hair inviting me to run my fingers through it. I blinked to find my senses. This tall, slender, fit looking, god-like person standing before me was the persistent, annoying, pigheaded stranger becoming an unstranger, the one wanting to acquire Gram's Cruiser bicycle? He was the color of azure blue, like a male morpho butterfly—determination and ambition—with a splash of ... light red passion and sensitivity. *What? Two color s?* That was indeed a rarity. I raised an eyebrow at him, impressed by his presence of being. 'So, you don't want flowers today?'

'No. Never in fact.' His voice was fruity, deep and strong in a pleasant way.

I breathed out the luring potion he offered. 'You know what flowers do—don't you?'

'Of course ... they die!' His lips curled up on one side.

I smiled. He was being obscure and intentionally annoying. I cocked my head and narrowed my eyes at him, then burst out laughing.

He frowned at me and smirked.

'Flowers are happiness, bundled into a bouquet—they are regret, an apology, a bridge to amends, friendship, thinking of you, *you make my heart sing*, they are the color at a funeral, get well soon, thank you, a surprise, a grand celebration ... I miss you—' *Was this really the man I had been writing notes to? He was stunning.* 'I love you.' I stopped speaking and swallowed. He was hard to convince. If he was a flower, he would be a Nigella damascena, otherwise known as Love-In-A-Mist, or Jack-In-Prison. The petals would definitely be in shades of blue, its flowers hidden in the misty foliage. In the language of flowers, Nigella damascena was equal to perplexity.

'Have you finished your rambling sales campaign?' He lifted an eyebrow at me.

I sighed. I needed to dig deeper. Who was this beautiful man who stood before me who wasn't responding to my sales tactics? They *always* worked.

'Flowers for a girlfriend?' I continued. Surely he had an elegant woman who graced the social pages.

No response.

'Boyfriend?'

He took a deep breath.

'Mother, or Grandmother?'

No response.

The phone rang. I held up my finger. 'Wait … one moment, and I'm yours again.' I picked up the phone and put it to my ear, and wrote down the flowers ordered for delivery. I finished the phone call and looked up at the beautiful Xander.

He let out an audible breath. 'Just take the letter. I need an answer.'

What's his problem? He seemed so arrogant. I took the letter from his hand, placed it on the desk and tapped it. Twice. 'I'll read it after the rush hour and get back to you.'

He nodded, removed a pink Peruvian lily from a container on a table to the right of the sales desk, and held it out to me. 'For persuasion.' He raised an eyebrow at me.

I half smiled, conscious of the warmth that flowed through me. 'Flowers don't work their magic on me. I live and breathe them five days a week. You're going to have find to something else. I hope your day gets better …'

He looked down at the flower and ran his hand through his dark hair, gazed into my eyes and pulled his eyebrows together. 'I don't think anything can beat the education about flowers you just gave me—but you forgot one description of them—they're beautiful, like you.'

I laughed more loudly than I intended. Conversations stopped around the store and people turned to look at me, then him.

He looked around and gave a nervous smile.

'Well played, Xander. The power of flattery. For a moment there, I almost believed you. Kindness and intelligence rank more highly on my list as a compliment. Beauty fades with age and fake beauty deceives and is all too abundant.' I stilled for a moment, looking into his blue eyes, and sighed. 'I'll give you an answer, later today.'

He put his hands into his pocket. 'I can't ask for anything more. Thanks.'

He gazed into my eyes for a little too long. My lips parted in response to his unexpected, intimate, eye connection. He narrowed his eyes at me, took a deep breath, turned and left.

I watched as he threw his backpack over his broad shoulders, then took long strides out the door. I frowned. He was dressed in a black, sleeveless hoodie and black jogger pants, but he had the walk of a man raised with wealth and privilege. What's his story?

A muffled scream sounded in the store. *Gram.*

I looked around for her, but she was nowhere to be seen. I rushed to her office and hesitated at the door, my heart thudding. When I opened it, Gram was sprawled on the floor, and blood was pooling near her head.

She was staring at the wall, her head held still.

I grabbed five sheets of paper towel and swooped down to her, and pressed them to her forehead to try to stop the bleeding, ignoring the poison of anxiety that tried to control me.

I watched her eyes. They were moving rapidly from side to side. *What's going on?*

'Enough of this. I'm calling the paramedics.' My voice was more forceful than I intended.

'No. I'll be fine, after a few hours—'

'Gram, you're bleeding! You won't be fine!' I tried to keep my panic from her.

Gram reached up to her head. The only part of her body that moved was her arm and hand. It was like she was a robot, the rest of her body fused into place.

Slowly, she moved her hand in front of her eyes, then vomited. Spectacularly. I squeezed my eyes shut while her body went into a spasmodic movement each time she expelled the contents of her stomach, numerous times.

'I can't do this anymore ... please help me ... please help me ... I can't do this anymore ...'

Tears streamed down my face. There was something seriously

wrong with Gram. I didn't want it to be sinister ... what would I do without my Gram? She meant everything to me.

I pulled my phone from my pocket with my free hand, and pressed some numbers. 'I need an ambulance ... please.'

Chapter Ten

He was at the door when I arrived at 7am, looking at his watch. He was a spectacular azure blue color. I faltered in my step, remembering that I didn't open his letter. I turned around and placed my hand on my forehead and closed my eyes for a moment. How should I explain why I haven't read his damn letter?

I turned back to him. His dark hair was manicured. He stood tall and confident, today in jeans and a white shirt with the sleeves rolled up to just below his elbows. His broad shoulders gave the impression he was an athlete.

As I got closer he lifted his chin and looked down at me, his pupils large. A curious heat rushed through me.

'You didn't read my letter, did you?' His tone was clipped.

I pushed past him to open the door. I was already twenty minutes late. The aroma of fresh coffee permeated the air and I took a welcoming deep breath.

'Why didn't you read it?' He was behind me, and I could smell his citrusy scent with a hint of liquorice, vanilla and ...

lavender, perhaps. It reminded me of fireplaces and winter and mulled wine—warm and comforting.

I stopped walking and closed my eyes. I wanted him gone. Do I tell him the truth or spin him an untruth to get rid of him?

Lie. I stepped forward with determination towards the workbench of flower imagination and reached for my apron, turned around and tied it on while I looked up at him. I pulled the top of my dress up, ensuring the scar on my chest was covered, even though I knew it was. He was frowning, his face filled with ... sadness?

Truth. 'Gram had vertigo and fell over. She split her head open. I went to the hospital with her.' I looked down and shook my head. 'I'm sorry. I'll read it today.' My eyes were wet, and tears gathered on my eyelashes. I blinked quickly to empty them from my eyes.

Xander put his hands into his pockets. 'It's me who's sorry. Can I help in anyway? I know some good doctors. I—'

'No. We have it sorted. Thank yo—'

'It could be serious. Don't wait to get the symptoms diagnosed. Your gram may ha—'

'We have it sorted. Thank you,' I said a little louder and sharper than I intended. He was annoying me.

Xander blinked at me. Not a slow calm blink. But short irregular blinks, like I had insulted him. I didn't mean to.

'Forget about the bike, and ah ...' He looked down and tapped his finger on the wooden workbench. 'I hope your gram is okay.' He took a deep breath and gazed deeply into my eyes. And that curious heat was there again.

'Me, too,' I whispered, my throat constricted.

He pressed his lips together and walked toward the door, running his fingers through his thick dark hair, then disappeared.

I knotted my fingers together, then turned to find Gram's famous bicycle.

It was in her office. I ran my fingers over it. It wasn't *just* a bike. It was the romance of my grandparents. And an heirloom.

I wheeled it through the flower store, through the French doors and outside, then leaned it against the antique-white storefront of Flowers for Fleur where it had sat for the last fifty years.

I walked with quick steps back inside and orchestrated a symphony of white, light pink, dark pink and golden yellow old-fashioned peonies for good health and prosperity. They were Gram's most favorite flowers. I returned outside and placed them into the basket. *Just for Gram.* I inhaled the scent—a heady mixture of sweet rose and clean citrus. I held my breath and closed my eyes, then blew out my scented breath with a prayer. *Just for Gram.*

The sound of running footsteps came close. I looked up and was greeted with a wide smile, framed by gorgeous flowing blonde locks, like mine once were, before I dyed my hair dark-brown.

My smile matched hers. 'Lucy!' Enthusiasm poured from each letter of her name as I said it. She was the color of bright, energetic orange—radiating warmth, happiness and cheerfulness.

'Yolande! Charlotte can't make it today, so Gramps sent me. He's at the hospital with Gram. They're testing for a brain tumor.'

My heart missed a beat. *No!* I knew it could be a possibility, but I didn't want it to be a reality for Gram! 'I'm not surprised really ... vertigo ... vomiting ... loss of balance.' I shook my head. 'Whatever it is, they'll be able to fix it!' I added as a silent request, brimming with sparkling hope.

'They will,' said Lucy. 'It could just be a virus, you know.'

'Really? That would be great ... I mean, it's bad, but, it's good, because the virus will go away, and we'll get our beautiful Gram back.'

My favorite cousin smiled at me. She linked her arm through mine, and pulled me through the front door of Flowers for Fleur.

The aroma of freshly brewed coffee hit me again. This time I let it caress me—comforting and soothing. Gram's dream of flowers, tea, coffee and books was visionary for her time, and was a huge success in this town of Tarrin, this town of "more".

The mad morning mayhem hadn't started yet, so I put on my barista hat and made myself a kind of cappuccino to soothe my heart, much to the dislike of Darcy. I carried it to the sales desk and placed it down and focussed on the to-do list. I sighed. The flower truck would be here in twenty minutes. No rest for the weary.

When I lifted my coffee to my lips I caught sight of the unopened letter from Xander. He said he didn't want the bike anymore, so I picked up the envelope and dropped it into the wastepaper basket. I wrapped both of my hands around the coffee mug and enjoyed the warmth of the brew before the day took over.

I frowned. Why would Xander deliver a letter in person instead of leaving it in the flowers of the bike like he had done previously?

There was only one way to answer that question. I retrieved the letter from the wastepaper basket and carried it over to the workbench, then flipped it over to open the seal. My phone buzzed. It was a text from Gramps. I placed the letter onto the workbench and looked at my phone ...

GRAMPS: *Singing softly to Gram at the hospital.*
I hope Lucy has arrived. xxx

I grinned and texted back: *Lucky Gram!*
Give her my love. Lucy is here with her
boundless energy. Thank you xxx

I pocketed my phone and opened the order book. I had ten orders of flower art to create and deliveries to be made. Not to mention the orders that had come in overnight—five of them. Gram had told me to start at 7am each day. Clearly, I would need to start much earlier to get everything done. At least Lucy was here today, and I had already given her my usual "to-do list".

I leaned over the order book and cupped my forehead. My

brain was used to logical processes and procedures. This creative gig was a struggle. Hopefully it would only be for a few more days after the doctors sorted out Gram's medical issue.

I crouched down to grab the florist tools from under the bench. As I reached over for the basket with the trimmers, shapers, wire, pins, floral tape and foam, I spied a book I had never seen before.

Fleur's Book of Fantastical Flower Designs

I pulled it out and opened it. Inside were the names of flower arrangements Gram had designed, with hand-drawn illustrations and labels. I flicked backwards through the pages of watercolor and ink beauty before I hovered over the contents page:

Flowers for ~

1 *Fabulous* - an astounding collection of flowers for life-long friends
2 *Fairy* - an eclectic mix of blooms for one who thinks they belong to a different realm, and wants to enchant another
3 *Faith* - a gorgeous congregation of florets reflecting the glory of heaven
4 *Fake* - for folk focussing on portraying someone they're not. I smell a rat!
5 *Family* - an assortment of flowers to impress
6 *Fancy* - like Grandmother Lawrence's underwear!
7 *Fantasy* - a bouquet of blooms for one who appears in your dreams and fantasies
8 *Farewell* - a combination of blossoms that gladden the heart of either the giver or the recipient - sad to see you go ... glad to see you go
9 *Fatality* - a garland of blooms for death caused by an accident - never nice to create

10 *Favorite* - a selection of flowers of the favorite
   colors of a person preferred over all others ...
11 *Fearful* - a posy of yellow flowers as reverse psychology
12 *Fearless* - an anthology of bold blooms that scream
13 *Felonious* - stolen moments in life. A combination
   of florets for one stealing another's love interest - boo!
14 *Fertile* - a gathering of blooms to invoke sensuality
   to set the mood for baby-making - ooh-la-la!
15 *Fervour* - a collection of passionate flowers for
   those eager for "more"
16 *Festivity* - an arrangement of flowers for religious
   and birthday celebrations
17 *Fetus* - a gathering of baby breath to celebrate conception
18 *Fibber* - a posy of florets to conceal a lie
19 *Fierce* - an assortment of blooms from a fiercely
   protective (and perhaps controlling) partner
20 *Fiery* - a gathering of blossoms for forgiveness
   after a bitter and somewhat vicious disagreement
21 *Fighter* - an arrangement of flowers for someone
   fighting to keep their love
22 *Finish* - an anthology of buds to celebrate finishing
   education, work, retirement, a race, a difficult journey
23 *Firsts* - a selection of blooms to celebrate firsts
24 *Fissure* - a collection of flowers to mend a fracture
   in a marriage or partnership
25 *Fix* - a bouquet of florets to fix a broken heart
26 *Fixation* - a combination of blossoms to present
   to a person you have an obsession with
27 *Flame* - a selection of flowers for that special
   someone who still lights your fire - perhaps an ex?
28 *Flatter* - a gathering of blooms to make someone
   feel special
29 *Flaunt* - an anthology of buds that shout of wealth

30 *Fleur* - a superb creation of peonies of course!

30 *Fling* - an assortment of flowers for a short affair

31 *Flirty* - a selection of blossoms to win a heart

32 *Florimania* - an insane collection of 100 blooms
for those who have a craze for flowers

33 *Flossie* - Roman Goddess of Flowers - say no more!

34 *Folly* - an arrangement of buds for someone who
has more money than sense - ka-ching!

35 *Fondness* - an assortment of flowers for someone
you like, really like!

36 *Fool* - a posy of blooms for someone who is an idiot!

37 *Forbidden* - a collection of buds that lure a lust interest

38 *Foreplay* - a combination of blossoms to encourage sex

39 *Forget* - a bouquet of flowers when you are in deep
trouble, or you want to forget the deep trouble

40 *Forgiveness* - an arrangement of blooms that
whisper words of "please forgive me"

41 *Fornication* - a collection of florets = sex

42 *Fractured* - flowers for broken bones ...

43 *Fraud* - an arrangement of blooms for a deceitful giver

44 *Frazzled* - an assortment of blossoms that release
an intoxicating fragrance that clouds the mind

45 *Freed* - a selection of 50 shades of flowers for the
soul who wants to cut ties or release chains

46 *Friends* - an anthology of buds that sing of love
and good times and memories never to be forgotten

47 *Frivolous* - a combination of trivial, silly flowers
for a superficial person

48 *Fruitcake* - a gathering of blooms for an eccentric
or mad person that balances their energy and calms

49 *Funeral* - a garland of delicate flowers for a man, woman,
child, baby or pet - always heartbreaking to make

50 *to be created*

I raised my eyebrows. Forty-nine flower arrangements that started with the letter "f", alphabetically. Who knew that Gram created magic from flowers every day in her floral boutique, then used them in mind persuasion with her customers' recipients? She certainly did have some fancy blooms and successful working formulas as a floriculturist.

I placed the book of flower secrets onto the wooden workbench and started matching flower formulas to orders. I hoped Gram didn't mind. Then I prioritized according to time of delivery. My work was mapped out for me this morning.

The shop was buzzing with business as soon as the doors opened at 8.30. Again, I noted that normal flower shops were never busy like this. It must have been the Tarrin factor of "more". Or perhaps, it was the coffee and tea that invited people in.

I glanced up from the workbench every now and again to see how Lucy was coping at the sales desk. She was fabulous.

By 10.30am, the last of the orders went out the door to their destination. I cleaned up the workbench and slid Xander's letter to the center of the workspace. I flipped it over to open the seal, and my phone buzzed.

GRAMPS: *Good news. No brain tumor.*
Talk to you later. x x x

ME: ♡ *Answered prayer x x x* Thank goodness.

I couldn't stop smiling. I went over to Lucy and held the phone message up for her to read.

She wrapped her arms around me in a tight hug and said, 'Now, get out of here for a thirty-minute break. I need to leave at eleven. I'll call you if I need you! But I won't.'

I ran my hands down my apron and looked around the busy flower shop.

'Go, Andi! Everything will be fine.'

I nodded, removed my work apron and put it on the back of the chair at the workbench, then touched the top of my dress to check that my scar was covered. The envelope from Xander caught my eye. I flipped it over to unseal it.

'Go, Andi! Before I chase you out of here with thorns from the roses!' Lucy called.

I held my hands up at my cousin, pushed Xander's letter to the side, grabbed Gram's *Book of Fantastical Flower Designs*, then left Flowers for Fleur and headed out into the sunshine. Tarrin's sunshine of *more*.

The central park was across the road, and the black, wrought iron park bench under the ancient oak tree looked like the perfect way to escape for a bit. Away from people. Away from flowers. But not too far that I couldn't call for help for myself if I needed it.

I looked down at my chest. My scar was covered. *Good.*

I opened Gram's flower design book to the first page, and the golden rays of the sun beamed onto it through the leaves of the aged tree. She had painted watercolor flowers and inked words in black:

❀ *Flowers are love*

❀ *Flowers are created with love*

❀ *Love isn't love until you give it away*

❀ *Actions speak louder than words*

❀ *Kind words conquer*

I nodded my head, agreeing with her words. This is how Gram lived her life, every minute of every day. And this is how I used to be, before that terrible day of the scars. And that is all good and dandy, until you look evil in the face. Then it's a matter of survival.

I stretched my fingers, stopping myself from touching the scar on my chest.

'Don't go there,' I whispered to myself, and suppressed the hate that tried to rise from inside. I repeated my survival mantra with whispered words:

Forgiveness does far more for me than for them, and, power over my own thoughts is my highest freedom.

Positive cognitive therapy could win.

I turned the page.

There were more flowers in an exquisite color palette, and words about a smile.

❀ *A smile is the universal welcome*
❀ *Use your smile to change the world; don't let the world change your smile*
❀ *A smile remains the most inexpensive gift I can bestow on anyone and yet its powers can vanquish kingdoms*
❀ *Today, give a stranger one of your smiles. It might be the only sunshine they see all day*
❀ *Every time you smile at someone, it is an action of love, a gift to that person, a beautiful thing*

I ran my fingers over the black ink script on the page ...*smile* ... my smile had disappeared that day. That day when I should have held on to Mia's hand tighter. I should never have let our grip slip, even as my blood dripped from my body, down onto the jagged ocean rocks below.

Bile rose in my throat. I swallowed hard to push it back down to where it belonged.

I divided my life into before the event, and after the event. One was full of color and laughter and music and love and life. The other, gray with an "a", although, I wished it was grey with an "e", like dark clouds and rain, like my heart was crying. But it was the color of gray with an "a". Nothing but tones of gray. My life was the color of broken.

My psychologist had told me to "Smile in the mirror. Do it every morning and you'll start to see a big difference in your life!".

I doubted it. What would she know? Had she been through what I'd been through?

The sun disappeared behind a cloud. I looked up at the silver lining. Some people claimed it represented hope. I claimed it was time to return to the flower shop where I would stop looking inside of myself where the darkness lurked and threatened to pull me under.

I closed Gram's book with care. This was surely an heirloom that would remain in the family until the end of earth time. And it was mine—for the pretend florist girl with the steel-capped work boots. I might start a fashion trend. You never know ...

I entered Flowers for Fleur with five minutes to spare. Lucy looked up and beamed me a captivating smile. Gram was right. A smile had power. Just like flowers. It touches your heart and soul and makes you think the world is perfect. Except it's a lie. The world is not perfect. Nevertheless, I drank in every positive speck of energy Lucy's smile offered me.

I walked to the workbench and donned my apron. There was Xander's letter sitting on the bench waiting to be opened. I picked it up and started to slide my thumb under the seal, once again. Done. I reached in to pull out the piece of paper.

'Yolande! I have a unique order for you to make up for Mrs. Smith,' Lucy called.

'Great. I like unique orders,' I said, hoping they didn't pick up on my sarcasm. I closed the piece of paper and wriggled it back into the envelope.

Mrs. Smith marched over to me at the workbench. I watched her carefully. Was she walking with confidence, or was she walking to confront me? She was the color of crimson red—determination and triumph.

I decided to try out a smile. If she was walking to confront me, it might disarm her.

Smile. 'Hi, Mrs. Smith. How can I help you? Are you celebrating?' *Keep smiling ...*

'Yes, I am. Today I made a mistake!'

'And you want to celebrate it?' I raised my eyebrows at her. This was incredulous. Mistakes weren't to be celebrated!

'Absolutely. Normally, when I make a mistake, I have a meltdown and dwell on it for days and think of all the things I could have done to avoid making the mistake and I lose sleep and I beat myself up over it—'

'That's not uncommon,' I interrupted. *I bet it's not as big as the mistake I made ...*

'Have you ever made a mistake, Yolande?'

At that moment, I wished Lucy had never called out my name to me. Mrs. Smith used it like she was a teacher lecturing me. I looked down and smiled in a grimace type of way, hoping it didn't look creepy. I looked back at her with a nice, pretend smile. 'Everyday— what can I create for you,' I said, trying to change the subject of mistakes, and trying to wash away her assumed accusation.

'You know, I thought today, it's okay to make mistakes ... it's not as if my mistake has killed someone ...'

I stilled and choked on my smile.

'I think I would like to celebrate with a bouquet of ...'

Fruitcake, I thought, *for the eccentric or mad person. She was making me mad! More than mad. She was making me angry. She deserved the fruitcake creation from Gram's book of designs. Or was she frivolous? She was making such a kerfuffle over something so unimportant in the big scheme of things. She really needed some resilience.*

What would Gram do? *Kindness.* The opposite of what I felt right now. But kindness is contagious, right? Just like a smile. Daisies, I decided. The blooms would just be daisies. They put sunshine into anyone's life—mistake or no mistake.

'Mrs. Smith. Please wander over to Darcy and order a tea or coffee while you wait. It's on the house. I have a wonderful creation of flowers in mind for you!'

Mrs. Smith clasped her hands together in front of her chest. 'Oh, thank you. That's so wonderful, dear!'

I nodded and tried out another smile, hoping it would encourage her to walk away from me while I put together her concoction of daisies. I didn't want her to watch me work. It would give away the fact that I'm a pretend florist. A fake.

It worked a treat. She about turned and marched over to see Darcy. When she ordered, Darcy looked over at me and raised his eyebrows. I nodded to him then disappeared into the cold room to collect a mixture of daisies for Mrs. Smith and her "mistake".

I returned to the workbench with ten yellow daisies, ten white daisies with a yellow center, and a single pink gerbera daisy for her mistake. I wrapped the stems with Hessian and bound it with string before I bundled the bouquet in natural brown paper. It was brimming with the simplistic beauty of daisies, plus a pink mistake. I stepped back and admired my creation. "Mistake of Madness"—that's what I'll call it. I took out my phone and photographed it for Gram. She would be pleased.

I picked up the flowers and Xander's letter and took them to the sales desk. I decided to read the letter while I waited for Mrs. Smith to finish her cup of tea.

I pulled the note out of the envelope and opened it up. I gasped. Xander's handwriting was flawless—every curl and swirl and dot and cross, written in black ink with a ... nib? Calligraphy. That's what it was—unlike his earlier notes. Did he write it?

Arms wrapped around me from behind. 'Time for me to go, my love,' Lucy whispered into my ear, twenty minutes later than eleven o'clock.

I folded the letter, put it down and turned around to Lucy. 'Of course it is. Thanks so much for helping out.'

'Anything for Gram. Good news is coming!'

'Yes. Yes, it is!' I smiled at Lucy. This time it was genuine, and my heart was lighter. 'See you later, alligator!' I said—our childhood farewell.

'In a while, crocodile!' she finished, smiled and scrunched up her nose at me, then left the store. I watched the bounce in her step. Energy followed her. It was contagious. I was eternally thankful for the time she spent with me after the scars came into being.

Mrs. Smith's face appeared in my line of vision. 'Ah—how was your cup of tea, Mrs. Smith?' People liked it when you used their name—apparently.

'Delightful, thanks,' she answered. She looked at the flowers I had prepared for her "mistake" celebration, and her eyes lit up. 'Perfect, Yolande. Your grandmother would be proud!'

'Naw ... thanks, Mrs. Smith. Would you like to pay with cash or credit card?'

'Cash please, dear. When you use your credit card, the government and Internet watchers know everything about your spending, hence your lifestyle, building a psychological profile about you,' she said. 'You watch. Buy something on credit card, and BING! advertising for the same product will come up everywhere on your computer as your browse the Internet! Sometimes I even wonder if they are listening in to our conversations ...'

I frowned. Mistake or no mistake, I think Mrs. Smith was onto something. Could she be right? Scary if she was. 'That'll be $40.00, please,' I said.

'Really? I was expecting $50.00 for these gorgeous flowers.'

I smiled at her. 'I'm celebrating owning and surviving your mistake with you. $40.00 is fine!'

'Bless you, dear!' Mrs. Smith said, and handed over the money.

'Enjoy your bouquet of sunshine, Mrs. Smith,' I said and smiled. Again. I wondered if it was possible to use up all of your stored smiles ...

Mrs. Smith's former, determined march, had transformed into a light step. Gram would be happy. I gave a customer smiles and sunshine. She'll be back to purchase flowers, tea, coffee or books in the future. Happy customers = booming store.

At 11.45am the store became quiet. It was the calm before the storm when people rushed into Flowers for Fleur in a flower buying and ordering frenzy during their lunch break. I looked around at the jobs I had to do in fifteen minutes, but I really needed to read Xander's letter. I looked over at Darcy. He was busy polishing glasses and coffee cups.

I leaned on my elbows and opened Xander's letter.

Dear Fleur and Andi,

I am formally requesting the private use of your Cruiser bicycle for the total time of four hours on Sunday.

It's my mother's 60th birthday. She means so many things to so many people. But mostly, she has been the greatest support of my life choices and I want to do something special for her.

Your bicycle is the exact same one she had in

her twenties. Since I cannot give the bicycle as a gift, I would like to use it to help return her memories of that time in her life.

Your consideration of my request is much appreciated.

Yours sincerely,
Xander

My heart dropped. What a sweet thing for a son to do for his mother. I stood up straight. Formal letters are all good and dandy, but Gram won't lend out her beloved bike if she hasn't met him. In fact, she would never let anyone use her treasured bicycle. It was her most precious possession.

I carefully folded the letter and slipped it back inside the envelope, then texted Gram.

ME: *Dear Gram. How are you?*

She replied almost immediately.

GRAM: *Darling Andi. I'm home and I'm tired but my head feels better than it was. I hope the flowers are behaving.*

ME: *They are blooming difficult! As soon as I have them out on display, they are gone. Business is good. Will you be here on Thursday?*

GRAM: *As long as I'm fit and able, dear.*

ME: *Great. I have someone you need to meet. Will 9am be good for you?*

GRAM: *Hmmm. I'm intrigued ... looking forward to it.*

ME: *Excellent. Thanks Gram. Rest up and take care of you. xxx*

GRAM: *Will do. xxx*

I found some floral paper and wrote to Xander.

Dear Xander,

Gram would like to meet you on Thursday, 9am.
Be prompt.

Andi

I folded the letter and placed it in an envelope, then wrote his name on the front. I hurried through the store to Gram's bicycle and placed the envelope in amongst the symphony of colored old-fashioned peonies in the basket. I hoped he hadn't given up on the idea. A contact number would have been good.

I returned to the store just before the flurry of patrons. It was a madhouse. I needed to speak to Gram about employing another fake florist.

The afternoon went by in a blur of customers, flower cuttings, orders, deliveries and invoices. When I finally closed the doors at 5pm, I still had work to do, not to mention the tally of the days takings and ordering of flowers for the next day.

The sun had long set when I locked the shop doors behind me. The female only taxi was already waiting for me, as I always planned. It was safer that way. I blew air between my lips. I couldn't wait to return to my own career and the cocoon and personal security it provided.

Chapter Eleven

Thursday arrived with an exclamation mark! Gram was back at the helm, her smile adding a surreal light to the store. She was the color of pink, like strawberry ice-cream on a hot summer's day—welcome and refreshing. She stood at her workbench of flower imagination, creating bouquets of beauty and elegance with a natural flair that was impossible to emulate. She was most certainly in her element and habitual happy place, miles away from the trauma that had happened a couple of days ago, and I prayed would never happen again.

The doors opened at 8.30am, and Flowers for Fleur was filled with a stampede of people. More people than usual. More than the regular café coffee and tea junkies. More than the daily flower addicted people and browsers. People came to see if Gram was okay. She was a much-loved local store owner who had served the township of Tarrin for fifty years. I'm sure she knew everyone's secrets.

'Flowers, tea, coffee or books?' It felt like the millionth time I had said it. I really needed to cut off the books word. No one came here to buy books!

The man standing before me lowered his head and gazed into my eyes, his pupils dilated. I stiffened as my heartbeat raced. He scanned me from my head to my waist, his eyes hovering over my chest for way too long before he made contact with my eyes again. He was the color of flashing dark, dark red. He was a fist thumped on the piano keys, numerous times. I found it hard to breathe.

'I did come to buy some flowers. But I think I found something better.'

I raised an eyebrow at him while panic raced through my veins, stinging me. 'Flowers for your girlfriend?' I asked, ignoring his insinuation, trying to be courageous. I clenched my jaw.

'They could be for you if you let me—'

'Can I help you with your purchase, sir?' It was Darcy's deep voice. It was blunt. I breathed a sigh of relief.

'Ah ... no. I was just asking for some flowers. Simple really.'

'Is it?' Darcy said. 'I know the flowers that will do the job for you.'

'You do. You like the same things as me?' The man narrowed his eyes at Darcy.

'No. But I know your type. I know what you need,' said Darcy.

He raised his eyebrows at Darcy.

'Men know men,' Darcy elaborated.

'Lead the way,' he said, dipping his head.

I watched as Darcy led the customer away. I couldn't call the customer a man, because real men don't treat women as objects or playthings. But Darcy ... he was my hero. I watched as he chose a bouquet of flowers and handed them to the thing inhabiting a human body, then took the cash from him.

I served three more customers before I saw Darcy walking towards me.

'How did you know?' I asked when he handed over the money.

'His foulness surrounds him like a visible stench. Men have radars for people like him and I could see you recoil at his presence.'

I closed my eyes and ran my fingers over my forehead trying to stop the flashbacks of three years ago.

'I also told him you were mine,' Darcy said, and smiled coyly.

'You did?' I said, raising my eyebrows.

'It was a test for him.'

'Did he pass?'

'No. He's bad news ... I'll stay with you until you get into your taxi tonight.'

A shudder vibrated through me. I visualized my self-defense moves and wriggled my toes in my steel-capped boots. I knew exactly where to damage him should he attack. 'Thanks, Darcy. You're the best.'

'I know,' he said, and smiled at me. Not a smile of happiness though. It was a smile of pity. I hated the pity smile. It made me feel more damaged than I already was. Damn the bloody pity smile! I hated people knowing any part of my story—what had happened to me. He only knew one part because of necessity, to stop him from thinking I was insane. He'd found me mid-PTSD—when I was trying to wash the blood from my hands. The blood that wasn't there. I was stuck in the loop of delusion and couldn't break free. He had pulled me away from the tap and wrapped his arms around me from behind.

'Stop, Yolande ... breathe,' he had whispered. He took me to a table and sat me down, then made me a cup of tea. I told him a fraction of my story. Not everything. He had gone pale when I told him about the blood. He left the table and went to the café kitchen, leaned over the bench and drank two glasses of cold water.

There were only five other people who knew limited fragments of what happened on that terrible day of the scars—my parents, grandparents, and my psychologist, Dr. Jones. No one else would ever hear the story from my lips. Ever. There was no use digging up the past. It was dead and buried ... *like* ...

I knotted my fingers together then smoothed down my apron. I had jobs to do. And so did Darcy. 'Let's knock off early tonight—5.30! Deal?' I said and took a deep breath.

'Deal,' Darcy said, and gave me a thumbs-up. He returned to the coffee machine and slipped back into his role as the kind-hearted barista.

Flowers for Fleur was insanely busy, and I found it hard to catch a breath between customers. I had just served the tenth person in 28 minutes and entered the sales data into the account book when I looked up at the next patron, and there he stood. Xander.

'9am. Like you said.' He gave me a crooked smile and lowered his head, his dark hair falling over his blue eyes. Today he was dressed in a long-sleeved, pale blue button-up shirt, and trousers the color of stone. My heart skipped a beat.

'I ... didn't think you'd come ... after you left the other day—'

'It's not about me.' He frowned. 'You did read the letter, didn't you?'

'Yes ... I did.' Why did he make me feel so self-conscious?

'Follow me.'

I left the sales desk and walked over to Gram. She was humming one of Grampapa's songs while she worked on a creation of flowers. My heart warmed. She looked up at me and then over my shoulder at Xander, where her eyes remained.

'Gram. I'd like you to meet Xander. Xander, this is my grandmother, Fleur Lawrence.'

Xander leaned forward and held out his hand to Gram. 'It's lovely to meet you, Mrs. Lawrence. I trust you're feeling better today,' Xander said.

I frowned at Xander and his formal words.

Gram took Xander's hand and held his eyes in hers for longer than necessary. Did she know him? 'Yolande, darling, please ask Darcy to make me a pot of tea, and Xander, what would you like?'

Xander turned to me. 'Coffee, please ... *Yolande*,' he said, and raised his eyebrows while he said my name.

I narrowed my eyes at him. He only knew me as Andi. It was only natural for him to react that way with my full name. 'Of course, Gram. Would you like to sit at one of the tables?' I asked, before I went to order their tea and coffee.

'Most certainly,' she said, filled with enthusiasm.

I left them to their conversation while I kept the wheels of the flower shop turning. Each time I glanced over at Gram and Xander at the cafe table, they were in deep conversation.

Forty-five minutes later, while I was tidying Gram's workbench, I heard my name called. I looked up to see Xander standing by the entrance. Gram was beside him, smiling. *What had she done?*

Gram gestured for me to join them. I put down the loose rose petals, brushed my hands down my apron, checked that my chest scar was covered, and walked over to them.

'Andi ... I have agreed for Xander to borrow my bicycle for Sunday, on one condition, which he has agreed to,' Gram said, touching Xander's arm.

'And that would be?' I couldn't keep the surprise from my voice. Gram had never trusted anyone with possession of her bike, not even me.

'That you accompany Xander to his mother's celebration to ensure the safety of my bicycle.'

BOOM! Right then and there my world darkened, and anxiety reached its ugly hands up to my throat to stop me from breathing. 'But, Gram, I—'

'It's all organized. Xander will meet you here at 1pm Sunday.'

'But, Gram, I—'

'I, what, dear?' Gram asked with both eyebrows raised at me. Her look told me that no excuse would do.

'I'll be here ...' I said in a quiet voice. I looked at Xander. 'Email me the details,' I said with the last of my breath, then turned on the heel of my steel-capped work boots and hotfooted from the store via the back exit.

I leaned against the brick wall and sucked in a sharp breath, then bent over, overcome with nausea from anxiety. 'No,' I whispered. 'I can't go to the party. I won't feel safe ... I won't *be* safe ...'

Footsteps crunched on the gravel then stopped. The shoes I could see belonged to Gram.

'I know what you're thinking. It's been three years, and nothing has happened to you,' she said sternly.

'Only because I plan everything meticulously before I go, and am surrounded by friends and family I know and trust to look out for me.' I kept my eyes on the ground.

'Yolande, you can't live your life in the shadows anymore. You are running in fear, every day. Everything you choose is based on fear. It's time to give it up. You are your own worst enemy. Now enough of this nonsense, we have all put up with it for far too long!'

Her words of criticism hit me in the chest and stung my heart. My eyes burned and I stood. 'You're right, Gram. I'm a terrified little girl inside this grown-up body of mine. I'm a worthless loser who has no right to enjoy my life after what happened.' I took off my apron and contained the sob that wanted to escape from me. 'I'm sure Charlotte or Lucy will come in to help you if you ask.' I threw my apron at Gram.

And ran. Fast.

'You can't keep running, Yolande. Face your fears and be bigger than them. Make sure you're here on Sunday at 1pm. It's an afternoon garden party. Think Audrey Hepburn. No safety boots!' Gram called out to me.

I kept running.

I didn't turn back. I just ran.

Chapter Twelve

I sat in the chair outside the psychologist's office. I'm sure it had a permanent imprint of my butt on it. My mother's hand was around my upper arm like a vice so I couldn't run. She knew me well. Thank God. I didn't want to be here, but I did. I needed to be here. Darkness had reached up to pull me under, yet again.

A woman in her thirties came out of the office. She had manicured nails, perfect hair, make-up, shoes that weren't steel-capped safety work boots, and a matching handbag. But I couldn't see what color she was. Not when I felt like this.

I pulled a face. I wanted a matching handbag. No, I didn't. I wanted the perfect hair and make-up. No, I didn't. I wanted to be her instead of me. She didn't look like she had any problems.

She turned her perfectly painted face towards me and smiled. One of those smiles that says, "I've got my shit together. I like me!" Maybe when I came out of my therapy session with Dr. Jones today, I'll come out looking a million bucks—like her. A new person. A new past. My baggage gone like it was permanently lost on a plane flight, or spewed out into space, never to return.

I swallowed. The bitter reality was, this is me. Fucked up. Because of two men. Two cowardly bastards. I hated them. I hated them with every fiber of my being. I hated what they had done to me, what they had done to Mia—what I had become.

I lowered my head and sobbed.

My mother shifted in her chair and handed me a tissue— my dear mother, who had the same blonde wavy hair and blue eyes like Gram and me. Except their hair fell to their shoulders, styled of course, while mine, dyed brown, fell to the middle of my back. Wild. I took the tissue from her and silently uttered a thousand apologies. Every parent deserved for their child to grow up happy—happy with a job, happy with friends, happy with themselves, happy with a partner, and babies. Not a self-loathing person like me. I should have d—

'Yolande.' Dr. Jones's voice was comforting, like a warm childhood blankie and a mug of hot chocolate by the fireplace.

My mother's grip loosened on my arm and I stood, eyes focussed on the floor. I took slow steps into the office. The familiar office. I'd been here so often I was wondering when she'd ask me to pay rent.

Dr. Jones put a light hand on my shoulder and led me to the couch. Usually, she asked me whether I wanted to sit on the chair or lie on the couch. Today there was no such question. She knew me well. For a moment I wondered if psychologists ever saw a psychiatrist or psychologist themselves? Who did they go to when they had a problem?

While my body molded to the curves of the furniture, Dr. Jones went to make of pot of tea. I heard the chink of the china teacups and saucers and the boiling water. I closed my eyes and rested my hands on my stomach. I knew what questions were coming. And I knew how to answer them so she heard what she wanted to hear, which was not necessarily my truth.

But today, I had decided, I was going to answer her questions, for me—for my truth, in the hope that it would set me free. My stomach quivered. *Courage. Step boldly.* I had to do this for me.

At the sound of approaching footsteps, I opened my eyes. Dr. Jones placed two teacups and saucers on the table in front of me. I reached over and picked up a cup. The warmth of the brew touched my lips and I relaxed a little. Aah ... tea ... *the magic key to the vault where my brain is kept,* according to Frances Hardinge.

'What brings you here today, Andi?' Dr. Jones asked, sitting beside me, so we weren't facing each other.

'The darkness within,' I said, and sipped on more tea. 'And fear.'

'Ah ... good old Darius Darkness. Your friend. What is he trying to tell you?'

'I deserve everything that happened. I almost believed him. But Darius is such a liar. He's relentless at times.'

'Well done, Andi. So, I'm assuming fear has jumped on board to weigh you down?'

'Yes.' I sipped on my tea. It warmed my throat and my stomach. I welcomed its warmth.

'Fear of?'

'Gram wants me to go to a garden party with a stranger to protect her bicycle. She told me not to wear my steel-capped boots.'

'How does that make you feel?'

'Terrified. I spiraled into a panic attack. I almost vomited from the anxiety it brought on. I took off my apron, and threw it at her, then ran. I ran away from Gram! I felt so terrible. She's not well you know, and I did this to her on top of what she's going through.'

'Why did you throw your apron at her?'

'She told me not to live my life in the shadows anymore. She said I was running in fear ... all the time. She said everything I chose to do is based on fear. She said, "that's enough of this nonsense, we have all put up with it for far too long!".'

I started to sob. I had failed everybody. I was a burden to everybody. I stole happiness from everyone who knew me. I felt like I was the color of black, absorbing everyone else's color.

'What did you think of your grandmother's words?'

I gained some sort of control of my crying. 'She ... she spoke the truth ... and it hurts.'

'I agree with your grandmother, Yolande. What you're doing day to day is surviving, not living. You're leading your life within tight, constricting walls you have self-imposed, squeezing your right to happiness from you. What happened to you and your friend is not your fault. Those men had choices. And they chose wrongly. It had nothing to do with you, or your friend, what you did, or didn't do, what you could have, or should have done. There was nothing you could have done to change the outcome of the events. The attackers were under a drug-induced psychotic state. You just happened to be in the wrong place at the wrong time.'

I closed my eyes and put my trembling hand over my mouth. I dragged my hand away and ran my fingers over my scar. 'I know ... I know all the facts and the results of the medical testing and psychiatric assessment of the bastards. The whole tragic event should never have happened. I want to go back in time and change the outcome. But I can't.'

'Have you visited Mia?'

'No.'

'It's something you need to do. There's a goal for you, Andi. I know you can do it. You have come such a long way since we first met, two and a half years ago.'

I sucked in a shuddering breath. 'I know.'

'Let's go back to the incident with Gram. Which is worse? Going to a garden party with a stranger, or not wearing steel-capped boots?'

'I think ... deep down ... it's not wearing my steel-capped boots. They're my safety net. I know they'll inflict serious damage if I kick someone with them in self-defense, and give me time to run.'

'I'm surprised. I thought going to the party with a stranger would rank higher than your steel-capped boots.'

I looked down at my faithful brown boots. I wore them with my jeans today and they didn't look so out of place, unlike wearing them with a dress at Flowers for Fleur. I wondered how they would look with an Audrey Hepburn type of old-fashioned dress that Gram suggested I wear. I touched the scar on my chest again. I was hit with the realization that a fancy, feminine, Audrey Hepburn dress would cover my scar entirely, and I wouldn't have to worry about the scar accidentally revealing itself to innocent guests, who would then stare at me after the initial shock of seeing it, then communicate a look of pity to me. Gram always thought of everything.

'At first, going to the garden party with a stranger was more terrifying, but when I thought about it, behind the stranger thing was that I had no one there to help look out for me, to be my extra eyes and ears in case of an attack. If I had my boots on, I'd feel safe. But when Gram added the no steel-capped boots, I felt cornered.'

'And that triggered other negative emotions and memories?'

'Yes.'

'So ... we return to the garden party and the boots. Knowing you, you already have a plan. What is it?'

'I have to wear a dress, with normal dress shoes. My fear is I have nothing to protect myself with. I think shoe throwing would be laughable.'

'It would still give you some time. Don't underestimate it. What else can you take that could be tucked into your bag?'

'Pepper spray. Hairspray. Whistle. Laser pointer. Self-defense safety rod. Mobile phone stun gun.'

'Have you considered telling your garden party partner your safety concerns?'

'Never. He knows nothing about me. He is literally a stranger, albeit one who has talked to Gram for close to an hour, and she's given him permission to borrow her bicycle for four hours as long as I go with him—something she has never done! And I still can't believe she has sacrificed my mental health in the equation.'

'Do you think he—'

'Xander—'

'Xander ... may feel the need to protect you if something unforeseeable happens at the garden party, considering you are going along as a guest? '

I closed my eyes. I had lost my trust in men. 'I honestly can't tell you. All I know is that I must be able to protect myself, no matter what, no matter who else is around, and never to rely on anyone else when it comes to my personal safety. I can't ever trust a man again.'

'That's a valid reaction considering your history.'

There was a short conversation silence. I could hear Dr. Jones madly scribbling notes into her file titled, "Yolande Lawrence-Harrison". I'm sure one of my therapy sessions will be on male trust, and learning to trust again.

'Andi, I want you to visualize this ... you've got your Audrey Hepburn style dress on, cleverly and safely covering up your chest scar. Your other scar is hidden, as you have perfected. On your feet are comfortable court shoes. I have chosen that style because you can run in them, or flick them off to throw, or to run faster from a possible threat.' Dr. Jones sat opposite me and handed me a sketch pad. 'I'd like you to draw a picture of yourself in your dress and shoes. Use any of the drawing implements that you feel will reflect how you feel about the situation.'

I took a calming breath and started to draw. Just a simple stick figure drawing of a girl in a dress with dress shoes. I used color. I added a stick figure of Xander, in blue.

Dr. Jones leaned forward towards my artwork. 'What have you drawn on your face, Andi?'

'It's my mask. I wear it every day, without fail.'

'Are you wearing it now?'

'No. I feel safe to remove it here.'

'Thanks. Would you now draw your handbag with all your safety tools inside it please? Visualisation is an important and powerful mind preparation tool.'

I drew a smallish bag, with only makeup inside it.

Dr. Jones looked at me and frowned. 'Where's your taser, laser light, mobile phone, pepper spray and self-defense rod?'

'On me. In my pockets. If I lose my handbag in an attack, I still have protection implements.'

'Clever.'

I picked up the black pen and gripped it in my hand. Hard. I let out a low scream between my gritted teeth and scribbled over the red mask on my drawing. Tears dripped from my eyes and landed on my drawing, making the ink run.

Dr. Jones did not speak. She did not react. After a while, she asked, 'What are you thinking, Andi?'

I sobbed. 'I don't want to keep wearing the mask ... I don't want to keep pretending everything is okay. I don't want to be this person that I am after what happened. I want the carefree, happy, energetic, kind and loving me back. Everyone says it will get better with time. But it doesn't. Why couldn't it have been me, instead of her? It should have been me!'

There was a long silence. And I hated it. We had been over this road a million times before, and I wondered if Dr. Jones was getting tired of it.

'Have you told her how you feel?'

'No.'

'Why?'

'Because then I would feel ungrateful for being almost okay, when she's not.'

'You need to tell her, Andi.'

'I know.'

'When?'

'Sometime in the future.' *I wasn't ready yet. Was I being unkind?* 'And don't ask me the magic wand question. There is no magic wand, so the question is pointless.'

'You're right. It is indeed a pointless question. So is wishing. If you want a wish to materialize, you have to act upon it and make it happen.'

'Agreed.'

'So, do you wish to go to the garden party with Xander in an Audrey Hepburn style dress with court shoes that you can either throw or fling off to run faster, and carry make-up in your bag while your self-defense tools are on your body and pockets to use in case your bag goes missing due to whatever reason?'

'No. I do not wish to go. So it won't be happening. Gram can accompany her beloved bicycle if she does not trust the very nice Xander to return it in one piece.' I sighed and looked down at my hands. 'I'm sorry for wasting your time today, Dr. Jones. Patients like me must be very frustrating.'

'On the contrary, Andi. Challenging is a word I might use. But I love challenges. My goal is to help you overcome your obstacles by giving you a mental toolbox full of effective strategies, so you will be able to live a life full of rich and rewarding experiences with happiness thrown in as the icing on the cake. I have total confidence that you will get there.'

'Some days are harder than others.'

'Are the hard days becoming less?'

I thought for a bit. I didn't like to look back into the past three years, but this question required it. 'Yes. I think they are.' I spoke in truth.

'You do realize you're looking a whole lot better now than when you came through that door an hour ago.'

Was she speaking the truth, or was she using psychological mumbo-jumbo on me? Words of persuasion. Whatever it was, her words did make me feel a little happier, and more like I could cope again. Maybe I wouldn't have to put that mask back on when I walked out her door today ...

'Before we finish our session, Yolande, can I ask who the blue stick figure is in your picture?'

'It's Xander.'

'Why is he blue?'

'I see people in ... colors ...'

'Like an aura?'

'No. I see their character as a color. The color is usually above and behind their head.'

'How do you work out their character?'

'Intuition, behaviour, tone of voice, dress choice ...'

'Can their color change?'

'Absolutely, with incidents ...'

'I'm glad you feel safe enough to disclose this ability to me. How long have you possessed this way of seeing people?'

'Since I was seven.'

'What color are you?'

I took a deep breath and twisted my fingers together. My stomach tightened. I cleared my throat. 'The color of broken ...'

Dr. Jones was silent.

I stopped breathing when anxiety rose inside me like a wall of lava, about to incinerate me. It was freaking me out that she now knew this about me, and that she had not reacted to the description of my color.

'And what color would that be?' she finally asked.

I breathed out through my lips, slowly, steadily, counting to five in my head. 'Gray with an "a".'

'There's a difference?'

'Oh, yes. Grey with an "e" is very different to gray with an "a".'

'How?'

'Grey with an "e" is like ... the rain clouds. It's melancholy, but an enjoyable melancholy that builds up until it releases, and then it's like petrichor, the smell of the rain after warm, dry weather. Satisfying. Grey with an "e" is also when deep thought, philosophy and ponderings happen. Everyone should experience grey with an "e", it helps to discover parts of you that you never knew existed, and it can vanish without leaving a bitter aftertaste.'

'Tell me about gray with an "a".'

I looked down at my knotted hands. 'Gray with an "a" is ... never enjoyable—it's a very dark gray. It's self-judgment, doom and gloom, forever hanging around and within. It wants to drag you into the dark abyss of the color black, that absorbs all colors ... the color of self-condemnation, the color of depression, the color of death of the physical body.'

'But not the spiritual body?'

'No.' I didn't want to add any more to this conversation. It was painful to talk about.

'So, me being a supposedly normal person, could I see your gray with an "a"?'

'No. Because I mask it. And my gray with an "a" is not a plain gray with an "a". It's a crackled dark gray, with other colors that seep out ... sometimes.'

'What colors would they be?'

'Drips of red for anger ... specks of black—' *for self-hate*, '—for my secret, blushes of pink for my love for Mia and my family, and explosions of turquoise that screams at me to love myself ...'

'That's very insightful, Yolande. It's highly intuitive. I'm curious ... when you look at me, what color am I?'

I hesitated before I spoke. I never told anyone the color I had appointed to them for fear of them running from me. But Dr. Jones, she was different, she would understand ...

'You are ... magenta,' I finally said. 'It's the color of a person who helps to construct harmony and balance in life, hope and aspiration for a better world—mentally and emotionally,' I said, and held my breath, waiting for her reaction.

She raised her eyebrows at me. 'That's an amazing gift to have in your mind toolbox, Yolande. Does it ever lie to you?'

I closed my eyes. The two men on that terrible day of the scars were blue—trustworthy—until a truckload of alcohol changed them to negative red—aggressive and domineering, and then the drugs made them a violent and brutal dark red. Shades of red. Every color had shades and positive and negative attributes.

I pressed my lips together before I answered her question. 'Alcohol and drugs change the essence of a person's color. But then I have to wonder whether their sober color is their true color at all, and the inhibition that a little alcohol gives, reveals their real color.'

'Do you think I should be serving up glasses of wine, rather than cups of tea?' Dr. Jones smiled at me.

'Clearly. If anything, it would make great research!' I grinned, wondering whether Dr. Jones would have a glass of red on the table for me next time I was here.

'Thank you for everything you have shared with me today, Yolande. For Sunday, use the mind tools I have given you. I'm confident that the afternoon will go well. And try to allow yourself to enjoy the event.'

'Thanks, Dr. Jones.'

We stood and walked to her door. She opened it for me, and

I left, without one of those smiles that said, "I've got my shit together!"

Chapter Thirteen

Sundays were my self-imposed "dare-to-be-bare" day. A day just for me. By myself. In my exposed emotional state. No public persona, no mask, no makeup, no steel-capped safety work boots, no judgment from others. It was a day when I could slip back to the Yolande before that terrible day of the scars. The Yolande who had no fear and saw the world as an amazing place to be journeying through life. The Yolande who was compassionate, kind, and full of laughter. The Yolande who had a positive bent on absolutely everything—there was never a problem that couldn't be solved. There was no person who couldn't be saved from their own self-destruction ...

When I was in Tarrin, I spent the entire day in my parents' studio, painting or drawing while listening to loud music and sipping on cups of tea, wearing nothing but the same oversized tank shirt and underwear each time, no bra. My right breast was often exposed to just below my nipple. I had an odd sort of belief that my "healing" art therapy would miraculously rectify my scars, and one day I would look down and find my scar gone. I know it was stupid and delusional, but it was my glimmer of hope.

But today, my cherished Sunday wasn't mine. It had been stolen from me by my bicycle infatuated grandmother.

My mother held my hand, walked me to the car and drove off. I sat beside her with my eyes closed, wishing I could escape. If I opened the door, I could activate my wish and fall out and run. After all, Dr. Jones said I could run in court shoes. Bloody pink ones at that!

I hung my head when she pulled up outside Flowers for Fleur. On a Sunday. When it was closed. I fingered both of my pockets for my self-defense tools, then lifted my head, pulled down the sun visor and looked into the mirror on the back of it, scrutinizing my makeup, particularly in one area on my face.

'You've got this, Andi,' my mother said.

'I know, Ma. Logically speaking, I have it planned and sorted. Rationally, I know I'll be okay. But anxiety causes irrational thoughts. I just have to get better at over-riding my errant mind.' I looked at my mother and pressed my lips together. I know she was pushing me out of my comfort level. And I know that is the only way I could improve.

I opened the door, stepped onto the pavement and brushed down the skirt of my Audrey Hepburn style floral print dress. It was in the vintage chic style, a 1950s flared skirt and sleeveless fitted bodice. The high neckline covered my chest scar. There were pink flowers with green leaves over a white background. I narrowed my eyes at my pale pink court shoes. Steel-capped work boots would have been so much better.

When I looked up, my gaze locked with Xander's. He was dressed in a white cotton button-up shirt, the sleeves rolled to three-quarter length, skinny trousers the color of jet mid-blue, a brown leather belt and matching brown leather shoes. He was the color of celestial blue, like the earth from space: peaceful, powerful, sacred. He gave me a slight nod with a crooked smile.

I looked away from him and towards Gram when that curious heat ran through me. She stood in front of her beloved bicycle, beaming me a smile that almost blinded me. She was happy. *Good.* As I moved closer, her expression changed a little, her face falling in just the slightest way. She wasn't as good as she was trying to portray.

I reached out and touched her arm. 'I made it, Gram, without my work boots. Anyone who tries to steal your bike will be battered by the lethal court shoe,' I whispered.

Gram moved her head a fraction as she gave a small smile. Her eyes widened, and she froze in place. Her usual magenta color of love was a pale apple-green of distress and worry.

She spoke to me without looking at me, her eyes kept in place without moving. 'I knew you wouldn't let me down.' She moved her hand and searched for Gramps but didn't move her head. The vertigo had returned.

'Go with Gramps, Gram. I'll let you know when I'm back. Xander will take good care of me and your bicycle,' I said in a calm voice, masking the anxiety inside me.

Gram held the look of terror in her eyes. I wanted to lean in and give her a kiss on the cheek and tell her everything would be okay. But I knew it wouldn't be, and I knew not to do anything that would make her head move while she was like this. It would make her vertigo worse, much worse.

I held back a tear that tried to betray me. Why did it always have to be on the right side of my face? I brushed my hand over Gram's in a gentle, affectionate gesture and my heart rate picked up in urgency. I knew she had to get home quickly, or she would be stuck here outside her shop on a Sunday, unable to move.

I caught the tear on my fingertip then turned to Xander. 'Shall we?'

'Yes, but I need to thank your grandmother first,' Xander said and started to walk towards her.

I put my hand on his arm to stop him and raised an eyebrow at him. 'Thank her later. She'll be appreciative.'

Xander looked at me and frowned. 'Sure,' he said, and cast an observative gaze over Gram.

My mother stood before us. 'Enjoy yourself at the garden party, Yolande. And Xander, look after my daughter!' It was an order, not a choice.

Xander gave a nod. 'I will, Mrs.—'

'Lawrence-Harrison,' I whispered.

'I will, Mrs. Lawrence-Harrison. And thank you for lending me your daughter for the afternoon,' he said.

I gave my mother a gentle hug before I turned to Xander with a frown. *What did he mean by "lending"?*

He placed his hands on the handlebars of the bicycle and started to walk. There were two bouquets of flowers in the basket today. One, I expected, was a gift for Xander's mother from Gram. It consisted of Peruvian lilies, and multi-colored roses. There were sixty floral blooms. I had counted them in our awkward silence while we walked, and inhaled the scent—a sweet spicy smell resembling meadow honey, with fruity notes, no doubt from the roses, as the lilies had no scent. The other flowers were blue, and absolutely not familiar to me. They looked like they had been stolen from a garden or meadow in passing.

We journeyed in a northerly direction and I felt every single step in my girly court shoes. Were they meant to feel so constrictive? Did I wobble about in them too much? I looked around for a car or truck to transport the bike. But there was none.

'Are we walking to the celebration?' I asked.

'Yes, Yolande,' he said, rolling the letters of my name over his tongue. 'It's a beau—'

'Don't say it—'

'Say what?'

I shook my head. 'Just don't say it.'

'I was going to say it's a beautiful day for a garden party ...'

'Then ... yes, it is.' I looked up at him, and he gave me a coy smile.

'Yolande ... it's a—'

'Don't say it!'

'Say what?'

'It's a pretty name, a beautiful name ...' I shook my head. I hated it when people said that. It felt so condescending.

'Then I won't. The name suits you.'

'Is that a compliment or an insult? Are you referring to my personality or the way I look?'

Xander took a deep breath and raised his eyebrows. 'Do you always dissect conversations?'

'You didn't answer me.'

'Now you're putting me on the spot.'

'And?'

'And I barely know you.'

'So?'

Xander stopped walking and looked at me. 'Can we start again?'

He was right. I wasn't being fair. 'Yes, let's.'

'Andi, thanks for coming to my mother's birthday party with me.' He looked into my eyes. He was being genuine.

I took a deep breath. I shivered, even though I wasn't cold. Heat rushed to my cheeks. 'Although I had no choice in the matter, I'll try to make the best of the situation,' I said.

Xander lowered his head. 'I'm sorry you had no say. That wasn't my intention.'

'You're forgiven. Gram is just ensuring her bicycle is returned. I happen to be the tag-along with the bike.'

'A nice tag-along, I might add,' he said with a slight smile.

My stomach backflipped. 'You may not think that by the time we return to the flower shop with the bicycle.'

Xander rubbed the back of his neck.

'Don't worry. I won't hurt you.'

'Physically or emotionally?'

'Both.' I smiled at him. He was unsure of me. I was in a good position. Or maybe I wasn't. 'Will your girlfriend be at the party?' I needed to change the subject.

'I don't have a girlfriend.'

'Oh?'

'Girls are too nosy. They ask too many questions,' he added.

'You mean they dig deeper instead of scratching the surface?'

He looked down with an amused smile.

'They make you feel uncomfortable? Are you scared of what they'll find—like the real Xander?'

Xander stopped walking again and looked at me. He moved his lips to form a word then closed his eyes and pressed his lips into a hard line. 'It's not that.' He started walking again.

'Can you explain how my mother is "lending" me to you for the party?' I asked.

'I'm "borrowing" you to get my father off my back.'

'I see. He wants you to have a girlfriend, to get married, and then to produce some grandchildren for him.'

'Yes and no. He already has grandchildren, but I'm the only son, and the only one who can carry on the family name.'

'Ah ... but why do you need me to appear to be your girlfr—' I stopped speaking when the realization hit me tha—

'Yes. He thinks I'm gay.'

'Are you?' *Tell me.*

'What do you think?'

I looked at him. If he was heterosexual, he would have denied being gay with conviction. Straight guys hated being accused of being gay. 'Truthfully?'

'Please.'

'Some gays you can pick by sight. Some you can't. Some, you

are shocked to discover their sexual preferences. With you, I really don't know. Whether that's the assessment you wanted to hear or not, I'm not sure. Why does your father think you're gay?'

'Because I've never had a girlfriend.'

'And I've never had a boyfriend. Pleased to meet you, Xander!' I held out my hand to shake his.

Xander's hand wrapped around mine and he smiled at me. I think we had met a midway point to start a friendship. I pulled my hand away from his when a tingle shot up my arm. I frowned, shocked by what I had felt. 'What's the plan with the bicycle for your mother's birthday?'

'My mother has always spoken fondly about her favorite Cruiser bicycle that she would ride everywhere. Even after her curfew. She would describe its every curve and color with a passion. And then one day she stopped talking about it. Like she had forgotten her memories. Even when we said little things about her bike, she never started talking about it again. When I saw this bike outside Flowers for Fleur, it represented hope to me. My siblings and I are afraid that our mother has early-stage dementia. We discussed in great deal the pros and cons of having this bike here for her birthday. In the end we took a vote and, here we are.'

I looked away from him. His family was taking a big risk. The emotional toll would be high if his mother showed no recognition of the bicycle. Couldn't they have chosen another day in private to test her out?

'What did you vote for?'

'I thought it would be best not to make such a big fuss about it ... with only family to witness her reaction.'

'I agree with you. Compassion matters.'

'Yes, it does.' Xander looked at me like he was trying to make his mind up about me. Whether he decided I was friend material or not, didn't matter after today.

'We're arriving a little later than the other guests. So, consider yourself pre-warned that everybody will think you're my girlfriend.'

I giggled.

'What?'

'This could be fun.'

'You think?' His eyebrows knitted together.

'Absolutely. I liked acting classes at school.'

'Well, then. You're hired.'

I looked down and smiled to myself. I hadn't felt this happy for a while. Xander was easy to be around. There were no expectations. No pressure.

'We'll wish my mother a happy birthday first with the bicycle, take photos, then mingle with the guests—if that's okay with you?'

'And eat birthday cake?'

'Tons of birthday cake.' He looked into the distance and a glorious smile spread over his face.

'Deal!'

We stopped at a double wrought iron gate at a private garden. Pink and white balloons floated effortlessly from the center. I could hear laughter and a little light music.

Xander pushed on the gate and we entered. There was a mass of colored balloons among the greenery in the distance, and the sounds of people engaged in conversation drifted in the gentle breeze.

Xander slowed his pace as we came closer. His walk became stilted, his body tense. He was anxious. He didn't want this to happen at his mother's birthday, yet here he was, delivering what could possibly be a blow to the hearts of those who loved her.

Guests looked at the bicycle with gasps of awe, then to Xander, and finally me, where their eyes lingered. I was the supposed long-awaited girlfriend. I wrapped my hand around Xander's bicep in a show of pretend affection. Xander glanced at me with a gentle smile. A smile that warmed my heart.

A shriek of excitement sounded. I turned my head to see a woman rushing towards us. Her hair was platinum-colored, straight, in a shoulder-length bob with a fringe. She wore a feminine floral dress that was rendered in dusty pink and peach florals. The skirt was long and floaty with a dramatic drape hem. It was a flattering fit and a delightful style for the garden celebration of her sixtieth birthday.

'Ma. Happy Birthday!' Xander said.

'My Andy!' She wrapped her arms around her son and hugged him, then stepped back and looked at me. 'And who is this delightful person? Have you been keeping secrets from your father and me?'

'This is my girl, Andi.'

Xander's mother leaned forward with her outstretched hand.

I took it in mine. 'Happy Birthday. It's lovely to finally meet you!'

'Thank you. You have no idea how pleased I am to meet you!'

I smiled at Xander's mother. Did she also think her son was gay? Gay or not, he was a good man. Someone to be proud of.

Xander picked up the small bouquet of flowers from the basket of the bicycle. 'Your birthday isn't complete without flowers from me.'

Xander's mother caught her breath as she looked at the blue flowers. Quite frankly, they looked like weeds to me.

'Andy, these are just like the first flowers you gave me when you were four years old. I could never forget them!' she said with a tenderness in her eyes.

Xander smiled at his mother. But the smile was tainted with sadness. I placed my hand on his shoulder.

Xander's mother pulled off a flower and ate it. I held my breath while Xander reacted in a different way: he doubled over in laughter.

'I'll never forget your face when I ate one of the flowers when you gave them to me. I was sure you had stopped breathing for ten minutes. Now hold these while I have a good look at this bicycle!' She handed the flowers back to Xander.

I placed my hand on the bicycle seat so Xander could hold the flowers. His mother traced her fingers over the handlebars, the frame, the pedals, the wheels. She placed her face against the frame of the bike and closed her eyes, like she was lost in memories.

I swallowed the lump in my throat and looked up at Xander. This was the moment he had been waiting for—perhaps dreading. He wiped a small tear from his eye.

'This is exactly like my bicycle, except mine had a white basket on the back rack.' She stood and placed her hand on the side of Xander's face. 'So ... which story do you want to hear?'

Xander smiled. A smile full of love. 'All of them!'

He was rewarded with an equally impassioned smile from his mother.

'Let's get photographs of you and the bicycle, and us kids, Ma.'

'Absolutely. You get the photographer and I'll organize your sisters.'

Xander turned to me. I was now holding the blue flowers and the bicycle. 'I'll be back soon.'

'Go for it!' I said. When he left, I reorganized the basket of flowers so that it sat on the back rack, like his mother's bike. I placed the blue flowers predominantly before the other collection of blooms.

Xander walked over to me with quick steps and cast his gaze over the bike. 'You are way too nice, Yolande. Come for the photos.'

'Well ... I am the tag-along with the bike. I don't have much choice, do I?'

Xander looked down, smiled and shook his head. That curious heat ran through me. He looked up at me. 'Actually, you do, but I want you to see my mother in her happiest place on earth, then your gram will know exactly why I asked to borrow this bike for the day.'

'Is her happiness contagious?' I asked. I needed a large dose of it.

'Absolutely,' Xander said.

'Then ... I guess I'll tag-along,' I said.

I stood behind the photographer while the shots were taken. I couldn't help but grin at Xander, his mother and five sisters.

The final shot had Xander's mother sitting on the bike holding the wild blue flowers. She oozed poise and sophistication. As she dismounted the bike, a round of applause broke out. Xander walked over to her, gave her a hug, and held on to the bike while she returned to her guests.

I walked over to him. 'You're right. Happiness is contagious. Thanks. What are those blue flowers?'

Xander frowned at me. 'You're the florist ... you tell me.'

'Actually ... I'm not a florist ... I'm a pretend florist, who, I thought as a child was someone who played the flute!'

Xander looked at me with a half-smile. 'It's Chicory. It used to grow wild in the paddock next to where we lived.' Xander looked around and an official looking man appeared before him. 'Andi, this is Smithy. He'll keep the bicycle safe at the party while we mingle.'

I frowned at Xander and shook my head. 'No. If anything happens to the bike, it's on my head. So—no!'

'Andi—'

I grabbed the handlebars of the bike and started to walk with it. Back to Flowers for Fleur. I was terrified about the fact that I wasn't wearing my steel-capped work boots.

'No, Xander. That wasn't in the deal.'

'Your gram knows about it. Please.' Xander placed his hand on my shoulder. 'Trust me about the bike security, and ... I need you here, with me.'

I looked up into his blue eyes. Those pleading blue eyes that I wished I could fall into.

'Please.' His voice was softer, and he placed his hands together in front of his lips.

I closed my eyes and inhaled. 'Okay. But I feel uneasy about it.' I faced Smithy. 'I'll be checking on you every minute.'

He nodded at me.

I leaned the bicycle against the tree and turned to Xander. 'You've got me for two hours. And that's it.'

Xander smiled at me and held out his hand. 'Thanks.'

I placed my hand in his. 'You might want to hold off on that thanks in case I'm not worthy.'

'Oh ... I don't know ... people look at you and smile.'

'Is my dress on inside out?'

His eyes wandered over my dress and down to my shoes. 'Not that I can see.'

'Have I got my shoes on the wrong feet? I've done that before you know!'

Xander laughed. 'How ca—'

'It depends on the shoes ... you know ... women's shoes— they're not designed for comfort.'

'Have I got something stuck in my hair that shouldn't be there? Curls tend to grab things and never let go ...'

'No. Relax. It's all good. You're doing—'

An arm wrapped around Xander, but he kept his eyes on me.

'Josh. How are you?' Xander asked without looking at him. *Odd.*

'Great. Who's this with you?'

'This is Yolande ...'

Don't say it. Please don't say it ... I mind communicated to Josh.

'Pretty name.' He said it! My blood warmed with annoyance at the word "pretty". 'Where did you meet Alexander?'

Alexander? His name is Alexander?

'She's a florist,' Xander said. He tilted his head to the side and grinned at me.

'Temporarily while my grandmother is unwell. I have a career in aeronautical engineering.'

'As a secretary?'

I blew air between my lips, stopping the anger from brewing inside me. I smiled sweetly at the irritating man. 'Actually, I'm an aeronautical engineer in the Defence Force. I'm on a team that oversees the blueprints to ensure that design and calculations are correct before we spend the multi-millions of dollars to build the prototype for testing.'

There was silence as he shuffled his position. I made him uncomfortable. He cleared his throat. 'What are you working on at the moment?'

'Four designs. That's all I can tell you due to my NDA. What do you do—play football?' I added the football remark to get back at him for his condescending secretary remark.

He cocked an eyebrow at me. 'Football is an avenue to reduce the stresses of reality for many fans. And no, I'm not a footballer. I work in marketing ...'

'Congratulations!' I dipped my head and grinned at him.

Xander's hand wrapped around my elbow. He leaned in close to my ear, 'Play nice!'

'Fine! I'll dumb myself down for you!' I whispered.

He led me to a group of young adults, around his age— twenty-seven-ish, perhaps?

'Alexander. Long time no see. How are you?'

'Never better, thanks, Adrian. I'd like you to meet Yolande.'

'Nice to meet you, Yolande.'

'As you.'

'As we stand here, I find myself in need of asking you a question.' I kept my face without emotion while I narrowed my eyes at him, hoping he didn't recognize me from the trial that took place. 'If you don't work. I would like to offer you a job—in my office ...'

I took a deep breath and ran my hand over my forehead. 'Thanks,' I smiled at him and scrunched up my face for a second. 'But I make paper planes for a living.' I smiled.

'Like ... origami?'

'Sure. It's lots of fun. Hey, nice to meet you.' I turned to Xander. 'Alexander,' I said, over-pronouncing his full name. 'I need the powder room—which direction?'

He lifted his chin and looked down at me. 'Keep walking straight ahead until you see a door on your left. It's that way.'

'Thank you, muchly,' I said, and walked off, leaving him alone with his friends.

When I returned to the party, Xander was waiting for me, leaning against a tree, his right foot crossed over his left. He stepped forward and put his arm around my shoulder in a show of pretend boyfriend possession. 'Can you find a middle ground with your answers. You can't go telling one person you work for the Defence Force, and another you make paper planes. If a guy asks you a question, please answer with politeness, not aggression.'

'Alexander, I will cease being hostile to men when women are treated on equal grounds. We are not created for men's sexual desires, nor as submissives to bow to men's lifestyle needs!'

Xander sighed, then frowned at me. 'That's a bit over the top, isn't it? Not all men are like that ... what happened to Andi from the flower store?'

'She's in the same place as Xander whom I met at the flower store ...'

He lowered his head and grimaced. 'Touché. The sooner we're done here the sooner we can escape the facade.' Xander rolled his eyes.

'What?'

'We're approaching my father—2 o'clock—call him Mr. Parker. Be truthful for when you meet him again for dinner one night, and in case he does a background check on you—'

'Why would he do that—'

'Father, it's great to see you again. I'd like you to meet Yolande,' Xander said.

Xander's father's eyebrows shot up before he gave me a wide smile, and something else. *Was it relief I saw?* He took my hand in his. 'Yolande, it's a pleasure to meet you.'

'Likewise, Mr. Parker,' I said.

'I trust you are enjoying the party and meeting family and friends,' he said.

'Very much so. It's the perfect location for a celebration.'

'I hear that thanks must go to you for the bicycle appearance, I believe.'

'Yes. It's my grandmother's most treasured possession.'

'I think I've seen it outside Flowers for Fleur. Is that where you work?'

'At the moment while Gram is unwell, yes, but normally I'm an aeronautical engineer in the Defence Force.'

'Wow. That's impressive. How long are you going to stay in the force?'

'For as long as I can. I'm happy there, and it's challenging, which I enjoy.'

'That's wonderful. You kids enjoy the party. I must keep circulating amongst the guests. It's lovely to meet you, Yolande. See you next time, for dinner.' Mr. Parker leaned forward and kissed my cheek, then pulled Xander into a tight hug and patted his back. I think it was a sign of approval.

Xander held my hand as we walked to the pop-up bar. 'Do you really work as an aeronautical engineer?'

He hates me now ... 'You told me to tell the truth.'

'Yes, I did.' He hung his head as we walked. His mood had just taken a dive.

'I'm still Andi from the flower shop, except I know exactly why planes don't fall out of the sky.' My voice was flat.

'I know. It's just ... I miscalculated you.'

I frowned at him. My heart started to ache. 'Meaning?'

He looked at me. 'I ... I—'

My phone vibrated. I pulled it out of my pocket and turned away from him as tears pooled in my eyes. I blinked them away as best as I could.

GRAMPS: *Gram is in hospital again.*
More tests. She has asked if you can open
the shop tomorrow. xxx

ME: *Sure.*

I lifted my head to the sky. I really wanted to return to the Air Force Base where my steel-capped work boots were part of the uniform.

He miscalculated me? What does that mean?

I really wanted to run. In my court shoes. Dr. Jones said I could run in my court shoes ...

'Is everything okay?' He was behind me, closer than I wanted him to be. I could smell his scent—citrus with a hint of liquorice, vanilla, lavender perhaps, and a touch of sandalwood?

I turned to face him. 'Gram's back in hospital. She's having medical tests.'

'I'm sorry to hear that.'

I shook my head. 'You know ... she was the only one who

believed in me when I said I wanted to design planes when I was little ... she would say, *You can do it, Landi. Girls can do anything!* Ma said I should pursue my career in ballet. But I was too fascinated by planes and helicopters. Gramps would buy me every book and magazine about flight that he saw.'

'I'm glad you followed your dreams,' Xander said.

'What about you, Alexander, you know heaps about me, but I know very little about you.'

He looked down and put his hands in his pockets. 'Not much to tell really. I work part-time and study—'

'Alex, we're about to cut the cake. Come at once!' a voice called.

Xander nodded and took my hand in his. I trailed along behind him through family and friends. I plastered a smile on my face for Xander's sake. The perfect girlfriend. With a dark secret.

I stood back and watched his father and siblings gather around his mother for the cake ceremony. Physically, they were a stunning family. Xander was fussed over no matter where he stood. Were they protecting him from something? Were they covering up something? Or was he the adored one? The child who was treasured the most?

Parents aren't supposed to love one child more than the others. But they do. Surely. I was the inconvenient one. The one who was problematic. A blemish on the family after that terrible day of the scars.

The guests broke out into a boisterous rendition of Happy Birthday. It was clear that Mrs. Parker was dearly loved. She made a magnificent speech that made me feel like life was indeed bearable. I wondered what it felt like to live a life of privilege as she has had—everyday filled with a blue sky and a sun shining down, carving a golden path to walk upon.

I looked at Xander. His eyes were on me. He raised one eyebrow and gave a small smile. I raised one eyebrow and smiled back, and that curious heat ran through me again.

There was a flurry of movement as guests descended on the tea and coffee cart. A barista had been hired for the event. I joined the queue and ordered two cups of tea.

I walked over to Xander and handed one to him. 'You look like you need a cup of tea.'

'Am I that transparent?'

'No. It's just the way your siblings fuss over you. You must be a tea drinker, not coffee.'

'Do I seem flustered?'

'No—annoyed—like they won't let you grow up.'

'And so you see the need to break away from the family. They can be suffocating at times. Did you learn to read people in the Defence Force?'

'No. Selling flowers teaches a lot about people types.' I sipped my tea and stuck my pinky finger out. It was something Mia and I always did to see how people would react. Most of the time they pretended not to see it. But Xander laughed, almost spilling his hot beverage.

I walked away and collected a large portion of birthday cake, then stood to the side and watched people. Just me and my cup of tea and a large piece of cake. A girl couldn't be happier. Well ... this girl, at least, with the mask covering her past and her dark secret. This girl for whom life was a struggle.

I watched as Xander roamed about the guests, chatting. Did he do that by choice, or was it his duty?

After a short while, he walked over to me. 'How's the cake?'

'Delicious, thanks.'

'Your two hours is up. Time to go,' he said.

'What?'

'That was the deal—the bicycle and you for two hours, plus to accompany me for dinner one night.'

Used. I felt used. I had an empty feeling in the pit of my

stomach. Suddenly, my tea tasted bitter. I put down my teacup, closed my eyes and ran my fingers over my eyebrows.

When I looked up, Xander stood with his head down, his hands in his pockets.

'I'll just go and say goodbye to your parents and sisters. Not because I'm pretending to be your "girlfriend", but because it's the right thing to do.' I cleared my throat.

Xander took my hand in his while we said our goodbyes. The perfect lie. I was an accomplice. In exactly what, I didn't know.

The return walk to Flowers for Fleur was quiet. I didn't have anything to say to him. He should have asked Gram if he could "use" me and the bicycle for his mother's birthday celebration—because that's what he did.

'Thanks for being a great tag-along, Yolande. Your acting audition as a girlfriend was believable.'

'Good. I hope it helped you in whatever way it was meant to. The truth always has a way of coming out, you know. And it will set you free.' I took the bicycle from him.

'I know ... but it has to be when the time is right for me.' He gazed into my eyes, then frowned.

While I secured the bicycle inside the shop and locked the doors, he left. Without a word.

I looked down at my pink court shoes. I should have worn the steel-capped work boots.

Chapter Fourteen

'Flowers, tea, coffee ... or books?' I was recording a sale in Gram's accounting book while the words flowed automatically.

'Sex.'

I froze. It was a male voice: deep, and to the point. It wasn't a question. It was a statement. A confident statement. Right then and there, I decided to *never* again ask the flower question without looking at the customer first.

I looked up. 'Ssssex? You have come here for ... sex?' *He looked familiar.* I cleared my throat.

'Yes. Flowers for sex. Flowers that will make my partner want to have sex.' He was the color of vermilion, an orange-red that spoke of desire, sexual passion, and a hunger for action.

I breathed a sigh of relief and frowned. Then I wanted to tell him that his partner would want to have sex because of him, not because of the flowers. But I didn't. 'Do you love her?'

'Him—yes!'

I hesitated. His unexpected answer threw me for a moment. I gathered my thoughts. 'If I was him, I would like the "I love you, flowers". It will make the sex more passionate.'

He tilted his head and narrowed his eyes at me. 'I think I agree.'

'Roses, tulips, sunflowers, carnations, azaleas ... orchids, perhaps. These are the flowers of love.' I waited while he thought and tapped my work boot to see if I was physically here. My pretend florist knowledge was becoming too real and too easy to regurgitate.

He pressed his lips together and nodded. 'Can I have a combination of all of those?'

'Sure. Which colors?'

'What's the color of love, according to a florist?'

'Red for passion and coral for desire and love, and pink. You can choose one, two or all.'

'Passion, desire, love ... I have to have a mixture.'

'In a mixture of flower types?'

'Please.'

'Sure. Have a complimentary tea or coffee while I create your flowers for sex. Go and say hi to Darcy and tell him that Andi sent you over. What's your name for when the flowers are ready?'

'Josh ... and are you sure about the complimentary tea or coffee?'

'Absolutely. Enjoy, Josh.' He was the one who wrapped his arms around Xander at the garden party.

He gave me a sly smile: lips closed, left eyebrow raised, then wandered off to the café.

I frowned, then recorded the order in the sales book and headed to the workbench. I pulled out Gram's *Book of Fantastical Flower Designs.*

Hmmm ... flowers for sex ... would it be under fondness, foreplay or fornication? Technically they weren't married, so it's fornication. But the word fornication doesn't sound like love. Fondness is more like what I think he feels. But then again, the flowers are acting as foreplay ... Ahh! A combination of the three. I studied the illustrated designs by Gram and created a new bouquet—*Amour, by Andi*. Perfect. Red and orange roses, tulips and carnations, with a touch of eucalyptus baby blue. I wrapped the stems in Hessian and string before I placed the bouquet into a fancy white paper bag. I added a "Flowers for Fleur" sticker to the front and the order was complete.

I smiled to myself and walked over to Josh. I stopped before him as he sipped on a coffee. '"Amour, by Andi". I hope you like my design,' I said.

His eyes wandered over the flower arrangement and he smiled, widely. 'I don't like them ... I love them! Thanks, Andi.'

'I'll keep them at the sales counter until you've finished your coffee.' I smiled at him, then returned to the sales desk where a queue of customers waited, and where I replayed the scene at the party where Josh put his arm around Xander. And where Xander refused to look at him.

My heart took a nosedive. I looked down at my steel-capped work boots and tapped them twice on the wooden floor. I now knew I would never have to use them with Xander. I was as safe as a girl could be with him, and Josh.

I looked up at my next customer. 'Flowers?' I asked.

'Hello, beautiful!' He was the color of gold: success, achievement and triumph.

I shrunk inside of myself. I couldn't be beautiful on the outside with my scars. And I couldn't be beautiful on the inside because I let go of Mia's hand. 'How can I help you?'

'I just bought a new car. So I need to buy some flowers for my wife. Win-win. You know ...' He winked at me.

I hated winks. It meant that he was either lying, or telling me a secret that I must not tell. He had just implicated me in his untruth, in one ... simple ... act. Of course, winks could also be a friendly gesture, like when Darcy winked at me. But not this wink—it was different ...

'Cool,' I said, finding my inner calm to override the annoyance I felt. 'What type of car did you buy?'

'A Bugatti Chiron.'

Wow! 'Color?'

'Red.'

'Niiiiice! Do you want red flowers for your wife, then?'

He took an audible breath. 'No ... I think a rainbow of colored flowers, thanks darl!'

I looked down to stop myself giving him the evil eye. I hated endearing names from men. They made me feel yuck, and it felt manipulative. 'Rainbow flowers coming up. Please have a complimentary coffee while I create a large bouquet of blooms for your lovely wife, Mr. ...'

'Peter—my first name.'

'Wonderful. I will bring your "win-win" flowers over to you once I have prepared them, Peter.'

'Thanks,' he said and walked away.

I had a plan. And it involved a pricey sum for flowers. Plus, a bottle of wine ... no ... champagne was the celebration drink, wasn't it? After all, his car status symbol wasn't cheap. His wife will think he is a wonderful husband.

Charlotte burst through the doors of Flowers for Fleur with her color of bumblebee yellow, innocently and infectiously happy. Timely. She was a lifesaver. Did Gramps call her in? She grabbed her apron and gave me a hug. I looked over at Darcy. Did he call her in?

'Thanks for taking over the sales desk. I have blooming designs to create ... you have no idea how thankful I am that you're here!'

Charlotte gave me a smile then turned her attention to the next customer.

I walked over to the flower art workbench and opened Gram's *Book of Fantastical Flower Designs*. I ran my finger down the contents page. And there it was. Flaunt. He was flaunting his wealth. Perfect. Page 29.

alstroemeria (lily of the Incas)
available in a rainbow of colors

I raised my eyebrows. Your wish has been granted, Peter the Bugatti owner. I entered the cold storage room and gathered twenty stems of alstroemeria, totaling sixty colorful flowers. I placed them into a clear bulbous vase and tied five strands of natural raffia around the neck of the vase. I spritzed the blooms with a flower preserver and went to the storeroom to fetch a lovely bottle of pink champagne, which I gift wrapped in a white carry bag. I took out my phone and photographed my creation. Gram would be delighted. This aeronautical engineer was getting the hang of this florist gig. I carried the Lily of the Incas-vased bouquet and champagne bag to Peter, who was sitting by the window in the café, gazing out at his new, red car.

'Presenting your rainbow of flowers, plus champagne to celebrate your "win-win". Please pay Charlotte at the sales desk before you leave. Enjoy your new car. And, ah … don't go trying to break the 42 second world record in your Bugatti …'

Peter looked at the flowers and then to me with a crooked smile. 'Perfect, thank you. How do you know about the world record?'

'I'm an aeronautical engineer pretending to be a florist to help out my Gram. Design and speed is my specialty.'

He raised his eyebrows. 'I'm impressed. I knew there was a reason I stopped at Flowers for Fleur!'

I smiled at him. 'Nothing is too expensive; nothing is too beautiful. We always work with the customer, as Bugatti does.'

Peter laughed. I had just quoted the Bugatti motto for his benefit. He would be back to buy flowers for his wife in the future.

'Enjoy,' I said, then returned to the workbench of flower

imagination. There were orders to fulfil and have delivered.

Darcy placed a cup of tea on the workbench for me.

'Thanks.'

'Do you know who that guy was that you gave the flowers to?'

'Sure, he's a Bugatti Chiron owner,' I said.

'And?'

'And that's all I know. Should I know more?' I asked.

Darcy narrowed his eyes at me. 'I guess that's all you need to know. I think Gram will be very happy with your customer liaison skills—especially with Bugatti owners.'

'Cool. Now, if you don't mind, I have work to do.' I raised an eyebrow at him.

'Geez, Louise. You're so bossy. No wonder you don't have a boyfriend!'

I looked at Darcy, then put my fingers over my eyes the moment I felt them burn with tears. After the day of scars, I would never be a wife or a mother. My heart was damaged. My body was damaged. A man won't be able to see past the physical scars, and he sure as hell won't want to deal with my psychological baggage.

'Oh crap! I'm sorry, Yolande. I had a brain glitch. Forgive me.'

I took my hands away from my eyes. I couldn't look at Darcy. I shook my head. 'Just go,' I whispered.

He tapped his hand on the workbench and left. I took a deep breath and tried to ignore the overwhelming sudden gush of heartache that flooded my body. I widened my eyes to stop the tears from falling. *Distraction.* I found the next floral order and focused on the details: a simple bunch of daisies. No fancy, convoluted or encrypted addends. Just friggin', bloody, daisies. White.

I let out my breath and ran to the cold room. The moment I opened the door I was accosted by the chilled air. It hit me like a slap in the face. I stilled for a moment, wondering if the chilled air would freeze my tears. I closed the door and put my hands on the top of my head and paced the small room. It was no good feeling sorry for myself. The pity party pit was a lonely, miserable place that reeked of rotten garbage, packed into my personal baggage. Whoever said life is beautiful hadn't suffered. I was filled with jealousy. I was filled with a deep sadness over my stolen happiness.

Life is painful. Messy. Hard.

I pressed my palms to my eyes. I couldn't let a tear expose me. Even a frozen one.

I sighed loudly. *Distraction.* It was the only way to climb out of the deep pit of despair. I looked around the room and found the frigging, bloody daisies. White. Then counted to ten before I left the room, without my self-pity.

My steps slowed when I saw Gramps at the workbench. I placed the white daisies next to the paper and ribbon.

'Grampapa, hi.'

'Hi back, Yolande.' He looked around the store. 'It looks busy this morning,' he said.

'It hasn't stopped since I opened the doors. How's Gram?'

Gramps closed his eyes for more than a moment. 'Still nauseous ... scared.'

'Scared?'

'Of another vertigo attack.' Gramps brushed his hand over his face. When he moved his hand away, he shook his head. His eyes were wet. He blinked numerous times.

'Surely there's a medication that'll make it go away?'

Gramps shook his head. 'The doctors can't even give us a diagnosis at this stage. The only certainty is that it's something to do with the inner ear ...'

'Well, that sucks. Why do ears have to be so complicated!' I started to wrap the daisies. White.

'Yolande. Where is Gram's bicycle?'

I sucked in a breath and tensed. I didn't put her bicycle out the front of the store this morning!

'Gram would be furious if she saw the bike was missing. You know what it mea—'

I put my hand on Grampapa's arm. 'I'm sorry, Gramps. From the moment I arrived this morning I've been in a rush—'

'Gram always did everything on her own and she always ha—'

'Stop ... stop, please.' My bottom lip trembled. 'I'm not a florist. I'm not a store owner. I'm not even a flowerologist who can read people's minds when they are requesting a particular type of flower for a specific occasion. I shouldn't even be here. I should be—'

'Forgive me, Landi.' Gramps closed his eyes and shook his head. 'Gram's illness is hard on all of us. Please hear me with sincerity when I say your grandmother and I are so very thankful you are here.' Gramps pulled me into a hug. He had no idea how much I needed it.

'I'll get the bicycle and add some flowers.' I pulled away from Gramps and put my hand on his shoulder.

'I'll do it!' Gramps put his hands on his hips.

I burst out laughing. 'Including the flower arrangement?' He was being incredulous.

He nodded. 'Certainly.'

'Make sure you prepare the flowers correctly, so you don't kill them!'

Gramps frowned at me. 'Oh-me-oh-my, Landi. Don't worry about that. I have a head full of knowledge about the flower science of keeping flowers looking handsome.'

'Really?'

'I certainly do. I don't need your help,' he said.

'Clearly,' I said, and gave him a sweet Yolande smile of the past, before that terrible day of the scars. 'Thanks.'

I cleaned the sales desk and rearranged the ornaments and plants to encourage purchasing while Charlotte was on her lunch break. I took a step back and assessed my new arrangement, not convinced that it looked tempting enough, then fussed with it some more, listening to the light footsteps that graced the floor in neither a feminine or masculine way. The scent of citrus with a hint of liquorice, vanilla, lavender, amber and sandalwood could be smelt.

Xander.

I looked up. He was the color of blue, deep, like the ocean depths, reminding me of slow motion, whale songs, dolphin clicks, and a halo of sunlight at the surface.

'Hey!' I said, and touched my chest scar to make sure it was covered. It was no use rolling off my usual flurry of words of flowers, tea, coffee or books. He never bought flowers—only stole them. He didn't look like a book guy, and I'm sure he wasn't here for the beverages.

'Hey!' he said.

'Are you here for flowers?' It was said in jest with a wry smile.

He smiled coyly, lowered his head then looked back up at me. 'Conversation ...'

I looked at him and waited.

'So ...' I encouraged.

'Thank you for being the one to enable me to use your gram's bicycle ... and for being the tag-along as my pretend girlfriend when you didn't want to be there.'

I smiled at him. Gram said smiling always helped to hide a myriad of emotions. I hoped my smile hid the confusion I was feeling. 'The cake was nice. I wish I could have had more though.'

'Granted.'

'Granted?'

'Wishes ... hey ... I have to go.'

'Sure ... no charge for the conversation!' I hoped he could see my sense of humor.

He frowned at me. 'Yeah ... so ... thanks again. I appreciate it.' Was he wanting to ask me something else? He seemed kind of nervous.

'See ya ...'

'Yeah ... bye.'

I watched as Xander turned, almost like a pirouette, then walked "step and point" for two steps before he fell into a normal stride. I narrowed my eyes. How odd for a guy to walk like that, unless he was—

'I'm back!' Charlotte said when she stood beside me.

'Good,' I said, picturing Xander ice-skating.

'Mmmm—he's delicious,' Charlotte said and let out a dreamy sigh.

'With an unpleasant aftertaste ...'

She spread her fingers out on her chest. 'Do you know him?'

'Once—for a little more than two hours of my life!' I looked at Charlotte and smiled at her.

'Two hours? I would have wanted more time with him.'

'Trust me, Charlotte. Two hours was two hours too many. He's complicated and confusing.'

Darcy headed out the rear door and locked it while I dimmed the lights to the store. This workday was a tiresome one. I stepped out of the double front doors, deadlocked them, and turned to catch my taxi; the same female driver each time.

I glanced at my watch. I was on time, but the taxi wasn't. It was never late. I tapped my right steel-capped work boot on the footpath, twice. It was my reminder that I was safe. I looked to my left and right at the main street of Tarrin. There was no one about. A wave of anxiety shot through me, burning my veins.

A black sports car stopped at the curb. Number plate: IMGR8.

A man stepped out of the car and stood before me. I knew exactly who he was. He had been at the store.

'Hi, Andi.' He was the color of dark red, and my alert to danger. He was a fisted hand slammed heavily onto piano keys. I needed to run from him. Fast.

'Did you need more flowers?' I tried to buy some time for the taxi to arrive.

He looked down and smiled. 'No. I've come to give you a lift home.'

'Really? What a nice idea ... but my cab will be here in the next minute.' My skin was tingling.

He shook his head. 'Your mother sent me to pick you up.'

Liar. My heart was beating double time. I had checked my phone texts before. None. I had a pact with my parents—if there were any changes to my taxi arrangements, they would text me.

Play the game. Play it better. I glanced over at his car. 'My mother was probably impressed by your sports car and thought I would be too.' I gave him a smile. A fake smile. 'But I'm fine. The taxi will turn up, any second now.'

He took a step closer to me.

I stiffened and held my breath.

'It *was* here ... but I sent it away, so I could give you a lift. I wanted to apologize for my poor manners when I met you.' He reached up and touched my hair. 'Come on, Andi. Let me make it up to you. I'm sorry.'

I tried to take a breath on top of my already held breath to still my shaking limbs. I let it out, then breathed deeply and felt my rage building. 'Step away from me.' My voice was low, and strong.

He reached for my hand, but I reefed it away from him. I took a step backward. 'Touch me, and I will kill you,' I said through gritted teeth.

The man laughed. 'Come now, sweet one. That's no way to talk to a—'

'Sorry I'm late!' It was Darcy. He was walking toward us, almost in a run.

I looked at my watch. 'Yep. Five minutes late!' I walked to him and hugged him. Tightly. He was my hero. Officially.

'Ow,' he said into my ear. 'You're standing on my toes.'

'I'm so sorry,' I whispered. I stepped back from him and looked down at my steel-capped boots. 'If you waited a bit longer, you could've seen my boots in action.'

Darcy smiled at me, put his arm around my shoulders and started walking with me away from the man. 'Hmmm ... I should have waited ... next time.'

'Next time?'

'Yeah ... the next time I have to rescue you.'

I shuddered, and a memory came, unbidden ...

Jack laughed. 'Look at what we have here ... two chicks!'

I clenched my fist. Chicks is such a demeaning word.

'You know why women hate some men, don't you—' I started.

'No more, Andi,' Mia whispered.

'Not that I would call either of you a man! Your violence shouts of your weakness,' I continued.

'Shut the fuck up, bitch!' The sharp bite of Jack's hand stung my already bruised cheek.

'Coward,' I spat.

'Andi, not a word more, you're making them angrier!" Mia said, her voice trembling.

Johnno looked down at the knife he held in his grubby hand and grinned.

'Andi—' Darcy's voice pulled me back from my memory. 'I

said … are you ready to go home?'

'How did you know to come back?' I asked, not answering his question as we walked. I looked back over my shoulder at the assailant and watched as he climbed into his black car and left.

'I saw your taxi leave before you closed the doors to the store. I thought another one would come. But when I saw the black car—'

'I forgive you.'

'For what?'

'Your comment today.'

He pulled me closer and kissed my head. 'You know I love you, don't you?'

'It depends on the day. Some days no one can love me. Not even me.' I wanted to add, *never me*, but I didn't.

Chapter Fifteen

'Flowers, tea, coffee ... or books?' I asked, wondering where Gram was. It was Josh who stood before me. He was the color of pink; hot pink, shouting of love.

'Flowers again, please,' he said, and stood taller.

'Again? Did the first flower arrangement not work?' I frowned at him.

'Oh—they worked a treat. This is a commitment bouquet.'

'Oh-my! Good news for you then! Did you have any particular type of flower in mind?' I asked.

'That's where I was hoping you would help ...'

I brushed my hands down my apron then touched the top of my dress up to make sure my scar was covered. Was Josh talking about Xander? Part of me needed to know if he was gay. 'In one word, how would you describe him—your partner?'

'Perfect. Spectacular. Favorite.'

'That's three words!'

He let out a heavy breath. 'I know ... I'm just so ... into him.'

I cleared my throat. The visual that entered my mind was too graphic. 'I think I know which blooms will represent everything you're saying,' *and a little more*, I wanted to add, but didn't. 'Can I grab your phone number or email so I can contact you when your bouquet is done?'

'I can wait,' he said.

'Up to two hours?' I frowned at him.

'Oh ...'

'Oh indeed. I'm waiting for help to arrive. Until then, new bouquet creations have to wait ... I'm sorry.'

He closed his eyes for a moment. 'Then, I'll just have to be patient, won't I?'

'I'm really sorry ...'

'I'll be back at 10.30.'

'See you then! And thanks for understanding,' I said as Josh left. I added his order to my list of things to do. Gram still hadn't stepped foot in Flowers for Fleur, and Charlotte hadn't graced the store with her presence, either.

'Good morning. How can I help?' I forgot to say the flowers, tea, coffee or books spiel, and guilt washed over me. I berated myself silently. A young woman stood before me. She wore a navy, short-sleeved A-line dress. She was the color of Parmesan yellow, full of anxiety.

'Flowers ... and a blank book, please.' Her voice was soft.

I smiled at the request for a book. My first one. 'Are you writing something?' I spoke in an upbeat voice to try and lift her mood.

'No. It's symbolic for me.' She twisted her hands together and moved from foot to foot.

Her nervous behaviour put me on edge. I looked around the store for anything odd. 'A good symbolic, I hope,' I said and looked back at her.

'It is. A blank book means a new start.'

'It does ... and you *are* the author of your life,' I said. *To a certain degree ... you can choose what you do, but you can't choose what others do to you*, I wanted to add, but didn't.

'It's my new life. I'm not going back to the old one.'

'Good for you!' I was starting to feel a little jealous of her. I wished I had the courage to start a new book for my life, where none of the past stories blemished any of the pages.

She leaned in a little closer. 'He made me keep a book, you know ...' Her voice was barely audible. Her eyes widened.

I paused for a moment. 'What type of book?' I nodded to her, encouraging her to keep talking.

'A mistake book. Every time I made a mistake, he would make me write it down.'

I shuddered and my chest tightened. 'Why?'

'So he could punish me,' she whispered, and looked down when she blushed.

I couldn't breathe. The sharp point of the bowie knife on that terrible day of the scars flashed in my mind. I had to distract myself to stop a panic attack. I reached over to a small watering can and poured pretend water into a plant displayed on the sales desk.

I placed the watering can down carefully and walked around to the young woman and guided her to the bookshelf. 'You must burn the mistake book.' The words came out in a whisper before I could stop them.

She pressed her lips together. 'I should. But it's the only evidence I have. It matches the secret book I kept—my punishment book.' She sucked in a sharp breath and looked to her side, wide-eyed.

'Is he here in the store with you?' I kept eye contact with her.

'No ...' Her eyes darted around the store. 'I ... I have to get back to the car before he finds out.'

I grabbed a blank-paged book off the shelf and handed it to her, then grabbed her hand and pulled her over to the flowers. 'Choose whatever you like.'

She picked up a simple bouquet of colored gerberas and looked around with wide eyes.

'I can hide you and help you get housed in a women's shelter,' I said.

'I can't leave him ...' She shook her head with wide eyes. 'I should go out to him ... he'll be real angry when he can't find me.' Her eyes darted around the store and outside. 'He'll be sort of kinder then, if he finds me sitting in the truck ... sort of. He needs me,' she whispered, as if the walls had ears.

I'd heard of victims like her, having a loyal connection to their abusers. I reached up and fingered my scar beneath my work dress—a habit that was hard to break.

'Okay ... but if you ever change your mind, I promise to help you,' I said.

A tear ran down the young woman's face. She wiped it away.

'You need to go. The flowers and book are a gift from me. Think of kindness when you look at them ... and ... whatever is happening to you, isn't forever. You can change the path of your life. You will know when the time is right. I won't forget you,' I said, trying to throw a life-line to her.

She turned and left Flowers for Fleur.

I stood, stunned. Staying with an abuser didn't make sense. It would be like me staying with the man who scarred me. I sent a silent prayer for her rescue and hoped that she would come back one day.

I returned to the sales desk and served people, taking money for ten pre-made wrapped blooms. The stock was getting low and I couldn't see a break from selling in sight, plus I had orders to create and deliver.

'Flowers, tea, coffee, or books?' I asked the elderly gentleman who stood before me in his grey trousers and blue button-up shirt. He was the color of indigo blue: relaxed, happy, and lovestruck.

'Flowers, for my wife,' he said, and smiled with a twinkle in his eyes.

My world slowed down, and everything seemed right. Peace *was* on earth.

'What type of flowers would your wife fancy, sir?'

'Roses. She loves roses ... but just in their closed-up form before the petals open, and then she watches them every day and photographs their miraculous unveiling, gifting their beauty to the world.'

I held on to his every word. This was what love was meant to be like. This was the poetry of love that sung to hungry souls who searched for the light. He was just like Gramps.

I placed my hand over my heart to hold the essence of his love for his wife in there. 'What color roses would you like?'

'Lavender ... if you have them.'

'Follow me.' I walked over to the rose corner, the corner of love. Right there was a bouquet of lavender roses in bud form. I had only bound them together late yesterday before I closed the store. I picked them up and handed them to the gentlemen. 'A gift for your wife—no charge. Please enjoy!'

'But I need to pa—'

'You have given me the gift of hope, so I'm giving you the gift of roses. Accept these with thanks and spoil your wife, please.' I gave him a kind smile, one that made him nod in acceptance.

'Well ... thank you,' he said. He left the store with an enormous grin.

They were the second bouquet of flowers I had given away today. I hoped Gram didn't mind.

Charlotte entered the store in a whirl, encased in the color of happy yellow. 'Darcy called me in,' she said as she went straight to the sales desk.

'He's a mind reader. Sometimes I actually wonder who runs the store.' I looked over at him, pressed my hands together in front of my mouth and bowed a thank you. He gave me a wink.

I wandered over to the workbench and pulled out the order book. Josh's "commitment bouquet" was top of the list. I retrieved Gram's *Book of Fantastical Flower Designs* and ran my finger down the contents page, looking for a word that was close to what Josh felt for his boyfriend.

Favorite—a person preferred over all others.

That was it. Josh used the word favorite when he described him. Favorite. Page 10.

Dahlia - the symbol of a commitment and bond that lasts forever.

I raised my eyebrows. I wondered for a moment if Gram's book was magical. I headed to the cold storage and found a spectacular looking dahlia that had pink outer petals that turned to orange then yellow in the center. It was called Kogana Fubuki. I grabbed eleven of them, and, as I turned to leave the cold room, a full orange dahlia caught my eye. It would be the perfect highlight in the creation. I looked at the name of them—Gay Triumph. There was that "more". Perfect. I chose four to take the total number of dahlias to fifteen, then returned to the workbench and arranged them together and wrapped them in natural paper and added a bow of raffia.

I delivered them to Charlotte for when Josh returned to purchase them. He would be pleased, though I was more pleased. I had managed to have them ready after the chaotic morning.

At 10.40am, I slowed my pace and glanced out the front doors on my return to the workbench. Josh was there, hugging a dark-haired guy. When they parted, I saw it was Xander. I looked down at my steel-capped work boots and pushed a stray lock of hair behind my ear. Secrets of a florist. Maybe I should grab one of the blank books that aren't exactly walking off the shelves and start writing a memoir.

I opened the order book and made a mental note of which flowers to collect from the cold room for the four orders I still had to create. One trip was better than four.

I paused for a moment on my return, with arms full of flowers. Gram was standing at the workbench.

'Gram. How wonderful to see you!' I put the flowers down with care before I wrapped my arms around her. With gentleness. She was back to a color the shade of pink today, reminding me of ballet shoes, tutus and pirouettes.

'As it is to see you, my darling!'

'You're sounding better—am I hearing correctly?' I stepped back from Gram but kept my hands on her shoulders.

'Oh—yes. My head is clear. My ears feel clear. No brain fog. I'm like a new woman. Whatever I had is well and truly gone.' Gram gave me a happy-go-lucky smile.

I dropped my hands from her shoulders. 'Great to hear. Welcome back!'

'Yolande, take the day off. You've been working so hard!'

'No, Gram. I came here to help you, and that's what I'll do.'

Gran waved me off. 'Take two days off. Scoot and enjoy yourself—I insist.'

I looked down at my steel-capped work boots. I guess I could go and hide in my studio. I had some unfinished paintings that would pull me into a time warp away from reality. 'Okay. Thanks, Gram. But if you need me—I'm a phone call away,' I said, making sure she heard me.

Gram nodded. 'Now go, before I bring in reinforcements!' Gram looked over at Darcy. She had him twisted around her little finger.

I untied my apron and hung it on the hook, then released my hair from its ribbon.

I walked over to Darcy. 'One cup of tea, one chocolate cupcake and one scoop of ice-cream, please.' I raised an eyebrow at Darcy and waited for his comment that was sure to come.

'You're doing that thing again, aren't you, Andi?'

'Yep!' I said.

Darcy turned and collected my favorite teapot and filled it with steaming water. 'Take a seat. I'll bring your order to you,' he said, and frowned at me. 'Have you finished work for the day?'

'Yep!' I said again. Darcy lifted his chin and looked down at me.

I turned and went to sit at my favorite table by the window and closed my eyes. My skin started to tingle. I didn't like surprises or changes of plans since that terrible day of the scars, and being given the day off was a surprise.

I jigged my legs up and down to burn some of the adrenaline running through my veins as I felt the beginning of my downward spiral. *Pull yourself out, Yolande,* I told myself. *Just because something has changed doesn't mean something bad will happen ...* I opened my eyes and cleared my throat. I had already decided I would go to my studio and paint for the rest of the day. My safe place.

Darcy placed a teapot, teacup and saucer, chocolate cupcake and scoop of ice-cream before me. I picked up my spoon and carved half of the cupcake out and added it to the ice-cream, then looked up at Darcy to see him wince.

'You have just committed a mortal crime, you know,' he said.

'The perfect crime. There will be no evidence by the time I finish.' I beamed a smile at him.

He shook his head. 'I like your hair down. It shows the true you.'

Little did he know it was the wrong color. My natural hair color was blonde. 'Messy?' I asked.

'No. Wild. And I suspect, like you once were.' He raised an eyebrow at me.

'Once upon a time, but not anymore.' I put my hand under my chin and looked up at him to stop myself from touching or pulling the top of my dress to cover my chest scar that was already covered.

'Nope. Once a wild child, always a wild child. Your inner giraffe will return when it's ready.'

I pinched my eyebrows together. 'Inner giraffe?' I scoffed.

'Yeah. I was going to say your inner lion, because lions are fierce and mighty. But a giraffe can kick a lion's head. You're a giraffe with steel-capped safety boots!'

A boisterous laugh erupted from me. 'Thanks, Darcy. I think.'

'I would like to think I'm a wild horse.'

I poured my tea and added milk, trying to see where his analogy was going. 'In what way?

'I can be tamed and bred.'

I frowned at him. Was he being facetious? 'I think you're more of a wild elephant.'

'What?'

'Of course, you're—you're slow to anger, you exude confidence and calmness ... and you're kind.'

Darcy pulled out the chair opposite me and sat down. He cupped his hands on the table in front of him. 'Do you like horses, Yolande?' He raised an eyebrow at me.

'Yes.'

Darcy's lips curled up in the corners. Smug.

'But not wild ones.'

He sat back in his chair and sighed.

'Don't you have work to do, Mr. Barista?'

'Yep,' he said. He stood, pushed in the chair then swaggered back to the kitchen, casting me a sideways glance as he strutted. I gave him a half smile for his effort.

I pulled out my phone to order my personal taxi, but hesitated when the sound of a bicycle bell caught my attention. I looked out the window, and there, just up the street at the bicycle store, were brand new bicycles set out on the footpath.

Hmmm ... could I? After all, I came from the family of the famous Cruiser flower bicycle at Flowers for Fleur!

I picked up my tea and savored it, looking outside the window trying to picture myself riding a bicycle instead of catching a taxi or being driven by family everywhere. I put my teacup down and dumped the rest of the chocolate cupcake into the ice-cream bowl. Would it be worth buying myself a bicycle? How long would I be here in Tarrin with Gram?

If I bought a bicycle, would I keep the bicycle style in the family and buy a girly Cruiser? Absolutely not! I didn't want to look dainty and vulnerable—the pretty girl riding a cute bicycle with her wild hair flowing behind her—an object for men to stare at. My only choice could be a men's road bike—a don't mess with me, I am capable thank you very much, type of bike. Black.

I balanced the ice-cream bowl on top of the teacup and saucer and picked it up, and with my other hand, I grabbed the empty teapot and went over to Darcy. I placed them onto the counter. 'Perfect crime executed, perfectly,' I said. 'Thanks. It was delicious!' I smiled at him.

Darcy frowned at me. 'What are you up to, Miss? Where is your taxi and, are you becoming a giraffe?'

'Nope,' I said. 'More like a lion ...' I turned and started to walk.

'But lions have courage and strength, Andi.' Darcy's voice was soft.

My blood boiled and I turned back to him. *Was he insinuating that I had no courage? Was he insinuating that I was weak? Did I appear weak to him? To everyone?* I'll be the first to admit I lived in fear. But who wouldn't be after what had happened to Mia and me.

I walked back to Darcy, slowly.

He stared at me, not moving. He was in deep trouble, and knew it.

'I ... saved ... my best friend ... from being ... raped. Would you call that courage and strength, Darcy?' My voice was low. I blinked away the extra moisture in my eyes.

He stared at the bench and shook his head. 'I didn't mean it that way—'

'No? What did you mean? Please explain!' I put my hands up in front of him. 'No ... forget it. I don't want to know.' I stared into Darcy's eyes and pressed my lips together. Disappointment. I was so disappointed with his comment. I turned and stormed out of the store. I didn't have to prove anything, but now I felt that I had to. *Damn you, Darcy!*

I walked up the street to the sports store and went directly to the bikes. At once I saw the bicycle I needed. It was a Raleigh—it had to be a Raleigh, that was a must—black. The Vantage RXW. I stopped before it and checked it out. This was it. This is what I needed. I ran my finger over the white, blue and lime green lines than ran across the frame.

'Andi, hi!' It was the store owner.

'Hi, Cooper!'

'That's a nice bike ... are you buying for yourself?'

'Yes.'

'Ahhh, nice ... the women's cycles are over here,' he said and started to walk toward the pastel-colored women's cruisers.

'I know, Coops ... but I'd prefer to ride this one,' I said, and looked up at him.

'Well ... okay then. Come this way and we'll size it up for you. When do you want to pick it up?'

'Now. I'm riding it home,' I said and smiled at him.

'Really? In those clothes?'

I looked over at the wall of cycling attire. 'Of course not. I'm also buying cycling shorts and a shirt and a backpack ... today.'

Great save, Yolande!

'Excellent. Let me grab my technician for a bike fit, while you choose your cycling gear and a backpack.'

'Great,' I said, and smiled at him, then walked to the wall of clothes. I grabbed black shorts and reached for a black shirt, but moved my hand to the multi-colored shirt—courage and strength, something that would stand out with boldness. Perfect for the lion inside me, and the kick-ass giraffe. I grabbed a black backpack with a splash of green to match my new Raleigh wheels.

Matt appeared beside me. 'Come this way so we can set up your bike.' He was young, handsome, and buffed, with way too many girlfriends in his life story to date. He was the color of red—pure red—energy and power. I followed him to the technician's area and placed my new clothing on a chair.

'You need to sit on the saddle, so I can set the correct height for you ... you'll have to hitch up your dress.' He frowned. 'Have you got your cycling shoes?'

'Yes. I'm wearing them.'

Matt looked down at my steel-capped work boots and chuckled under his breath. 'Those boots are not—'

'They're the shoes I'll be wearing. Now turn around while I sit on the bike.' I made a swirly gesture in the air before him.

He turned away from me. I pulled up my dress and cocked my leg over the bike and pulled myself up onto the seat, then pulled my dress down so my underwear couldn't be seen.

'Ready, Matt.' I watched as he turned to face me.

His eyes started at my boots, then followed my leg up to the top of my dress. He ran his hand through his hair. 'Okay. Start peddling so I can see your leg extension ... good ... and stop.' He wrote down some notes. 'I need to look at the saddle angle ... ummm—'

I didn't want him putting his hand on the seat between my thighs. 'It's fine as it is. I'll come back to you if the cycle doesn't feel right. Just adjust the height of the seat and we're done.'

'Are you sure you want a road bike? You look more like a Cruiser girl,' he said.

I raised an eyebrow at him.

'Right,' he said. 'Go pay for your stuff and I'll adjust your bike and have it there in a jiffy.'

'Thanks,' I said. 'Look away while I get off the bike.'

Matt rolled his eyes at me and turned around. I climbed off the saddle, smoothed my dress down, picked up my new bike clothes and backpack and went to the sales counter.

'Does this mean you won't be catching a taxi at six o'clock every evening now?' Cooper said while he processed my purchases.

'Maybe,' I said. I didn't realize he knew my schedule, and it rattled me a little.

'I'm surprised you didn't get a bike similar to your Gram's,' he said.

I looked down and smiled to myself. 'Gram's bike has a love story attached to it. Mine doesn't. I love my grandmother, but we're very different.' I waved my credit card over the machine.

Cooper smiled at me. 'That may be true, but you have the same heart.'

'She's ready to go,' Matt said, holding the bicycle beside me.

'Thank you, to you both, for your help,' I said, and walked out the door with my shiny new bike.

I went back to Flowers for Fleur and parked the bike outside before I entered and made my way to the powder room, where I changed into my riding shorts and shirt.

'Bye, Gram. Call me if you need me!' I called as I left the shop and disappeared out the front door, then jumped on my new black bicycle with my new backpack and left.

It had been an age since I rode. They say riding a bike was something you never forgot how to do. It was true. The breeze blew onto my face like a kiss from an angel. It ran its fingers of air through my hair that trailed behind me.

I sucked in a deep breath when I was taken back to my tenth birthday, when I received my pink Raleigh Breeze. I was so ridiculously happy.

Mia's eyes had lit up when she saw my shiny new bike. But then she ran off. I didn't understand. I thought I had done something wrong. All of a sudden, I wasn't so ridiculously happy anymore. I rode my bike home and put it in the garage. I didn't want it if it meant I didn't have a best friend anymore. I shut the garage door and started to run to the big tree in my backyard where I could sit and hide my tears, when I heard a dinging bell. I turned to see Mia. She had the biggest smile on her face, and a bike, exactly like mine.

'Now we can ride together, Yoyo!' Mia said.

I squealed and hugged my best friend. 'We'll be like twins, you and me!'

'Yoyo and Meemee!' Mia said and giggled.

A car beeped its horn as it went past, pulling me from my ten-year-old self. I so wanted to stay in that memory, when everything was right in the world. I turned into the street where I lived with my parents, temporarily, and at the same time, I decided I wouldn't hide in the studio and paint for what was left of the day. Perhaps I could visit Mia.

Dear Mia.

Or head to the beach. Just me and my bicycle and my steel-capped safety boots.

I cycled the streets of Tarrin, hoping my new wheels would give me some direction. But I found myself feeling lost. And then I stopped behind a fence. A familiar fence. The same fence I had stood behind, hundreds of times with my grandfather—at the airport.

I watched the planes take-off and land, and a couple of

helicopters, too. The pure power and feeling of exhilaration vibrated through me, feeding my passion of flight. I never felt that same passion with flower designs. My heart longed for the metal hangers and lecture rooms and flight simulators and top-secret projects that challenged my intellectual cravings. I sighed. It wouldn't be long until I found myself back in my Defence Force uniform. Gram was well now, and wouldn't need me for much longer.

I turned my bicycle around when the sun started to cast long shadows. I positioned my foot on the peddle to start riding, but stopped when a text from my mother came through ...

Ma: *You need to go back to the store tomorrow.*

Me: *Is Gram unwell?*

Ma: *She's had a car accident.*
I'll talk to you when you get home.

I shoved my phone into my pocket and mounted the bike. I hit the pedals hard to get home. Fast.

Chapter Sixteen

The day yawned and stretched when I arrived at Flowers for Fleur. I dismounted my bike and leaned it against the wall while I unlocked the door and turned on the lights. I wheeled the black beast into Gram's office and pushed her bicycle out to the front, then set about arranging a floral bouquet of peonies to adorn it. I returned to the shop, donned my florist apron and started on my list of necessary jobs before I even thought about putting flowers in metal buckets outside the store to welcome the day.

I ran my hand over my forehead. Wild, wicked, Wednesday. That's what I called it. Gram called it wonderful Wednesday. This is the day all the market flowers came in. It was also the day older blooms were prepped and placed outside the store for a quick sale.

I heard the jangle of keys and the back door creaked. Darcy was here. He was the color of grey with an "e" today, like the rain clouds—melancholy, deep thought, philosophy and ponderings.

'Morning, Andi,' he said, his tone flat.

I gave him a thumbs-up. It's all I could muster after yesterday's conversation.

'I thought you had the day off?'

'I did. Gram was in an accident. She's in hospital.'

Darcy stopped walking. 'Is she okay?'

'Mostly, I think.'

'I'm sorry about your Gram.'

'Me too.'

Darcy headed over to crank up the barista machine and start the process of baking muffins for the morning rush.

The back door creaked again. This time Charlotte walked through with liquid sunshine following her. It should be illegal to smile that brightly at this time of the morning.

She walked over to me, her smile fading. She gave me a hug. 'Sorry about your gram.'

'Thanks ... and thanks for coming in on wild, wicked, Wednesday!' I couldn't hide my sarcasm.

Charlotte burst out laughing. 'I call it weird Wednesday. It's like the entire store takes on a new look. Everything changes, and you have to relearn the store all over again.'

'That's for sure.'

'Hey. Let's put flowers in our hair!'

I smiled at Charlotte, hiding the shiver that traveled down my spine. Memories do that.

'Keep your head down, Mr. Johnson will see us!' Mia said while we laid on our tummies in the clover field.

'But there's a bee!'

'Bee bee bumble bee. Be still and it will go away, Landi.'

'Do you think we're invisible enough?' I asked.

'Has Mr. Johnson got his glasses on?'

I lifted my head and peeked in Mr. Johnson's direction. 'No.'

'Then we're invisible!'

'You know we're trespassing ...'

'Mr. Johnson knows us, so it can't be trespassing ...' Mia finished making a head garland out of clover flowers. She lifted it up and placed it onto my head. 'Now you're a princess. Tell me, eight-year-old Princess Yolande, who will be your prince?'

I rolled onto my back and looked up at the clouds. 'I would rather have the dragon than the prince.'

'A dragon?'

'Yes. It breathes fire and I can sit on it while it flies high into the clouds ...'

'Yolande! How on earth will you live happily ever after?'

'I will.' I took the clover garland off my head and placed it onto Mia's. 'Now you are a princess. Tell me, eight-year-old Princess Mia, who will be your prince?'

'That's easy. My prince will be that boy at ballet class. The tall one with the dark hair.'

I gave Mia a smile and giggled. 'You can have him. He's got boy germs!'

'Very nice boy germs!'

'Eeeew! Mia.'

'Princess Mia to you!'

'Yolande?' Charlotte's voice pulled me back to the store.

'Sure. Let's go with a daisy or two. Super flower power!'

Charlotte grabbed four daisies. She put two in my hair at the back and two in hers at the side. 'It's a good thing your Gram isn't here. She wouldn't approve of our frivolity.'

'I don't know,' I said as I looked at myself in the reflection of the window. 'We might start a trend and increase the profit margin.'

'True,' Charlotte said, and gave me a cheeky smile as she went to the sales desk to her job list.

I opened the order book and ran my finger down the page.

The aroma of coffee alerted me to Darcy's presence. He placed the brew on the workbench. 'Coffee is like a hug in a mug,' he said.

I looked up at him. He was frowning.

'It's better with a dash of whiskey, then the hug in a mug becomes a caress to stop the stress!' I said.

Darcy shook his head at me, slowly. 'The floral hair is very becoming.' He reached around and touched my daisy. 'Do girls still use daisies for "he loves me, he loves me not"?'

I closed my eyes and shook my head for a moment, trying to block a memory from returning.

I looked up at Darcy. 'It's a necessary game that prepares girls for analyzing potential partners. If one moment the man of your life loves you, and the next moment you're saying, he loves me not, he doesn't love you enough. End of story. End of relationship. End of conversation. I have work to do. Thanks for my whiskey-less coffee.' I lifted the mug to my lips and took a sip of the coffee. I closed my eyes as I tasted the cappuccino laced with chocolate. More chocolate than a mocha, and a teaspoon of raw sugar. It was more than delicious. It was like a love potion for my body and mind with an added kick of fantasy.

When I opened my eyes to thank Darcy, he was walking to the café with his hands behind his head. Was he frustrated? That would be a rare occurrence for the calm, patient and wise man. Perhaps I rattled his bones with the daisy talk?

At 8.20am, I carried the "hot sale" flowers to display outside the store in their tin buckets, and arranged them for a visual explosion on the eyes. Satisfied, I turned to re-enter the store, when I saw a note nestled in the peonies in the bicycle basket.

I walked over and removed it. It was addressed to "Yolande" in inked cursive handwriting. *Xander.* He was the only one who wrote with a nib pen. I slipped the note into my apron pocket and re-entered the store for the morning onslaught.

I went directly toward the sales desk. Charlotte was busy with a customer at the daisies, arranging one in the customer's hair. I smiled. Maybe we could start a trend.

'Flowers, tea, coffee or books?' I asked. The person in front of me was elderly. She held a tissue box and dabbed at her eyes while she sobbed. She was the color of happy yellow, yet her behaviour was the color of black.

'Flowers ... for a funeral,' she said.

'I'm so sorry for your loss. Who are the flowers for?'

'On top of my husband's casket.' She started to cry.

I breathed out my sadness. 'How long were you married for?'

'Fifty-five years.' She dabbed at her eyes, again. 'I want the flowers to celebrate.'

I swallowed and looked down, opened the order book, then looked back at the woman.

'These aren't tears of grief, my dear, they are tears of relief! He made me stand on the scales every morning so he could check my weight, then he would tell me what I could eat for the day, *if* I could eat!'

I watched her dab away more tears. How sad was her story? Perhaps I *should* write "Memoirs of a Florist"? 'What type of flowers would you like Mrs. ...'

'Williams, Mrs. Williams. Black roses would be perfect, except I have to play the role of the mourning, devastated wife to fulfil the requirements of the will.'

I felt a heavy burden for Mrs. Williams, her late husband was controlling her behaviour, even after his death. 'So then, to keep up the facade, I'm thinking you need flowers for a beautiful remembrance—yes?' I said, trying to make sense of the situation.

'Oh, yes, dear.'

'We'll deliver them, Mrs. Williams. Please write down the details of the date and place of delivery. Then enjoy a complimentary pot of tea while I choose some flowers I think will honor your late husband.'

'Oh my, how sweet of you. Thank you.'

I left Mrs. Williams to fill out the details while I went to the workbench and found Gram's *Book of Fantastical Flower Designs*. I flipped through the pages and stopped at funerals for men, husbands, fathers and sons. There was one design that looked like the perfect arrangement for Mrs. Williams's little pretence.

I joined Mrs. Williams at her table. 'I believe I have found a fitting arrangement.' I showed her the illustration. 'It contains orchids, protea, anthurium, lotus pods, pittosporum, aspidistra, salal and ti leaves. It has a beautiful blend of red, yellow, orange and green colors that oozes warmth from your heart. It's quite stunning.'

'It looks and sounds as wonderful as this pot of tea. Thank you, dear. I have left the date, time and place on the paperwork for you, as well as invoice details.'

'Perfect. Enjoy your tea, Mrs. Williams, and I'll be thinking of you as you celebrate your husband stepping into eternity.'

I returned to the sales desk and entered the details of Mrs. Williams's order.

My phone vibrated. A text.

GRAMPS: *Gram had a vertigo attack while she was driving. That's why she crashed the car.*

ME: *No ... she said she had no more vertigo. She said it was gone. For good.*

GRAMPS: *Only in her dreams and wishes. She will lose her driver's license for certain.*
ME: *This can't be happening! Is she okay?*

GRAMPS: *I know. I can't believe it either.*
She's sore and sorry for herself and the doctors
are keeping her in for more tests.

ME: *Good. I hope they diagnose her this time.*

GRAMPS: *Me too ... me too.*

ME: *Gotta go. The store is busy.*

GRAMPS: *Of course. Thanks for coming in on your day off.*

ME: *No problem.*

I pushed my phone into my pocket and looked up. 'Can I help you?'

'Ah ... flowers ... please.' He shuffled from foot to foot. He was nervous. He was young. He was the color of rose red, filled with love.

'Hmmm ... girl's love flowers,' I said. 'Are they for anyone special?'

'Ummm ...' He looked from the left to the right then leaned in closer. 'For my girlfriend ... well I want her to be my girlfriend ... I'm going to ask her to be my girl.' He blew air out between his lips.

I nodded my head at him and smiled. 'I would love for a guy to give me flowers and ask me to be his girlfriend.' I tucked a lock of hair behind my ear. 'It will make it even more memorable. A good choice, I say,' I said to the young man.

He seemed to relax a little.

'How long have you known her?'

'Er ... eight months.'

'So, you know her well then ...'

'Er ... no.'

'No?'

'I see her every day on the train ... that's all ...'

'Aaah ... so she's the girl on the train?' The corners of my lips rose.

He gave me a crooked smile and looked down. 'Ah ... yes.'

'Nice,' I said. 'Okay ... so you want to play the flower game to win her over—right?'

'That's the plan.'

'Roses are a no go—they are an assertion of love, and you don't want to declare your hand yet. Daisies are too innocent and not impressive enough to make a statement. So, I'm thinking a bouquet of ranunculus. They come in ... like a paint box of colors ... and are quite exquisite!'

'Sounds good.'

He followed me to the ranunculus display. 'There's many to choose from. It's all yours from here. Please pay at the sales desk, and ... good luck!'

'Thanks.'

Done. A funeral full of lies and a girlfriend to be. I was finished at the sales desk. Charlotte could charm people for the rest of the day. I had new flowers to refrigerate, a never-ending list of orders to make up and send out for delivery, stock to order, and displays to replenish.

At 2pm, I stepped outside to catch some sun rays. I was about to re-enter the store when I heard my name.

'Yolande?' The voice belonged to a man who wore white clothes and a white apron with The Last Cupcake in blue on the front.

'Yes?'

'I have a delivery for you, with the instructions to hand it to you personally.'

'Oh?'

He held out a pastel green box. On top of the box was a note with the handwritten words "wish granted". It was Xander's handwriting in black ink.

I smiled and took the box from him. 'Thanks.'

When the delivery man left, I opened the box. Inside were three large slices of cake. Exactly what I needed on this super-busy, wild, wicked, Wednesday. I wondered if Xander knew he had perfect timing.

By 4pm the daisies were totally sold out. Somehow, daisy hair became a thing today. Gram would be more than pleased.

I wheeled Gram's bicycle into the store for the night at 5pm, after giving away my two daisies to a little girl who walked by holding her father's hand. I watched as a sunshiny smile lit up her face, filling me with joy.

I rubbed my thighs. My legs were tired after the maniac of a day. Perhaps it was the bicycle riding making my muscles ache. I sighed, wondering where I would get the energy to ride home. I had an hour left to do the books and clean the store ready for business tomorrow. I had gained a new admiration for Gram. She had been working in her store for fifty years and never had she moaned or groaned about the amount of effort it took.

I yawned as I removed my work apron and hung it up on the hook behind the sales desk. I patted down the pockets to check for anything that shouldn't be left in there, like wire, scissors, ribbon, pens, twine or bloom satchels. I stopped when I found the note from Gram's bicycle bouquet. I had totally forgotten about it. I removed it from the pocket and opened it up. Two tickets fell from the folded note. I bent down and picked them up off the floor. They were ballet tickets. I opened the letter from Xander.

Dear Yolande and Mrs. Lawrence,

I would like to thank you both for supporting me by allowing me the generous use of your bicycle for my mother's birthday, and to you, Yolande, for being a wonderful birthday party bicycle supervisor and my tag-along partner. We learned that my dear mother does not have Alzheimer's or dementia, and that every memory of her bicycle days are indeed intact.

It would be remiss of me to not return your kindness with kindness. So, please enjoy a night at the ballet, on me. I can guarantee you that it will be a magical evening for you both.

Thank you, from my sisters, my father and myself,

Xander

I put my hand over my heart. What a sweet thing to do. But Gram—how could she watch a ballet with her unpredictable health?

Swan Lake was three days away. Perhaps she would be well enough to go by then?

'What time is your taxi coming tonight, Andi?' Darcy called.

It was 6pm. That was my routine. The taxi would arrive at 6pm exactly, every single workday that I was here. 'It's not,' I said, and wheeled my bicycle out from Gram's office.

Darcy whistled. 'Could this be the new chariot?' He walked over and cast his eyes over the bike. *My* bike.

I stood on the tiptoe of my safety boots and smiled. 'Yes. Welcome to my velocipede.'

Darcy leaned over and ran his hand along the frame. Slowly. Like he was enjoying caressing my bike. 'Your ... *velocipede* ... is a fine specimen.'

'Indeed,' I said. 'Did you know the bicycle is one of the most efficient inventions in the history of mankind.'

'Human power—there's nothing more efficient than that.' Darcy stood upright. 'Please forgive me for my insensitive comment yesterday. It was harsh—'

'You're forgiven. But only because you added extra chocolate to my coffee this morning.' I gave him a crooked smile.

Darcy narrowed his eyes at me. 'You're way too easy to win over!' He looked out the windows. 'You'd better get going before it gets too dark.'

'Yes. I'll see you tomorrow.'

'Tomorrow it is.'

Chapter Seventeen

'Flowers, tea, coffee, or books?' I know I didn't need to ask the question, but I was trembling inside when I saw him ... and Gram *did* want me to ask that question, each and every time.

'Flowers ... for Fleur,' Gramps answered, not blinking. I had watched him walk toward the sales desk with a stooped posture. I looked into his red eyes and swallowed the lump in my throat. He was the color of orange smoke, like a flare. It was his distress signal.

'She's bad, Landi. Real bad. I want to fix her. But I can't.' His voice cracked, and my throat constricted once again.

Any ounce of happiness inside me evaporated. 'Peonies are her favorite,' I said, my voice flat.

'I know. Make it a white bunch. Pure, like her heart.' Gramps hung his head and walked away from the sales desk and over to the workbench. I followed him with slow steps, my heart crying in silence.

Gramps ran his hand along the timber bench. 'There was

one test that was brutal, for Gram. The doctor said it was usually well tolerated ... but not for Gram.' He looked up at the ceiling, trying to stop his tears, I suspect. 'The fear in her eyes was—' He stopped talking and swallowed. 'She was so brave ...' He leaned his elbows on the workbench and put his head into his hands. 'I want it to be me, not her. Not my love.' Gramps lifted his head and looked at me with wet eyes.

A tear slid down my face. On that side. The side of my face that always betrayed me.

And I ran. In my work boots.

The door to the powder room banged when I pushed it open. I didn't mean to push it so hard. I swooped down and grabbed my concealer makeup. I wanted to sob. Deeply. But this wasn't the time, nor the place. I had to hold myself together to serve at the flower store. For Gram.

I stood tall and looked in the mirror. I held my eyes in my own before I looked to my right cheek. And there it was, partly exposed from my tear. The scar. The scar of terror and broken dreams. I lifted my chin in defiance and applied the make-up. I was good at making the scar look invisible. Three years' experience works a treat. I moved my face from the left to the right, checking my scrupulous application.

I took a deep, calming breath and left the powder room and walked back to the workbench. Gramps was sitting in the corner on a chair, his hand under his chin. 'Sorry,' he mouthed.

I gave him a thumbs-up. I couldn't speak to him. Not yet.

I gathered the white peonies, blinking away my tears. Gram didn't deserve this. Bad things aren't meant to happen to good people. And Gram was the best. I grabbed a white square tin as a vase and placed the peonies into it. White on white. Pure white. Pure. Like Gram's heart.

Gramps was in front of me then. 'Beautiful. Thank you.'

'Created with unending love, for Gram.' I sniffed an ugly

sniff, trying to stop the flow of tears. 'I want to know the details of the tests ... when it's just you and me. Come at closing time.'

Gramps breath shuddered. 'That would be best. I'll be here.'

I walked around the workbench to Gramps and pulled him into a tight hug. 'Good things are coming. We have to believe it.'

'I know.'

'Give my love to Gram. Tell her I'm thinking of her every minute of every day, and sending healing, Godspeed.'

Gramps pressed his lips together and picked up the peonies. 'I will. Love you, Yolande.'

He left through the front double doors. He stopped at the bicycle and ran his hand over the handlebars with a look of despair. He shook his head, took a deep breath and walked off.

Flowers for Fleur. Love for Fleur. A cure for Fleur ...

I brushed my hands down my apron and closed my eyes. I had to be strong. For Gram.

I walked to the sales desk. Jobs to do. People to serve. With kindness and a smile.

Like Gram. For Gram.

'Flowers, tea, coffee or books?' The man who stood before me was in good physical shape. A gym junkie to be succinct. He was the color of dark orange: deceit.

'Since I'm florally repenting, I'll need flowers,' he said without blinking.

'Florally repenting?' I asked, filled with disbelief at the words I heard.

'Aaah ... yes.' He placed his hands into his pockets. He wasn't florally repenting at all.

'Really?' I narrowed my eyes at him.

He touched his mouth then frowned. 'Yes ... yes I am.' He pointed as he spoke. *Liar.* He needed a good dose of flowers for a fibber.

I looked down and nodded my head. 'For him?' I knew it

would be a she, but I wanted to stir him a little.

His eyes bulged for a fraction of a second before he stepped back, looked away and shook his head. 'Always for a woman,' he said, his voice stressed.

'Repenting, as in an apology?'

'Hmmm ... no. I'm not sorry for what I did.'

I tilted my head to the side a little and frowned at him. 'I'm confused ... you're ... florally repenting, but you're ... not sorry— is that correct?'

'Exactly.' He raised his eyebrows at me.

'So ... these flowers are to—'

'Say sorry for what I did, even though I'm not sorry. But I need to act sorry for hurting her feelings,' he explained.

'Because ...'

'To look good in front of her friends, and to make her look good in front of her friends. It's simple.'

'Clearly.' *Not.* I frowned. 'You're in luck today. I've created a display of "sorry" bouquets, over in the right corner of the store.' I pointed to the colorful tulips, perfect for apologies.

He looked over and smiled, then pulled out cash to pay for his floral repentance.

'Thanks,' I said, and watched him sashay over to choose a bunch of tulips. He chose white, and left the store.

Arms wrapped around me from behind and I stiffened. 'Are you okay?' It was Charlotte. I hoped my chest scar couldn't be seen.

'Yes, just confused,' I said, and pulled the top of my dress over my chest higher to make sure my scar was hidden.

'Confused?' Charlotte repeated.

'Yes. That guy wanted to say sorry for what he did, even though he wasn't sorry. He said he was "florally repenting", to use his term ... can you believe it?' I shrugged my shoulders. 'He's bad news!'

'Hmmm ... wouldn't it be good if women saw a warning color or something with those types,' Charlotte said.

'Yeah,' I said, and raised my eyebrows. What would she say if she knew of my color visions?

'And then we would all stay away from those deceitful "bad boys",' she said.

'Absolutely,' I agreed. Mia liked those smooth, deceitful, bad boys. She reveled in playing the flirting game with them. That's how we got into our situation on that terrible day of the scars. Only, she didn't realize how truly bad those two men were, until it was too late ...

'Thanks for coming in again, Charlotte. If it was just me and Darcy, I'd go insane!'

'I don't know ...' Charlotte looked over at Darcy. 'A good-looking man in the kitchen who can make a killer coffee and bake cakes is a win-win, I think.'

I looked over at Darcy. He was a keeper. My protector in the store and therefore my hero. 'Yep. He has all the boxes ticked for husband material,' I said.

Charlotte looked at me. 'Your husband?'

'No.' My eyebrows snapped together and I shook my head. He knew too much about me and what I had been through. 'He feels like ... a big brother to me.'

Charlotte tilted her head to the side and considered him. 'Maybe for you, but I think he's rather cute!' She waggled her eyebrows at me.

I smiled at her and picked up a piece of paper. 'Here's your list of jobs to do between flower sales. It's considerably less than yesterday—so it's a bit of a cruisy day!' I smirked at her, then walked away to the workbench. It felt like I had a trillion orders to make and have delivered.

The rain started its gentle pitter-patter when I closed the store doors at 5pm. By the time Gramps arrived at 6pm, it was a heavy and burdensome deluge, apt for Tarrin's "more".

Gramps shrugged off his coat and hung it in the wet room. I walked over and embraced him. When I stepped back, I watched as he wiped a tear from under his eye.

I felt an ache at the back of my throat as I tried to stop my sadness from surfacing. 'Tea?'

'That would be best.'

I walked over to Darcy. He should have left by now. But I had been here long enough to know that he never left before me—like my security guard. I assumed he did that for Gram as well.

'I'll bring you a large pot of tea, two teacups and cupcakes. Sit by the window,' he said with soulful eyes.

'Thanks, Darcy. Are you a mind reader?'

'No. Just observative. When your Gramps walked in at 6pm, he could only be here to have a conversation with you that can't be said on the phone ... tea is liquid wisdom, it will help you through the conversation ...'

My stomach quivered. I had invited Gramps back to the store because I needed to face him and read his emotions while he spoke. I twisted my fingers together. 'I'll clean up after we finish. Or maybe ... I will sit and wallow and scoff the rest of your cupcakes ...'

Darcy raised an eyebrow at me. 'You know that Yolande with a belly full of cupcakes is bad news. I suggest you refrain from over-indulging on my baking, for the sake of everyone you know.'

'Advice heard and considered. Time for tea with Gramps. See you tomorrow!' I placed my hand on his arm. His skin was warm and sent me a strange soothing comfort, like having a warm blanket wrapped around me on a freezing winter's day.

When I turned to my preferred table, Gramps was already sitting there, looking out the window, lost in his thoughts. I took one step towards him and stopped.

Anxiety rumbled in my stomach. I stretched my hands to use some excess energy from the anxiety, then continued my path to sit opposite Gramps.

Darcy placed our teapots, teacups and cupcakes onto the table once I had sat down. Gramps turned his attention to the teapot. He turned it three times to the left, and three times to the right, then poured our tea.

'Meniere's disease,' Gramps said, stirring sugar into his amber brew.

'Many what?' I picked up my teacup and wrapped my hands around it, absorbing all the warmth I could while a shiver ran down my spine. *Gram has a disease ...*

'Meniere's disease,' Gramps repeated. 'There's no cure.'

Everything inside and outside of me froze. Except for the tear that slid down my face. On that side of my face, revealing my past. 'No cure!' I said in a whisper that cracked my heart. I put my teacup back onto the table.

'Debilitating vertigo, hearing loss, tinnitus, nausea, brain fog, loss of balance, depression—'

'Gram will go deaf?' I stood with an abruptness that caused my chair to fall backward onto the floor, landing with a bang. 'She can't, Gramps—she lives to hear your voice. It's how you met. When you sing, she floats around with a beautiful smile on her face and ... and—'

'That's enough, Yolande! Sit down and listen.' Gramps ran a hand over his face.

My expression fell as I up-righted the chair and sat on it gingerly. I wrapped my hands around my teacup again, lifted it to my lips and took a sip. A long sip.

My erratic heart rate returned to a calmer beat, and I watched Gramps stir his tea, unnecessarily.

'How did Gram get this ... this ... Meniere's disease?' I asked.

'No cause,' he said. His voice was low.

'No cause, no cure!' I pinched my eyebrows together in frustration, then wiped a tear from my face.

'Yesss …' It was an exasperated yes from Gramps. He put his hands over his eyes. 'One of the tests was brutal, Landi …' He dragged his hands over his nose until they rested together in front of his lips, like he was praying.

'What did they do?'

'It was an electronically controlled chair that rotated from side to side … Gram had a severe vertigo episode because of it.'

'But that's good … right?'

'I guess so. The doctors could truly see how debilitating her vertigo was.'

'Where's Gram now?'

'In hospital. She's been started on some new medications to see if it helps alleviate the symptoms.'

'And if it doesn't?'

'Once they have exhausted all oral medications, comes the invasive intervention—grommets, injections into the middle ear, a vestibular nerve section, where they cut the balance nerve to the affected ear … or they remove the inner ear, Yolande … *remove it*!' Gramps frowned and shook his head, then continued, 'A labyrinthectomy—'

He stopped speaking and looked out the window. 'Why has this happened to my beautiful Fleur? Why is this … this … Meniere's disease even in existence? Why can't the doctors fix it?' Gramps took a long, deep breath, and looked back at me. 'What are we going to do, Andi?'

There. Right there. That is when the heavy weight fell onto my shoulders and crushed me, and any hope I had of returning to my career. I looked out at the storm. I missed my old job. I missed the high security. I missed my uniform. I missed my dog tags, and I missed everyone I worked with. I especially missed the intense meetings at the round table.

After an almighty boom of thunder, the rain stopped. The storm clouds broke, and a rainbow appeared. Perhaps it was a sign. A promise. Gram would make it through her storm.

What are we going to do, Andi? I looked back at Gramps and put my hand over his. 'We give to Gram what she has always given others—love, care, kindness and hope. We take each day as it comes and work together to get Gram well again, even doing our own research to find something that will help her. She needs to know, above all else, that we are here for her, fighting the battle with her, and that she's never alone,' I said with resolution.

A tear rolled down Grampapa's face. My chest tightened, and I swallowed the sob that rose from my chest. He looked into my eyes and gave me a nod.

'Let's celebrate, Gramps,' I said, eyeing off the cupcakes.

'How can you even think of celebrating after this news?' His voice cracked.

'The doctors know what Gram has, and that means we can educate ourselves about the disease and start to work towards her wellness. That's what we're celebrating!' I handed him a cupcake. He held it up and I touched my cupcake against his.

'To Gram!' I said, then shoved the entire cupcake into my mouth and savored the taste.

Chapter Eighteen

Grampapa's operatic singing filled the house. I could see Gram, but she couldn't see me. She was sitting in her teal-blue wing chair. Her dress was a beautiful combination of pastel colors with its floral pattern, as it should be, since Gram *is* Fleur the florist from Flowers for Fleur. Her dyed blonde hair fell gently around her face, making her stunning blue eyes stand out.

'I hope you don't have those ugly work boots on, Yolande!' she called. She was the color of a fuscia lipstick kiss of family—warmth, acceptance, and unconditional love.

I smiled to myself and looked down at my feet. Yep, there were my work boots; steel-capped and capable of inflicting serious pain, enabling me time to get away from any assailant who decided I was the weaker sex and thus fair game. I lifted my boot up and stretched it from behind the wall so she could see it.

'I demand you remove them at once, young lady!' she said.

I stepped out in front of her, grinning from ear to ear. She was being bossy. That meant she was feeling better. Maybe the medications the doctor had her on were working. I twirled around in my dress—a black floor length, high neck, sleeveless gown to hide my safety boots and the scar on my chest. It was perfect.

'Yolande ... you look stunning! Are you going somewhere?'

I walked over to her and curtsied before I gave her the ballet ticket. 'Yes. I'm going to the ballet ... with you.'

'Caleb Lawrence, come here at once!' Gram called.

Gramps stopped singing. He was in trouble. Big trouble.

'You should keep your natural hair color, dear.' Gram's comment to me was curt. She was annoyed.

'No, Gram. I like my hair dark.' I had dyed my blonde hair dark brown after that terrible day of the scars. Dark haired girls didn't get the amount of attention that blonde haired girls did, in my experience. And I liked it that way. It made me feel safer.

Gramps stopped before Gram with a tea towel over his shoulder. 'Yes, dear?' He was the color of blue, like a clear sky, giving a sense of peace and calm.

'You knew about this ... this ... ballet scheme.' Gram waved her hand in the air. 'That's why you said I should dress up tonight ... and the candlelit dinner ... it was all a part of the plan, wasn't it?'

'No, Gram,' I butted in. 'Xander left tickets for the ballet in the flowers of your Cruiser. It's a thank you gift for allowing him to use your bicycle. It was my idea for Gramps to do the candlelit dinner and to dress up ... I thought you might stress about going out to the ballet if you knew too soon ... and it might ... you know ...' I looked down.

'Oh, Landi ... that's so sweet of Xander. But I can't go ... just in case of ... you know ...'

I looked up at her. 'I know. But your medication is working, and you sound like your normal self ... I have arranged the seating so we're close to an exit, just in case of ... you know ...'

Gram stared at me as though my words were toxic. But she

stood, as if testing how she was feeling. She closed her eyes for a moment and let out a sigh. 'No. I'm sorry. I just can't do it, in case of ... you know ...'

'But Gram ... look at you—you are radiant and standing taller than I've seen you stand for a while now. Some of the research about Meniere's disease says the vertigo comes in clusters and then goes away for a while. You might even be in remission now that you've started on some medication.'

'No.'

'But you love the ballet ... remember when I was young, and we would see every ballet that came to the theater with my mother, and she would sit there giving me a million reasons why I should choose a career in ballet instead of engineering.'

'No.'

'No, you don't remember, or no, you won't go.'

A tear ran down Gram's cheek. I had said too much. 'No. I won't go.'

I closed my eyes and brushed my hand across my forehead.

'It's fear, Yolande. I know you will understand, perfectly.'

I turned away from her and caught my tears on my fingers.

'Too well,' I said, my voice quiet.

'Please face me when you speak, so I can hear you ...'

I turned back to her. Gram was losing her hearing. 'How long have you had this disease for?'

'Seven years. I managed to hide it from everyone except Gramps, and you. But it's getting worse instead of better. At least I have a name for it now.'

'And medication that can help,' I added.

Gram gave me a weak smile.

'Surely your fear of spinning, and my fear of being attacked, combined, will make us a dynamic duo.'

'More like a formidable one ... aaah—yes, I'll go to the ballet with you. If you're digging deep for courage, then I can do that too! Besides ... the medication *is* making me feel better.'

I held out my hand to Gram. She took it in hers. 'I'll look after you,' I said.

'I know.' Gram squeezed my hand. *The same hand that Mia once held on to ...*

'We'd better get going then. Gramps, will you drive us to the theater? I don't think my bicycle is built for two girls with party dresses!' I said.

❧

'Sit on my right side, dear, so I can hear you.'

I sat in my allocated seat once Gram was comfortable. I looked around for the exit, should we need to use it, but prayed that we wouldn't have to. I relaxed and looked up at the stage. A thrill traveled through me. Once upon a time I was a ballerina. Once, a very long time ago. Never in a theater like this, but still, good memories.

'*Swan Lake* was the first ever ballet I saw, remember, Gram?'

'How could I forget. And then you were stuck on Tchaikovsky's *Dance of the Sugar Plum Fairy* for what seemed forever.'

'I still love that music,' I said, feeling the warmth of reminiscence hug me.

The theater darkened, and a hush descended. The audience clapped as the conductor arrived and bowed. There was silence for a moment before the first piece of orchestral music began, and Princess Odette appeared out of the shadows on the stage to pick up the first flower. Our night of magical ballet had begun. I cast a glance toward Gram. She sat with a serene smile on her face. She was in a happy place.

I watched with interest as Princess Odette was transformed into a swan, then the scenery changed, and out came the male ballet danseurs. Gram touched my arm and I stiffened. *Was she having a vertigo attack?*

'Who do you think Prince Siegfried looks like?' she whispered.

I looked closer and kept my eyes on his every movement. I gasped. 'It can't be Xander, could it?'

'If it's not him, he certainly has a doppelganger!' Gram said.

Suddenly, *Swan Lake* became even more interesting. I looked over at Gram. She had her eyes closed. 'Are you okay?' I whispered.

'Most certainly. I'm listening to the *Swan Lake* Waltz, and feeling it vibrate through my body. I want to memorize the sound and feeling for when I can't hear anymore.'

I lifted my chin to contain the tears that threatened to fall for Gram. I couldn't even begin to imagine what it would be like, knowing you were going to lose your hearing. Although, I suspected she had already lost some of it, but I didn't know to what extent. I turned my attention back to the ballet, and allowed myself to be carried away with the magic of the fairy tale, thanks to Xander.

'Oh, to be young again,' Gram said, and placed her hand in mine.

I wrapped my fingers around hers. 'I'd like to go back just three years, before ... you know ...' I said.

'I know, and I wish we could. Things would be different for you then, my darling.'

We walked in silence for a bit, hand in hand. *Would I be here? Would I be married? Would I have a baby by now? What mischief would Mia and I be up to?*

'Do you think it was him?' Gram asked.

'Who?'

'You know, Prince Siegfried ... was it our Xander?'

'No. I had a look at the dancers' names on the program. There was no Xander or Alexander. Prince Siegfried was performed by

Zan Lucas.'

'Prince Siegfried was a very handsome prince!' Gram said, her eyes dreamy.

'If not a little too perfect,' I added. 'You know, like, too perfect becomes an imperfection, if that's possible at all ... like stripping away their personality because all you can focus on is their perfection?'

'Do you think that's possible?'

'Maybe ... I don't know. But I tend to think physical perfection would be a burden.'

'How's that?'

'Think about it, Gram. You'd have the pressure to stay perfect, at all costs. I think it would wear you down emotionally. No matter how hard you try, or the amount of money you spend, age catches up in the end, one way or another.' I opened the car door for Gram. She sat in the front seat and beamed Gramps a smile.

I grinned and sat in the back.

Gramps turned to me. 'Andi, I'm going to alter a pair of court shoes for you so they have steel caps. Those work boots of yours just look out of place with that beautiful dress.'

'It's all right, Gramps. I can decorate a pair of my work boots with glitter if I have to.'

'How was the ballet, girls?' Gramps asked.

Gram talked at a million miles an hour. She was floating. I let her keep talking and looked out the window. Tomorrow was Sunday. My painting day in the studio. My "dare-to-be-bare" day. The color red came to mind. I had to paint something red. Like the color of ... blood. There, I said it. It was a necessary evil to combat my panic attacks of all things associated with blood, just like on that day ...

Chapter Nineteen

I dipped my fingers into the red paint and held them above the white canvas. Red droplets fell, one after the other and splattered, just like that terrible day with Mia. I dipped my fingers into the paint pot once again. Twenty splots of blood wasn't enough. Twenty splots of blood would never be enough! I turned my head to the side, fighting the memory that came unbidden, but at the same time, desperately needing to remember. I gave in, and let it fill my internal vision. I frowned and shook my head while the scene replayed in my mind ...

'Ugh!' I moaned, as my breath was punched out of me when I became wedged on a tree jutting out from the cliff. I groaned when I felt a terrible, sharp pain every time I inhaled the salty air. It was impossibly hard to breathe.

Mia's hand was still in mine. I could feel it. Gripping tightly. I looked down. Firstly, at the jagged rocks far below beside the sea, then at my hand holding on to Mia's. It was covered in roads of blood. My blood.

Mia was dangling mid-air, our terrified eyes connected.

My chest constricted. The pain in my ribs was unbearable and my shoulder was screaming at me to move. I couldn't keep hold of her for much longer ...

I watched as a drop of my blood dripped onto her face. Right there, in the middle of her forehead, like she was marked. Another drop of blood fell. She turned her head and it landed on her cheek. Like the kiss of death.

She turned her eyes to mine. 'I'm scared, Oliander,' Mia said, using my childhood nickname. Her voice was filled with terror.

'I've got you, Mamma Mia,' I replied with her nickname.

'Tell my parents I love them ... and my brother.'

'You tell them yourself, Mee. Hear those sirens?'

Mia's hand slipped a little more. A little closer to death.

There were shouts from above, and hope bloomed. Just a little longer and we'll be rescued.

Just a little longer ...

My chest tightened, and I began to suck in short, fast breaths. I wiggled my hands and feet as they started to tingle. An anxiety attack was coming on. Fast. I pinched my arm numerous times then concentrated on breathing in for a count of five, holding my breath for a count of seven, then exhaled for a count of nine—*inhale-hold-exhale, inhale-hold-exhale*, on repeat until I felt calm. I was a pro at it. And it worked. Every. Single. Time.

Dr. Jones said my fixation for hands and fingers and blood and the color red was understandable after the tragedy. She said it was related to my post-traumatic stress disorder. She said educating myself about PTSD was essential. I did that, and the three therapies.

She was also the one who introduced me to art. When words weren't enough, or I had nothing but indescribable, devastating emotion, she always guided me to the paper and pencils, or crayons. And that was enough to release what I needed to express at that particular time. Even if it didn't make sense to her, it made sense to me.

But now I had paint. And for two years I had been painting. Every. Single. Sunday. Hidden in my parents' studio here at Tarrin, or in my room at the Defence Force Base.

I touched my red fingertips to the paint splots on the canvas and closed my eyes. I lifted my chin and went inside my mind and heart to feel the depth of despair, of pain, of love, of loss of the ways things used to be. The past is done. You can't change it. You must accept it. Mia would understand, wouldn't she?

Dr. Jones said life was a journey. In the six months after the "tragedy", as she called it, "that terrible day of the scars", as I called it, I wanted my journey to end. Every waking moment was too painful to bear. I wanted my earth journey to end ...

Dr. Jones said life was a story, and we were the main character of our book. Dr. Jones said we could control the story of our life, and instead of letting things happen to us, we could take control. But I wasn't convinced. You may be able to control yourself, but you can't control others. So, in the end, you spend your time being proactive and reactive towards events and people.

I pushed my dripping red fingers onto the canvas and moved my hand, working with the emotion. The darkness. The anger. The fear. The hate. The guilt. The loss. Of myself ... of *my injured soul.*

I slumped in the chair when emptiness consumed me. I wanted to change my memory. But I couldn't. It would betray Mia. And besides, it would be a lie.

I dropped my head and squeezed my eyes shut. I had to do more red art work.

Red. Like blood.

I grabbed another canvas and dipped the paintbrush into the

pot of red paint, then covered the entire surface. *Done.* I placed it next to the free-form finger painting I had created and stepped back.

More. I needed more red. I pushed my hand into the red paint and placed my hand on to the canvas to leave a red hand-print, like a hand covered in blood. I repeated it over and over again, until I had thirteen hand-prints.

Thirteen—the number of betrayal.

I leaned the canvas next to the previous two artworks and grabbed another canvas and a stick of charcoal. I sketched a bowie knife then added blobs of red paint. Like blood. My blood on that terrible day of the scars.

I let out a sob. Just one. Then held my breath before I released it heavily.

Another canvas. I needed another one. This time I drew my eye with pencil, and a trail of red down the canvas that ended in a pool of blood.

Done.

I drew two hands, gripping on to each other, the one above holding on to the one below. And trails of blood. Like on that terrible day of the scars.

Done.

And finally, in exhaustion, I painted a delicate blood-red heart of love. *For Mia ...*

I stood back and looked at the seven complete canvases. They told a story. A violent story of two people. A story that ended in love; for my love for Mia would never end, and I would *never* forget.

I had one more painting I needed to do before the sun set. One for Gram. I was absolutely fascinated by the fact that the inner ear, the cochlear, was in the same formation as a shell—like a nautilus cut, or a snail shell. And if you followed the path of the shell formation, it was like spinning, round and round.

Vertigo.

I wanted to paint a spectacular spiral for Gram. One that would help her to associate something beautiful with her cochlear, and the vertigo. I blew out my cheeks. The word vertigo left a bitter taste in my mouth.

I needed to plan my artwork first, so I opened my sketchbook and drew a spiral. And another and another. I opened my laptop and researched the inner ear and shells and spirals in nature and discovered the Fibonacci spiral. The more I researched the more captivated I became. It was then that I realized Gram's painting was going to take quite a few Sundays of focussed artwork.

When the natural light in the studio dimmed, I closed my laptop and my sketchbook. But that was okay. I knew the image I needed to create for Gram would come and draw in my mind in its own time. The brain is ingenious in the way it works.

I cast my eyes back over my red pieces of artwork. I was more than satisfied with what I had achieved. I pulled out my phone and photographed them. Dr. Jones would love to analyze what I had done.

I could even imagine her almost breaking into a smile.

Chapter Twenty

Dear Xander,

The ballet was absolutely enchanting.
Swan Lake was the first ballet I saw as a child,
but watching it as an adult was pure ecstasy.

A passionate thank you from Gram and me.

xx Andi

I folded the floral paper in half and wrote Xander's name on the front. I slid it into my work apron to put into the bouquet of flowers in Gram's bicycle basket when I went out the front to refresh the flowers.

I placed a gerbera in my hair. Today was a good day. Gram was here and she was on top of her game. The store seemed to inhale a big breath of fresh air, and release a combination of relaxing meditation notes to enhance the flowers, like a magical mist had descended the entire store, like Tarrin's "more".

'Flowers, tea, coffee or books?' The words rolled off my tongue like poetry. The young man standing before me was the color of bubblegum pink—happy and caring.

'Flowers ... I'm meeting my girlfriend's parents.'

'Are the flowers for your girlfriend?'

'No. For her mother. I want to make a good impression.'

'Aaah ... that's a lovely gesture. This girl must be important to you, then.'

'Yes. She's the one.'

'The forever one?'

'Yes.'

I smiled at him. Young love. 'Flowers and chocolates, then?'

'Depending on the price.'

'How much were you thinking of spending?'

'$25.'

'I have the perfect combination. I'll be back in a moment.'

'Sure.'

I took quick steps to the freshly prepared popular flower arrangements, then grabbed a box of handmade chocolates. It came to $32.00.

I returned to the sales desk. 'Smell these flowers. They are divine. Your future mother-in-law will adore them.'

I watched as he moved his face closer to the flowers and inhaled. I laughed inwardly at his response. It was a typical male response to the perfume of flowers. He just didn't get what all the fuss was about. He blinked, four times, quickly.

'And these are chocolates to die for,' I added. 'That's $22.00 please.'

He raised his eyebrows when I said the price, then handed over the money.

'Good luck. Be yourself and you'll be fine!'

'Thanks.'

'Happy to help.'

He walked out of the shop with a quick step. I wondered for a moment whether I should have recommended wine instead of chocolates. But no. His fumbling indicated he was a chocolate gift type of guy. He wasn't smooth and sophisticated to gift wine. Yet. But it would come as he matured.

'Landi?' Gram called.

'Yes, Gram,' I called back, then walked to her.

'Let's have a pot of tea. I have something to tell you.'

I frowned at her, wondering what needed to be said over a pot of tea. 'Here, or at a table?' My question was answered when Darcy arrived with a tea tray. He placed it on the workbench, being careful not to make a sound with it, and poured two cups of tea.

'Thank you, Darcy,' Gram said.

'What she said,' I said to Darcy, and gave him a pat on the back. He held a stern face and raised an eyebrow at me. I raised an eyebrow and shot it back at him.

Gram waited for Darcy to leave. *What was it she had to say that he couldn't hear?*

'I don't need you at the store anymore.'

'What?' My heart rate picked up.

'I'm completely better. Cured in fact!'

'How?' I narrowed my eyes at her.

'The meds are working. I feel like my old self, before the disease started. I have so much energy I could run a marathon!'

'Gram ... what meds are you on?'

'Aah ... betahistine dihydrochloride and prednisone. It's the cure!'

I took a sip of my tea and studied Gram. This was not her true self before the disease. This Gram had too much energy. Was it the steroids? It didn't matter. She was feeling one hundred percent better and that's what mattered.

'Once you finish your cup of tea, Andi, you're dismissed!' Gram beamed me a smile.

'Are you sure?' Anxiety rattled through me, and I controlled my breathing.

'Absolutely. You've devoted enough of your time here for me. Go back to your career. I can call Charlotte if the store gets too busy.'

I picked up the florally decorated cupcake Darcy had placed on our plates and took a small bite and frowned. 'I'll miss you, Gram.'

'And I'll miss you, Landi.' Gram walked around the workbench and wrapped her arms around me.

My throat felt scratchy and my eyes watered. When I woke this morning, I had no idea I would be saying goodbye to Gram, Gramps and my parents today. But elation soon flooded out the gloom. Gram was feeling well, and I could return to the job I loved the most in the whole world.

'Let me sell one more bouquet of flowers, and then I'm happy to go,' I said. I needed to feel like I had earned my leave.

Gram stepped back from me and placed her hand on the side of my face. 'I'd love you to do that!' She walked to the other side of the workbench and took her fill of tea and ate her cupcake, while I finished mine.

I walked to the sales desk and waited. A dark-haired man walked towards me. He wore a dark blue suit, white shirt, burgundy tie and brown leather shoes. A businessman, I would guess. He was the color of navy blue: knowledge, power, and seriousness.

'Flowers?' I asked. He didn't look like a tea or coffee drinker, nor a book reader for that matter, so I didn't say the rest of the usual question.

'Please,' he said, then ruffled about in his pocket and pulled out his cell phone. 'Hello …' He turned his back to me while he conversed. Then he faced me again. 'Yes, flowers please.'

'Would you like a prepared bouquet, or we can create you something special to suit your flower landscape.'

'Flower landscape?'

'Yes … you know … flowers for the office, to get well …'

He smiled at me and started to nod his head. 'I see. My flowers are for a marriage proposal.'

I smiled and raised my eyebrows. 'How exciting!'

He looked down with a grin. 'Thanks.'

'Go over to Fleur at the workbench to your left, and let her know that you need flowers for a marriage proposal. She's the best. Your girlfriend won't be able to say no when you present her with a Flowers for Fleur bouquet.'

He took a deep breath. His strong business persona had wavered a bit. 'That's what I'm hoping.'

He strolled over to Gram. I watched Gram interact with the man, mesmerized by the happiness glowing from within her. This store and the people she served was everything to her. It was her life.

I gazed dreamily at the handsome man. A marriage proposal. That's something I will never experience—a man down on one knee before me, asking for me to be his wife. Sacred promises and vows—not with my scars. I could never be beautiful. Not after what happened. And babies … I don't want to bring any souls into this troubled world. It wouldn't be fair, and besides, I couldn't bear to watch my own flesh and blood suffer when poisoned arrows came their way, injuring their souls, hearts and minds.

I sighed and removed my apron for the last time. I grabbed the letter out of the pocket for Xander and held it in my hand, then walked over to Darcy.

He looked at me and frowned. 'Are you quitting, Andi?'

'No. Gram fired me! She said she has been cured.' I shrugged.

Darcy's eyes widened. 'That's a little hard to believe.'

'And too quick, what—three days?'

'It must be a miraculous kind of drug she's taking.'

'Hmmm ... steroids. And you'd better check to see if she has a stash of marijuana out the back!' I gave him a smile.

Darcy chuckled. 'I guess you'll be going back to the Base?'

I nodded my head. 'Tomorrow.'

'Good. Those safety boots won't look out of place there!'

I looked down at my brown steel-capped safety boots. Were they really that bad? It didn't matter. They made me feel safe.

'Take care, Darcy!'

'You too, my sweet!'

I turned and went to Gram's office and grabbed my bicycle and walked through the store with it, glancing around and absorbing the colors and perfumes of the flowers. I think I must have had some kinda love for flowers. After all, I'm sure I had inherited the flower love chromosome through my genetic makeup.

I stepped outside the store and went to Gram's bicycle basket. I placed Xander's letter in amongst the flowers, then took out my phone and took a photo, for memories sake. I must admit, receiving and sending letters through the flowers was exciting, even for a non-romantic like me.

I paused and looked through the window at Gram one last time. She glanced at me. I kissed my fingers then blew the kiss to her. She lifted her hand and pretended to catch it, then kissed her hand and blew her kiss to me. I lifted my hand and pretended to catch her kiss like she had done, then I placed it over my heart. I loved her. Unconditionally.

I pushed my bicycle a little further before I mounted it and rode to my parents' house. There, I changed out of my floral work dress and threw on jeans and a t-shirt and started to pack.

There was a knock at the door.

I looked up and stopped packing. My mother leaned on the

door frame. She was the color of soft pale pink, reminding me of a warm blanket, wrapped around a newborn baby with the overflowing, unconditional love of a mother.

'Dr. Jones wants to see you. There's an appointment at 2pm,' she said. Her eyes tracked my facial movements, wary.

'You knew, didn't you!' Tears welled, and I blinked them away.

'Gram called and spoke to me about her decision late last night.'

'And you agreed with her? You, of all people know that with medication for chronic illness, you need to take it for a while to see if it works the way it's supposed to. Three days is too early to know whether her meds are right!'

'I agree. I tried to talk her out of it, but you know Gram when she's off with the fairies and unicorns!'

'I don't need to see Dr. Jones! Cancel the appointment!' I said, then resumed packing my belongings.

'I disagree. You were talking in your sleep last night.'

I stopped and looked up at my mother. The world slowed down, and sorrow crept into the crevices of my fractured heart.

'No, Ma ...' This time my tears fell. Talking in my sleep was a bad sign. It was the forerunner to a depressive episode. A shiver ran through me. Darkness was not my friend. It was nobody's friend. I hung my head. I didn't want to take medication anymore. Every morning when I used to pop that pill into my mouth, it reminded me of the event on that terrible day.

I looked up at my mother and brushed away my tears. 'This is the last time that I will see her.'

'Okay.' My mother's voice was soft.

'Okay,' I said with firmness.

I rode to the quaint little white house with the pretty flower garden that was my psychologist's office and sat in my regular chair. The one with the imprint of my butt on it. I was aware for a while now that I associated this place with negativity, and the ever reminder that I was damaged. Emotionally and physically.

The door opened smoothly and silently. Dr. Jones was dressed in a dark grey pants suit with a white button-up shirt. Her black court shoes were particularly shiny.

'Yolande.' Dr. Jones's voice was comforting, like the smell of cupcakes baking and my mother's warm smile as I walked in the door after school. Perhaps I was over-thinking the negativity of visiting my psych doctor.

I stood and followed her into the office. The familiar office.

I faltered in my step. Dr. Jones had repainted her room. She now had a sky-blue feature wall. I liked it.

Dr. Jones put a light hand on my shoulder. 'Would you like to sit on the sofa or lie on the couch today?'

'I'll take the sofa.' I gave her a smile, covering the nervousness that bubbled in my stomach. What would she uncover and explore and make me face today that would have me squirming?

I hugged three cushions when I sat on the sofa while Dr. Jones went to make of pot of tea. I heard the chink of the china teacups and saucers and the boiling water. I closed my eyes and rested my hands on my stomach. I had a plan for today's psych visit. And that was to spend as little time possible here, and to walk out, victorious.

At the sound of approaching footsteps, I opened my eyes. Dr. Jones placed two teacups and saucers on the table. I reached over and picked one up. The warmth of the brew touched my lips and I relaxed a little. Aah ... tea ... *liquid wisdom*. If the good doctor served the truth serum of wine, she would end up learning a whole lot more about me ...

'What brings you here today, Andi?'

'My mother,' I said.

'Indeed. But you must agree with her to be sitting here on the new sofa.'

'Yes and no.'

'Yes?'

'I have started talking in my sleep again—usually a sign of doom and gloom about to come, but this time, I don't feel it.'

'What do you feel, Yolande?'

'Normal ... but scared—the precedent has been set.'

'Sleep talking, the medical term—somniloquy—is a sleep disorder defined as talking during sleep without being aware of it. It can be triggered by stress, or depression, or sleep deprivation, or alcohol. Or, it could not. Did you do anything on Sunday that was noteworthy for you?'

'Perhaps ... I painted a series of seven canvases, to stop my obsession and panic attacks with the color red, and blood.' I pulled out my cell phone and showed her the photos.

'Can you tell me about each of the art pieces, Yolande.'

I took a deep breath. 'The first canvas began with dripping red paint from my fingertips.' I looked up at Dr. Jones. 'You know why.' I looked back at the image. 'This painting was the gatekeeper of my emotions, and I opened that gate. It resulted in a flood of despair, pain, love, defiance, and of loss of the ways things use to be. It clearly told me the past is done, I can't change it, and I have to accept it.

'The second canvas is red. Just red. But not *just* red. It's an emotionally intense color. I loathe red because it's the color of blood. But this canvas ... this one is full of blood, and fire, and energy, and war, and danger, and strength, and power, and determination.

'This one, the third, is about betrayal, and how I feel I broke my word with Mia.

'The knife is what happened to me, as well as the next one with the eye and the tear of blood ... for me it means guilt and death of my former self.

'The two gripping hands decorated with blood are what would have changed everything, if I was strong enough to hold on to Mia's hand.' I stopped speaking and swallowed my sadness. 'And the red heart ... it's my forever love for Mia.' I put my hand to my heart, feeling it beat precious life-giving blood through me.

'The emptying of blood which leads to death seems to be a recurring theme on your canvases,' Dr. Jones said.

'Blood means life, or lack of blood means—death. The last painting signifies love, and throughout the entire seven canvas story, love remained. The realization of that revelation, was terrifyingly freeing from the chains that bound me,' I elaborated.

'Art is a powerful instrument of expression and of exploration. It has a way of releasing energy when words cannot unlock what you feel. It can lead you to some insightful conclusions about yourself,' Dr. Jones said.

'I think ... for me ... these seven canvases are about confronting my fears ... conquering my fears, and ... trying to ... create something physical from nothing but memories.'

'Does it feel empowering to you?'

'I feel ... stronger in myself, and I feel a sense of ... freedom, and calmness ... healing even.'

'Let's go back to the earlier question about talking in your sleep. You said sleep talking for you was a sign of doom and gloom to come. But this time you don't feel that it is. Tell me, Yolande, did you talk in your sleep as a child?'

'Chronically. I was a regular sleep talking chatterbox.'

'Then I would like to suggest to you, based on your journey of the seven art canvases, that perhaps your recent sleep talking is natural for you, and not an indicator of depression to come.'

I nodded my head as I considered her analysis.

'Are you taking your medication regularly?

'No. I stopped taking it.'

Dr. Jones stopped writing and looked at me. I didn't know whether she was happy or angry or disappointed.

'I'm confident that you have considered the ramifications

of stopping medication with detail, knowing you. I have also given you alternative strategies to help you through a period of difficulty.'

'You have, Dr. Jones, and I'm grateful for that. It's also what helped me to decide to go medication free. I feel stronger ... emotionally.' I wasn't telling the entire truth. It was mostly because I couldn't stomach taking anti-anxiety medication anymore. I wanted to be me, without a chemical sense of security. I wanted the real me back.

'Let's go back to the topic of death, Yolande.' Dr. Jones didn't look at me. She was scribbling something in her notebook. I waited for her next statement. It always followed a pattern. She would declare the topic, pause, then ask me to tell her about it.

'Taking the data from numerous sessions, you seem to have an abnormal fixation with death. Tell me about it.' Bingo. There it was—the question.

'No. Not death itself ...'

'Then what?'

'Dead people never come back,' I said.

'That's a fact. But they live on in your memories—'

'What? Do you think it makes it less real? Or better? Or solves the whole finality of death?' I was fuming.

'Tell me about death.'

Did she mean physically or spiritually? 'You stop breathing. Your body stops functioning. Your personality, or whatever makes you, you, is gone. You no longer have a consciousness of earthly matters.'

'Is it what you look like that makes you who you are?'

I closed my eyes. That was a tough question. 'No. Nobody chooses the body they are born with. What we look like is physical deception, hiding the real you, inside. I think ... what we look like, can shape how we act, once we're aware of society's acceptance or rejection, but it's not *who* we are.'

Dr. Jones was focused on her notepad, madly writing.

'Imagine a world, Dr. Jones, where people had sight, but they couldn't see what they looked like—because there were no reflective surfaces—how would people be different then?'

Dr. Jones raised her eyebrows at me, then smiled after a moment. 'That's an interesting question and scenario, Yolande ... tell me, what attracted you to Mia?'

Silence. How did we end up on the topic of Mia? And where was she going with it?

I pressed my lips together in a hard line before I spoke. 'The very first time I met her was when we were eight years old. She was on a seat, sliding her green rain boots on.'

She stood and buttoned up her raincoat and ran into the rain and jumped in puddles. I wished I could be like her. Not afraid of the mud. My mother hated mud. And so I hated the mud. She stopped jumping and looked at me, then walked towards me, her hand outstretched.

'Come and play,' she said.

She pulled me into the rain and we jumped in puddles and spun around and around and around with our arms outstretched, our faces towards the dark clouds, rain splattering our faces. I felt free. For the first time in my life.

'We stayed best friends until I was ten, and then I saw her no more because my family moved ... until, I accidentally knocked the study notes out of a girl's hand at the new high school when I was thirteen.'

The paper scattered on the ground like paper from a party popper. I scrambled to pick them up for her, apologizing profusely. When I gave the papers back to the girl and looked up, she was smiling at me.

'I'm so sorry,' I had said to her.

'Hi, So-Sorry, I'm Mia. You remind me of myself.'
'What's that? Clumsy?'
'Yes, in fact.' We both giggled.
I paused and stared at her. 'Mia?
'Yolande?

'We squealed, and click, there was our immediate bond. Our paths had crossed again.' I stopped talking and let out a deep breath.

'So, you connected over an incident?'

'No. We connected over our similarity.'

'Perfect!'

'Perfect what?'

'Have you got any other friends like Mia—who you can connect with?'

I shifted on the sofa. I didn't want to talk about Mia and friends. 'I have friends—but no one will ever be my best friend like Mia, or maybe ... Indigo, perhaps.'

Dr. Jones looked at me and tapped her pen on her notepad.

'Why do you hand write notes when you can type them straight into a computer document?' *Great deviation from the subject matter, Yolande!*

'I've tried both. Handwritten notes have an extra depth to them. I remember more from my handwritten notes. I can think with clarity, analyze, ponder and ... I feel more connected to the patient and the notes.'

I nodded my head and looked over at the white coat that hung on the wall near her degrees. That was new! Was it symbolic or something? Did she ever wear it?

Dr. Jones followed my line of gaze and smiled. 'My private joke.' She shook her head then looked at me. 'Have you spoken to Mia?'

'No.'

'You need to.'

'I can't, yet.'

'Why?'

'It makes it more real.' I looked down at my trembling hand. I swear I could still see the stain of blood on my fingers. My blood. The same blood that dripped onto Mia's forehead like she was being targeted by a marksman for a fatal shot.

Dr. Jones was writing madly. I think she needed a red pen to write the word "denial", because when it came down to it, that's what I was doing to the ending of that terrible day of the scars.

'When do you go back to the Base?'

'Tomorrow.'

'How does that make you feel?'

I shook my head. I was getting tired of analyzing how I was feeling. 'Excited but worried.'

'More information.'

I sighed. 'I'm excited to be going back to Base to work as an aeronautical engineer, and worried about fitting into the routine again and about catching up on what I have missed out, especially on critical data that will be needed to make decisions, plus, I'm worried about Gram's health.' My voice was flat.

'That's not uncommon to feel multiple emotions,' she said.

Please, not the magic wand question ...

'If you had a magic wand, what positive changes would you make to the situation?'

I scratched my eyebrow to stop myself from rolling my eyes at her. Magic wands didn't exist, and never will! 'Without a doubt, I would use it to cure Gram's Meniere's disease.'

'Is that all?'

'Yes.'

'Yolande, here's my personal number. Call me at any time if you need to talk. I take texts too, if you prefer to use that form of communication in particular situations.'

I took the card from Dr. Jones. Our session time had ended. If she had a magic wand to make any positive changes, what would she choose to do?

'Thanks for your support, Dr. Jones.' I stood and shook her hand. I was hoping this would be the final time I would ever see her. She was so mentally exhausting.

'It's my pleasure, Yolande, and, thank you for sharing your artwork with me. I know they're very personal to you. Take care.'

'I will.'

Dr. Jones walked out of the consultation room with me, as she always did with her patients.

I turned to her before I left.

She smiled at me, and then and there, I decided never to return for another psych session.

Ever.

Chapter Twenty-One

'Flowers, tea, coffee ... or books?' The words rolled off my tongue like I'd never left the flower store while I entered data into Gram's accounting book. In the two weeks that I was back on the Base, I had managed fall deeply into analysis and design. My happy place. Somehow, flowers weren't so exciting ... or tea, or coffee, or books.

'Yolande.' It was a man's voice, deep and strong, caressing the letters of my name. I looked up. Xander stood before me, his lips curled into a smile.

I took a deep breath to calm my erratic heart. He was the color of blue. A mesmerizing blue like the sea, reminding me of summer holidays and salty air, sand between my toes, running along the beach and kicking up cool water.

'Alexander ... Gram's not here. She's unwell again.' I sighed.

'I know.'

I frowned. 'How?'

'Everyone in town knows when she isn't well.'

'Is it a grape vine of town gossip?' I asked, my voice more abrasive than I intended.

'No ... your grandfather stops singing,' he said and winced.

I held my breath to stop the hurt from cutting through my heart. Gram's Meniere's disease—it didn't just affect her, it affected everyone around her. Including me. I let out a broken breath.

'How can I help you?'

'I need to buy some flowers.'

'Really?'

'Yes.'

'I thought you never bought flowers. Let me recall—"No. Never in fact."'

He looked down and grinned. 'It's true. I usually harvest them ... from gardens.'

'You mean *steal*?'

'Yes.'

'So, who are they for—the person must be important if you're purchasing them.'

'They're for a partner.'

'He?' *Like Josh?* I wanted to ask, but didn't.

'She,' he said, and lowered his chin.

I raised my eyebrows. I thought he and Josh were together.

'What would you like?' I asked.

'That's why I'm here.' He put his hands into his pockets and gave me a coy smile, sending that curious heat rushing through me.

'Hmmm ... would she prefer flowers by color, perfume, or by type of flower?'

'See, this is why I don't buy flowers!'

'So ... when you *steal* flowers from gardens, how do you choose which to take?'

'Color.'

'Now we're getting somewhere.'

'Flowers for ... friendship ... a favorite ... a fixation ... a flame ... fondness ... friends ... sex?'

He gave me a look of mock horror. 'Sex? People buy flowers for sex?'

'Correction ... *men* buy flowers for sex.'

'No way!'

'Yes way!' I was confused. Josh had bought flowers for Xander, twice, hadn't he?

He smiled and pulled his hands out his pockets, and threaded his long fingers together. 'It's for dancing.' His voice was gentle.

'Nice. Let's see what I can rustle up for you.'

'Well, I hope she's my dance partner. I haven't asked her yet.'

'So, the flowers are for persuasion?' I raised an eyebrow at him.

'I guess so ... if you were to receive flowers, what would you like, hypothetically speaking?'

I frowned at him and pressed my lips together. 'Hmmm ... if I was to receive flowers ... I would prefer the wild garden variety that bloom without competition with the others. They smell much nicer. For your purpose though, flowers from Flowers for Fleur is necessary. Do you trust me to create something special for you?'

He smiled and crossed his arms. 'You? Andi the pretend florist?' He cocked an eyebrow at me.

'Yep!' I said. 'Fake it until you make it!'

He looked down at the floor and then lifted his eyes to mine. 'Okay ... how bad could they be? They won't be flying flowers, will they?'

I narrowed my eyes at him, ignoring his comment, resisting the urge to pick up the nearest flower and throw it at him. 'What type of dancing?'

'Does it matter?'

'Yes—for instance, hip-hop dancing flowers would be different to say ... classical ballet flowers ...' I was testing his reaction to classical ballet. Gram was right, Xander did look like the Principal

Danseur in *Swan Lake*. He didn't flinch or react in any way at the mention of the words.

'I hadn't thought of it that way. I was only thinking of my dance partner, well ... hopefully my dance partner ...'

'So, what type of dancing?'

'Ballroom.'

I raised my eyebrows at him, surprised his answer.

'What?'

'I just never pictured you as a ballroom dancer!'

He shifted his weight onto his other foot. 'Me neither. But I'm giving it a go ...'

I nodded my head at him and narrowed my eyes. 'I've got it!'

'Got what?'

'I have a vision of the bouquet you need to persuade the woman to dance with you.' They were roses, peonies and ranunculus—orange, light pink and dark pink, with some dark green foliage.

'Really? Just like that?'

'Yes. Simple really, as compared to avionics, or potential dangers of new aircraft technologies ...' *Had I said too much?*

He cleared his throat. 'Yes. When you put it that way—simple really ...' His penetrating gaze probed.

My heart skipped a beat. 'Look around the store to see if there's anything else you'd like to add for power of persuasion, while I gather the blooms for your dance proposal.' I breathed out his energy traveling through me.

'You're good at this, aren't you?'

'Good at what?'

'Selling.'

'No ... I'm just trying to get rid of you so I can create your magical bouquet filled with the word "yes".'

Xander grinned at me and I whooshed him away with my hand.

At the workbench I opened Gram's *Book of Fantastical Flower*

Designs to see if she had anything fancy in her flower journal. I ran my finger down the list and stopped at the word "flattery". He needed to flatter the woman he was targeting as a dance partner to persuade her to dance with him. I turned to page 28, and looked at Gram's illustration and list of flowers and greenery. Her design was similar to my vision, but she also added a couple of gerberas.

I closed the book and went to the cold room and gathered the collection of blooms, then returned to the workbench and constructed the bouquet of persuasion. I tied pale pink ribbon around the stems then wrapped them in brown paper and added a bow of natural hemp twine. It was sure to impress.

Xander was at the bookshelf flipping through a book.

'Sir, your order is ready.'

He turned and faced me, his blue eyes capturing me.

I took a calming breath. 'The "yes" bouquet will work wonders. When she sees you with your hands behind your back, her heart will soften ... but when you reveal the flowers, her heart will melt, and she will say yes to anything you suggest. That's what flowers are—persuasion,' I said in a theatrical voice, and took a bow.

Xander raised an amused eyebrow at me and took the flowers, his fingers exquisitely brushing against mine. 'How much do I owe you?'

I rubbed my hand where his fingers had touched mine. 'Nothing ... and the story that goes with the "yes" bouquet is free.' I smiled a little and battered my eyelids at him for dramatics. I wanted him to take the flowers and go. He made me uncomfortable. I wanted to run from him.

'Do you always talk so much?'

My cheeks warmed. 'Only when I want to get rid of someone. Is it working?' I stiffened to stop the sting of his criticism.

'Yes.' His blue eyes caressed mine, drawing my soul closer to his.

I took a deep breath. 'Good luck,' I said, and walked away as

I built a fortress to protect my mind and heart. I added him to my mental list of people I never wanted to see again—him and Dr. Jones.

I wrote the bouquet off as a loss of in Gram's accounting book, then busied myself in the store, tidying and replenishing, breathing out the Xander potion that chipped away at the fortress around my heart.

Three minutes later, Xander appeared before me, with his hands behind his back.

I pulled the top of my dress up higher over my scar, even though I knew it wasn't showing. My skin burned with anxiety.

'Did you need something else?' I wanted him to go away.

He took a step towards me and looked towards the floor. When he lifted his eyes to mine, he held the flowers out towards me; his eyes soft and vulnerable. 'Yes ... will you be my dance partner? You did say you did ballet at my mother's garden party.'

'Oh.' I put my hand on my forehead and looked down at my steel-capped work boots. My insides clenched with dread while my heart raced. I felt a little faint.

'Please.'

I walked to the window and focussed outside. I hadn't danced for three years. Not since I let go of Mia's hand. He did ask what flowers I would like if I was receiving some ... and here they are. I had just fallen into a net.

My eyes started to burn, so I looked up and blinked to stop my tears from falling.

Xander stood behind me. Today he smelled like a spicy blend of cedarwood and cocoa-vanilla. It reminded me of carefree hot summer days, wearing groovy sunglasses, arms outstretched and looking up at the blue sky. He was so close I could feel his body heat. And right now, I was lost. Utterly and completely.

I snapped out of his potion. 'Did Gram put you up to this?' My voice wavered.

'No.'

'My mother?' I asked.

'No.'

'What would I have to wear?'

'A ball gown, designed to how you wish.' His voice was gentle.

I reached up and fingered my scar through my florist dress. Ballroom dancers were beautiful. Blemish free.

An empty feeling filled my stomach and I tried to control the panic that crept through my veins. I breathed out—slowly, steadily, and gently, until my last drop of breath was released.

'You won't need your work boots with me. I'll look after you.' His voice was tender.

My eyes filled with tears again.

Can I dance again? Can I enjoy my life when Mia can't?

'Please,' he whispered.

I wiped my tears, turned around and faced him. He lowered his chin and gazed into my eyes. Deeply. He really wanted this.

I swallowed the lump in my throat. 'I'll consider being your partner, but there's one condition.' My stomach started to quiver, but I ignored it.

'Being?'

'That you forgive me for waffling on with nonsensical unnecessary words.'

'What if I like your nonsensical unnecessary words?'

I shook my head at him. 'I'll make mistakes ...'

'We all make mistakes.'

'I'll forget steps ...'

'I'll help you to remember them.'

'I've never done ballroom dancing ...'

'Neither have I.'

I shook my head in the slightest of movements, scared of being vulnerable.

'Please,' he said again. His blue eyes seemed to glow with

light, a light I wanted to capture and inject into my heart.

A heatwave flooded my body and I inhaled a slow, steady breath. The warmth was as thrilling as it as it was frightening, flashing through me like an electrical storm. I closed my eyes and opened them again. 'Yes.'

What have I done?

The regular chair still had the imprint of my butt on it.

The door opened without one sound of complaint. Dr. Jones was dressed in a long dark blue skirt and jacket with a white button-up blouse. Her black ankle boots were stylish, unlike my steel-capped safety boots.

'Yolande.' Dr. Jones's voice was calming, like having my Gram's arms wrapped around me. She was on my list of people to never see again, but somehow, here I was.

I nodded before I stood, then followed her into the room. Dr. Jones put a light hand on my shoulder. 'Would you like to sit on the sofa, or lie on the couch today?'

'The sofa ... thanks.' I made myself comfortable and hugged a cushion. Dr. Jones went to make of pot of tea. I heard the boiling water and the chink of the china teacups and saucers. I closed my eyes and knitted my fingers together before I placed them on my stomach. I still couldn't believe I was back in this office. I needed to talk about something, but I wasn't sure what. Well ... I had an inkling ... of something ...

At the sound of approaching footsteps, I opened my eyes. Dr. Jones placed two teacups and saucers on the table. I reached over and picked one up. The warmth of the brew touched my lips when I sipped it and I relaxed a little. Aah ... tea. I was reminded of a Chinese Proverb—*a hasty man drinks his tea with a fork*. Such an odd thing to say …

'What brings you here today, Andi?'

Our session always started like this. Predictable. Safe … I guess. 'Xander asked me to dance with him.'

'How does that make you feel?'

As if I didn't already know. But saying it out loud took away its power, apparently. 'Anxious … terrified.'

'Of dancing, or of Xander?'

Xander. 'Dancing.'

'Why do you think that is?'

Make it up. 'Because I haven't danced since … you know …'

'It's okay to enjoy your life again.'

I feel like I can't. 'I know.'

'Do you think Mia wants you to miss out on enjoyable moments in life?'

Mia … does she always have to mention Mia? 'No.'

'You were an exceptional dancer, once. I believe you're more than capable of being Xander's dance partner. What type of dancing is it?'

'Ballroom.'

'Is that a problem for you?'

No. 'I'm not sure …'

'Yolande … is your anxiety more to do with Xander?'

Yes. 'I'm not sure … I think that's why I'm here.'

'Let's explore that more … is it Xander himself, or the fact that he's male?'

I let out a deep breath. *Truth* … 'I don't think it's Xander, because I'm 50% sure he prefers men, so in that regard, I feel safe with him. But, on the other hand, he is male.'

Dr. Jones wrote at speed on her notepad. She looked up at me. 'Yolande … are you scared of men?'

Yes. 'No. I'm angry with them.'

'Putting aside what happened to you and Mia on that day,

what other reasons could you be angry with them?'

'Well ... the male-dominated power structure and the fact that some men don't think rules apply to them, and they think they can do and say anything to women that they like, without considering the emotional, physical or psychological repercussions ... and, I distrust them and what is behind their intentions. Since that day ... I can't trust any man whom I do not know. I look at them and think they are lusting after a woman—women to be used and discarded after they have had their wicked way combined with their power trip.'

'Do you know any good men? Good in the way that they treat women with respect?'

'Yes—my father, my grandfather, my brother, quite a few men at the Base.'

'Do you know what signs show that a man is respectful of a woman?'

'I'd like to think I do. But I feel like my vision is tainted forever, after ... you know ...'

'Observation is the key. You need to observe him and whether he looks at your face and listens when you speak. Does he treat all people and animals kindly? On the other hand, a man you must avoid is one who looks at your chest, speaks down to others, or gives you very personal comments without knowing you.'

'That's exactly what I know, but I analyze and over-think and build my walls to protect myself, even with the "good" men ...'

'Yolande ... go with your intuition, your gut feeling, the colors you see, and if you're not sure, ask someone you trust. Your grandmother has met Xander, hasn't she?'

'Yes.'

'Perhaps a conversation with her about Xander would be wise. She may be able to give you more information about him. Do you consider your grandmother to be a good judge of people?'

'Absolutely.'

Dr. Jones gave me a slight smile. 'I think this ballroom dancing opportunity will be good for you. There is no doubt you'll have to step out of your comfort zone, but you can do it. You have your Cognitive Behaviour Toolbox at your disposal, any time of day or night. Print out your CBT Alternative Action Formulation to list your coping strategies, and journal your emotions. You have made significant progress from the first day we met, Yolande. I believe you can do this ... and I know Mia will approve.'

I finished the last of my tea and gazed out the window. There were no warning bells sending shrills of anxiety through me. Dr. Jones was right. I had everything I needed to cope with the anxiety, and feelings of guilt.

If only I hadn't let go of Mia's hand ...

One soft light was on at Gram and Grampapa's house when I arrived. It was in the bedroom on the second floor of their Gothic Revival home. I rested my bike against the hedge near the gate of the house I loved to visit.

Every. Single. Time. It was filled with beautiful memories, and warmth, and unconditional love, and hot chocolate, and baking cupcakes.

I looked up at the familiar steep-sloping roof, decorated bargeboard, cross gables, and Gothic windows, then walked up the four steps to the porch and knocked on the wooden door with the stained-glass panels.

And waited.

I knocked again. I heard the squeak of the internal steps, and after a moment more, the door opened, a little, and Gramps peeked through the crack.

'Gramps. It's me ... Yolande.'

He opened the door a little wider. My breath stopped when I saw his face. His eyes were swollen and red. He was the color of midnight blue; a profound sadness that rattled the bones.

Filled with dread, I pushed hard on the door and stepped inside.

'Go home, Landi ... Gram isn't well.' His voice cracked as his eyes watered.

I shook my head at him and made my way up the steps to their bedroom. Gram was lying on her side on the bed, staring at the wall.

'I can't do this anymore ... I can't do this anymore ... please, make it stop ... I can't do this anymore ...' She sobbed between phrases of words.

I knelt on the floor in front of her, out of her line of vision, filled with utter and complete devastation.

'Gram.' I had no other words. What do you say to someone who is debilitated, unable to move? I reached over to her hand and held it. *Take my hand ...*

'I'm sorry, Gram. I wish I could make it better.' Tears filled my eyes and I let them fall, unbidden. 'This is so unfair. Bad things aren't supposed to happen to good people.'

Gram vomited. Violently. And although she had nothing to expel, she continued to vomit, so what she spat into the container was nothing but white froth. I handed her a tissue and she wiped her mouth and dropped it into the container.

'I hate this ... I hate this damn disease—' Gram vomited once again.

I sat on the floor, holding her hand. 'How long have you been like this, Gram?'

'Five and a half hours of the room spinning around me and vomiting, of staring at the same place on the damn wall to try to stop the bloody vertigo.' She took short breaths, breathing them out forcefully between pursed lips. I knew what she was doing.

She was trying to stop the nausea. 'Five and a half hours of absolute, bloody hell … I'm so tired, but I can't close my eyes …'

I squeezed my eyes shut as Gram vomited forcibly. When she stopped, I looked at her, and was rattled to the core by her wide eyes filled with fear.

'The most ridiculous thing is … I know the room is not spinning, yet, everything in my damn body and mind tells me it is. It's such a lie … *a lie*!' Her voice broke.

I squeezed Gram's hand and shut my eyes. 'Dear God, please take this wretched disease from Gram, and give it to me—'

'NOOooo!' Gram yelled.

I jumped.

She was furious. 'You can't have it, Yolande!' she cried. 'I would NEVER wish this upon anyone, not even my worst enemy.' She made a high-pitched noise, and vomited, but nothing was expelled from her stomach. She went limp as she wept with a stuttered despair, still staring at the wall.

I stroked her hand with a gentleness from within. 'Gram … I'm worried about dehydration. I need to take you to the hospital?'

'No … don't take me there! I can't move. I don't want to move. It'll make me spin more and I'll vomit again. Please … no … just let me lie still, here … in my own home …' Gram's voice was husky, probably from the relentless vomiting.

'Fleur, my love,' Gramps said, standing in the doorway of the bedroom. His voice was gentle, but filled with pain. 'I've already made the call for the paramedics. Your signs of dehydration are verging on dangerous.'

Gram gave a loud sob. 'I can't do this anymore …' She released a breath like it was her last.

Heavy, silent tears rolled down my face. This scene before me was unbearable. Grandparents are supposed to age with grace, smiling with a gentle knowing of everything, like they had figured out life, and had decided that indeed it was good, even after all they had seen and done.

The flashing blue and red lights of the ambulance intruded the bedroom. Within moments the paramedics were talking to Gram.

And then she was gone.

Exactly where she didn't want to go ...

Chapter Twenty-Two

stopped in the middle of my conversation with Charlotte at the tapping sound on the glass of the front door. It was 7.45am. I ignored it and continued discussing today's job list at Flowers for Fleur. The tapping sounded again, louder. I glanced over at the door at the dark-haired man with a sweeping curl over his forehead. It was Xander. He held up a piece of paper against the pane of glass.

Little pig, little pig,
Let me in!

I wrote on a piece of paper and held it up.

Not by the hair of my chinny-chin-chin!
Open at 8.30am

He raised an eyebrow at me, then looked down to write again. He held it against the glass.

You have a beard?

I giggled and walked to the front door and unlocked it.

Xander stepped inside. He was the color of baby blue today, reminding me of the awe and beauty of the blue tone of a winter frost that I loved. I inhaled his citrus scent with a hint of liquorice, vanilla and lavender, and felt an inner glow.

'How do I leave a note for you if Gram's bicycle isn't outside?' he asked.

My eyes widened and my inner glow vanished. Gram's bicycle. She was fanatical about it. The day wasn't right unless her bicycle was on display out the front and there were flowers in the bicycle basket!

"This is our florist signature, Andi. It's not Flowers for Fleur without flowers in the bicycle basket!"

She had said those words one hundred and one times. I had been so busy I had forgotten all about it. Slipping back into the role of the store manager was harder than I thought. There was so much to organize and do before the doors even opened.

I held up my finger to Xander. 'Wait one moment.' I rushed to the office and wheeled her bicycle through the store, out the front doors, and leaned it against the antique white storefront where it had been for the last fifty years.

I stepped back into the store and held my finger up once again. 'One more moment.' I hurried to the cold room and grabbed peonies in a rainbow of colors and took them to the workbench. I needed to prepare them for the bicycle basket.

Xander stood opposite me at the workbench. 'Do you need help?'

I stopped and looked up at him. His words were so unexpected.

'Okay ... can you go to the room by the back door and pour a bottle of water, please.'

'Too easy,' he said, and left for a moment, but his citrusy scent with a hint of liquorice, vanilla, lavender and ... sandalwood perhaps, remained.

I was binding the stems together with twine when he returned with the water.

'Thanks.' I poured the water into the custom-made glass vase and placed the flowers stems into it, then grabbed some brown paper to wrap around the flowers to present them with the flair of Flowers for Fleur.

'Gram is unwell again,' I said and lowered my head. I pulled my eyebrows together. 'It is, so, not fair.'

'I'm sorry to hear,' Xander said. 'If there is anything I can do—'

'It's incurable. There's nothing the doctors can do, except try to manage the symptoms, which is hit and miss. It's a matter of elimination, trying to find what works. So far, no medication is effective.' I pressed my lips into a hard line, then picked up the blooms and walked briskly through the store to place them in the bicycle basket.

Xander followed. 'What's her diagnosis?' he asked.

'Meniere's disease.' My breath shuddered and I shook my head, my eyes burning.

Xander frowned. 'That's a vestibular disease, isn't it?'

I looked up at him, surprised by his use of the word vestibular. 'Yes. Have you heard of it?'

'No. I'm just thinking of Dr. Prosper Menière, who studied diseases of the ear.'

'Why would you know that, and I don't?'

'Well ... you know ... I come from a family of doctors ... dinner table discussions and all.' He shrugged.

I caressed the petal of a pink peony. It felt like a soft marshmallow. 'Well, here are the flowers in the basket of the bicycle. You can put your note in there now.' I looked up into his deep blue eyes and felt their pull on me. I held my breath as a kaleidoscope of butterflies fluttered inside me, then breathed out the addictive feeling.

He kept his eyes connected to mine while he placed his note into the flowers. 'Done.'

I moved my hand to the note without breaking our eye contact. 'Delivered.'

'But not read,' he added, his eyes caressing mine.

'Work before pleasure,' I said.

'My notes are a pleasure?' He cocked an eyebrow at me.

'Well ... not at first, but then, after a while, I looked forward to reading what you had written.'

He smiled at me. 'I had no idea you were the one reading my letters at first. I thought Andi was a guy.'

'Good.'

'Good?'

'Yes. If you had known I was female, your words would have been crafted differently, and your handwriting neater ...'

He raised his eyebrows at me. 'True. And I would have entered the store to speak to you in person earlier.'

'What? Because I'm a girl?'

'Yes.'

'So you could charm me?'

'I tried that. It didn't work. You laughed at me, remember?'

I grinned. I couldn't help it. 'Perfectly!' I looked at my watch. 'Gotta go. The flowers are calling.'

He pushed his fingers through his hair. 'Talk to you later.' And then he was gone, leaving a trail of his citrusy scent with a hint of liquorice, vanilla, lavender and sandalwood.

I opened his note while I walked back in to the store.

Dear Yolande,

Thank you for being my dance partner.
It means more to me than you know.

I'll be here at 5pm to organize our dance schedule.

✿ Alexander

Tarrin, the town of "more". I smiled and tucked the letter into my pocket and returned to Charlotte to go over her job list. We had a busy day ahead: me at the workbench of flower imagination, and Charlotte at the sales desk.

At 4.45pm Charlotte left, fifteen minutes before closing. I flitted around the store tidying while I could. I bee-lined to the sales desk when a well-dressed man entered the store. Hipster? Yes, definitely. And he was the color of dark orange—deceit.

'Flowers?' I asked.

'Two sets,' he said, grinned and stroked his dark manicured beard.

'Lovely. Who are they for, so I can tailor the flower bouquets accordingly?'

'What do you mean?'

'Well … it's highly unlikely that you would want to give flowers of love and passion to your mother.'

'Aye.' He looked around the store, then leaned in closer and spoke with a quiet voice. 'I have two girlfriends … I'm trying to work out which one to ditch.'

I narrowed my eyes at him. 'You know it will never work. If you stay with one, you'll forever wonder if you should have chosen the other.'

'That's what I'm afraid of.'

'And when they find out you're dating another girl at the same time, you'll lose both ...'

He hung his head.

'So ... two bouquets to end your tangled web?' I watched his face carefully.

He took a step back from the sales desk and pulled his eyebrows together while he put his hand over his heart. He looked at me like I had fired an arrow into his chest. He let his hand fall and closed his eyes for a moment. 'I think I have some serious thinking to do,' he said.

'You already knew that. I just had to verbalize it for you ... come back and see me for one bouquet of flowers when you know where your heart belongs,' I said.

He pressed his lips into a hard line and nodded. 'Sure.' His eyebrows knitted together, and he looked up at the ceiling, then turned and left.

Sorry, not sorry. Better now than later when he is in deeper. Jealousy is an ugly emotion.

Xander almost bumped shoulders with the two-timing guy as they passed. He stopped before me. 'What did you do to him?'

'Nothing. He did it to himself ... you're early.'

'I know.'

'I have work to do. We don't close until five.'

'Can I help?'

'Then I'll have to pay you.'

'No need ...'

'No deal, Xander. You'll slow me down.'

He put his hands up, palms outwards towards me. 'I'll wait then.' He looked over at the café. 'Join me at a table once you're done.'

I looked over at the tables, most of them empty at this time of day, and tried to guess which table he would choose—one by the window, surely? 'Okay. See you in ten.'

I got back to work, bringing flowers in from outside, Gram's bicycle, serving the last of customers.

I looked over at Xander. He was sitting at the table in the center of the café. The table where you could see everything and everyone in the store. He sipped on a hot drink while his eyes found mine every now and again, sending that curious heat flowing through me.

At 5pm I closed the store, checked that my scar was covered, then went and sat opposite him.

'I could have done some of those jobs, you know.'

'I didn't want you to.'

'Why?'

I didn't want to tell him that I would feel like I owed him something. And I didn't want to be in debt to anyone, physically or emotionally. 'You don't work here.' That was a logical reply; one he couldn't oppose.

Xander looked into my eyes and took a deep breath. 'I like stubborn.'

'Stubborn is hard to like, especially when you're trying to persuade.'

'Apparently, flowers are persuasion ...' he gave me a coy smile and my heart skipped a beat.

'Touché!'

Xander lifted an eyebrow at me and opened his diary. 'Friday and Saturday morning is my only time to practise our ballroom dancing this week.'

'Friday morning? Don't you work? After work suits me better after dealing with the rebellious blooms.'

'I can't do nights right now, and I have lectures and study to do in amongst other important things.'

'Study? What are you learning about?'

'Anatomy—the human body, and how to fix it when it goes wrong.'

Gram ... 'Will Josh be jealous of me spending time with you?'

Xander straightened his back and frowned. 'No.'

'Is he why your dad thinks you're gay?'

Xander ran his fingers through his hair and sighed. 'Yes. That and something else that he despises.'

'Being?'

'I dance ... classical ... according to him, all male dancers are gay!'

'But that's not true! Little does your father know that most male dancers are more sure of their masculinity than other men.'

'Yes. Thanks for sticking up for me.'

There was silence then. A static, sticky silence.

'Are you using me?' I asked.

'What?'

'To convince your father that you're not gay, like you did at your mother's birthday party?'

'No!' He looked up at the ceiling then back at me. 'The truth is ... I need you as a dance partner. I want to enter the ballroom competition to prove that I'm not just a classical dancer. And, I want to dance with someone who's not in my dancing fraternity.'

'So are you—'

'What?'

'Prince Siegfried from *Swan Lake*?' I held my breath.

He stilled, lowered his head and looked up at me through his eyelashes. 'Yes.' He lifted his chin higher and kept eye contact with me.

I smiled, and it grew wider as I replayed his grace on the stage. 'Ballet perfection. I couldn't fault you on any technicalities when you danced. Plus, the emotion you put into your character to make him real. You were magnificent!'

He flipped the pen from end to end in his fingers. 'Thanks.'

'When did you start dance classes?'

'When I was six. My father hated it.'

'And yet you continued.'

'My mother was my biggest supporter, and still is. My father likes to pretend his son is not a dancer.'

Now it made sense why his sisters seemed to protect him and fuss over him at his mother's birthday celebration.

'Sorry, not sorry.'

'Huh?'

'I'm sorry about your father, but I'm not sorry about your dancing.'

Xander took a deep breath. 'Let's get back to our dance schedule. Now you know why I have limited time, with all the dance preparation and rehearsals. Can you do Friday and Saturday morning?'

'No and yes.'

He looked at me and shook his head. 'You need to try harder than that ...'

'For how long?'

'Three hours.'

'I'll see if I can get Charlotte to cover Friday morning for me.'

'Good.' Xander looked down and wrote in his diary.

'You're welcome, Prince Siegfried.'

He looked up at me with narrowed eyes. 'Don't go all gooey on me because I play a prince.' He shook his head.

'I'm not. I'm just surprised.'

'Good. I don't like it when girls go all la-la on me.'

'La-la?'

'Yeah—you know—dreamy eyes and I love you and all that, like I have a magic love potion I sprinkle over them.'

'Don't worry. I don't do gooey la-la over guys.'

'Good,' he said, but his eyes told me a different story.

'I'll let you know if I can make it on Friday morning.'

'Give me your phone,' he said and held out his hand.

I gave it to him, and he added his number to my contacts then handed it back to me. 'Oh, and aaahhh ... no work boots.'

I smiled at him and raised an eyebrow. 'We'll see.'

He put his shoe over my work boot under the table. 'See you 7am, Friday morning at the community hall up the road. I'll be waiting for you.' He stood and turned to walk out.

'Not if I'm there first!'

He stopped and turned to face me. 'Is that a challenge, Yolande?'

'Maybe, Alexander ...'

He smiled crookedly at me, turned and left.

I watched him take confident strides, his feet slightly turned out, but not in the classical walk that would be ingrained from years of dancing. He was probably trying to walk like a normal person, which he would never be. He was almost too perfect.

What was his weakness? His flaw? What secrets did he have? If there was one thing I knew about perfection, it's usually the result of hiding something you didn't want others to see. I should know. I lived it every day of my life since I let go of Mia's hand ...

Chapter Twenty-Three

'Gram!' I called. She was outside Flowers for Fleur, fussing about the blooms in the basket of her bicycle. She was the color of blush pink—acceptance and calm. Her presence at the store was totally unexpected. 'Gram!' I called again, but she still did not respond.

I dismounted my bike, stopped beside her and touched her shoulder. 'Gram. You're here!' I smiled a double smile if that was at all possible—one smile for her being here at the store, and the other was because I could hear Grampapa's singing: *E lucevan le stelle.*

She turned her head towards me. 'Oh, Landi. I didn't hear you. How are you?'

'I'm well ... and you?'

She turned her body, holding her head still and faced me. 'It's a good day today. I'm feeling much better after my short stay in hospital.'

I put my hand over my heart. 'That makes me happy.' I kissed her on the cheek. 'Is that what I think I can hear?'

Gram looked at me with furrowed brows. She turned her

head to the left, listening with her right ear.

Her face relaxed and she smiled. 'Yes. It's *E lucevan le stelle*. It's magnificent.' A tear ran down Gram's cheek, and my heart broke a little. She had most definitely lost some hearing, if not a lot. She wiped her tear away and took a deep breath. 'Now go inside and start on your job list, Yolande. We have a busy day!'

'Yes, Gram.' I wanted to add that every day was busy here, but I didn't. I opened the door to the store and Grampapa's voice poured out, loud and clear. I put my bike in the office, then went to Gramps and gave him a long hug. He was the color of tawny brown—reliability and endurance.

'I didn't think Gram would be here today ... should she be here?' I asked.

'No, she shouldn't. But you know Gram. I can't stop her, so I have to support her and be there for her when it all crumbles.'

'We're all here for her, Gramps.'

I found my apron and put it on, checked that my scar was covered, then got on with my list of jobs. I opened the front doors at 8.30am, then made my way to the sales desk. I looked over to my right at Gram. She was working at the workbench of flower imagination with a beaming smile on her face.

'Flowers, tea, coffee or books?' All four words rolled off my tongue, as Gram insisted on me saying. The older gentleman was the color of pineapple yellow—optimism and joy.

'Flowers. For my wife.'

I smiled at him. 'Are you celebrating?'

'Well ... my wife is having her cochlear implants turned on today. She'll be able to hear again after twelve long years. It's such a ... a ... miracle!'

I swallowed. Hard.

'It'll be the first time she will hear her grandchildren's voices.' The man looked down and smiled, then wiped his eye. It was a big moment for them.

They needed to commemorate with the most beautiful flowers we had. This called for the "flossie"—the Roman Goddess of Flowers. 'Let me organize an extraordinary gathering of blooms to honor your grand celebration. Please enjoy a complimentary hot drink at the café. Tell Darcy that Andi sent you.'

'Really? Thanks,' he said, and ventured to his right, over Darcy's way.

I approached Gram and stood by her left side. 'Can you create a "flossie" please, Gram.'

She looked at me. 'Bossy? Have I been too bossy?'

I berated myself after forgetting that she couldn't hear so well with her left ear. Maybe she needed a cochlear implant? I walked around the workbench and faced her. 'No, Gram. I have an order for a "flossie" bouquet. You know ... in your special book, the Roman Goddess of Flowers.'

'Oh—of course! I'll get on to it right away!'

'Thanks, Gram.' I tucked a strand of hair behind my ear. Her hearing had deteriorated. It was like she was guessing at what I had said. I returned to the sales desk.

'Good morning. Flowers, tea, coffee or books?' A young woman stood before me. She wore an emerald green empire waist dress that matched the color of her eyes. Her red hair was tied into a high ponytail. She was striking. I looked at her a little longer to see her color. She was a gray-blue, that gray with an "a"—deep sadness.

'Flowers.'

'For?'

'Why should I tell you that?' She was defensive.

'So I can organize the right type of flowers for you. It's no good giving you roses when I should be giving you sunflowers?'

She looked away and held her breath. I knew exactly what she was doing. She was stopping her tears from falling. I had lost count of how many times I had done that in the last three years, after that terrible day of scars.

'They're for me ... for my broken heart,' she finally said, her voice breaking.

I wanted to go and hug her. I wanted to tell her that it gets better, but I couldn't. I was still waiting for the pain of my broken heart to lessen.

'I'm so sorry ... it's an indescribable pain, and a grief process. It's okay to feel every emotion and express it, if you can. There's nothing you can do to avoid what you're feeling. It's what makes us human.' She needed nurturing. She was feeling the color of broken. Fractured. We needed flowers for "fractured". 'Let's walk around in the flower garden and create a unique bouquet, just for you.'

I took her hand in mine with a gentleness, like a sister would. The same hand that once held Mia's. Together we looked at flowers, lifted them and smelled their perfume, and collected them in a basket. I took her to the workbench and gathered the palest pink ribbon and a clear jar-like vase, and together we added the blooms, tending to the flowers with care, like tending to her heart.

Some people believe that flowers have magical healing properties. At this moment, I believed it was true. I wrapped the pale pink ribbon around the top of the vase, then added a thin wire of fairy lights into the creation and turned it on.

A smile spread over her face. A happy smile that warmed my heart. Before she left the store, I gave her a hug. I waved away her offer of money. I didn't help her because I wanted a sale. I wanted to help to make her heart feel lighter, to lessen her burden. And I think I did, because my heart felt full—full of glitter and sparkles. But ... would Gram approve of my generosity?

I returned to the sales desk and sold a few bunches of flowers. I turned my head toward Gram to check on her. She walked toward Darcy with an unfamiliar gait. She didn't walk with her usual grace. Her walk was unsteady, like she had had a few too many drinks. Did she? I watched as she ordered herself a cup of tea, then turned, keeping her entire body stiff as she did so. It was an odd thing to do. On her return to the workbench, she stopped beside me at the sales desk and put her hand on my back.

'The rain is coming, Landi. Put the umbrellas out.'

'But it's sunny outside!'

'Trust me. It's going ... to rain. My brain fog is back, and my ear feels full, the tinnitus is roaring, and moving my head is like doing it in slow motion, plus it makes me feel nauseous. The rain ... is coming.'

'Oh, Gram. I had no idea the weather affected you like that.'

'Just another wonderful part of this disease—the unique meteorologist ability it grants ... that was a lovely thing to do for that young woman, by the way,' she said.

Guilt rose inside of me. 'I gifted them to her, Gram. I couldn't take any money. Helping to ease her pain was more important than the money. If I took money from her, it would have felt false.'

'You have a heart of gold, Andi.'

'Just like you, Gram.'

'That's why I have you here in the store with me.' She smiled at me, but it didn't reach her eyes. I watched as she continued to the workbench, where she stood motionless for a little bit, and took a deep breath. I shook my head. Gram shouldn't be here. She wasn't as well as she was pretending to be. She only proved one thing—it's harder to fake being well, and it takes a lot of effort. She's using up energy that she will need later.

I moved about the store in double time, replenishing flower supplies and restocking shelves. I did as much as I could so Gram would have to do little. She needed to conserve her energy.

I waltzed out the front of the store to spritz the blooms for longevity, and looked over at the flowers in the basket of Gram's bicycle. There was no note from Xander, not that there should be one. My heart sank. I returned to the sales desk and pulled out my floral notepad. I would write to him instead:

Dear Alexander,

I was going to give you a quote about dancing, but you would know them all.

I must thank you for awakening my dancer soul from its eternal slumber. A new energy is flowing through me and I can't wait to use it.

What have you done?

❀ *Yolande* ❀

I folded the letter and wrote Xander's name on the front. I walked out to the bicycle flower basket with a grin and placed it between the blooms. I looked up at the sky. Dark clouds had gathered overhead, just like Gram had predicted. I returned to the store and grabbed the umbrellas, and placed them by the flowers at the storefront for people to purchase.

I turned my gaze to Gram, looking through the windows. The glow of the store lights illuminated her. She looked like she was an angel while working on a magnificent, artistic flower creation. I placed my hand over my heart as it overflowed with love for her. A sad smile formed on my lips as I thought of all she was going through. In the next moment my breath stopped. Gram had dropped to the floor with a loud thud. I screamed.

My breath trembled like an aftershock and I ran through the store and around the workbench. Gram was lying on her back, staring at the ceiling. She swallowed hard and then her chin began to quiver. A tear rolled down the side of her face and disappeared into her hair.

'I hate Meniere's disease!' she said between clenched teeth. 'I feel like I've been cursed!'

I knelt beside Gram. 'Are you spinning? Is it the vertigo?'

'No. It's another symptom of this despicable disease—a drop attack ... I am so filled with the ugliness of hatred, and I don't know who or what to hate. Do I hate me, fallen man, or the disease itself?'

My eyes burned. Gram filled with hate? This wasn't my gram. She was always the personification of grace, love and kindness. She was the epitome of the color pink!

'Are you hurt?' I asked while I blinked fifty million times to drain away my hot tears. I placed my hands around her back to help her sit up.

'I'm sure something will hurt in the coming days. Right now, it's my ego that's hurting the most.' Gram put her hands over her face and sobbed.

'I hate this. I so, so hate this!' She lifted her face to the ceiling, her eyes closed, tears rolling down her cheeks. She placed a shaky hand on her forehead. 'I'm at the mercy of this disease. I have no control over it and it does what it likes, mocking me in the process.'

My heart cried for her. 'I'll be back with a stool for you to sit on, Gram. You can't drop to the floor if you're already sitting. It will be safer that way ...' *I hope.*

I placed the stool before the workbench and helped Gram onto the seat. Darcy arrived with a glass of water and a look of concern.

'Thanks, Darcy. Gram's okay. The water is much appreciated.' I gave him a small smile then turned my attention back to Gram.

'Thank you, dear Darcy,' Gram added and took a sip of the

water.

'Shall I call Charlotte in, so I can work here by your side?' I asked.

'Slide? No, I didn't go for a slide. I fell, remember?' Gram looked at me as if I was bonkers.

I went around and stood on her right side—the ear she could hear with. 'Silly me,' I said. 'Of course, you fell. I'd like to call Charlotte in to work, and I'll stay at the workbench with you.'

Gram looked at me. Her eyebrows crinkled, and tears filled her eyes. 'Has is really come to this ... to Grammy-sitting me?'

I put my hand over my mouth to cover my gasp. *Yes.* I removed my hand from my mouth and swallowed, hard. 'Gram, you are more precious to me than all the flowers in the world. Working side by side with you is an honor, not a duty.'

Gram held my hand in hers and squeezed it. 'Tactful, my dear. And I thank you for it. Let's finish this flower work of art.'

'Yes, Gram.' I watched as she arranged the Japanese magnolias, camellias, kumquats, loropetalum, and bottlebrush—whites, pinks, yellows, dark pink, blues, orange and red—with greenery to set it off, all in a metal goblet vase with handles, humming while she worked. The fragrance of sweet candy flowed around the flowers. It was a breath of loveliness from the magnolias.

'Does your humming add extra love into the creation?' I asked.

'Perhaps ... it's more for me, to try and tune out the incessant loud tinnitus that haunts my ear non-stop. Five noises! It's louder than anything else I can hear, even when I go to a live performance!'

Oh ... how hideous to be afflicted like that. I looked down at the flowers, consciously trying to listen to my own hearing for any tinnitus. *Nothing.* 'Do you have a name for this floral revelation by Fleur?'

'Yes ... I'm calling it "Faith by Fleur". It's for those who feel they no longer have control over their lives as everything is taken away, piece by piece.'

'Like you?' My voice was soft as I felt my heart break for her. I looked up at the ceiling and widened my eyes to stop a deluge of tears.

There was a pause before she spoke in a hushed tone. 'Yes.' Gram lifted her chin higher.

There was an ache in my chest. 'If faith was a picture, it would look like your flowers, Gram, the buds blooming to show their inner beauty, despite being culled from their life source of harmony and happiness, and opening, in the knowledge that someone was still watching over them with grace.'

Gram turned to me, anguished, and looked into my eyes before she wrapped her arms around me.

'I see them ...' she whispered into my ear, 'those suffering like me ... and I want to be the one to stop it for them. Nobody deserves this ... this ... manic, violent, debilitating, depressing, disgusting, deplorable, despicable, devastating, damaging, distressing, diabolical monster of a disease that makes you vulnerable and defenseless. It takes everything, *everything* Landi, and *never* gives back ... it takes everything.' Gram's voice was tainted with a restrained anger.

'Except your family. It can't take away those who love you.'

Gram started to sob into my shoulder, and I held her tighter. I wanted to take the Meniere's monster from her. I should be the one with it, not her. I was the one who had done something unforgivable on that terrible day of the scars. Gram had done nothing but give joy and happiness to others.

I handed tissues to Gram when she sat back on the stool. I looked over, and there on the bench were two teacups and a teapot. Darcy was an angel with a red beard. I poured the cups of tea and added milk. 'Let's find a cure, Gram.'

'There is no cure!'

'Where there's life, there's hope. Where there's hope, there's a will, and where there's a will, there's a way … I'll look into it for you.' I sipped on my tea and watched as Gram lifted her teacup to her lips, her hand with a slight tremble.

A shadow passed over her eyes. A very dark shadow. My skin prickled. *Intuition*. Dr. Jones had spoken about it. Gram was in a dark place. I knew, because I had been there, and still hovered there at times. Sometimes I wondered if it was easier to go to that place and feel sorry for myself, rather than to step boldly, and live with courage.

Darcy collected the teapot, cups and saucers, once we had finished. I gave him a silent nod of approval and thanks. He raised his eyebrows, asking in silence whether Gram was okay. I creased my eyebrows together and gave a quick small shake of my head. He frowned with a sadness in his dark eyes, and backed away to return to the café.

Charlotte and Darcy kept the store going while I spent the rest of the day "Grammy-sitting", as Gram so accurately described. At 5pm, Grampapa took one step inside the store and scanned the space for Gram. He was the color of dark blue: reliability, radiating security and trust.

When he caught sight of her, he smiled, then walked over to her and kissed her on the lips. He then sat at the sales desk and started to sing, his tenor voice filling every physical object, vibrating at a resonance that felt like it penetrated the very essence of life.

I took a calming breath and looked over at Gram. She was standing at the workbench with her eyes closed, and her hand over her heart. My throat tightened. Their love story would not end the way it started, with Grampapa's singing. Gram's hearing was being taken away from her, and one day, she would never hear his passionate voice again.

I walked over to her and put my arm around her, then rested my head on hers.

'*La fleur que tu m'avais jetée,*' she whispered, 'from the famous opera, "Carmen".'

'Beautiful,' I whispered back.

'We need to talk, Landi. Let's finish up with our closing jobs and sit together at the table to discuss things.'

My muscles tensed. I didn't want to hear what she was about to say. 'Okay.' My voice was too quiet, even for me.

I left Gram, knowing that Gramps would be watching her, helping her, caring for her, and started the store closing routine, including preparing for the next day.

At 6pm, I sat at a table by the window. I cast my gaze outside at the rain and tried to ignore the waves of dread that came and went. Gram and Gramps sat opposite me and held hands. It was like the calm before the storm to come.

Gramps leaned over and kissed Gram on the forehead. 'I want Gram to finish up at the store.'

Gram looked at Gramps with wide eyes. She pulled her hand away from his. 'No, Caleb. I can't leave the store. It's my life! It's everything to me!'

'Fleur, I want you better. What if it's the stress of running the store that's causing the vertigo attacks, and what if, you stop working here and the vertigo stops. If the vertigo stops, you won't lose any more of your precious hearing.'

Tears rolled down Gram's face. 'I'll try reducing my hours, and if that doesn't help, then I'll take some time off, and see how it goes.'

Gramps wiped away her tears and took her hand in his and kissed her fingers. He looked at me. 'Yolande, can you stay on a little longer? I know it's a big ask, with you putting your career on hold ... again.'

I looked at Gram. Her eyes were dark pools of fear. She was the one who had spent every single night with me when I couldn't cope with life anymore after that terrible day of the scars. She was the one who knelt and prayed by my bed every single night. She thought I was asleep, but I wasn't. I knew every word of her prayers by heart. She was the one who gave me hope in a violent world that I despised and feared, and didn't want to be a part of anymore.

'Without a second thought, yes, of course,' I said, and wrapped my fingers around Gram's.

'Thank you,' she whispered. A heavy tear dropped from her eyelashes and hit the table, spreading out like a flower, her namesake.

'Take the rest of the week off, Gram. I have everything under control here.'

'You're under house arrest, my dear. Now let's go home.' Gramps stood and held out his hand for Gram.

She took it and stood. 'Thanks again, Landi.'

'My pleasure, Gram. Now go and get started on destressing to get well again.'

I watched Gramps walk Gram out of the store like she was his princess. He loved her more than life itself.

I turned and walked to the office to fetch my bike to ride home in the rain. As I was about to lock up and leave the store, I heard Darcy's voice.

'Gramps doesn't know about what happened today, does he?'

I shook my head. Gram called it a *drop attack*. It looked and sounded as scary as hell. 'See you tomorrow. And thanks for always being here for us. I don't know what we'd do without you.'

'That's what being a man is about—caring and protecting, always.'

'I wish all men were like you,' I said and stepped out of the store with my bike, locking the double French doors behind me. Darcy would leave via the back doors, as he always did.

I mounted my bike and rode into the rain. Hard.

Chapter Twenty-Four

I flipped his letter between my fingers while I sat outside the white hall as the sun cast its first golden rays over the land. The crow of a rooster sounded in the distance, reminding me I was in the township of Tarrin. I looked down at my steel-capped work boots, danced them around a bit and smiled.

I opened Xander's letter to read, for what felt like the fiftieth time. I don't know why I did; I knew it off by heart. I had found it amongst the flowers of Gram's bicycle yesterday afternoon.

Dear Yolande,

I hope your dancer soul hasn't woken from
its eternal slumber with a wild side.
Nonetheless, I will tame it if it has.

✿ *Alexander*

I held my shy smile while I folded the letter with care and placed it into my pocket for safe keeping. I looked up when I heard the sound of stones crunching under footsteps.

'You're early,' he said, and gave me a coy smile.

'So are you,' I said, noticing his color of baby blue had turned to the color of yellow, like liquid sunshine. He was filled with happiness.

He pointed to my bike. 'Did you cycle here?'

'Yes.'

He looked down with an amused smile. 'That's exactly the type of bike I thought you'd ride.'

'Do I take that as a compliment?' I stretched out my leg and moved my safety boot from side to side, so he couldn't miss it.

He looked at my footwear. 'It is a compliment now ...' He looked at me with a half-smile.

'Good,' I said and stood, then followed him to the door, inhaling his spicy blend of cedarwood and cocoa-vanilla scent. He unlocked it and we entered.

I walked ten paces into the hall and spun on the tip of my boots. It was just like the hall I had learned to dance in when I was eight. I inhaled deeply, dragging the old wooden butterscotch pinewood smell into my lungs. I walked to the side of the room and sat on an old pew and placed my backpack onto the floor.

Xander planted himself beside me and started to take off his sports shoes. 'We're doing two dances—a waltz and the foxtrot. We'll work on the waltz first.' He put on dance sneakers, then stood and took off his jumper, revealing his black t-shirt that matched his black track pants. I tried not to stare at his distinct danseur physique as he proceeded to warm-up and stretch. He had broad shoulders and lean, defined arm muscles.

When he looked my way, I cast my gaze onto my shoes as I undid the laces on my safety boots and removed them. I put on my dance sneakers, then stood and discarded my jumper. I was dressed like Xander—black t-shirt and track pants. I walked around for a bit trying to shake off my anxiety, before I did my warm-up and stretches, ingrained from many years of ballet.

Xander waited for me in the middle of the dance hall. His hands were by his side and he stretched his fingers, closed them, and stretched them again.

I strolled over and stopped in front of him, my stomach a quivering mess.

'Let's do the basic steps, so we're comfortable with each other.' He lifted his left hand, and I placed my right hand into his, our skin intentionally touching for the first time. I swallowed as I felt the warmth of his skin and gentleness of his touch. I took a half step closer to him, and he put his right hand around to my left shoulder blade. I placed my left hand onto his shoulder.

'It's okay ... relax ... shoulders down.' His voice was calm, reassuring.

'I feel like you've been set up in a dare ... that you have to prove something to the guys ... you know—to dance with "that" girl.'

He frowned at me. 'I would never do that. I'm not "that" type of guy, and you are definitely *not* "that" girl.'

I focussed on Xander's throat, then moved my eyes up to his. Our eyes connected, and I felt myself falling. I think he did have the magic love potion. I could feel it traveling through my veins. Suddenly I was filled with nervous energy.

What am I doing here?

'Breathe, Yolande,' he said, keeping his eyes on mine, his pupils large. Did he know what I was feeling? Did I know what I was feeling?

He took the first step and I followed his lead. We fell into an easy rhythm and soon added the rise and fall—down, up, up, down, up, up—and continued in the pattern for half an hour until our dancing belonged to each other.

We stopped to hydrate, and Xander grabbed his phone and played a video of the waltz dance he wanted us to do, but he would add his own tweaks to make it ours.

We danced some more then, working on fancy steps and moves.

At 10.30am we stopped. I sat on the pew and changed back into my safety boots.

Xander sat next to me, looking at my footwear. 'Is that a Defence Force thing?'

'My safety boots?'

'Yeah.'

'No. It's a Yolande thing—no explanations. Just accept it.'

'Okay. But I have a theory,' he said, and looked deeply into my eyes.

I stopped breathing to resist his charm. 'About my work boots?'

'Yes.'

'Go ahead,' I said, and released my breath.

Xander looked at my brown steel-capped boots and cleared his throat. 'You have really hairy feet, like a hobbit.' He raised an eyebrow at me.

I snickered. 'Hmmm ... hobbit feet. That would be insanely awesome!' I looked at my watch. 'Time for work.'

I picked up my backpack and Xander followed me to my bike.

'I'll send you the link to the waltz music. I want you to listen to it numerous times before we meet tomorrow morning ... and go to YouTube and watch ballroom dancers waltzing. Plus, I'll send you my choreography notations to make the process easier,' he said.

'Sounds fair. See you then. Same time?'

'Yes.'

I pushed off on my bicycle and rode to Flowers for Fleur.

Life had just become complicated.

Chapter Twenty-Five

The door to the community hall was open when I arrived. I stilled when the sound of the sharp crunch of my apple bounced off the walls. I didn't expect it to be so loud. Xander peered over at me while he was stretching. I grimaced at him and took another noisy bite of my sweet juicy apple.

I sat on the pew and put my apple down to remove my work boots, then put my dance shoes over my hobbit feet.

Xander sat beside me. He smelled citrusy today, with a hint of liquorice, vanilla, lavender, amber and sandalwood. 'The dance comp is in two weeks.' I heard the crunch of my apple.

I looked up at him and took my apple from him. 'Two weeks?' He was trying to achieve the impossible. I couldn't be ready in two weeks, and I hadn't even started organising either of the dance gowns.

'It's my last performance of *Swan Lake* tonight—do you want to come ... and to the celebration afterward?'

'Yes to the ballet—thanks—no to the party.'

He frowned at me. 'Why not the party?'

'Aaah ...' *How could I tell him I don't do parties after that terrible day of the scars, with the exception of his mother's birthday, which I had no choice about.* 'You're such a big star and you'll be busy interacting with everyone. I don't want to slow you down in any way. I'll get lost in the crowd and I'll be standing against the wall looking for you ... or looking for the exit so you don't have to worry about me.' *And people will look at me and wonder why I'm there with you, when you could have chosen from a million beautiful women. Unbroken women.*

Xander smiled at me. 'If ... after the ballet ... you change your mind, I'd like you to be there.'

'Thanks,' I said to be nice, not letting him know there was absolutely no chance of me being at the celebration.

'Did you do your homework?'

'Of course ... can I ask you something?'

'Go ahead.'

'Why don't you have your real name on the ballet program?'

Xander threaded his fingers together and looked down. 'For my father's sake.'

'You mean, he doesn't know how successful you are, or how hard you've worked?'

He took a deep breath. 'No ... let's learn our waltz.' He stood.

'I need to warm up and stretch ... do you think two weeks is enough time to master two dances?' I breathed through my anxiety.

'Yes. We can practise all day tomorrow and then every night from Monday.'

'But aren't you moving on to the next destination in the *Swan Lake* tour with the company?'

Xander blinked slowly and took a deep breath. 'No. I'm taking a break.'

I nodded. My intuition told me he didn't want to talk about it. So I let the conversation end and moved away from him to stretch. My ballet body was more out of shape than I thought it was. Muscles hurt where I had forgotten I had muscles.

Xander stood in the middle of the dance hall and waited. I walked over to him, shaking my head.

'What?'

'I still can't believe I'm crazy enough to be doing this with you.'

'What do you mean?'

'Dancing with the famous, Prince Siegfried ... if I knew who you were, I would've said no.'

He winced. 'Because?'

'Look at you, then look at me—a somebody and a nobody.'

'There's something about you, Yolande, that's why I chose you.'

'I think you made a mistake.'

'Now, that's where we're similar ... you cross analyze everything before you make a decision, and that's exactly what I do too. I *know* I haven't made a mistake.'

I stopped before him and raised an eyebrow with disbelief at his words. He reached out his hand so I could take it. He put his other hand around my back while I put my hand onto his shoulder. I looked at his chin before I moved my eyes to his.

'The music is the key to remembering the steps, learning layer by layer, until you have muscle memory for our dance.'

'And visualize it before going to sleep and it will be second nature ...' I added—*words from my own ballet mistresses.*

'Exactly.' Xander pulled a remote control out of his pocket and pushed a button. He placed it back into his pocket and we took the waltz pose once again, then the music started ... *Once Upon a Dream* ... our second practice session had begun.

My steel-capped boots were covered by the hem of my high-necked dark blue evening dress. I ran up the steps of the theater and entered the doors while the sun set, casting a brilliant canvas of oranges and reds. I had arrived on the dot of seven. That way I wouldn't be standing around by myself. Alone.

I sat in the seat Xander had gifted to me, again, and my muscles melted, allowing little sparkles and stars to travel down my spine. I hadn't felt like this since before that terrible day of the scars. And it scared me.

The theater darkened, and a hush descended. The audience clapped as the conductor arrived and bowed. There was silence for a moment, before the first piece of orchestral music began, and Princess Odette walked out of the shadows on the stage to pick up the first flower. The night of magical ballet had begun, again. It never got old.

When I sat here with Gram I had watched every ballerina and ballerino. But not tonight. I had eyes for only one danseur— Prince Siegfried. I watched his every grande allegro and pirouette, adagio, changements, plié, relèvé, port de bras and grand jete, and everything in between and over and above and beyond. He had phenomenal power, strength, extreme flexibility, balance ... and grace. He had amazing grace. I wondered what could be so important to him to stop dancing after tonight. He would miss it—the exhilaration, the attention, the addictiveness, the pure ecstasy of the performance and the fans who worshipped his every move, his every nuance. He would miss his dance family.

My heart tightened as I watched the final curtain call that continued for twenty-five minutes. When Xander stepped forward on the stage alone, he covered his heart with his hand and bowed gracefully. An almighty applause broke out with boisterous cheers. My eyes watered, and I looked towards the ceiling of the theater to stop my tears from falling. My own final ballet performance, in the local hall when I was eighteen remained as a strong memory, small as it was, compared to this. It hurts to stop doing something you love. Even when you're moving on to a new passion. Perhaps that was it? Perhaps Xander had a new passion?

'Bravo, Xander, bravo,' I whispered as I stood and clapped for my ballroom dance partner. I was honored, and proud to be present.

Rose petals rained down on the stage adding to the magical evening. My heart sank. What a come down for him, from dancing with a beautiful Principal Ballerina to dancing with me. *Broken me ...*

I remained in my seat until the last person had left the theater. When the workers entered to clean, I left and ventured into the foyer. It was busy with chatter and laughter and merrymaking. Dancers were floating amongst the theater goers, interacting and thanking them. I smiled. I remembered well, the mixed feelings of finishing a production—the sadness, yet the extravagant, intensified feeling of elation.

I held the door exit in my sight and started to walk towards it. My taxi was waiting. A warm hand wrapped around my mine and I tensed, but when I heard the timbre of his voice I relaxed.

'Yolande!'

I turned to him. He was the color of scarlet, filled with energy, enthusiasm and a love for life.

'You look amazing!' he said with sparkling eyes.

I wanted to run from him, but it would be bad manners. So I dug deep and found the politeness that was ingrained from my upbringing. 'Zan, congratulations on another brilliant performance!' It felt weird calling him Zan. But that was his name on the program.

He lifted my hand to his lips and kissed it, leaving my skin burning where his lips had touched. 'Thank you for coming. It means a lot to me!'

'Ah—but I'm just one of thousands of adoring fans.'

'Yes, but you're the most important one.'

I looked at him and tried to catch my breath. A crowd of gushing fans started to form around him. It was time to leave.

'Thanks for inviting me. I should leave you to your admirers. I'll see you tomorrow,' I said.

'Please come to the celebration with me!' His eyes widened, then his brows drew together.

I took a step back from him. 'I'm sorry.' I shook my head. 'I can't.' I pulled my hand away from his and our spark of disconnection hurt. My reaction to him shocked me. He and I could *never* be a "we".

He looked deeply into my eyes and I held my breath. Did he do that with all the girls?

'Tomorrow then,' he said.

'Tomorrow,' I repeated, then fled in my clunky safety work boots, out the door and down the stairs to my waiting taxi, thankful I didn't lose a work boot as I descended the steps. I wasn't Cinderella, and he wasn't a real prince. Fairy tales didn't exist.

I stood before the closed door of the hall, full of incredible, crippling self-doubt. Why was I standing here? I was not in his league! I would be the one to blemish his god-like status. I had to bail out now while he could still find another partner.

I pushed on the door. It was locked. I walked around the building and found a window that was ajar. I reached up and opened it wide, then threw my backpack through the window before I jumped up and latched on to it and pulled myself up, using the tread on my work boots to get enough grip to propel me upward and through the window. See—safety work boots were practical.

I dawdled over to the pew and sat. What could I say to him?

Could I use looking after Gram as an excuse? He will hate me! But it would be better than falling from ballerino grace ... I had to save him from damaging embarrassment.

I looked up at the sound of the creak of the door. Xander walked in with a spring in his step. He was the color of sunshine yellow. He was still probably high after last night's performance and celebration.

He saw me and grinned, but all I could manage were burning eyes and down-turned lips. His expression changed at once to one of concern. I had successfully managed to sour his mood.

'Are you okay?' he asked.

'I can't do it, Xander.'

'Do what?'

'Dance with you.'

'But you must! You're the only one!'

'I'll make you look bad—'

'*We* will look good.'

'I'll make mistakes—'

'I won't let you.'

'I'll fall down.'

'I'll lift you up.'

'I'll be a jittery mess of nerves.'

'I'll take them from you.'

'I'll let you down.'

'You won't.'

He held out his hands to me. I looked at his long fingers, the ones that had wrapped around mine with warmth and strength and reached into my broken heart while we danced. I lifted my hands to his and he pulled me to my feet. He wrapped his arms around me and hugged me with a gentleness that made me believe in miracles.

'Dance with me,' he whispered, like a magical spell that wound its way into my heart and mind, changing my outlook on life, so that the sun shone so brightly it changed the colors of the world, and beamed rays of supreme happiness and everlasting love.

I couldn't answer yet. I wanted to bathe in whatever it was that he was injecting me with.

'Dance with me,' he whispered again.

'Yes,' I whispered back, 'but please forgive me for my inadequacy.'

'Are you going gooey la-la on me, Yolande?'

Was I? I hoped not. I never went gooey la-la over a man! 'No. Just realistic about my skill level as compared to yours.'

Xander stepped back from me. He reached for my hand and placed it over his heart. 'Feel my heart beating?'

'Slowly, yes.' I gazed into his beautiful eyes.

'It means I'm human and will make mistakes. That makes us even. Change your shoes on your hobbit feet, warm-up and stretch, and let's nail our dancing!'

I looked down at my work boots, smiled and nodded.

'How did you get in?' Xander asked.

I sat on the pew and started to remove my boots. 'Through the window!'

'Of course, you did!'

'Yeah—I'll have to add break and enter to my resume!'

'That's an employable skill to have ...'

'Clearly.' I stood after I put on my dance shoes and walked away to warm up and stretch.

Xander followed soon after.

'How was the party?' I asked.

'Happy. Loud. Tipsy. Freedom. It was a person short, though.' He looked at me and raised his eyebrow.

Oh ... me ... 'I would have been the walking dead.'

He nodded his head. 'A zombie could have been an interesting addition.' He held up his outstretched left arm. I placed my right hand into his left hand. His right hand came to rest just under my left shoulder blade, while I placed my left hand on his right shoulder.

The music began, and we took our first dance step.

Our third practice session had begun.

Chapter Twenty-Six

'Flowers, tea, coffee or books?' The words rolled off my tongue without a second thought. I tapped my work boot on the floor, annoyed at the long question Gram insisted on being used each time. People only came to the sales desk for flowers, otherwise, they headed over to the café if they wanted tea of coffee. It was a no-brainer, really. Yet, for Gram, I continued the facade.

The neatly dressed man before me stared with a confused look. I couldn't blame him really. He snapped out of it and shook his head. 'I find myself standing in a flower shop with uncertainty. Why should I buy flowers?' He was the color of dark, dark gray with an "a", turning black—sadness, spiraling into a depth of numbness of emotion.

'Well …' I took a deep breath, trying to stop the burn of heated dread filling me. 'Flowers are mood-enhancing, production-boosting powerhouses if you're in business, or, they're a reminder of you. They are sorry, thank you, sympathy, condolences … love. Who are they for?' I was rambling on, trying to drown out the alarm bells ringing inside of me.

He pressed his lips together. 'They are for ... incredible happiness, and, for ... unbearable sadness.' He stiffened and held his breath. 'New life, and ... death ... at once.' He released his breath and his eyes reddened.

My heart felt heavy. Too heavy. I felt like collapsing in a heap on the floor from grief. The man before me was in incredible pain. I swallowed the lump in my throat. 'A celebration of new life, and a celebration of a life,' I said, trying to find a way around the devastation, almost choking on my words.

He cleared his throat. 'Yes,' he said as a released breath, almost as if his saying yes out loud would make it come true.

I slid a piece of paper along the sales desk. 'If you could write the details of the flower arrangements on this paper, I will create them for you while you have a cup of tea in the café. Tell Darcy that Andi sent you.'

The man blinked at me and started to write. I closed my eyes, wishing not to see the details of the death. So final. With words left unsaid. Love shattered. Hearts broken. I opened my eyes when I heard the paper slide along the desk top.

'Thank you ...' I looked at the paper for his name, 'Mr. Anderson. I will do these at once for you.'

He pressed his lips together and walked over to Darcy.

I cast my eyes on the piece of paper. There was only one name for the recipient of the flowers. A baby. With the same birth date, and death. I crouched on the floor behind the sales desk and hugged myself. There were no words. There could never be any words. Only a crushing heartfelt pain for this spirit-destroying event.

After a moment, I stood and dragged my feet over to the workbench, my mind numb. There was no way I could create a hello/goodbye arrangement of flowers for a beautiful baby. I opened Gram's book of designs and slid my finger down the contents page, slowing at the word fatality ... no ... it wasn't a fatality like that ... funeral—for a baby - girl - pale pink roses and pink mini carnations offset by baby's breath, ivy and lush greens. An ivory plush bear, a sheer white ribbon and a pink ribbon with "Little Angel" in gold metallic lettering.

I left Gram's book open and headed to the cold room. There, I gathered the flowers and greens and stilled. I hugged the flowers to my chest and sobbed, holding a tissue against my right eye. I hated the mortal earthly sleep. I had to remind myself there was also an everlasting spiritual life. It is when the mortal became immortal. *Just like* ... I squeezed my eyes shut and turned my head to the side and blocked out a memory.

After a long moment I straightened my back and lifted my chin. I had a job to do. And I would lather the creation with love and adoration to honor the baby and her grieving parents and family and friends. On the way to the workbench, I chose the ivory plush bear with care, choosing the one with the most adorable face. Then I got to work at creating a masterpiece.

Mr. Anderson appeared before the workbench as I put the finishing touches on the arrangement. 'Thank you. How much to do I owe you?'

I shook my head. 'They're a gift from Flowers for Fleur, created with heart.' *And tears*, I wanted to add. But I didn't.

Mr. Anderson put his hand over his chest. 'Thank you.' He picked up the flowers and teddy bear with care, turned and left, holding his head high, and I suspect, stopping the flow of tears from his broken heart.

I hung my head. If it was a perfect world, there would be no terrible tragedies. No death, no war, no disease, no hate, no evil ... I swallowed the lump in my throat and returned to the sales desk and the next person waiting to purchase flowers.

The rest of the day was filled with joyous flower sales. I needed it. I couldn't even begin to think what it would be like working in a funeral parlor where you dealt with only death. How did those people do it?

At 5pm I closed the front doors and sighed with relief, then got on with the jobs I had to do before I could leave and meet Xander for dancing.

At 5.45pm there was a knock on the French doors. Darcy answered the door and took care of the delivery. The smell of curry awakened my hungry stomach when he walked closer.

'Yolande. Dinner for two. See you at the table in two minutes.'

'But—'

'No buts. Two minutes.'

I finished listing the orders for tomorrow and closed the three books I had been working in. I walked to a table Darcy had set up with plates, glasses, cutlery, a candle and flowers.

'Stolen flowers!' I said as I sat opposite him, wondering what he was up to.

'Borrowed,' he said. 'Eat and enjoy.'

'What have I done to deserve this?'

'You work too hard, and you've lost weight.'

'Oh, so you're trying to fatten me up?'

He lifted his chin and looked down at me, gazing into my eyes. 'Yes. Someone needs to take care of you.'

My blood began to boil. I didn't need a man to take care of me. That was my job, and my job alone. 'Darc—'

'It's what a real man does.'

I looked at him and decided to bow out of the disagreement. He was being kind. 'Thanks,' I said, and placed a bite of food into my mouth to make him feel good.

'I'm taking you to a movie afterward.'

I stopped eating. 'I'm sorry. I can't. I have dance lessons every night this week.'

His eyebrows crinkled together. 'Since when do you dance?'

'Since forever. It's only been the last three years that I haven't danced.'

Darcy looked down. 'Oh.'

'But thanks for the movie invitation. After the dance competition has finished, I'll go with you.'

'Good,' he said, unconvincingly. 'Who's your dance partner?'

'Xander.'

Darcy put his cutlery down and placed his hands under his chin and looked into my eyes with a frown. 'Is he any good?'

'He's okay, I guess.' He obviously didn't know that Xander was a danseur. His secret was well hidden. I finished eating and took a long drink of water. 'I have to go. I'm late.' I put my hand over my heart. 'Thank you ... for all of this.' I waved my hand over the table. 'After the comp—dinner and a movie ... I promise.'

'Without your work boots?'

I stilled. 'Not yet.'

'One day,' Darcy said, and gave me a small smile.

'One day,' I repeated, wondering if that day would ever come.

Xander was waiting for me outside the hall. He was the color of fire orange; a flamboyant mix of energy and happiness. A handsome smile grew on his face when he saw me.

'For a moment I thought you had changed your mind,' he said, when I ascended the steps, two at a time.

I shook my head. 'No. But I do prefer entering via the window.'

'I thought you would. How am I supposed to tame you and turn you into a dancer?' He smirked at me.

I gave him a light punch on the arm. He pulled an "ouch" face. 'You'll keep,' I said, and stepped past him to go to the pew, where I sat to change into my dance shoes.

Xander stood before me. He smelled like a spicy blend of cedarwood and cocoa-vanilla today. 'I'll pick you up at work and drive you home afterward from now on.'

I sat up and looked at him. 'I'm fine riding the black beast.'

'It's just ... I don't want anything happening to you before the comp.'

'Conceded ... and thanks.' I stood to begin the warm-up and stretch routine. 'Sorry I'm late. Darcy decided to feed me before I left. He works at the store.'

Xander warmed up and stretched opposite me. 'With candles and flowers on the table?'

'Yes, why?' I slowed my stretches.

'He wants to be *more* than your friend?'

'No, no, no. We work in a flower shop. There are flowers everywhere, and candles are already on the table.'

Xander raised an eyebrow at me. 'We'll see. If he asks you to a movie ...'

That, he had already done. 'He's not my type.'

'What is your type?'

'One who doesn't ask so many questions.'

'You mean who digs deeper instead of scratching the surface?'

I looked down and smiled. He was repeating my words from when I went to his mother's birthday party with him.

'Do the questions make you feel uncomfortable? Are you scared of what they'll find—like the real Andi?' he continued.

'Oh—stop it!' I smiled at him and put my hands on his chest to give him a push. He placed his hands over mine and held them there. 'Let's dance, shall we?' He bowed to me.

I bowed back and gazed into his mesmerizing blue eyes, and the world slowed down. *Once Upon a Time* started, and we fell into step for the waltz, cementing the steps we already knew, building layer upon layer until our minds responded to the music with muscle memory. We danced for an hour and a half, and it seemed so effortless.

And then I stumbled, and fell.

Xander wrapped his arms around me to lessen the impact of the fall. He eased me down by holding me and lifting me in our forward motion as the floor approached. I landed with only a slight bump, but lied flat on my back, staring up at the ceiling. Xander slumped down beside me.

'Sorry, and thanks,' I said. A tear rolled from the corner of my eye towards my ear.

'No problem, and no problem,' he said. 'Are you okay?'

'Yeah ... it's just ... my mind went off on its own tangent.' I turned my head to look at him. 'There's no cure for Gram's disease. If I leave the flower shop, my grandparents will close it down because they want to keep it strictly as a family business, passed down through the generations. Gram's heart will break, and I can't do that to her ... so here I am, the only aeronautical engineer trying to make flowers fly.'

'What about other family?'

'Apparently, they don't have the same "heart" that I do,' I said, punctuating the air with inverted commas. 'I don't blame them ... there's nothing worse than working in a job that you didn't choose. And why should another person's dream destroy your own dream?'

'And your dream?'

I took a deep breath. 'I'm too kind-hearted, and my grandmother means the world to me.'

'Even over your own career?'

'Yes. And that's why I am determined to find something that will halt her disease, and then I can return to what I love to do!'

Alexander closed his eyes. 'I'm sorry,' he said. 'On the other hand, we're both stuck here in Tarrin, together. Maybe you can invent a flying machine to get us out, fuelled by flowers!'

I started laughing. Deep belly laughing. 'Sounds like a deal!'

'Done!' he said.

I drew an imaginary rocket in the air above my head, and

pushed it over to Xander. 'Gramps use to sing in the forest not far from here once, practising for the opera. His mother threw him out of the house because he was too loud.'

'I'll bet,' Xander said and smiled. He gathered my imaginary rocket in his hands, then moved it towards his lips, and blew it away.

I drew an imaginary heart next, and pushed it towards him. 'Gram was walking by the road when she heard his voice and searched him out. It was love at first sight, according to Gramps.'

'Nice ... a true love story.' Xander captured the heart in his hand and pressed it to his chest.

My breath hitched.

He rolled onto his side and looked at me.

'Do you know what the worst thing is about Gram's disease? She's going deaf. She won't be able to hear the one thing that brought their hearts together ... I catch her crying when Gramps sings now, and at the ballet, she closed her eyes and listened to the music to put it to memory for when she can't hear anymore.' Another tear slid down to my ear.

Xander wiped it away. 'Being present is the kindest thing you can do for her. It shows that you love her, and she needs to know that.'

'Hmmm ... a prince with sensible advice.'

Xander stood and reached out his hands to help me off the floor. 'You're welcome.'

We assumed the waltz position and started again, working smoothly as one, like we were made to dance together.

At 8.30pm, Xander closed the door behind us. He held my bicycle while I hitched my backpack over my shoulders, then watched while I rode away.

'I'll pick you up at six!' he called.

I lifted my hand and gave him the thumbs-up.

Our fourth practice session had finished.

Chapter Twenty-Seven

'Flowers, tea, coffee or books?' The words rolled off my tongue with a melodic sound. Gram was here, with a flamingo pink color surrounding her—love, acceptance and calm.

'Pink flowers, please,' said a middle-aged woman in a coral colored double layered dress. She was the color of lavender—femininity and grace.

'Of course. Would you like dark pink or light pink, and what type of flower?'

The quiet-natured woman shook her head. 'My friend has been diagnosed with breast cancer ... what flowers do you recommend?'

'I'm so sorry to hear. Let's go over to Gram. She will create something beautiful for your friend.'

I stopped on Gram's right side so she could hear me. 'Gram—could you make a floral bouquet for someone who has been diagnosed with breast cancer, please.'

Gram looked at me. 'Absolutely. Landi, what flowers would you use, if you were making the arrangement?'

I looked at Gram and raised my eyebrows, surprised by

her question. She was in charge of the workbench of flower imagination and all designs today, now that she was feeling that a vertigo attack was not imminent.

'Hmmm ... possibly pink roses, pink Matsumoto asters, white daisy poms, pink mini carnations, a couple of pink gerbera daisies, and ... myrtle. What do you think?' I asked.

'It sounds wonderful. Would you mind collecting the blooms and bringing them to me, please.'

'Of course.' I disappeared into the cold room and collected the said blooms and returned to Gram and placed them on the workbench for her, then returned to the sales desk.

I looked up from the sales book to see Charlotte floating in the front doors like a spring breeze. I expected to see butterflies following her. She was a perpetual color of happy bright yellow.

I gave her a quick hug. 'I'll be back in a couple of hours. Thanks for taking over for a bit.'

'Happy to help,' she said.

I jumped on my bicycle and rode to the quaint little white house with the pretty flower garden that was my psychologist's office, and sat in my regular chair. The one with the imprint of my butt on it. The door opened smoothly and silently. Dr. Jones was dressed in a flowing floral dress today. Her shoes were red and textured.

'Yolande.' Dr. Jones's voice was comforting, like the sound of rain on the roof at night.

I stood and followed her into the office. The familiar office. Dr. Jones put a light hand on my shoulder. 'Would you like to sit on the sofa or lie on the couch today?'

'The sofa ... thanks.' I made myself comfortable and hugged my usual cushion. Dr. Jones went to make of pot of tea. I heard the boiling water and the chink of the china teacups and saucers. I closed my eyes and knitted my fingers together like I always did before I placed them on my stomach. I had chosen to be present today. I needed to talk to her.

At the sound of approaching footsteps, I opened my eyes. Dr. Jones placed two teacups and saucers on the table. I reached over and picked up one. The warmth of the brew touched my lips when I sipped it and I relaxed a little. Aah ... tea. I was reminded of an English Proverb—*a man without a moustache is like a cup of tea without sugar.* Odd ...

'What brings you here today, Andi?'

Our session had begun with the same question as usual. Predictable. Safe. 'When I went to the ballet, for the second time, I felt a sensation I haven't experienced for a long time.'

'What did you feel?'

'It was like little sparkles and stars had traveled down my spine. I hadn't felt it since before ... you know ... and it scared me.'

'Was it a pleasant feeling for you?'

'Yes.'

'So why did it scare you?'

'Because I felt happy.'

Dr. Jones smiled at me. 'That's nice to hear. What is your definition of happy, Yolande?'

I hated when she asked me to analyze concepts. I took a deep breath and let it out before I spoke. 'Not feeling sad.' *There. That should do it.* I smiled inwardly at my devious answer. She wanted more information, but I didn't want to give it to her.

Dr. Jones raised an eyebrow at me. She knew I was playing games. 'Why did it scare you?'

'Because I don't deserve to be happy, after ... you know ...'

'Yolande, this isn't about Mia. You alone, are the one who can give yourself consent to be happy. It isn't something someone gives you, or allows you, it's all up to you. Don't keep punishing yourself for something that was out of your control.'

'But was it?'

'You know it was. Be kind to yourself, and go and visit Mia.'

'Do you really think it will help?'

'Absolutely.'

There was a silence then. Of course, I knew I had to go and visit Mia. But I just couldn't bring myself to do it yet. I sipped on my tea. It allowed the pause in the conversation that I needed, and had a wondrous, calming effect.

'Happiness is ever-growing and ever-changing, Yolande. It will take on several different meanings for us throughout our lives. Something that made you happy once, may not make you happy anymore.'

'Is that why people always seem to be wanting to find happiness?'

'Perhaps. They keep searching outside of themselves, for an external source. They need to understand that happiness comes from within, with your own permission. Happiness from material things is temporary. So those who try to find happiness through material objects will never find happiness.'

Dr. Jones continued, 'Happiness is a state of mind that can be created by us. Here's an interesting fact. Our brains have trouble telling the difference between real events and imagined events, and our brains process imagined events like they're real. So, if you imagine yourself as happy, you will feel happier.'

'I have to work on the part where I give myself permission to be happy. That's the part I'm having trouble with.'

'That's not uncommon. It's *okay* to be happy after everything you've been through. You're not at fault with what happened. You have the right to be happy ... I have some homework I want you to do—I want you to visualize yourself being happy, now and in the future. And I want you to visualize Mia smiling at you, being happy—that's a big one, an important part of your homework.'

I nodded my head. I decided to try, if not today, within the next few days.

'Is there anything else you'd like to talk about today?'

'No. I think I'm done. Thanks.'

I walked out of her office holding my head a little higher.

I sat on my bicycle and started peddling. My bicycle made me happy. But I knew it was a material object, and I understood perfectly that there would come a time when it would not make me happy anymore. Like about now, when I had to cycle hard to ascend the road incline, and my legs would ache with the lactic acid build up. That's when I wished for a car. A car to make me happy.

But I didn't want a car. I wanted Mia, my best friend.

I rushed into Flowers for Fleur so Charlotte could leave. I had only been gone for an hour. She kissed my cheek then left. I sent all the fancy flower bouquet requests over to Gram while I concentrated on the selling the pre-made blooms and restocking the store with fresh flowers and ornamental gifts.

Gram left at 2.30pm to get some much-needed rest, as we had planned. At 5pm the store closed, and I started carrying the flowers in from outside to place in the cold room, then moved other ornamental decorations inside.

The absolute final front of the store job, as prescribed by Gram, was to bring her bicycle into her office for the night. The moment I stepped onto the pavement there was a citrusy scent with a hint of liquorice, vanilla and lavender. I hesitated in my stride and looked to my right. Xander stood beside Gram's bicycle and had begun to push it toward the doors of the store.

'You're early,' I said. 'I was expecting you at six.'

'I know. I was hoping we could get started a little earlier.' He lifted Gram's bike up the steps like it was a featherweight. I followed him as he pushed it through the store. He was the color of cerulean blue, glowing, like in the northern lights on rare occasions.

Heat rushed to my cheeks and I took a moment to collect myself. 'It goes in her office, to the right ... thanks,' I finally said, then left him while I went back to finish the closing jobs so the store would be ready to go in the morning. I opened the accounting book and updated it, then found the on-line flower orders for tomorrow, printed them and placed them into the order book.

At the workbench, I tidied and wiped down the workspace, looking over to the cafe when I heard male voices. Xander was talking to Darcy over the steam of his drink.

I went to Gram's office and grabbed my backpack, then walked toward the boys. They stopped talking and looked at me. I didn't know who to look at first. I chose Darcy, only because I had known him longer.

'See you tomorrow, Darcy!' I said, then looked at Xander. 'I'm ready to go.'

'See you, Andi,' Darcy said, raising his eyebrows. He gave me a small smile.

I turned and walked toward the front doors of Flowers for Fleur. I heard Xander's quick footsteps as he caught up to me. He reached forward and pushed the door open then followed me out. I turned and frowned at him.

'What?' he said.

'I can push the door open myself.' I lifted the key to double lock the store doors.

'I know ... I have old-fashioned manners.'

'Thank you, then,' I said, thinking that is what an old-fashioned woman would have said.

He led me to his car and opened the door for me, and closed it once I had sat in the passenger seat.

'I have arms,' I said when he sat in the driver's seat.

'I've noticed that,' he said.

'I can open doors myself,' I said.

'And climb in windows,' he added, 'arms are good for that!' He looked at me and gave me a lopsided grin.

I smiled and averted my gaze as that curious heatwave passed through my body. I didn't want him opening doors for me. I saw it as a power game, one that said men were dominant.

Xander pulled up outside the community hall. 'Stay,' he said.

'Like a dog? Is that a challenge?'

He tilted his head to the side and closed his eyes, then opened them and gazed into mine. 'Please.'

'Perhaps. You never know, maybe I can follow orders ...'

Xander laughed.

'What?'

'Can't you see the irony—you work for the Defence Force where you *have* to follow orders.'

I looked around outside. 'It doesn't look like the Defence Force right now, so those rules don't apply.'

'Conceded.' Xander exited the car and walked around to my door and opened it for me. I got out and shook my head at him, then waved my hands about. Xander raised an eyebrow at me and closed the door.

I waited for him at the entrance of the hall while he collected his gear for dance practice. He unlocked the doors and we walked in.

'I think it's quicker for me to ride here,' I said, waiting for him to bite.

'You'll thank me after a couple of hours,' he said while he set up the sound system.

I sat on the pew and changed my footwear, checking out my hobbit feet. 'Did you have a good conversation with Darcy?'

'Yes, why?'

'Just wondering ...'

Xander sat beside me. 'Wonder no more.'

'Okay.'

'Okay? No more girly digging questions?'

'No.' I stood and went to my spot to warm up and stretch.

Xander followed me to my space and mirrored my warm-ups and stretches, plus he added a few more.

He cleared his throat and I looked up at him. 'Darcy told me he would come after me if I hurt you.'

I stilled and frowned at Xander. 'Are you scared?'

'No. I'm not going to hurt you, and I can look after myself. That's another thing being a danseur has taught me.'

I nodded at him, thinking of all the bullying Xander would have copped over the years for his ballet gift. 'That's why danseurs are the best.'

Xander narrowed his eyes at me. 'Is that a compliment, Yolande?'

'Maybe, maybe not. I didn't elaborate on what they are the best at ...' I walked to the center of the hall ready to start polishing our waltz.

Xander followed me and stopped close. He held up his hand for mine and placed his other hand just below my shoulder blade, while I put my hand upon his broad shoulder, and the music began ...

After an hour and a half, we took a break. I sat on the floor and drank deeply from my water bottle.

'Have you bought your dancing gowns?'

'Yes. For the waltz, I'm wearing a white gown with a waterfall of colored flowers, and for the foxtrot my outfit is white with a rose vine creeping over the shoulder ... the flowers are for Gram. Is that all you need to know?'

'Yes.' Xander stood and proffered his hands.

I waved my hands in front of him. I could get up by myself. I didn't need his help.

His face fell. I rolled my eyes and sighed, then placed my hands into his. He pulled me to my feet and gave a little bow. I curtsied to him.

Once again, we took the waltz position and the music started. We had our dance perfected, with head movements and fancy feet movements, but we continued for another thirty minutes, to solidify our performance.

A flash of lightning brightened the hall, followed by the rumble of thunder, startling me.

'It's a good thing you didn't ride your bicycle,' Xander said in a smug voice as we continued to dance.

'It's a good thing you gave me a lift,' I said, noting to check the weather each day from tomorrow.

'You're welcome.'

'I didn't thank you.'

'You will,' he said, and twirled me around. We connected again and continued the waltz step until the hall plunged into darkness. We stopped dancing. Anxiety spiked through me. I needed my work safety boots. Now.

'I'll get my phone. It'll give us some light,' Xander said as he held on to my hand. A flash of lightning lit the hall for a fraction of time. I tagged along behind Xander, hoping not to trip over anything.

When he stopped walking I felt around for the pew and sat on it.

Xander located his phone and turned it on. 'There's a severe storm warning telling people to seek shelter immediately. We'll stay put.'

The sizzle of lightning sounded, followed by instant thunder and a vibrating of the foundations of the hall. I slid off the pew onto the floor and crawled towards the center of the room to get away from the windows, and lay on my back.

Xander was beside me at once.

'I love storms,' I said.

'Me too.'

There was silence. A comfortable silence. And I felt safe, even without my safety work boots.

'Tell me the story about your gram's bicycle and the basket of flowers.'

I smiled in the darkness. 'Gramps bought her the bicycle to get around while he was out of town, singing opera. He delivered it with a love note in the flowers he had put in the basket. It was quite a statement in the 1950s. Gram was the first woman in Tarrin to have a bicycle.' I smiled again. 'I can just imagine a young Gram riding along in her old-fashioned dress. She was a brave velocipedestrienne.'

'A what?'

'A velocipedestrienne ... bicycles were known as a velocipede, and women who rode them were known as *velocipedestriennes.*'

'Of course, you would know that!'

'Is that an insult?'

'No. I like your nerdiness. Go on ...'

I rolled onto my stomach and leaned on my elbows. 'Did you know some men believed that if women went around straddling bicycle seats, they would start having orgasms from the shocks and vibrations of the road?' I giggled.

'Hmmm ... intriguing ... so do you?'

'Do I what?'

'Have an orgasm while straddling the seat of your bicycle?'

'A young lady would never reveal such personal information!' I said in a dramatic voice.

'It depends on the young lady ...'

'True ... anyway, Gram and Gramps had the most beautiful flower garden in all of Tarrin, and for miles around. After numerous requests for bouquets of her flowers, she started selling them, and that lead to the opening of Flowers for Fleur. Gram would ride her bicycle to work every day. She would leave her bicycle out the front of the shop with flowers in the basket. It became a well-known icon on the street.'

'And it's still there to this very day,' Xander added.

'Yes. But Gram stopped riding it to work about seven years ago.' I stilled. *Her vertigo. She said it started about seven years ago ... so that's why she stopped riding her bike!*

I rolled onto my back again and listened to the heavy rain and rumbling thunder.

Xander's deep voice was gentle. 'It's about respect you know, and caring, and tenderness, and manliness, and romance. It says that you're important, and worthy.'

'What are you talking about, Mr. Parker?'

'Opening doors for women, Miss Lawrence-Harrison. It means you're highly thought of.'

'I disagree, Parker. I think men tend to open doors for women who are pretty.'

'I disagree, Harrison. I would open a door for any woman, no matter what she looked like.'

'Somehow, Alexander, I don't think you are like the majority of men.'

'Is that a good thing?'

'It means you're too nice. Sometimes, a man opening a door for you is their initial form of flirting, like a pick-up line.'

'Really?'

'Yes ... I think you have been smelling too many ballet shoes. You need to get out amongst the commoners more often, and listen and watch what goes on.'

'What if an older man opens a door for you, do you accept it?'

'I do—depending on my intuition.' *And the colors I see ...*

'And your intuition tells you ...'

'Whether a man is dangerous or not, whether his intentions are pure.'

'What does your intuition tell you about me?'

'My gut reaction about you when we first met, or now that I

know you a little more?'

'Both.'

'Are you sure you want to hear it?'

'Absolutely.'

'Nah—I'll keep that information to myself.' I pointed my toes like I once did in ballet. I had forgotten how good it felt.

'Tell me about when you began dancing,' I said.

'I started when I was six, with my sisters. My father thought it was cute at first, expecting me to quit soon after. By the time I was ten, he was taking me to football games and enrolled me in a football team, again hoping I would quit the "girly" dancing. But I didn't, and here I am.'

'And he still doesn't know you dance?'

'No. When you really want something, you get good at going about it, so it goes unnoticed. My mother has been an instrument to my success, supporting me all the way, and shutting my father down when he suspected something.'

'How do you feel about your father rejecting something you love and have excelled at?' *Now I was sounding like Dr. Jones ...*

'I used to beat myself up about it. But not anymore. I used to get jealous of the other guys whose fathers were proud of them, and would come to watch them dance. But not anymore. He has his life to live, and I have mine.'

'I'm sorry it's been like that.'

'It's okay. His rejection made me stronger, and it made me stop seeking his approval.'

'But it still hurts ...'

He was silent for a moment. 'That, it does.'

'Let's dance by the light of the storm, Xander ... I've never done that before,' I said.

He turned his head toward me. I could see the whites of his eyes. 'Me neither ... another first with Yolande Lawrence-Harrison.'

'Another?'

'The fourth in fact.'

'The fourth?' I couldn't for the life of me think of what four things could be a first for this famous dancer beside me.

'Taking a girl to a party, buying flowers, ballroom dancing, and now this ...'

'Gosh, Alexander Parker, you really are living on the dangerous side ... you'd better be careful, or you'll be making distance-breaking paper planes next.'

He smiled, then stood. When lightning lit up the hall, I could see his proffered hands. This time I didn't wave my hands around in protest, I just placed my hands into his and enjoyed the moment. I was starting to like this fleeting happiness feeling.

'Can you hear our music in your mind?' His voice was gentle.

'*Once Upon a Dream*—yes,' I whispered.

'Yolande, will you dance with me?'

I took a deep breath, unsure of what I was feeling, and breathed out the heat that seared through my body. 'Yes.'

Chapter Twenty-Eight

'Books, coffee, flowers or tea?' I had rearranged the words alphabetically, just to see how they felt and sounded. I smiled inwardly at the result of my boredom with saying the same phrase over and over.

'Coffee ... but tell me why I should buy flowers?' The woman asked. She was the color of dark blue—knowledge and power.

'As an experiment ... to see how they change the behaviour and mood of the recipient.' It was worth a try to get some more flowers out the door for Gram's business.

'That's interesting. I've never thought of it that way.'

'Do you have anyone in mind—someone who rarely smiles, is grumpy, or is the one who is left out?'

'Sounds like you're describing someone who gets bullied.'

'Perhaps I am ... or someone who has a chronic illness.'

'Let me think on that while I have a cappuccino.'

'Sure. Darcy is the master cappuccino maker. He's over to your right. Enjoy!'

'Thanks. I will,' she said, and left.

I looked over at Gram. She had flowers lined up on the

workbench of flower imagination. That was new. With a lull in customers, I collected the spritz spray bottle and went outside to freshen the flowers. I went over to Gram's bicycle flowers last, as I always did, and stopped before I gave them a burst of water spray. There was a note. From Xander.

I picked it up and opened it.

Dear Yolande,

I would like to cordially invite you to dinner at my parents' house, tonight.

8pm – after dance practice.

Hoping you'll say yes.

xx Alexander

P.S. Call me Alexander tonight, please x

Oh ... I needed to call him Alexander because of his father, perhaps. My mind went into a whirl. I didn't have the right clothes to wear to his parents' house, and I don't think they would appreciate my safety boots.

I rushed into the store and stopped in front of Gram. 'I need to go home for a moment.'

Gram looked up at me. 'Is everything okay, Andi?'

'Yes. I have to get some clothes for after dancing with Xander tonight.'

Gram smiled. 'That sounds interesting.'

'Not really. It's just something we agreed on when I went to his mother's birthday.' I shook my head. Yolande the "pretend" girlfriend and tag-a-long was back.

'Go, my girl, but don't take too long!'

'I won't,' I said as I removed my apron, went to the office, changed into my cycling gear, grabbed my bicycle and exited via the back of the store.

Within thirty minutes, I had arrived at my parents' house and raced upstairs and stopped before my wardrobe. A dress was needed for dinner at Xander's parents' fancy house. So, a fancy dress it would have to be. And fancy shoes. I grabbed my Audrey Hepburn vintage style navy dress with white polka dots. It had no sleeves and the neckline would cover my scar. I looked down at my limited shoe selection: running shoes, safety boots (3), white girly shoes, black girly shoes and my pale pink court shoes. I took a deep breath. The black ones will have to do.

I picked up the black court shoes and a clutch purse and put them into a backpack, then took the dress, still on the hanger from the wardrobe. I pulled out my phone and called a taxi. It would be better to leave my bike here since Xander was picking me up from Flowers for Fleur each night for dance practice now. I left the house and waited for the taxi, which didn't take long in Tarrin, and returned to Gram at the store.

I entered through the back door. 'I'm back, Gram!' I called as I whizzed past. But there was no answer from Gram. She was still working on the flowers she had lined up in a row. Either she was lost in designing, or she didn't hear me.

I hung my dress in the office and left my backpack beside my dancing backpack, then walked over to Gram and stood in front of her at the workbench.

She looked up at me. 'You're back! Did you come through the back door? You should have told me ... I wanted to see what you had chosen to wear.'

My heart sank. She didn't hear me at all. 'I put the dress in your office. Do you want me to get it?'

'Yes, dear.'

I returned within the minute and held the dress up for Gram to pass judgment.

'That'll be perfect. What shoes are you wearing?'

I looked down at my safety boots.

'No! I forbid you to wear those!'

I smiled at her. 'It's okay, Gram. I have black court shoes in the office.'

'You're learning!' She gave me a gentle smile.

'I'll put the dress back, and then I want you to tell me what you're doing with those flowers.'

Gram waved me off and I took quick steps to her office.

'Andi!' It was Darcy. I looked up at him and he walked toward me. 'I'm going to a movie tonight. Would you like to come?'

'Sorry, Darcy. I'm going out to dinner tonight.'

'Is that why you have that dress?'

'Yes.'

'It'll look amazing on you ... where are you going?'

'To Xander's parents' house.'

'Oh ...' Darcy looked down.

'It was something we agreed on when I went to his mother's birthday celebration with Gram's bicycle. It's to make his mother and father happy ...' *Why was I explaining it to him?*

'What?'

I walked closer to him and whispered. 'They think he's gay?'

'Is he?'

'I don't know, and it doesn't matter if he is.' It was the truth. I really did not know. The only thing I knew was that his best friend was gay. But did that make Xander gay as well?

Darcy shook his head. 'If he is, you are supporting his lie by pretending to be his girlfriend.'

'You spoke to him, Darcy, what did you think?'

'He could go either way.'

'And that's why I don't know.'

'A movie with me would be better,' Darcy said with pleading eyes.

'I'm not so sure ... this evening could be interesting—watching expressions, lie detecting, observing interactions ...'

'If you like that sort of thing,' he said.

'I do.'

'Let me know how it goes.'

'Oh ... so you want to be up on the gossip?'

'If it's about Xander, yes!'

I frowned at Darcy. That was an odd thing to say. 'We've both got work to do. I'll see you later.' Darcy nodded at me and went back to the café.

I sold a few bundles of blooms before I returned to Gram. 'What's the plan for these?' I asked, waving my hand over the row of flowers. She had green trick, caspia, curly willow, mini carnations, and wax flowers—pinks, purples, hues of green.

'I'm designing a new type of bouquet. It's a bit tricky as I don't want the flowers to move once they are in the vase—I want them to go in a spiral.'

'How about while they're laid flat, run tape along the stems, and then roll them so they're like a spiral.'

Gram looked at me. 'Let's try it.'

'What are you going to name it, Gram?' I asked while I retrieved the tape.

'Fury. It will be number 50 in my book of blooms.'

'Fury?'

'Yes. The vertigo makes me furious. I needed to express the vertigo in a creative way so I can laugh at the dark beast.'

'That makes sense!' I ran the tape along the stems. Gram started to roll the flowers until she got to the last flower. When she held it up it was a perfect spiral of colors and a mass of beauty.

'Wow!' I said. I looked down and fiddled with a fallen petal.

'Tell me, Gram ... what's the vertigo like?'

Gram frowned and closed her eyes. She pressed her lips together. 'The world is spinning around me, like ... one hundred and twenty times a minute, maybe faster. It doesn't stop, for hours on end. For some people, it lasts a shorter amount of time, for others is can last for days. The spinning, for me, is in an anticlockwise direction, and it goes on for between three to five hours each time. I can't close my eyes because it's like spinning while falling in the pitch-black darkness where there's no end. I fixate my eyes on one place because I'm trying to stop the spinning, but I can't.'

Gram tied two ribbons around the stems: silver and gold. 'And the nausea,' she continued, '... while I'm spinning, staring at the wall, I'm also trying to concentrate on my breathing to stop the nausea and vomiting, but I fail, every single time.'

Gram turned her new "Fury" creation in her hands. 'And I can't walk. It's impossible. I have no orientation of where my body is in relation to what is around me while the world spins. Lying down is the only option.'

Tears ran down Gram's face. 'Afterwards I'm exhausted. I feel like I've been running for days. I have nothing left. I'm empty, but filled with fear of another attack, which is impossible to predict when it will happen again.'

Gram turned to me, put down the flowers and clutched my hands in her. 'It's so hideous, Yolande, I would never, *ever*, wish it on anyone, not even my worst enemy!'

I looked into Gram's eyes and shook my head. 'So, if I sat on a swivel chair, or lay on a playground roundabout, and was spun around, would that give me the sensation of the spinning you experience?'

'Yes ... but for me it's when the chair or roundabout stops, and it looks and feels like the world is spinning around you, and your eyes feel like they are moving from side to side and you have no control of them ... that's what it feels like, for hours and hours on end, with no rest from it, and you can't stop the ride to get off.'

I sucked in a deep breath. This was hard to hear. I looked out at the park across the road and saw a little boy and girl with their arms out, spinning round and round and round until they fell over. They sat on the grass for a moment, staring, before they stood again, then did it once more. And that was the last time they did it.

Gram twirled a ribbon around her finger. 'Sometimes my head feels whooshy all the time. It's like being drunk without having a drop of alcohol to drink ... and then there's the loud tinnitus and hearing loss ...'

Gram put her hand over her forehead. 'And the fear—it's soul destroying,' she whispered. 'I've never been so scared in my life. I have absolutely no control of my body when I'm having a vertigo attack, whatsoever!'

A wave of dread washed over me. I reached up to check that my chest scar was covered. Listening to Gram describe her vertigo and other symptoms was difficult. Meniere's disease was so much more than just the debilitating violent vertigo we had witnessed.

'The only consolation is that I won't die from it, and it's not contagious,' Gram added.

'No cause, no cure,' I whispered. I ran my fingers along the gold and silver ribbon of Gram's new flower creation. 'Fleur's Fury is perfect!' I said with a heavy heart. I looked back up at Gram. We were similar in that we both used creativity to deal with something negative in our lives. The healing power of creativity— it was a real thing.

Gram left Flowers for Fleur at 2pm. She was exhausted. How precious was that time I had spent with her?

There was a lull in the busy-ness of the store, and I grabbed the chance to write a note to Xander.

Dear Alexander,

I would be delighted to accompany
you to dinner tonight.

I have found my cleanest, sparkliest
work boots for the occasion.

xx Yolande

I folded it at once and went outside the store and placed it into the flowers in the basket. Today it was pink sunflowers. I hoped he would collect the note before I had to bring the bicycle in at closing time.

❦

Xander knocked on the double French doors at 6pm. I opened one door for him, casting my eyes over his blue color.

'Hey!' I said.

'Hey!' he said, tapping my note against his fingers.

'I'll get my stuff.'

He nodded.

I grabbed my dress and two backpacks, then returned to Xander. He took both of my backpacks. I wanted to carry them myself, but in the end, I decided to go with the flow and make him feel like he was helping me. Not that I wasn't capable myself.

'The dinner to seal the deal ... right?' I said, referring to when I accompanied him to his mother's birthday.

He frowned at me. 'Our deal?'

'The day of your mother's birthday,' I said, and then changed my tone of voice to try to mimic his voice. '"That's the deal—the bicycle and you for two hours, plus to accompany me for dinner one night."'

He smiled. 'Ah, yes ... but that was then, and this is now.'

'Meaning?'

'Then, you were the convenient tag-along "pretend" girlfriend. Now you are ... more.'

'More?' *What did he mean?*

'Yes. You're my dancing partner now.'

'True.'

We walked outside and I locked the doors. I turned to find Xander standing at his car with the door open for me. I waved my free hand about at him.

'I know you can open the door yourself. Just humor me, please.'

I sighed at him. Humor him I could do.

There were candles in the dance hall. They weren't lit, but they were there.

I looked at Xander with questioning eyes.

'There's supposed to be another storm tonight, and we can't lose practice time.'

I nodded and sat on the pew and changed into my competition shoes.

'Smart move,' Xander said, as he put his competition shoes on. He handed me some paper. 'Here's the dance notation for our foxtrot and the link to the music.'

'Thanks,' I said, and tucked it into my bag to look at later. I moved away from the pew and warmed up before I stretched. Xander joined me. After ten minutes he went and stood in the middle of the dance hall.

Our sixth dance session had begun ...

'Turn around while I change,' I said after we had finished dance practice. Perhaps it would have been better for the power to go out during the storm that rumbled overhead.

It started to rain.

'I get changed around ballerinas all the time. It's no big deal,' he said.

'Turn around!' I said once again. 'And stand further away.'

He rolled his eyes and walked to the other end of the hall. I made sure his back was towards me, then stripped out of my dance attire and put on my navy dress with white polka dots, and some perfume. I felt the neckline of my dress carefully and checked that it covered my scar.

I walked over to him. He had changed into his trousers. I stood in front of him, so my back was towards him. He zipped me up without a word spoken between us. He stood closer and his body heat warmed me. I took a slow breath in. He lowered his head and inhaled gently against my neck. An exquisite current flowed between us, making my heart flutter.

'I like your perfume,' he said, his voice low.

I turned to face him after a moment. 'Thanks. Better than smelling like two kinds of body sweat.'

'Two kinds?'

'Yours and mine.'

Xander's lips turned up in a half smile. 'I kinda like that you would smell of me.'

I narrowed my eyes at him and shook my head. 'Put your shirt and shoes on. I'll see you outside.'

'Bossy.' His eyes were smiling.

I went to my bag and grabbed my make-up to retouch my face, and added a little lipstick to look a bit dressier for Xander's parents. I let my hair down and wrestled it into some sort of okay, then changed my footwear.

I gathered my gear and went and stood at the front of the hall under the cover from the rain. I placed my bags beside me and put my hands behind my back and rocked to and fro on my steel-capped work boots.

Xander ran from the car and stopped before me. He grabbed my bags and put them into the car and returned to me. 'You look—'

'Don't say it!'

'Say what … nice?'

'Oh … that's okay to say. Thanks.' I didn't want him to use the word beautiful. I put my leg out to the side and slid my foot around in front of me and back beside my other foot. I was waiting for him to say something about my shoes.

'I thought you were going to wear sparkly work boots.'

'Nah—I changed my mind.'

'Sparkly would have been better.'

'I know.' I looked down at my work boots and then back at Xander. 'Am I still your "pretend" girlfriend?'

'More so than ever.'

'Really? Please don't hate me.'

He stilled. 'Why would I hate you?'

'Because of what I might say at dinner …'

He stood taller and looked to the side. He looked back at me. 'Somehow, I think my parents will love you.' He held out his hand. 'Come,' he said. 'Let's go to the Parker residence.'

I placed my hand in his and we ran to the car in the rain. He opened my door and closed it after I got in, then went around and slid into the driver's seat. He was more than a little damp from the rain. I watched as a droplet of water fell from a curl of his dark hair onto his forehead.

We drove for fifteen minutes and arrived at a large wrought

iron gate. Xander entered a code and we proceeded onto the opulent property. The driveway was flanked by trees on either side, reminding me of a country drive. And then the space opened.

I mouthed a silent "wow" when the house came into view. It was a sprawling, two story French country home. It had an exterior of stone with multiple gables and a double entrance. It exuded elegance, and wealth.

Xander stopped the car under a high roofed covered entrance, a little way from the large double front carved timber doors. A butler approached the car and opened my door, and when I climbed out of the car, Xander was already waiting for me. He was the color of pale yellow, an anxious color.

A shot of anxiety flowed through me at his unexpected reaction to his parents' house. He offered me his arm and we started to walk to the front door. I took a deep breath to calm my nerves.

'I like your shoes,' he said.

I had sneakily changed into the black court shoes while he was driving, concentrating on the road in the heavy rain.

'Thanks,' I said. 'You smell like rain,' I added.

'Sorry,' he whispered.

'I love rain,' I whispered back.

He looked down at me, his eyes dark, and swallowed. 'Me too.'

The front doors opened, and we stepped inside. Xander's mother appeared at once, dressed immaculately in a stylish light pink, long-sleeved tweed dress. She held out her hand to me. I placed my hand in hers and smiled.

'Andi, it's lovely to see you again. Welcome.'

'Thanks, Mrs. Parker. Your home is beautiful.'

'Thank you.' She smiled then stepped forward and hugged her son. 'It's so good to see you, my darling Andy.' Xander dipped his head like he did in *Swan Lake* and my heart melted.

Mrs. Parker took my hand and lead me through the house. I looked behind my shoulder at Xander, who gave me an amused smile. When she stopped walking, we were in a generous sitting room with the largest drapes I had ever seen, plus furniture that looked fit for royalty.

I stood beside Mrs. Parker, and within a second, Xander positioned himself on the other side of me.

His father, well dressed in black trousers, a white button up shirt and a black tie, stood from his seat and moved toward Xander. A proud smile grew on his face and his wrapped his arms around his son. 'Now my evening is perfect! All of my children are here.' He stepped away from Xander and gazed at me.

I looked at him with a polite, practised smile. Gram said smiles were like magic.

'Yolande. I was hoping I would see you again.'

'It's lovely to see you again, Mr. Parker,' I said.

A butler stood before me with a tray of martinis. I nodded slightly and took one off the tray with absolutely no intention of drinking it. I was very good at lifting a glass of alcohol to my lips, but never tasting it. It avoided the host thinking I had bad manners by not accepting their offer of a drink.

Xander took my hand in his and lead me over to his sisters and their partners. And with polite greetings, the evening of deceit had begun.

I, Yolande Lawrence-Harrison, now had an astronomically famous superstar ballet dancer boyfriend, who was unknown to his father in any shape or form as a dancer, and who was possibly gay, or not, but my presence would prove that he wasn't, for the sake of his mother and father.

I took a pretend sip of my martini and looked at Xander. He seemed tense and was unbearably quiet. Somehow, this evening was harder for him than me. And at that moment, I vowed to be the best pretend girlfriend I could ever be. Just for Xander.

I placed my hand on his shoulder. 'You look divine,' I whispered.

Xander looked at me with questioning eyes.

I raised my eyebrows at him and gave him a barely noticeable nod of my head. He seemed to snap out of wherever he was in his head.

'Not as divine as you,' he said, and kissed the back of my hand, sending heat running through my veins. He stood. 'Come. Let me show you through the house.'

I placed my martini next to his on the mantel, held on to his hand and strolled casually behind him as he took the lead.

The house was far more extravagant than I realized. After five minutes of walking, Xander slowed and opened some French doors. We walked outside onto a terrace, decorated with copious flowering pots and a muted light.

He leaned against a white column and put his hands into his pockets, exuding a hot masculinity that made my stomach quiver. I wanted to touch him, my skin to his, but I resisted.

'Is this where you grew up?' I asked, feeling something deeper that seemed to come dangerously close to touching my soul.

'Yes.'

'Which is your bedroom?'

'It's over in the west wing. I haven't lived here for seven years.' He looked deeply into my eyes, sending a warmth rushing through me.

'Really?'

'My father said I couldn't live here once I quit football ...' Xander stared out into the distance and my heart fell.

'I'm sorry.'

'It's okay. It was easier because I didn't have to cover up all my dancing lessons and rehearsals for productions, telling lie after lie about where I was going and what I was doing.' Xander laughed. 'I didn't even get on the paddock to play one game of football. I virtually sat on the sidelines every single year.'

'What did your father say about that?'

He shook his head. 'Nothing. He was too busy being a doctor to get to a game. He was happy that I was "playing" football like any other boy.'

There was a dinging sound. I looked around. 'What's that?'

'Time for dinner.' He smiled, and I gave him a look of mock horror. 'It's easier to summon the kids like this when the house is so large.'

'Do you feel like you have been conditioned like Pavlov's dog?'

Xander burst out laughing. 'I love that you're here with me, Yolande Lawrence-Harrison.'

'I'm glad too, Alexander Parker.' I performed a simple curtsy for him, suddenly aware that no one is born with perfection—it is shaped, by both internal and external factors.

He smiled coyly and took my hand in his, and we made our way to the dining room. Xander pulled out my chair for me to sit on, like an attentive boyfriend would.

I had never sat at such a grand table with polished silverware and fancy fresh flowers from Flowers for Fleur worth $200 as a table decoration. I had never felt so prim and proper. I sat taller on my fancy chair.

I spoke so only Xander could hear. 'My sparkly work boots would have been perfect for this room, Alexander.'

He smiled, and a dimple appeared on his cheek. 'Absolutely,' he whispered back, and I melted in a floral symphony of feelings.

'Yolande, I'm sorry your grandmother couldn't be here tonight,' Mr. Parker said. 'We wanted to thank her for allowing us to borrow her bicycle for the birthday celebration.'

I lowered my chin a little. I had no idea Gram had been invited. 'Gram has been a little ... unwell lately ... and it was her pleasure. She likes to show off her bicycle, and for the record, Alexander is the only person she has ever entrusted with it.'

'I heard you work in the flower store, Yolande,' Mrs. Parker said, looking over the top of her wine glass.

Mr. Parker butted in, 'Hmmph ... flowers are over-rated, and expensive, my dear.' He shot a look at the flowers in the center of the table.

I gave Mr. Parker a small smile and looked directly into his blue eyes. 'Flowers are a sensual gift that express emotion so simply, Mr. Parker. They are the art of romance and speak a secret language that women understand perfectly that men seem to stumble over when expressing their feelings,' I said, wondering if I was being too outspoken.

'Here, here,' Mrs. Parker said, and gave me a triumphant smile.

I looked down at my dinner plate, feeling like I had said too much. The lamb and vegetables were a work of art. A tingle of anxiety shot through me. I tapped my court shoes on the carpeted floor, remembering that I needed to be the perfect girlfriend for Xander.

'I thought you said you were some type of engineer at the party, Yolande,' Mr. Parker went on.

I looked back up at him. 'Yes, I am, sir—an aeronautical engineer.'

'Ah, yes. That's right. Quite an unusual occupation for a woman.'

'It is. But I always wanted to be involved with flight, beside my other love.'

'And what would that be?'

'Ballet. I had to choose between becoming a professional ballet dancer or going to university to study engineering. My mother wanted me to keep dancing.' I saw Xander lift his wine glass to his lips in my peripheral vision.

'Why?'

'Oh ... it's romantic, I guess ... and because of the danseurs, she loved watching them with their athleticism. They are classified as professional athletes.'

'No chance of a boyfriend there though, eh?' Mr. Parker said with a smirk, followed by a slug of wine.

'Why's that?' I crinkled my brows at him. I knew exactly the direction he was going in as I had manipulated the conversation that way, and he had taken my bait—hook, line and sinker.

'Well, aren't male ballet dancers gay?'

I laughed at his comment. 'You're just assuming they are because male ballet dancers threaten the perceived masculinity of men. Some fathers become concerned that they may have passed down a homosexual gene with epigenetics. Perhaps you know of that, being a doctor?'

He cleared his throat and looked at Xander. 'It's an interesting field of research.'

'Working on your line of thinking, Mr. Parker, and meaning no disrespect at all, if my chosen career is male dominant, would that make me homosexual?'

'Point taken,' he said, and put a large forkful of food into his mouth.

I think he was finished with the topic. But I wasn't. 'Thank you ... I grew up with quite a few ballerinos—danseurs. All but one was heterosexual ... it just seems the press makes a big thing about the very few homosexual ones, and they shouldn't. They should be judged on their technique and emotional interpretation of the ballet, not their personal lifestyle.'

'Well explained, dear,' Mrs. Parker said.

'Yolande,' it was Xander's sister speaking. 'What do you work on?'

'At the Base I work as part of a team. We can be working on a number of things at one time. Before I left recently, we were investigating and designing safety in planes and helicopters, analyzing pilots' reactions to flight troubles and implementing training to alleviate any split decisions in time that are crucial to survival. We've got some pretty awesome flight simulator programs happening.' I couldn't stop the smile that spread over my face.

'That sounds a little different to working at the flower shop,' she said.

'Yes, but working in Flowers for Fleur can be challenging.'

'How's that?'

'Trying to work out the type of flower the customer needs to project their emotions.'

'Who buys the most flowers?' she asked.

'Men.' I smiled. 'Plus, they tell me their stories ...'

'Any juicy ones?'

'Many, and of women too, of which I can't tell you, as that would be a betrayal of trust. But for the men, it's always about love and forgiveness. With women, it's about love and compassion and celebrating.'

'Alexander, how's your study going?' Mr. Parker asked.

'Hard work as always, Pa. I just have finals, and then I'm done,' Xander said, and smiled at his father.

'Good to hear, son.' Mr. Parker raised his glass of wine. 'To finals, to male ballet dancers, to people who excel in their profession, and to family.'

We held up our glasses and touched them to each other's, the clinking sound echoing around the room with the sound of acceptance. When my wine glass touched Xander's, he held my eye contact and nodded his head to me. I think he was pleased with his "pretend" girlfriend. And I hoped I was convincing, for him.

After dinner we moved to the sitting room again. I sat next to Xander, who took my hand in his, sending a searing heat rushing through my skin. I breathed in deeply.

'Thank you,' he said after a while.

I looked up into his eyes, where I could see the flames of the fire reflected in them.

'I love having a smart girlfriend,' he said. 'I haven't told you, but I remember you when I was younger ...'

I shook my head. It was impossible. 'Where from?'

'Ballet classes. I was ten—'

I went back in time to ballet lessons, here in Tarrin. 'And I was eight.' *You were the one Mia had a crush on ...*

'But then you left.'

'My parents moved interstate.'

'That makes sense.'

'I saw your football boots at ballet lessons one day ... and I really wanted to know how it felt to wear weird looking shoes like that.'

Xander smiled at me. 'I reckon you could swap your work boots for football boots!'

I burst out laughing. 'Only with long stripy socks!'

'Of course!'

'Any chance of taking off soon. I have to get up early to work.'

'Sure. Let's go.' He stood. 'Short goodbyes are the best ones. Follow my lead.' Xander threaded his fingers through mine, and I floated on the intimacy of our contact. He announced to everyone we had to go. At once, they came to us with hugs and kisses, and then we were gone.

He was right. Short goodbyes are the best.

Chapter Twenty-Nine

'Flowers?' It didn't look like she needed tea, coffee or books. *I'm sorry, Gram,* I whispered with my mind voice. I hoped she didn't hear my omission of words from the workbench. The young woman before me was the color of dull yellow—emotional fragility.

She caught a tear on the end of her finger. 'I don't know really. I stuffed up with my boyfriend. Guys buy their girlfriends flowers for forgiveness, but what do women buy their boyfriends?'

She had me there. What do women buy to make it up to their boyfriends, or husbands for that matter? 'Hmmm ... how about ... a jar of notes, like handmade vouchers ... back massage, movie, pizza, golf, video games, football tickets, a surprise bottle of whatever he likes to drink each day for a week, little love notes ... stuff like that ... unless he likes flowers, then that would be special.'

She tilted her head to the side and put a finger under her chin. 'The jar idea could work. Thanks,' she said.

I nodded. 'We have jars, and a variety of colored paper and teeny envelopes over by the open French doors.' I pointed to the French provincial side table with cabriolet legs, two drawers and a white distressed finish with a timber top.

She walked over to the collection of jars and colored papers. In a moment she was back wearing a carefree smile.

'Anything else I can help you with?' I asked while I put the sale through the register and wrapped her purchases.

'No—but thanks a heap!' She left through the front doors with a bouncy stride. Gram will be happy with my non-flower sale.

Darcy walked past with a pot of tea. It was for Gram. When he returned to the café, I went over to her.

'I love having you here,' I said as I gave her a gentle hug.

'I love being here,' Gram said, and looked up at me with a smile that didn't reach her eyes.

'Why didn't you go to the Parker's for dinner last night?' I asked in a gentle voice.

Gram looked through me for a moment. 'I don't do social gatherings anymore,' she said, and lifted her chin slightly.

'Since when?' I asked. Gram was invited to occasions every week, and had been for years. She never missed them.

'For the last three years.' Gram snipped a few stems of roses.

I caught my breath. 'Why?' Gram loved people.

Darcy stopped before us and placed a new pot of tea and a cup and saucer for me onto the bench, without making a clinking sound. The sound that Gram hated. She said she had hyperacusis, or sound sensitivity, when some sounds are unbearably loud. It didn't make any sense to have that when you were losing your hearing. 'Thanks,' I said and tried to hide the distressed look on my face.

He looked into my eyes and gave me a knowing nod. On the way back to the café, he stopped at the sales desk and served a customer who held a bouquet of flowers.

'I don't want to talk about it!' Gram snapped.

I poured my tea and took a sip as my heart hurt. 'You're as bad as me. Remember when I loved to party? It was the highlight

285

of my life until … you know …'

'I remember, Yolande, but the difference is … you will love to party again, when it feels right for you.'

'It will be the same for you, Gram!'

'No, it won't! I can't hear anyone properly … in restaurants, or group gatherings, or parties. All I can hear is the murmur of voices. I can't tell what the heck they are talking about and I can see they get tired of me saying "sorry—can you say it again". It's always an imposition for them to repeat it, and then they end up saying, "it doesn't matter", when it does matter—*it does matter to me!* I *want* to know what they said, it's important to me. All I do now if I *do* go out, is smile and nod, without knowing what they're saying. And do you know how stupid I look when they're talking about something bad or sad, and I'm smiling and nodding—I feel like the biggest idiot!'

Gram closed her eyes and a tear escaped. She wiped it away and looked around the store. 'And now, I hardly receive invitations, and when I am invited on the rare occasion, I don't go to save from embarrassing them, and myself.'

Gram took a slow, deep breath. 'I hate Meniere's disease, Yolande. I hate everything about it! I hate that people can't see what I feel and suffer. I hate that it's an invisible illness. Some of my friends even think I'm faking it! Little do they know I am faking being well … it's exhausting!' Gram brushed her hands over her face. Her beautiful face. 'It's *so* exhausting!'

My heart went out to Gram. Not only was her ability to hear being taken away, but her social life was too, without her approval. At least my social life had died by my choice. I closed my eyes while I finished my cup of tea. I placed my teacup onto the saucer and placed my hand on Gram's. 'I wish I had a magic wand to cure you.'

'Me too, Andi. Me too … I pray every night for a cure … God hears you know.'

'I know, Gram.' I wondered why God didn't hear my prayer on that day with Mia. I wondered why God let bad things happen. 'God didn't hear my prayer for Mia ...' I whispered.

Gram stopped arranging a bouquet and looked at me. 'He heard you, Landi.'

'Then why didn't he stop those evil men ... why couldn't I hold Mia's hand for longer ...'

Gram placed her hand on the side of my face. 'We don't live in a perfect world. Humankind has free will to choose whether to love, or not to love. The day will come when sickness and pain and suffering is eradicated, and people will be held accountable for what they have done. True justice will be served.'

'But, Gram ... how can you still belie—'

'All will be revealed in God's time, and then you will be filled with understanding ... be still and know ...' Gram said with a gentle voice, where peace flowed with abundance.

I watched Gram for a moment longer as she returned to her flower bouquet.

'I'd better get back to the sales desk. It looks funny with people taking their flowers to Darcy to purchase over at the café, although, I think he is selling more tea or coffee with the flowers.' I put my hand on Gram's shoulder. 'Maybe we should sell the flowers from there ... it could boost sales in the café, hence overall profit for the store.'

Gram narrowed her eyes at me. 'Let me think on that one, Andi, and I'll let you know.'

I smiled at Gram, then returned the teacups and pots to Darcy.

'Everything okay with your gram?' he asked.

'Yes. We were just solving the problems with the world,' I said.

'Good. There's a lot of problems to solve.'

'Way too many. Thanks for the tea.'

'Pleasure,' Darcy said.

'Sorry about the people paying for their flowers here with you.'

'No problem. I sold more beverages than normal,' he said.

'That's because no one can resist your barista charm when they come closer!'

'In that case ... will you come to the movies with me tonight?'

'I can't, I'm sorry. I'm busy every night for a little bit longer.'

'With Xander?'

'Yes. Is there a problem with that?'

Darcy looked down and shrugged. He looked back at me. 'I need to know that he will look after you.'

I raised my eyebrows at him. 'I can look after myself, remember ...'

'Do you really need to see him every night?'

'Yes. We're entering a dance comp, remember?'

'Ah, yes.' Darcy looked down and shook his head slightly.

'I know. I can hardly believe it myself.'

Darcy looked up at me and narrowed his eyes. 'That you're dancing again, or that you're dancing with him?

'Both,' I said.

'I heard he was a professional ballet dancer. Did you know that before you started dancing with him?'

'No. If I knew I would have said no.'

'Why's that?'

'Look at him, then look at me ...'

'He has looked at you. That's why he chose you.' Darcy raised an eyebrow at me.

'He didn't want to dance with any professional dancers ... that's why he chose me. I'm surprised he hasn't given up yet. I'm pretty awful.' I laughed at myself.

'I bet you're not,' Darcy said, and narrowed his eyes at me.

I held up one of my heavy safety boots so Darcy could see it.

'But then again, they aren't the most beautiful dancing shoes.' He grinned at me and my heart grew arms to hug him.

I smiled. 'Work to do. Chat later.'

'Sure,' he said, and gave me a warm smile.

I returned to the sales desk and looked at my watch. There were only three hours until Xander would be here.

5.45pm.

I sat on the steps of Flowers for Fleur and waited for Xander to appear. When I saw his car, my heart raced. Why was I nervous? Was it because of the new dance? Was it because of the music he had chosen?

He pulled up at the curb and I stood. He vacated the car and stood with the passenger door open for me before I could get there. I waved my hands about, and he tilted his head to the side and smiled. I narrowed my eyes at him and sat in the passenger seat. He really didn't need to open and close doors for me.

In the dance hall, it was routine now to go to the pew, sit, change into dance shoes and then warm-up and stretch. But this time, when we were about to start practising our new dance, Xander's phone rang. He looked at the caller ID and answered it. He held up a finger. He would only be a moment. He ran his hand through his hair as he talked.

My breath hitched. I wanted to do that.

He turned away from me and continued his conversation.

When he was longer than a moment, I walked over to the piano and sat on the stool. I lifted the lid of the keys and tinkered on them ...

'Landi, let's play the duet you taught me!'
I stopped playing the classical piece of music and looked up at

Mia. She battered her eyelids at me with a goofy smile on her face.

I took a deep breath. 'Alright then ...'

Mia sat next to me on the stool, our legs touching. She bounced up and down on the seat like a child waiting to open her birthday presents.

'Ready?' I said, and placed my fingers on the keys.

'Set,' Mia said with a squeal.

'Go!' I said and started to play the more complicated low notes, while Mia played the easy high notes.

'Oliander,' she said while she played the wrong notes, 'my fingers have a mind of their own. They're creating a magical piece of music that will mesmerize the boys and have them chasing after me.'

'Mia Pizzeria, they will be chasing after you away from the piano to stop you from playing!' I said.

Mia laughed hard and fell off the chair ...

I smiled at my memory, and placed my fingers onto the keys and played *Comptine d'un autre été - L'après-midi*. I closed my eyes while I played, and after a little while, I could feel the heat from Xander's body close to mine. I inhaled deeply and smelled his citrusy body scent with a hint of liquorice, vanilla, lavender, amber and sandalwood. I stopped at once.

'I'm sorry,' I said, not wanting to waste his time.

'No. I'm sorry you stopped. Please ... play it again.' He sat on the piano stool next to me, our thighs touching. A delicious warmth grew on my leg where we touched.

I cleared my throat. 'Okay.' I positioned my fingers on the keys and played the piece of music through to the end, with Alexander Parker sitting close, watching and listening. There was silence between us when I finished, and neither of us moved for a moment in time.

'I'd like to dance to that. Tonight. When we finish learning our foxtrot ... please.' His voice was gentle.

'No,' I said.

'No?' he asked with raised eyebrows.

'No,' I repeated.

'Why not?'

'Because I won't be able to watch you dance ...'

'I'll video it, just for you,' he said.

My heart hammered against my chest. 'Okay,' I whispered.

He held out his hand. I placed my fingers in his hand and stood. We walked to the center of the hall and restarted our warm-up stretch routine.

'Did you look at the dance notation for the foxtrot?'

'Yes.'

'Did you listen to the music?'

'Yes.' I frowned at him.

'What?'

'*Perfect*?' I couldn't believe he had chosen that song. I hated *everything* about that song!

He frowned at me. 'Yes. Ballroom dancing is romantic. We need an emotionally charged song ... *Perfect* is ... well, perfect!'

I turned away from him and continued to stretch. I closed my eyes. I could never be loved like in that song. Not after—I should have held her hand for longer, just a couple more minutes ...

'Did you visualize the dance notation to the music?'

I turned back to him. 'Yes.' *While I cried.*

Xander held his hand up to start our practice session. I placed my hand in his while he placed his other hand on my back. I put my left hand on his shoulder and held my breath. I looked at his Adam's apple then up to his perfect chin, perfect lips, perfect nose, and then his perfect blue eyes that drank me in and caressed my soul.

'Breathe, Yolande,' he whispered.

I blinked and obeyed his words. Then we took our first step of hundreds to the new song that I hated with all my heart.

Halfway through our dance session I stepped back from Xander, and buckled over in laughter.

'What?' he said, frowning at me.

'I'm so imperfect at dancing to *Perfect*!'

Xander's lips curled into a slight smile. Surely he could see the irony? I performed an elegant ballerina's curtsy, known as 'reverence', just for him, and for a moment in time, I was transported back to when I was seventeen, when the world was uncomplicated, when Mia and I would make up stories about the danseur she had a crush on at the time, and I would add a dark twist to their story.

I looked up at Xander after my curtsy. He put his right hand over his heart and gave me a simple bow, his eyes connected deeply to mine, then he held his hand out for me. His hypnotic elixir of swirling emotion raced through me, and my walls of self-protection almost came crashing down. I took a deeper breath and placed my hand in his and we started the foxtrot again. This time we danced like we were one. And our seventh dance session was evolving into a dream.

On the final round of the foxtrot, Xander spun me around in a pirouette.

'You should take up ballet again,' he said.

I shook my head. 'My decision was made when I was eighteen.'

'You can change your mind.'

'I don't miss the pain from ballet.'

'Hmmm ... we'll see.' Xander walked over to his bag and pulled out a GoPro. He set it up in the corner of the hall and did a test recording, then went and checked the vision. 'Yolande Lawrence-Harrison, please play the piano again,' he said. 'I need to dance to that music!'

'Okay,' I said as I walked to the piano. I sat, then turned around to him to see if he was ready to dance.

'I want you to play it twice. The first time I will listen and feel the emotion of the music, the second time I will dance.'

'Okay,' I said, turned on the seat and placed my fingers on the keys of the piano. As I played, I felt each note move through me, with the energy and emotion of the music. I poured my heart and soul into the music for Xander. Just for Xander.

When I finished the piece, I rested for a moment, before I started again. While I played, I could hear his feet as he danced. I knew when they touched the floor and when they didn't. The music flowed from me like it was part of my soul, like being on a different spiritual plain.

After the last note, I removed my hands from the piano keys and lowered my head. I was emotionally exhausted. In a good way. I wanted to cry, but I didn't. Not here, with Xander.

Arms wrapped around me from behind. Xander hugged me tightly. 'Thanks. That was immensely satisfying.' He released his arms from me, and I turned to face him.

I had no words. All I could do was nod at him. He held his hand out to me. I placed my hand in his and stood.

'Do you want to see me dancing to your music?'

'I would love that,' I said, my words barely audible.

'Come,' he said.

We sat on the pew and Xander held his GoPro between us. I watched his dancing: music expressed in body movement, connecting human existence to vibrations of sound, the language and art form of music and dance joined—compelling, beautiful, moving. My heart felt full of life, overflowing with the color spectrum of love, transcending time and space.

'Beautiful,' I whispered when the vision finished. I caught tears on my fingers to stop them trickling down my face.

'Thanks for playing for me,' he said, and placed a finger under my chin and lifted my eyes to his. 'I'm blown away by your hidden layers. When I first met you, I thought you were just a florist—a girl selling flowers in her work boots looking at life through rose-colored glasses.'

'And then, like a rose bud I unfurled, revealing many petals ...' I said with a dramatic tone and expressive hands.

'Of beauty,' he added.

'I wouldn't go that far,' I said, my cheeks warming with embarrassment. 'I was trying to be sarcastic!'

'Hmmm ... sarcasm, the highest form of intelligence. It goes perfectly with who you are.'

'Now who is being funny!' I started to change my dance shoes to put on my work boots, but decided to leave my dance shoes on for the short drive home. 'Oh ... do you still have my bag in your car from last night?'

'No. It's in my room at the university. I can bring it tomorrow.'

'Do you mind if we get it tonight. I have some sketches in there that I need.'

'Sure. I'll pack up and we'll go.'

He opened the car door for me again and I shook my head at him. He simply raised his eyebrows at me. I think I just needed to accept his door opening as a Xander-ism.

Xander drove, heading north out of town for thirty minutes before the university campus appeared on the horizon. It was large with historical architecture, making it seem more important.

He pulled the car up into a circular driveway, then walked around the car and opened my door. 'I don't want to leave you alone in the car. You'll have to come with me.'

'I'll be fine. You won't be long, will you?'

He looked around. 'I can't risk anything happening to my dance partner. Not this close to the competition date.'

'Alexander Parker, you are being ridiculous! We're on a university campus—'

'It's not immune to incidents. And you're not immune to incidents!'

I sighed. He was right. I got out of the car, only because I didn't have my work boots on.

'Girls aren't allowed in our dormitory. So, don't speak, and if I ask you to do something, do it without questioning. Got it?'

I widened my eyes at him, then rolled them. 'Yes.' I had no other choice.

Xander took my hand and I walked closely behind him so as not to be seen. We entered the centuries-old door and along long hallways and stopped at the bottom of steps that lead up a multitude of floors.

Xander turned to me. He held his fingers to his lips. 'I need to piggyback you from here. If anyone hears two sets of footsteps going up the steps at this time of night, doors will open to see what's going on,' he whispered and held a finger to his lips again.

I gave him a disbelieving shake of my head. I definitely did not want him to carry me up flights of stairs. He turned around and crouched down so I could latch on to him. I put my arms over his broad muscular shoulders and wrapped my legs around him, my breasts pressed against his back. He held on to my legs and straightened up, and started moving up the stairs, faster than I thought he would.

I started to giggle at the ludicrousness of the entire situation. Xander shushed me.

After the fourth flight of steps, he stopped outside an oak door. I slid down his back until my feet touched the floor. He held his finger to his lips once again, then inserted a key into the door lock. The moment he pushed the door open, he ushered me into his room, quickly, and closed the door behind us and turned on the soft white light.

'Do you smuggle girls into your room frequently?' I asked in a quiet voice, conscious of the need to be unheard.

'No. You're the first and only one,' he replied.

I narrowed my eyes at him. I wasn't sure I believed him. I

looked around his tidy room. There was a window in the center of the wall on the right. To the left of the window was a single bed, while on the other side was a dark oak study table. A tall bookshelf was within close reaching distance to the desk. On the opposite wall to the window was an oaken wardrobe and a doorway that led to a bathroom, I assumed. My backpack was placed in the corner of the room.

'Is your room serviced?' I asked as Xander walked over and picked up my backpack.

'What do you mean?' He handed me my bag and our fingers touched, sending a warmth along my skin.

My breath hitched. 'It's so tidy!' I managed to say after I re-scrambled my senses.

'No. That's just me. Between dancing, studying and lectures, I don't have time to mess it up.'

I looked around at his bed, desk, bookshelves, bathroom and wardrobe, once again. 'I'm ready to leave,' I said, needing to get away from him and the way he was starting to affect me. I wasn't looking forward to being piggybacked down the stairs.

He nodded and turned to the door. He opened it a fraction and peered through the gap. There were male voices and footsteps and chairs scraping the floorboards. He closed the door and leaned against it with his hands behind his back and looked at me.

'It looks like the boys are settling in for a game of cards.' His voice was barely audible.

Great. I looked towards the window as an escape route. But I didn't have my work boots on. We were four stories up and I was now stuck in a dorm room, with the beautiful Xander.

'Out the window isn't an option,' he whispered. 'There's a long drop and a pool that juts out ...'

'I can swim,' I said.

He shook his head.

There was a knock on the door followed by a British sounding voice. 'Soon to be, Dr. Alexander Parker, we need you for our card game.'

Dr. Alexander Parker?

Alexander lowered his head and spoke through the door. 'Not tonight. I'm behind with my study.'

'No you're not! You're the proverbial goody-goody, academic student. Open the door!'

Xander looked at me with wide eyes. He pointed to the space between the wall and where the door would open to. I dropped my backpack on his bed and scrambled to that place and flattened myself against the wall.

Alexander took a deep breath and opened the door, then stood in front of the gap to hide me completely.

'Aaaah, Dr. Parker, where are your study books? And your computer isn't turned on. Plus ... there's a girl's bag on your bed!'

I closed my eyes. We had just been caught out. Xander would be disciplined.

'I found it in the park on the way home. I was just about to look through it to find the owner, before I settled in to study,' he lied.

If there ever was such a thing as the power of invisibility, I wanted it. NOW!

There were footsteps around the room and the sound of the window being opened, then closed.

'I'll give you the benefit of the doubt, Alex. Now come and join us for a game of cards.'

'What's the wager tonight?'

'The winner has their drinks paid for an entire month.'

'Let the game begin then,' Alexander said. 'I'll be there shortly.'

I shuddered. Alcohol. Drunkenness. Abuse. Violence.

One set of footsteps left the room. Xander closed the door and turned to me. 'They'll be less suspicious if I join them ... only for a while, and then I'll take you home,' he whispered.

I nodded to him. I didn't have a choice. At least he had some sort of plan.

But my plan was different to his ... the window ... four stories high ... I could do it.

He left and closed the door. A cheer went up. Male voices. I walked around Alexander's room and stopped at his bookshelf. Medical books. I took two steps to his study desk. Apple laptop, stationery. Painfully clean and ordered. I took three more steps to the window and opened it, leaned out and looked around. There was a small drop to the roof below. Good. I went to Alexander's bed and grabbed my backpack and pulled it over my shoulders. I had learned if you wanted something, you had to do it yourself instead of waiting for other people.

I climbed out the window and dropped onto the roof, cushioning my landing by bending my legs to absorb the impact, then stilled so the noise of my landing didn't cause a stir and curious eyes.

I walked around the rooftop with care, ducking under windows so not to be seen. One edge of the roof ended with a drop into the pool below, like Alexander said, one ended in a drop onto cars, and another ended in a drop onto hedges. I inched closer to the last edge, and looked over the side. There were rocks. Jagged rocks, like on that terrible day of the scars.

I closed my eyes and saw my drop of blood fall onto Mi—I opened my eyes before it landed in my memory. A tingle of anxiety bloomed in the center of my chest and threaten to spread into a panic attack. I looked around to name five things I could see. Out loud I said, 'Roof tiles, windows, trees, moon, clouds.' The distraction method worked, pushing my anxiety back inside its dark place. I let out a loud breath. I had nowhere to go but back to Xander's room.

I moved back from the edge of the roof and returned to Alexander's room, where the window was closed! I let out a low groan of annoyance and sat below it, turned my head and cussed. I had to play the waiting game for Dr. Alexander to return. He couldn't play cards all night, could he?

Two hours later there was a scraping sound above me. I looked up to see the window being opened, followed by a hand reaching down to me, waiting for mine. I gazed over his hand, lean and strong with defined contours and shape, even in the muted light of the night. Of course, he would have beautiful hands. They matched his attractive genetic pool. Lucky him. No one had a choice with what body they were born into.

I closed my eyes. I wanted his hand to go away. I didn't need his strength to get up. I didn't need his help. I didn't need his anything.

'It's a gentlemanly gesture,' he said.

I opened my eyes and looked at him. 'The card game or the hand?'

'My hand,' he said and narrowed his eyes at me.

'Thanks, I guess. I don't know whether to take it as an insult, or a compliment.'

'Insult?'

'Yes—that you're implying women are incapable and weak.'

He hung his head and chuckled. 'Oh, we're back to that again.'

What? I frowned at him.

'There are no weak women, just those who act weak and incapable, purely for the sake of a man's ego—manipulative, conniving, fake. Puke,' he said.

I laughed out loud at the word puke.

Alexander placed his fingers over his lips. 'Sssshhhh!'

I placed my hand into his and was rewarded with an instant

flashback—my rescuer's hand as he dangled beside the cliff face with his safety harness on. Nausea surfaced. When would the flashbacks stop? How I hated them with every ounce of my being and every drop of bile in my gut. Shit happens. But why did it have to happen to Mia and me?

His warm, strong hand tightened around mine, and I felt the uplift. Once I was on my feet, I placed my other hand on the windowsill and clambered inside his room, our fingertips still touching. I let go of his touch and sat on his study chair.

'And the compliment?' he asked.

'You ... may—' I took a deep breath. I didn't want to say it. I didn't want to think that he liked me. I didn't deserve for him to like me in any way, shape or form. Not a smart, good-looking doctor, a beautiful danseur like him. He wouldn't like me if he knew how damaged I was. 'Like me ...' There. I said it. I released a long breath.

He connected his eyes to mine. 'Hmmm? Like you,' he said, like he was testing how the word, like, felt on his tongue. 'I do like you ... I like your honesty, your wit, your engineering brain, your flower shop manner and design, that you like to solve problems, that you shun fashion trends. I love your work boots that you wear everywhere.'

'Except when I really need them ...'

'Like now?'

'Yes.'

'To protect yourself from me?'

I blew air out between my pursed lips. 'No ... not from you.'

'From what then?'

He was digging. Deeper. I looked down because I couldn't look at him. I couldn't show him how vulnerable I was.

'Trust me, Yolande. Let me in ...' he said in a whisper that almost mended my broken heart.

I swiveled his chair towards the bookshelf. 'What books do

you need for study?' I asked, changing the subject. I couldn't let him in. I couldn't let his light inside my darkness, exposing me.

'*The Brukner & Khan's Clinical Sports Medicine: Injuries, vol. 1*, thanks.'

'Oh, Dr. Parker, you are way too polite!'

'Compliment or insult?'

'Insult—how can I make fun of you? You're too nice?'

He shook his head. 'I have been called many things, but never "too nice".'

'Really ... oh, yeah ... at first, I thought you were totally arrogant, entitled and cold,' I said.

He smiled at me. 'Because of the letters in the flower basket of your gram's bicycle, or the first time we met ...'

'The second. The first time was when I spoke to you at the front of the store, one stormy morning,' I recalled.

He ran his hand through his hair and narrowed his eyes at me. 'Oh yes ... I remember now. I laughed at your steel-capped boots—at a flower shop of all places!'

I leaned forward and gave him a punch on the arm. 'No one insults my work boots!'

'Ow!'

'You deserved that.' I found his medical book and handed it to him. 'I want you to pass those exams, Dr. Parker.'

He took the book from me. 'I want to pass them too.'

I vacated his study chair and sat on his bed. 'How long do you think I'll be imprisoned here in this clean and ordered room?'

'Compliment or insult?'

'Neither. Just an observation,' I said.

'I'm not talking about the state of the room. I was talking about the use of the word "imprisoned".'

'And?' I asked.

'It carries a negative connotation.'

'Well ... I'm in a small room and I can't leave—that's like a prison.'

He leaned back in his chair and looked at me under hooded eyes. 'Am I that bad to be around?'

'On the contrary. You're okay for a guy, and that's saying a lot in my books.'

'You have books of men?'

I shook my head and smiled at him. 'You'll keep!'

'I hope so.' He held my eyes in his, and there was something deep that seemed to come dangerously close to touching my soul, again. And I wanted it to touch, so I could absorb his soul light to vanquish my darkness. But I couldn't let it happen. What I felt for him scared me. I pulled my eyes from his and crawled back inside to my darkness, my friend.

'Trust me,' he whispered, again, his words pleading to my heart.

I looked back into his eyes. 'Trust is earned, never given,' I whispered back.

'Then I'll earn it.'

I took a deep breath. He had earned it already, but I couldn't tell him, and I still couldn't let him in.

Loud laughter sounded from outside the door. The card game was still going.

'How long will they be?' I asked. I needed to go home.

Xander looked at his watch. 'Sometimes they're there until 2am.'

'Great,' I said.

'I'm sorry.'

'You weren't to know.' I pulled out my phone and texted my mother, then I went to Xander's bookshelf and pulled a book out to read. I sat on Xander's bed and laid on my side to read the book—*The Soul of Medicine: Tales from the Bedside by Sherwin Nuland, MD*, while he studied.

I started to get tired after an hour. It was late. 'Do you mind if I catch some shut eye while you study?'

Xander looked up at me from his textbook. 'Go for it,' he said.

I pulled back the covers of his bed, took off my shoes and my t-shirt that I wore over a sleeveless shirt, and climbed into his bed and turned onto my side.

I looked up at Xander as I got comfortable. He was staring at me, at the top of my chest, and it scared me.

'Nice scar. What happened?'

Anxiety shot its poison through me. I looked down and quickly pulled my shirt over to hide the part of my scar that was visible. *A nice scar? How can a scar be nice?* A scar is the result of pain. Scars are marks for life, reminders of an event that can never leave your body or memory. Scars mean you are damaged. Physically. And for me, it meant emotional scars and crippling guilt.

'I didn't do anything. It is neither an accident, nor self-inflicted.' I closed my eyes to stop the memory from returning.

'Who did this to you?' He sat on the bed beside me. He was angry. 'A man?'

I looked out the window and into the distance. 'I can't tell you.'

'Can't, as in you don't know who did it, or won't, because you don't want to tell me?'

'Can't, as in I don't want to remember!' My words were forced through gritted teeth. 'And won't, because I don't want to tell you ... or anyone.'

I rose from the bed and stood by the window. It had started raining. Like my heart. Tears for the sad earth. Except the tears from the clouds gave life and strength. Human tears are supposed to give strength too. But I wasn't so sure about that. I held my tears in, only because they would run down the scar line and he would know more than I wanted him to know about my damn bloody scar. I didn't want to tell him about the bastard who had done this to me. I hated him with a passion, and I hated the ugliness of hate that lived within me. I truly was the color of broken.

Alexander's hand wrapped around mine and he pulled me back to the bed. 'Give me a closer look at your scar. There may be something that can be done for it.'

My head told me to run out the door. This was way out of my comfort zone. I wished he'd never seen it. He knows that I'm damaged now, and I could never be perfect to him, like in our foxtrot song.

I closed my eyes and sat on the bed beside him, like I was in slow motion.

His finger traced along my raised scar. I screwed my eyes shut at the pain. Not the physical pain; the emotional pain. This moment was too hard to bear. He didn't trace the scar any further than the top of my shirt, and for that I was truly thankful.

'Your scar tissue is called a keloid. Laser treatment has effective results, and cryotherapy ...'

Anxiety flooded through me. I knew everything he said was true. I had researched it over two hundred times. But I couldn't part with my scars. They were my reminder. They were my punishment. *I shouldn't have let go of Mia's hand ...*

Then his finger continued to trace my scar. I saw him hold his breath when he realized it wasn't just on my upper chest. I put my hand over his to stop him before he continued down my breast to where the scar stopped at the start of my areola, around my nipple.

'Who did this to you?' he asked between gritted teeth. 'Tell me!'

I lifted my head higher, trying to find my inner-strength. 'There are only six people who know little bits—my parents, grandparents, Darcy and Dr. Jones.'

'The psychologist?'

I breathed out deeply. I didn't want to have this conversation with Alexander. 'Yes.'

'Darcy knows?'

'Only some parts … he doesn't know everything. He doesn't know the entire story, and he hasn't seen as much of the scar as you have.'

'Good.'

'Good?' *How can that be good?*

'The only man who should know about this scar is someone you trust implicitly. Someone who will never betray you. Someone who loves you unconditionally.'

Alexander looked out at the rain and then back to me. 'Now I know why Darcy is so protective of you. If no one knows the full story of the event, Yolande, what are you scared of?'

I squeezed my eyes shut and tried to bury the pain inside of me. The pain of guilt and rejection. 'That whoever I tell will judge me … and will leave me. It's the fear of rejection, I think, and that the person will look at me with different eyes and create a wall between us.'

A tear ran down Alexander's cheek. 'I need to know, Yolande. It is killing me that you have been through a trauma that has profoundly affected you and I don't know what happened. Trust me … please,' his voice cracked as he spoke.

'I can't … I can't tell you. I don't want you to look at me with pity. You already know too much.' My heart fell. 'Please … just leave it be.'

Alexander looked deeply into my eyes. I didn't want him there. I looked away from him, ashamed that he knew about my chest scar. His opinion of me, whatever that was, would change. I would be able to tell by the way he looked at me from now on. I counted how many days we had left together. There were four or five more practice sessions and then the competition.

And that night would be the last I ever saw him. It was better that way.

'You should get back to your study,' I said.

'I should,' he said, his voice monotone.

He got off the bed and sat in the chair at his desk and returned to his textbook. I lied back on his bed and faced him. I really wanted to face the wall so he couldn't look at me. But I needed to face him, so I could detect any movement that might come my way. It was a self-preservation thing, like wearing my steel-capped safety boots.

After a while of watching him study, I closed my eyes. I regretted it at once. Part of my memory of that terrible day of my scars came flooding back to me with a vengeance, and I had no way to stop it ...

The point of the knife pierced my skin. I closed my eyes as I felt the sharp cutting of my flesh, with a searing pain that screamed at my core. With a slow, torturous speed, the tip of the knife traced the path of my tear ... I held my breath as the knife went in a direct tear path towards my nipple—piercing, cutting, tearing ...

I sucked in a loud sharp breath and my eyes flew open, wide. I pushed my hand over my chest scar, checking to see whether it was bleeding, like on that terrible day of the scars, dripping onto my feet and pooling onto the ground.

Alexander was there by my side at once. He wrapped his arms around me and held me tight, so tight I hoped he could push all my broken pieces back together. But then, that would require a miracle. And there were no such things as miracles.

Not to me, anyway ...

Chapter Thirty

The stars disappeared one by one when Xander drove me home. The sky was an impressive color of rosy pinks and sandy yellows, and then whispers of a blue bouquet when we arrived at my parents' house. He opened the car door for me and we walked along the slumbering garden pathway together. The morning birds did not sing, and the roosters did not crow. It was as silent as my hurting heart. Xander walked me to the front door and knocked on it. He said he wouldn't leave until my mother was with me. I turned and watched as he got back into his car and left, his tires leaving tracks on the wet road.

Tears slid down my face.

'Are you okay, Andi?' my mother asked. My dear mother, the color of forever pink, like my grandmother. I loved her with all my heart.

'More than okay,' I said.

'Then why are you crying?'

'He's the most beautiful man I have ever met.'

'Does he know about ... you know?'

'No. He would run from me if he knew.'

'Oh, Landi ...' My mother hugged me. She thought she knew

how deep my pain was. But no one could *ever* truly know. And that's the way I wanted it.

I showered and got ready for work. It was going to be a long day. In fact, it was going to be a long six days until the competition was over.

Gram's bicycle was not out the front of Flowers for Fleur when I arrived. I unlocked the doors and entered the store. The first thing I did was to wheel her mulberry-colored 1950s Cruiser bicycle out the front, then created a bouquet of pink peonies to place in the basket.

I returned inside the store and started on the list of pre-opening jobs.

Darcy walked in through the rear shop door. He was the color of earthy brown today, secure and comforting. 'Good morning, Andi!'

'Morning, Darcy!'

'No *good* morning, today?'

'Not today.'

'Good things will come.'

'Yeah,' I said. But I wasn't so sure.

I pulled the top of my work dress higher over my chest scar. Since last night I had become acutely aware of it again. And I hated it!

Charlotte entered the store early with yellow sunshine following her, leaving a trail of sparkles wherever she went. Perhaps she should be the one dancing with Xander. She would fit his *Perfect* song, perfectly. And she didn't carry a truckload of baggage with her. She was every man's dream girl. She was *that* girl a man falls madly in love with. A keeper. The marrying type.

I left her to the sales desk and took over Gram's workbench of flower imagination since she wasn't here this morning. I opened the book of yesterday's orders for today, then activated the computer to download overnight orders that had come in. There was a lot to do. At least I wouldn't be able to dwell on my misery while I concentrated on creating bouquets of beauty.

I pulled out my phone and texted Gram. I needed to know if she was okay.

ME: *Hi Gram. How are you today?*

GRAM: *Not so good today. Brain fog.*

ME: *Brain fog?*

GRAM: *Yes. I can't think. I can't make decisions. I can't find the right words at times. Just Google it. It's so hard to explain. It's like being lost in a fog ... searching but not finding.*

ME: *I'm sorry to hear. I'll Google it.*

GRAM: *And I feel like I have a bobble-head ... and I have head lag. It's like I've turned my head, but my head doesn't know it yet ... and then it catches up to my body. Makes me so nauseous. It's just not a good day.*

ME: *Oh Gram. Sending masses of hugs and love. I hope you feel better soon.*

My heart sank. How often had Gram come into the store feeling like that? She always looked well, except when she was having a vertigo attack spewing up her insides for hours and hours on end. I sighed. Invisible illnesses were the worst. People could never understand what the person was going through. Even I was grappling at what brain fog must feel like ... and I hoped I never knew. A shot of guilt hit me. Was I being selfish?

I needed a dose of sunshine. So I looked up at Charlotte. She stilled and looked at me, then her mouth curved into a contagious smile and her eyes twinkled. I smiled back. Gram was right. A smile had power. Just like flowers. It touches your heart and soul and makes you think the world is perfect. Even when it's not.

At lunchtime I disappeared from the shop.

I walked through the white gate of the quaint little white house with the pretty flower garden that was my psychologist's office, and sat in my regular chair. The one with the imprint of my butt on it. The door opened smoothly and silently. Dr. Jones was dressed in a black suit today. Her shoes were a smooth, orange and brown, colored like a giraffe's coat.

'Yolande.' Dr. Jones's voice was comforting, like sleeping with my childhood teddy bear.

I stood and followed her into the office. The familiar office. Dr. Jones put a light hand on my shoulder. 'Would you like to sit on the sofa or lie on the couch today?'

'The sofa ... thanks.' I made myself comfortable and hugged my usual cushion. Dr. Jones went to make of pot of tea. I heard the boiling water and the chink of the china teacups and saucers. I closed my eyes and knitted my fingers together like I always did before I placed them on my stomach. I had chosen to be present today. I needed to talk to her.

At the sound of approaching footsteps, I opened my eyes. Dr. Jones placed two teacups and saucers on the table. I reached over and picked one up. The warmth of the brew touched my lips when I sipped it and I relaxed a little. Aah ... tea ... *a bath refreshes the body, and tea refreshes the mind*—a Japanese proverb.

'What brings you here today, Andi?'

'Xander knows about my chest scar.'

'How does that make you feel?'

'Scared ... ashamed ... damaged ... undeserving of his attention ... deceitful.'

'Which of those feelings is the worst for you?'

'The deceit.'

'How have you deceived him?'

'By allowing him to think there was nothing wrong with me. Xander is perfect—skin, body shape, manners, kindness, beauty, dance—he is luminous, *so* luminous, and I feel like I don't measure up to what he thought I could be.'

'How did he react when he saw your scar?'

'He was angry. He wanted to know who did it. He wanted to know the details of how it came to be.'

'Did you tell him?'

'No. I couldn't. I didn't want him to see me as a damaged person. But I fear it's too late.'

'Is it making you feel anxious?'

'Yes. I want to be someone more than the story of my past. I want a new beginning. But now I can't do that because he knows about the scar.'

'Did he have any other reaction to it?'

'Yes. He touched it and told me the type of scar it was, and how it could be fixed, but I already knew how it could be minimized.'

'Do you think you would feel better if no one could see your scar if it was uncovered?'

'Like a secret hidden inside of me, tucked deep into the darkness, never to see the light of day, the truth?'

'Nobody needs to know what happened to you. It's none of their business.'

'I know.'

'I think if you have cosmetic surgery on the scar, you won't have to worry about others seeing it and asking questions. It's definitely worth consideration, Yolande, particularly where your emotional and psychological healing is concerned, and moving forward with your life.'

I nodded. She was probably right.

'What are you hoping for with Xander, in terms of your relationship?'

'I just don't want him to dislike me because of something that happened to me. I don't want to lose our friendship.'

'There are people who can see past the scars of life. You will see whether he is one of those by how he treats you from now on.'

I lowered my head. She was most definitely right. I nodded.

'If he distances himself from you, he's not worth having around. It's as simple as that.'

I nodded once again.

'Was there anything else you needed to talk about, Yolande?'

'I think not. I just needed to hear your advice. It will stop me from over-thinking and adding a negative slant on the situation, as I always do.'

'I'm always here to talk things through with you.'

'Can I ask you something, Dr. Jones?'

'Anything ...'

'Will you come to watch me dance with Xander at the Ballroom Dancing Competition?'

'I would love that. Email me the details.'

I smiled at Dr. Jones. I wanted her to see something I loved.

'I will,' I said and stood, as did Dr. Jones after me. We walked to her door and I left her room that held the secrets of many in its walls, and returned to Flowers for Fleur.

As I walked past Gram's bicycle there was a note in the flowers. My stomach churned.

Xander had left me a note instead of talking to me in person?

It could only be bad news. I took the note out of the flowers and pushed it into my pocket. I couldn't deal with a rejection right now when I had to put on a happy face for the sake of the customers. I returned to the workbench, donned my apron and got on with the work of a florist.

After an hour, I went to the powder room and opened the carefully folded paper. I had to know what he had written. It was eating away at me, and I had to get it over and done with, to move on.

Dear Yolande,

I'm so sorry for last night and the way I reacted.
I was overcome with the intense need to protect you,
and to make everything right for you.

Please forgive me.
I'm looking forward to dancing with you tonight.

X Xander

I looked up to the heavens that was the powder room ceiling, and breathed a sigh of relief. I pushed the letter back into my pocket and returned to the workbench with a smile.

Darcy was right. Good things did come.

Xander stood in the middle of the hall for our eighth dance session. He was the color of blue, like the light blue sky during the blue hour of sunset. It reminded me of deep and trustworthy heart to heart talks while walking along a beach as the sun sank below the horizon.

He raised his left hand and I placed my right hand into his. He put his right hand just under my shoulder blade while I rested my left hand on his shoulder, and we waited for the music to begin.

'Why didn't you fight back?' Xander asked.

What? I took a deep breath as anger filled me to the core. It was best to be honest with him. 'Xander, being ... knifed ... stopped my best friend from being raped ... that's why I didn't fight back ...' I kept my eyes on him. Would he run from me now?

Xander stilled, then stepped back from me. I watched as he bent over, putting his hands on his knees. It was like I had punched him in the stomach. Hard.

When he stood up and looked at me, he had tears in his eyes. 'I'm so sorry. I cannot even begin to think what you've been through.'

'I don't want you to think about what I went through. It's in the past, and that's where it needs to stay.'

He brushed the side of his face with the palm of his hand then ran his fingers over his chin, his eyes connected to mine.

'And don't feel sorry for me ... okay?'

He took slow steps and stopped before me, and we resumed our foxtrot stance. 'Okay,' he said, and then the music began, as did our steps to the song.

When I gazed into his eyes as we danced, I saw something new in the windows of his soul.

It wasn't pity.

It wasn't sorrow.

It wasn't sadness.

It was understanding, and dare I say, some sort of adoration.

He was closer somehow.

He was a good man; a man I could trust implicitly, and who I knew cared unconditionally.

Chapter Thirty-One

Iopened the doors to Flowers for Fleur. I took one step inside and instantly knew something was wrong. It wasn't that Gram's bicycle was still in her office. I had passed it on my way in, adorned with pink roses that infused the air with a bold, fruity fragrance with hints of fresh lemon and raspberry. It wasn't that Darcy was late: the smell of coffee and baking cupcakes consumed the store. It was the trail of flowers knocked over and water pooled on the floor. I followed the path of destruction through the store to the door of the powder room.

I paused and closed my eyes before I entered, then took a slow, tentative step, through to the sound of Gram vomiting. Violently. And crying.

It was gut wrenching, and my heart broke. Nobody should see their grandmother like this. Grandmothers were supposed to be warm and happy and smiling and oozing with love that flowed around you and hugged you tightly, squeezing every bit of sadness from you.

I texted Gramps.

ME: *COME AT ONCE. IT'S GRAM.*

I didn't need to add any more details. Gramps would be here, like the knight in shining armor that he was.

I pushed my phone back into my pocket and my muscles tensed. Gram was sprawled on the floor lying in a pool of vomit. Her lips flattened and she heaved again, screaming as she did.

This was torture. Absolute torture.

'Gram!' I cried, a deep sadness rising from within me. At first, I was confused. I didn't know whether to grab toilet paper to soak up the vomit she was laying in, or to just be present for her.

She let out a soul-destroying sob and held up her hand towards me. She wanted me to hold her hand. I looked at her fingers stretched out to me, and in a mind flash, I saw Mia's hand, covered in blood. My blood. Mia's desperate hand that was filled with terror, and hope. Terror from what could happen next, and hope that I could save her.

Anxiety reared its ugly head, with its grip of tingles in my chest and fingers, and inside my head. I focussed on Gram while my stomach quivered. I was filled with the most insane feeling of incompetency as time seemed to slow down. I wanted to save Gram from this hideous vertigo that was robbing her of quality of life. I wanted to reach inside her body with a bright white healing light to incinerate the Meniere's monster that was ravaging her, destroying her very essence.

But I felt empty. Numb ...

I wrapped my fingers around Gram's hand, and she cried. Deeply. Staring at one constant place on the wall. I closed my eyes and knelt behind her, and cried with her. Deep, painful soul cries. Ones that were beyond words and feeling and actions. Ones that tried to reach out to our Creator, pleading and begging for mercy.

I lay down behind Gram and put my arm around her, without moving her, as I knew it would make the spinning impossibly worse, and she would vomit, again. I placed my head on the floor behind her, my hair in the vomit. I closed my eyes and sent a silent prayer to our heavenly Father. "He always hears," Gram had said. *He always hears …*

I heard the creak of the door opening, followed by Gramps anguished cry.

I sobbed again. Deeply.

'My darling Fleur.' Grampapa's voice broke. I listened as he pulled out his phone and called an ambulance. He sat beside Gram then, and held her hand and started to sing. His tenor voice filled the powder room with a heartbreaking tune and my heart shattered. Could Gram even hear him?

I held on to my beloved grandmother, lying in her vomit with her, even as the paramedics entered the powder room. One of them lifted my arm from her and told me that it would be okay now. I wanted to believe him, but I knew it wouldn't be true. As they rolled Gram onto her back to move her to the gurney she vomited once again, yelling as she did so. Then she stared at the ceiling.

In my numbness, I looked into her eyes. The forever light of life and love that she gave freely to others was gone. My beautiful Gram's soul light had gone. She was there in body only, breathing to remain alive.

She was the color of broken. Like me.

Anger flared inside me. I flicked the vomit from my clothes, then stood and ran.

I ran out the back door and along the streets in my work boots, my hair dripping with Gram's vomit. I ran until I could run no more. Then I collapsed in a field of wildflowers and I didn't want to get up.

Ever.

I just wanted to stay there. Alone. Sinking into the eternal hate of life that I tried to bury inside of myself since that terrible day of the scars. The day I let go of Mia's hand …

I rolled my eyes when I heard slow, heavy, footsteps crunching the living flowers. Death of beauty. Like what Meniere's disease was doing to my gram. I could see it was Darcy as I stared up at the clouds. But I didn't look at him.

He lay beside me but didn't speak.

Good. I had no words. I lifted my right hand to my hair. Gram's vomit had dried and hardened, sticking strands of hair together. Vomit hair artistry. It was a real thing ...

After a while, Darcy held onto my left hand. I wanted to yank my hand away from his. I was sick to death of hand holding and all its connotations: of saving, of comfort, of love, of support, of safety, of friendship.

But I left it there. Not for me. For him.

He pulled out his phone and texted, then put his phone away and stared up at the clouds, like me.

'Gramps said Gram is sedated. She's sleeping and not suffering at the moment. He was worried about you. I told him you were safe, and I was with you.'

I swallowed. 'Thanks.'

'I put Gram's bicycle back into her office.'

'Thanks.'

We said no more. Even while Darcy walked me home and left once I entered the house.

The closed sign hung at the front of Flowers for Fleur when I arrived at 6pm. For the first time since its opening, fifty years ago, it was closed all day on a weekday. I sat on the steps of the store and waited for Xander, for our ninth dance session, my heart completely devastated for Gram.

I stood as soon as I heard his car approaching, I moved towards the car. I didn't want him to open the door for me today.

It didn't feel right.

I slumped into the passenger seat and stared out the windscreen. 'What do we get if we win this comp?' I asked.

'Money.'

'I'm donating my half to medical research.'

'You can have it all. I don't need it,' he said.

I looked at Xander. How can someone not need money? Then I remembered that he came from a wealthy family.

'I'm sorry about your Gram,' he said.

'What? You know?' Anger bubbled inside me.

'Everyone knows, Andi.' He winced.

'So, everyone in this whole freaking town knows everything about everyone?' I was furious.

'No. It's not like that. Your grandmother is dearly loved. When an ambulance arrives, and the store is closed for an entire day, people need to know that your gram is okay.'

'Well she's not okay!'

'I can drive you home if you don't want to practise tonight.'

I let out a breath and closed my eyes. 'I want to dance for my gram. I invited her to watch the competition. If she derives some sort of pleasure out of the evening, then it's worth it.' I opened my eyes and looked at Xander. 'I'm sorry for being angry.'

'No need to apologize.'

'Yes, I do.'

'Apology accepted.'

Xander turned on the car engine and we drove in silence to the hall. We put our gear on the church pew. I changed my shoes and warmed and stretched in silence oblivious to everything around me.

When I looked up and became aware of where I was and what I was doing, Xander was waiting for me in the center of the hall.

I walked over to him and we took the foxtrot pose. I focused on his Adam's apple, then traced my eyes over his chin, his lips, his nose and to his eyes. I wanted to tell him how much I hated the song we were dancing do, but I decided to hold my tongue in case my words came out with added venom.

When the music started, we took our first step, but Xander pulled away, taking steps back from me, his feet in first position. It must have been his default foot placing after many years of ballet.

He dragged his hands down his face. 'I need to change the beginning of our dance, and add other changes.'

I didn't say anything. I just worried. The competition was too close for changes now.

'I want you to be facing away from me, head lowered with your hand over your scar for the start.' Xander raced over to his bag and pulled out the dance notation. He sat on the floor and I sat next to him. He scribbled the new steps onto the paper, then he added a lot of spinning moves to the rest of our dance. He gazed up at me. 'For your gram.'

I looked at him with wide burning eyes. I covered my face and burst into tears, and turned away from him. I picked up the hem of my t-shirt and pressed it to my right eye to stop the tears from washing away my make-up. As I tried to control my tears, Xander wrapped his arms around me. 'And for you, Yolande.' His words made me cry more.

'Thank you,' I whispered once I had settled my sadness. 'Just give me a moment and then we will start again.'

'Take your time.' He kissed the back of my head and stood. I watched through my splayed fingers as he practised the new dance steps by himself with an invisible me.

I grabbed a tissue and dabbed at my tears, then checked my face. My make-up covered what it needed to cover. I returned to the dance notation and visualized the new steps, then went and stood where I needed to be for the start of the dance—head lowered, hand over my scar. But I hated it there, so I put my hand over my heart. For Gram.

Our song started. *Perfect* was perfect as he said it would be, only because I changed the words to be about a guy instead of a girl. It made the song easier for me to dance to. With Xander. Because ... he was perfect.

We danced until past midnight, ensuring our foxtrot was powerful. When the song ended for the last time, Xander pulled me close and held me. I needed it more than he knew. Or perhaps he did know, that's why he did it.

I breathed in his citrusy scent with a hint of liquorice, vanilla, lavender, amber and sandalwood, plus a good lavishing of Xander body sweat, putting it to memory.

After the competition was said and done, we would part ways, and he would become just a beautiful, perfect memory to me, once upon a dream ...

Chapter Thirty-Two

'Flowers, tea, coffee or books?' The words rolled off my tongue with a melodic sound. For Gram. Just for Gram. She was home, resting, with Gramps spoiling her. I had placed her bicycle out the front of the store early with one of every single type of flower Gram had in the cold room. The blooms were magnificent, and the floral scent was profoundly magical.

'Flowers, please. In fact, Fleur had a bouquet of spiral looking flowers in a vase the other day. I was wishing for one of those, if you have one?'

'Not at the moment, but I can make one for you.'

'That would be perfect, dear.'

'Please go and have a complimentary tea of coffee at the café. Just tell Darcy that Andi sent you.'

The mature-aged woman smiled at me. She was the color of olive green—peace. 'Thank you,' she said and left.

I began to panic. There was a queue of customers with flowers in their hands like we had never seen before. How was I going to create "Fleur's Fury" and serve everyone?

Like an answered prayer, Charlotte weaved her way through the store, the sun's rays frolicking behind her. She was the perpetual color of happiness: yellow. She grabbed her apron and tied it on. 'Morning, Yolande!' she said, and placed a gerbera in her hair.

I laughed, remembering our crazy hair day on wild, wicked, Wednesday. I followed suit and grabbed a gerbera and threaded it through my hair, then left to create "Fleur's Fury" at the workbench of flower imagination. I pulled out Gram's design book and ran my finger down the contents—Fury. Page 50.

I turned to the flower recipe and noted the ingredients to the spiral creation, then went to the cold room at once and collected the green trick, caspia, curly willow, mini carnations, and wax flowers—pinks, purples, hues of green. I laid them in a tight row on the workbench as Gram had done, then ran tape along the stems and rolled them so they were like a spiral. I then added the gold and silver ribbons—the Meniere's ribbons.

'Perfect,' I whispered. The spiral of colors were a mass of beauty. Pleased with myself, I meandered my way through the store to the café to the woman and presented them to her, much to her pleasure.

I returned to the workbench and worked on orders that needed to be delivered, including my own special creation to be delivered to Gram, then set about ordering more flowers as they were disappearing fast.

At 5pm, I closed the doors to Flowers for Fleur and took a breath like it was my first for the entire day.

I hugged Charlotte. 'Thanks for rescuing us, yet again. Will you work for us full time until we know what is happening with Gram?'

Charlotte pressed her lips together. 'Hmmm ... I'll do some shuffling of my diary, but yes, I'd love to.'

'Thanks. See you at 7am.'

Pleased with Charlotte's commitment, I walked over to Darcy and wrapped my arms around him. 'Thanks,' I said.

'What for?'

'Being you!' I said.

'My pleasure, Yolande.'

'Can we talk, after I finish preparing for tomorrow?'

'Sure,' he said with a frown.

I dashed off and attended to the must do's that I did each evening before Xander arrived. At 5.55pm I sat opposite Darcy at a table. A pot of tea and cupcakes were between us.

'I want to raise money to find a cure for Gram's disease.'

Darcy looked at me and nodded his head. 'Go on ...'

'We add some items to the menu with wacky names that suit the symptoms of Meniere's disease. The sales from those items are donated to research, one hundred percent.'

'What were you thinking of?'

'I'm leaving that in your capable creative baking hands. Do some research, then create a menu to match.'

Darcy nodded his head and raised his eyebrows. 'Sounds like my type of challenge.'

'I thought so, and ... ah, don't tell Gram what we're doing.'

Darcy raised his hand and gave me a three-finger salute. 'Scout's honor.'

I frowned at him. 'I didn't know you were a boy scout!'

'I wasn't. I just always wanted to do the three-fingered salute!'

I smiled at Darcy and punched him on the arm. 'Gotta run. See you tomorrow!'

I grabbed my backpack from the office and left through the front doors, locking them behind me, then walked to Xander's car. He stood there holding the door open for me.

'Thanks,' I said as I slid into the passenger seat.

He gave me a nod before he went to the driver's seat, started the engine and drove to the hall for dance session number ten.

'You should invite your father to watch you dance,' I said while we sat on the floor and stretched.

Xander pressed his lips together and shook his head ever so

slightly. 'He's not ready.'

'But it's not ballet, and you're dancing with me. He'll think we have something going on ...'

'True.' He let out an audible breath.

'Think about it. I'm happy to say that I asked you to dance with me, and that you went along with it, begrudgingly ...'

We stood.

Xander held his hand out to me. 'We're doing just the waltz tonight, three times without a foot wrong. Tomorrow night it's foxtrot, then full-dress rehearsal the night after ... and ... I'm taking you to a movie tonight.'

I narrowed my eyes at him, wondering if there was a motive behind his movie plan. 'Darcy won't be happy,' I said, placing my hand into his.

'Is Darcy your boyfriend?'

'No. But he keeps asking me to go to the movies with him, but I'm always with you.'

'Good,' Xander said, and we took our positions and waited for the music, *Once Upon a Dream*, to begin.

After four rounds of waltzing, we had finished for the night. I sat down to change back into my work boots.

'No work boots, Yolance,' Xander said. 'You don't need them when you're with me.' He looked into my eyes and raised his eyebrows at me.

I put my dance practice sneakers back on. 'Can we stop at my place on the way, so I can change?'

'Sure.'

I hooked arms with Xander as we walked to the movie.

'Is your father, right?' I asked.

'What do you mean?'

'Do you prefer men, and I'm your cover-up?'

'Does it matter who I prefer?' he said.

'Yes, and no.'

Xander looked down at me and frowned.

'No—it's the way you treat others that matters, not your sexuality, and yes—if a woman really, really likes you, she needs to know if you're unavailable.'

He gazed deeply into my eyes and my body filled with warmth.

'Yolande, I'm—'

'Alexander! It's so good to see you! Join us at the bar! Josh is there too!'

'He is?' Xander said. I watched Xander's face light up at the mention of Josh's name. He had just answered my question.

I looked down at my feet. I didn't have my safety boots on. A wave of anxiety washed through me. I pulled out my phone.

'Go to the bar with your friends, Alexander. I'll make my own way home,' I said, filled with disappointment. It had nothing to do with not seeing a movie. I unhooked my arm from his.

He found my hand and held it. 'Come with me ... just one drink ... and then we'll go to the movie,' he said. 'Please.'

'I don't want to make you look bad. Please go without me.'

Xander shook his head at me and frowned. 'Let's go.'

I followed behind him, my head down, preferring not to accompany him.

There was a great raucous when he entered. Josh ran over to him and hugged him, way too generously. Xander let go of my hand, and I watched as he struggled out of Josh's hold. I looked away, embarrassed for him.

I went and sat on a stool at the bar. Out of earshot. Out of inquiring looks. Out of Xander's way while he socialized with his male friends.

Xander kept glancing over at me. Each time I held up my

thumb to let him know I was okay.

As I sipped on a glass of iced water, Josh appeared beside me.

'You know I don't like you, don't you!' Josh's words were curt.

I took another swig of water. 'Now I do,' I said, not making eye contact with him.

'You're stealing the man I love.'

'I'm just dancing with him. It'll be over soon, and you can have him back,' I said, and looked him in the eye. If I could have stepped off the edge of the earth into eternity I would have chosen now—except there is no edge. Imagine how many people could have chosen that option if the world was flat.

A hand rested on Josh's shoulder: Xander's. 'Josh, I'd like you to meet Yolande.'

Josh held out his hand. 'Nice to meet you, Yolande!' he said, changing his entire voice, body posture and attitude.

I didn't place my hand in his. 'We've already met, remember? When you were buying flowers for your boyfriend at Flowers for Fleur!' I gave him a smile, then looked up at Xander. I clicked my fingers pretending to try to remember something. 'Who did you say the flowers were for again?' I knew very well he didn't mention his boyfriend's name at the time.

'Matt,' Josh said. 'He's over there if you'd like to meet him?'

I was confused and looked up at Xander. I was one hundred percent sure the flowers were for him. 'No. It's all good,' I said.

'Are you scared of our type?' he asked.

'Not at all. I just don't like being threatened, as you did to me.' I took a sip of my water.

'Josh?' Xander said.

'Just marking my territory, Alex.'

'And that would be?'

'You.'

Xander raised an eyebrow at Josh. 'I'm not yours, Josh. Best friends, remember.'

I wanted to step out of this conversation, now. I looked at my fingernails. Something I never did, but it reminded me I should have them manicured for the dance competition.

'If you'll excuse us, Yolande and I are going to see a movie.'

I looked at Xander at the mention of my name. He took my hand in his and we left.

Xander took long strides as he walked with a quickened pace.

'I'm sorry. If you were alone that would never have happened, and you would still be with your friends,' I said as we walked.

'It's not your fault. Josh gets insanely jealous of my friends. I thought he would stop once he and Matt connected. But apparently not.'

'I don't blame him. I would fight for my best friend, too.' I gazed ahead of me, looking but not looking. I did fight for my best friend, Mia. That, I did do right.

Chapter Thirty-Three

*D*arcy slid a piece of paper in front of me. It was the additional menu to raise money for medical research for Meniere's disease.

Beverages

Tea with a Teapot Spin
Coffee with a Spoon Swirl
Sundae Milkshake with a Flavored Spiral

Cakes & Other Deliciousness

Vanilla Swirl Cupcake
Blueberry Swirl Cupcake
Chocolate and Cream Spin
Dizzy Fairy Bread
Vertigo Meringue
Meniere's Monster Cookie

'Nice!' I said. 'I'm impressed!'
'Thanks,' Darcy said. He pushed a tray of foods towards me.

'This is how they look,' he said.

Each of the menu items were either in a spiral, decorated with a spiral, or created with a spin. 'They're for sale from today while we have the increasing volume of people entering the store.'

'Gram will be over the moon!' I said. 'Thanks, Darcy. You always go above and beyond. I'll be interested to see how they sell.'

'Me too.'

I looked out to the front of the store. It was busy with people. 'It looks like we're about to open early today. Do you think Gram would mind?'

Darcy shook his head. 'No. It's what Gram would do. She's about kindness to others.'

Any doubt that was in my mind about opening the doors before 8.30am were erased by Darcy's comment.

I walked over to the double French doors and opened them wide, and greeted everyone with a smile as they entered Flowers for Fleur. I looked over at Charlotte. She gave me a mischievous grin as she placed a garland of flowers on her head. I smirked at her, remembering what day it was; Wednesday—wild, wicked Wednesday! I walked over to her with a spring in my work boots, lowered my head, and was rewarded with a matching garland. I looked at her and curtsied. She curtsied back and inclined her head with a giggle, before I went to the workbench. There was a mountain of orders to fulfil.

I leaned against the French doors when I closed them after the last customer had left. The day had been relentless. The flower business was booming, and I had sold out of Fleur's Fury, the flowers arranged in a spiral. Charlotte had requests for garland flower classes, which was something to consider. Gram had decisions to make.

I hurried about cleaning the store and finalizing paperwork so the day could start afresh tomorrow. I looked down at my work boots. I couldn't wait to take them off.

Headlights of a car lit up the road. I grabbed my backpack and said goodbye to Darcy then disappeared out the front doors, locking them after me. Xander held the door open for me and I slid into the passenger seat with relief. I put my head against the headrest and closed my eyes.

'Are you okay?' Xander asked.

'Just tired after a maniac of a day,' I said. I opened my eyes and looked at him. His brow wrinkled. 'What?'

'I need you to be rested for the comp.'

'I'll have Saturday to rest ...'

Xander looked ahead, stretched his hand on the steering wheel and started the engine. I closed my eyes for the short drive to the hall. It was dance session number eleven. Foxtrot night, danced until perfection ...

I fell into bed exhausted.

Xander was sitting on the steps of Flowers for Fleur when I arrived at 7am, an hour late. He was the color of blue, like looking up at the sky at midday while lying in a paddock amongst the golden wheat. Peaceful and satisfying. I slowed my stride as I came closer to him. I didn't have time to talk.

He held out a bio-cup to me. 'Drink this, then eat this!' He handed me a brown paper bag. 'I want you well for the comp.'

What happened to good morning? I took the drink from him and took a sip. 'Hot chocolate?'

'Yes. I chose endurance foods for your energy.'

'Come inside,' I said and unlocked the doors and entered. I

put my backpack in the office and walked to the sales desk to grab the list of morning jobs. 'Talk to me while I get the store ready for opening ...' I looked over at Darcy. 'Morning, Darcy!'

'Morning, Yolande—no good today?'

'Way too busy to be good,' I said.

Xander put his hand on my shoulder and stopped me. 'You need to eat.'

'I will, as I work.'

'No. Sit down and eat, or I'll carry you there!'

I lifted an eyebrow at Xander. He was being ridiculous. I turned to continue to Gram's office and took two steps, when suddenly, Xander picked me up and put me over his shoulder.

He carried me to a table, pulled out a chair and sat me on it. 'I'm not leaving until you've eaten the breakfast I've made for you.'

Darcy stopped at the table with a spoon. 'You're in on this too?' I said to him.

'Xander has a point,' he said, and returned to the coffee machine.

'Fine!' I said, and opened the bag. I pulled out a container of warm porridge and a container of blueberries. I poured the blueberries over the porridge and started to eat.

'The cherries, bananas, walnuts, bagel with peanut butter and pasta with sauce are for you to eat throughout the day. Darcy will bring you tea and chocolate milk to keep you hydrated at given times,' Xander said. He pushed a lock of hair behind my ear, his touch sending a tingle down my spine. 'Full dress rehearsal tonight.'

'I remember.' A twinge of anxiety shot through me, surprising me. 'Can you take Gram's bicycle out the front for me ... and ah ... thanks for the food,' I said.

When Xander re-entered the store, I held the empty porridge bowl up to show him, then poked my tongue out at him. I went to the workbench, grabbed my apron and tied it on while I went to the cold room to collect flowers for Gram's bicycle. When I returned, Xander was leaning on the workbench. 'Anything I can do to help?'

'Here's my list.' I held it in front of him.

His eyes widened. 'Now that's a list! I can take flowers out the front for you.'

'That'd be great, considering I'm late today and you made me sit and eat breakfast.' I looked up from the flowers I was arranging and frowned at him.

'Is there a problem?'

'Are you okay with taking the flowers outside?'

'Yes, why?'

'It's kind of a girly thing for a guy to do ...'

'Yolande ... I'm a ballet dancer. I'm beyond worrying about what people think of me.'

'Are you?'

'Am I what?'

'Do you prefer men?'

He rolled his eyes at me. 'Yolande ... I'm—'

Arms wrapped around me from behind. It was Charlotte, her sherberty perfume floating around me.

'Xander, this is Charlotte, my partner in crime, as fake a florist as they come, like me.' I smiled at Charlotte and she beamed back at me with the warmest light in her eyes.

'Actually, Landi's fakeness is far superior to mine. She may even hold a bit of floral knowledge in that crazy head of hers.' Charlotte grinned and held out her hand to Xander to shake. I watched as Xander placed his hand in hers, Charlotte almost incinerating on the spot.

Charlotte looked back to me; her cheeks flushed. 'Catch you later, Andi, we better get organize d before Gramps comes in and berates us.' She looked back at Xander and inclined her head.

'Nice to meet you, *dearest* Xander!'

Charlotte turned and walked to the sales desk, leaving a trail of virtual glitter flowing behind her.

I gazed up at Xander and shook my head at him.

'You have just witnessed someone going gooey on me.'

'I'd hate to imagine how many girls fall at your feet. Do they know they're wasting their time?'

'They all fall at my feet except for one—you.'

'Is that a problem for your ego?'

'No. It's refreshing, and I like that you're not like the others.'

'Compliment or insult?'

'Compliment ... now, which flowers am I taking outside?'

I picked up the bouquet of various pink pastel flowers I had just made for Gram's bicycle basket. 'These ones. You know where they go. I'll do the others. See you tonight—and ah ... thanks for the food.'

He took the blooms from me and his fingers brushed over mine. My pulse skipped a beat, and I took a moment to collect myself.

He stilled and frowned, while looking deeply into my eyes. I didn't want to go all gooey on him, but I feared it was too late.

'Looking forward to it, and don't forget to eat,' he said, then left.

I blew air between my pursed lips. He was *just* my dance partner, right? I picked up a spray of miniature lilac roses and put them into my hair. Then took a spray of miniature pink roses over to Charlotte.

'He's been in the store before, right? I remember you watching him walk out the doors,' Charlotte said while I decorated her hair with roses.

'Yes. He's my dancing partner.'

'No way! You get to touch him?'

'Yes.'

'He looks a bit like Prince Siegfried from *Swan Lake*.'

'That's because he *is* Prince Siegfried from *Swan Lake*!'

'No. Way! I can't believe it ... so you're dancing with a prince?'

'Something like that ...'

'Has he kissed you?'

'No ... it's professional. We have a competition on Saturday and then we say goodbye.'

'How do you feel about that?'

'Good,' I said. But I knew it wasn't going to be good. I liked him more than I cared to admit.

'What type of dancing are you doing?'

'Ballroom—a waltz and a foxtrot. But I did ballet until I was eighteen.'

'Did you get to kiss the ballet boys?'

I grinned at her. 'I've kissed a good share of danseurs in my time.' I giggled. 'Mia and—' I took a breath. Saying Mia's name out loud still hurt, '—Mia and I ... use to kiss the guys we thought might be gay, to see if we could convince them to go straight.'

Charlotte burst out laughing. 'What's it like kissing a gay guy?'

'Hmm ... it was so long ago I can't remember ...'

'Yes you do. You never forget!'

'I don't kiss and tell.' I wrinkled my nose at Charlotte. She was my favorite fake florist and flower power sister.

'Is Xander gay?'

I pressed my lips together and wobbled my head. 'I'm not sure. I've asked him, but we're always interrupted when he's about to answer my question.'

'I hope he's not,' Charlotte said, her eyes shining.

'It doesn't matter if he is. He's a beautiful dancer, and that's all that matters.' I looked down at my work boots, not believing a word I had just said. 'We'd better get back to work or the shop won't open on time and Gram will be furious! We don't want

Gramps turning into a fire-breathing dragon.'

Charlotte lowered her head. 'I think she's already furious that she can't be here in the store ...'

'I know ... but we have a plan to raise money for research now.'

Charlotte wiped away a tear. 'Let's do this and make your gram well again!'

'Absolutely!'

I returned to the workbench and checked my list of jobs. A pot of tea and a teacup appeared in my vision. I looked up at Darcy. 'Thanks.'

'Are you going out with him?'

'With whom?' I asked.

'You know ... Xander.'

'No, why do you think that?'

'He opens doors for you, he brings you breakfast, and this morning he helped you with flowers. No guy would help you with flowers unless they were trying to impress you.'

'He's being nice to me because I'm his dance partner. That's all.'

'You think?'

'I know!'

'And I know, because I'm a guy!'

'Well, you're wrong. He's just a gentleman who will do anything for anybody—' I stopped talking, lifted my chin and narrowed my eyes at Darcy, 'Much like you.'

Darcy lowered his head and smirked. He looked up at me again. 'I'd better get back to my barista self.' He tapped the workbench twice, turned and left.

I shook my head while I watched him walk away. He was the most backward guy at coming forward. Maybe he needed a dose of liquid courage.

I wiped the crumbs from my lips before I sat the in the car. I had saved the best food till last - the bagel with peanut butter. I had eaten everything in Xander's paper bag today. Just for him. And I had created a paper plane out of the paper bag. Just for him.

Xander sat in the driver's seat and turned on the engine, then looked at me. 'Did you eat everything?'

I tilted my head to the side and threw the paper bag plane at him.

It hit him on the arm and fell into his lap. He picked it up and turned it this way and that. 'You know you could improve the aerodynamics with this ...'

'Is that a challenge, Mr. Parker?'

'Perhaps it is,' he said. 'But for now, we have some dancing to do.' He pulled out onto the road and drove to my parents' house, where I gathered my two dancing gowns and shoes.

We arrived at the hall and Xander unlocked the door and pushed it open.

'Ladies first,' he said with a slight dip of his head.

I stepped inside and stopped. My breath caught. There were fairy lights everywhere. It was beyond beautiful. It was magical. It was like a fairy tale ... except fairy tales weren't real. But here I was with Prince Siegfried ...

I swallowed the lump in my throat to stop myself from crying, and turned back to Xander. 'Did you—'

'Yes.' He gazed deeply into my eyes. Warmth flooded my body, and I closed my eyes.

I shook my head. 'You didn't need to do this—'

'I wanted to make our dress rehearsal special,' he said, and frowned at me.

Had I hurt his feelings telling him he didn't need to decorate the hall?

'It's ... it's amazing and wonderful and ... magnificent, like you.'

'And like you,' he said, his voice gentle.

'Thanks, Alexander Parker. You're a girl's dreams come true!'

Xander smiled at me, took my hand and walked to the church pew with me.

I put my backpack on the seat as I always did.

I turned toward Xander when he started to speak. 'At the dance venue, the first thing we will do is change into our competition clothes, warm up and stretch, like tonight. Tomorrow night is our final practice. It will be short, so we can rest.'

'Okay,' I said. 'Now stand outside the front door while I get changed into my waltz gown.'

'Yolande, I'm used to being in dressing rooms with ballerinas, remember?'

'Please ...' I said in a quiet voice. I didn't want him to see my chest scar again.

'For you, I'll go to the other end of the hall and turn my back, if you like.'

'You won't peek at me?'

'Not until you tell me I can turn around.'

'Okay. But if I see you peeking when you're not supposed to, you're out that door!'

Xander smiled. He grabbed his costume and walked away from me. When I was comfortable with his distance and the sight of his back, I found the opposite corner of the hall and changed into my gown. I looked down at my chest. The scar was well covered. Good.

I walked towards Xander. 'You can turn around now,' I said.

He turned and faced me. He looked damn good in his black dance suit. He lowered his chin and swallowed as he looked at me. A shot of anxiety flared through me. Perhaps I had chosen the wrong gown to dance in.

'Can you zip me up, please,' I said and turned around for him.

I felt the light touch of his finger against my spine as he fastened my gown. My body tingled along the trail he left. It traveled through me, warming me.

'Thanks,' I said, and walked away to put on my dance shoes.

When I stood, fully dressed to dance, I looked over at Xander. He was in the middle of the hall with his hands in his pockets, waiting for me, looking every bit a high-profile fashion model would. No wonder women were spellbound around him. Even I had to fight his magical potion of allure.

As I came closer, I gazed into his blue eyes. He made a deep connection to my eyes and held them, even as I stood in front of him.

'I want to say you look beautiful, but you don't like the word beautiful, and pretty isn't suffice—'

I put my finger over his lips. He didn't need to say anymore. I didn't need to hear words of flattery. 'Will you dance with me?' I said.

'I'd love to,' he whispered, and then the music began ... *Once Upon a Dream*.

Romantic dance session number twelve had started. First, the waltz until three times without error, then a change of ball gown to dance our foxtrot, three times without error.

It couldn't be any more beautiful than dancing under the fairy lights that adorned the hall.

Did he truly know what a gift he was?

Chapter Thirty-Four

What the mirror reflected was a lie. What the mirror showed me was a flawless face with artistic make-up for ballroom dancing, which, like a mask, was hiding the real me ... the one who let go of her best friend's hand when she needed me the most ...

I leaned closer to the mirror, inspecting the face before me. It appeared unblemished. I applied one last burst of hairspray to my hair. Charlotte had created a beautiful up-do with loose curls framing my face, and added miniature roses from Flowers for Fleur.

I brushed my hands down my waltz ball gown, rechecking that my chest scar was completely concealed. I turned while I looked at myself in the mirror. The colored cascading flowers looked perfect on the white gown.

Flowers for Fleur. For Gram.

I hoped she was here to see me dance with *the* Prince Siegfried.

I stepped out of the make-up room and looked for Xander. He was talking to a dancer, dressed just like him. Tonight, he was the color of red, of passion, of love, of power, of sensuality. I sucked in a shuddering breath.

The dancer's eyes moved from Xander to me. Xander followed the dancer's gaze and turned to face me. He stilled, and his breath hitched. He placed his hand over his heart and bowed a little, then took two ballet steps toward me before he corrected his walk to that of the other ballroom dancers.

He stopped before me. 'Wow!' he said. 'Beautiful.'

'Wow, yourself,' I said back, ignoring his use of the word beautiful. He reminded me of the world saving prince in all the fairy tales. But when I looked around the room, it was filled with princes. Maybe they weren't so unique after all ...

He took my hand in his and kissed the back of it, his lips warm and soft. Warmth rushed through me like a warm apple cider on a freezing cold day. I wanted to capture the "Xander Effect", bottle it, and keep it forever, for I knew it would all come to an end after midnight.

'Let's warm-up,' he said. I wanted to tell him I was already warm, but I didn't. He took my hand in his and I followed him closely, inhaling his scent of citrus with a hint of liquorice, vanilla, lavender, amber and sandalwood.

'Does anyone here know who you are?' I asked while we stretched.

Xander looked around. 'There's only one other ballet dancer I recognize. But we'll keep each other's secrets.'

'You gave yourself away, Zan.'

'When?'

'The first two steps you took towards me were the steps of a danseur.'

'That's because I was distracted,' he said.

'By what?'

'Whom ...'

I rolled my eyes at him. 'Whom?'

'You.'

I turned my face to the side as I felt my cheeks warm. I looked back at him. 'That's because you were waiting for me to throw a paper plane at you!'

Xander narrowed his eyes at me. 'Yes. I had to be on alert in case of an incoming bomber.'

We warmed-up and stretched for fifteen minutes and rehearsed a couple of our steps. Xander looked up at the dance call board and our names were illuminated. Our final waltz was about to begin.

Xander took both of my hands in his. 'This is when the magic happens, when you and I become one. Don't think, just feel ...'

I wanted to tell him the magic had already happened. But I didn't.

Xander stood beside me and took my hand in his. The doors opened, and we stepped out onto the dance floor. An applaud echoed through the theater and Xander dropped my hand as we separated for the start of our waltz. It would be spectacular, there was no doubt. Xander was a gifted choreographer and he had incorporated some clever ballet moves into our routine. It definitely gave our performance the "wow" factor.

I stilled in my position and waited for the music ... *Once Upon a Dream* ... and then it began. My nervous energy transported me into another dimension, where it was just me and Xander, dancing in a magical castle where no past existed, no future, just the present, in a way I chose to be.

Within a minute and a half our waltz had finished. I inhaled deeply, like I hadn't taken a breath during the entire performance. When I looked into Xander's eyes, they were bright with unadulterated passion. I wanted to keep my eyes connected to his, swimming in pure delight. It would hurt to break our deep soul contact, one I had never known before. I felt like I was tied to him by an unknown force, but I had to break it, before I fell too deeply.

Xander stood from his kneeling position, stepped closer and closed his eyes, then kissed me on the forehead. 'UN-believable,' he whispered through smiling lips as he stood next to me while we bowed to the judges. He took my hand in his, and we walked with grace across the dance floor, smiling, like seasoned professional ballroom dancers did.

'UN-believable?' I asked once we were in the warm-up room again. *Had I done something wrong?*

'Yes. I never knew you could dance like that.'

Oh ... that ... 'I disappeared into the music and let it transport me to another place and time.' *Away from the last three years of my life, to a time where the sun shone brightly, and no dark clouds ever entered my life.*

He gazed into my eyes. 'You blew me away!'

My stomach fluttered. 'Good.'

We parted ways and I went to change into my foxtrot gown.

Xander was standing by the window, looking out, a million miles away.

'Hey,' I said from behind him. My foxtrot gown was white with a red rose vine that grew from the hem and up and over my shoulder.

Xander turned around. 'Hey,' he said, 'look at you—perfect ... stunning!'

'Look at you—black pants and a white button up shirt!' I wondered if he received my sarcasm. There were a million and one ballroom dancing gowns for women to choose from with twenty million color variations. But men could choose from suits or pants and a shirt, with limited color variations for the waltz or foxtrot.

'I know ... sexy, hey?'

'On you, yes.' I meant what I said, and took a deep breath.

He looked down at my white dancing shoes, 'No sparkly work boots?'

'Do you think we'd get extra points?'

'Definitely!'

I gave him a small smile. 'Let's go and warm up.'

'Let's,' Xander said.

I wished time would slow down while we rehearsed our steps. After this dance, Xander and I had no need to see each other.

When our names illuminated on the dance board, my heart dropped. This dance would be bittersweet.

I felt Xander's fingers wrap around mine and I calmed. 'For Gram,' he said.

I almost crumbled in an emotional blob. I held Xander's hand tighter. 'For Gram,' I whispered.

We walked onto the dance floor and our fingers lingered in connection before they parted. I moved to the corner and lowered my head, and put my hand over my heart, then waited for the music ... *Perfect* ... I took a deep breath when it began.

For Gram.

I could barely remember where we were when the music finished. I was completely lost in Xander and his touch, his eye connection, his emotion, his gentleness, his passion, and his presence that I had melted into as we danced, like our two souls had become one and we were the only people in the room.

Xander put his arm around my waist, and we bowed to the judges.

'You nailed it, Yolande,' he whispered, then smiled.

'You think?'

'I know.' He kissed me on the forehead, and we turned and left the dance floor, walking with grace to a loud applause.

I was filled with a dancer's high. I was so unbelievably high that I never wanted to return to reality. Maybe I could just float away into the heavens and remain in that state permanently.

Xander threaded his fingers through mine when we were ushered to the green room to wait for the dancing results. I looked around at the professional ballroom dancers.

Did they know I was a fake ballroom dancer? I stilled in that moment, wondering how Xander and I were able to compete against the elite around us.

Xander grabbed my hand and we ran. He, in his black trousers and white button-up shirt, and me, in my foxtrot dancing gown. We stopped underneath the ancient tree in the field outside the arts theater. I looked up at the light bulbs hanging artistically from the lower branches while trying to catch my breath, and smiled. It was beyond beautiful.

'Take your shoes off,' Xander said. 'Let's climb the tree!'

I looked at my shoes, my protection, even though they weren't my work boots.

'I'll look after you,' he said. He crouched down and loosened the buckle on my dance shoe. When he lifted my leg, I placed my hand on his shoulder while he slipped the shoe off. He did the same with the other shoe. Somehow, it felt intimate. I took a deep breath to calm his magical potion flowing through me.

The grass was cool and soft under my bare feet. It had been a long time since I had felt the caress of grass against my skin, the last time being when I stood beside Mia by the ocean cliff, three years ago.

Xander rose smoothly and slowly to standing position before me, his eyes dark. My hand was still on his shoulder, something I had done a million times when we danced. But this felt different, somehow.

I felt nervous. And scared. Scared of my heart being hurt.

'You go first. I'm right behind you. I'll catch you if you fall.' His eyes were connected to mine like he was looking into my soul, and that curious heat traveled through me.

I looked up at the tree and smiled, feeling free. Feeling happy.

I inhaled deeply, then hitched up my ball gown and started to climb, giggling, until I found a thick branch where Xander could sit with me.

Xander smiled as he inched beside me, our thighs touching, my heart melting.

'What?' I said. Maybe it was the thrill of climbing a tree. Or maybe he was still high from dancing?

'I love your giggle. It's nice to hear.'

He was right. I didn't giggle that much, or laugh for that matter. 'I still can't believe we got placings in our dances with all those professionals!'

'That's why I chose to dance with you—the judges had never seen you dance before, so they would really focus on you. Someone new and fresh and invigorating ...'

'And you—'

'No. They knew I was a danseur. I saw the recognition on their faces when we walked onto the dance floor.'

'How did we even get to dance there? It isn't the norm for unknowns to compete with the knowns in a competition like that!'

'I was handed a wild card for the event. And I wanted to try something different.'

'Nice,' I said, and smiled at him. 'I must thank you ... I loved every moment of the ballroom dancing! I haven't felt this happy in a long time.'

Xander lowered his head and grinned. 'That would be the endorphins ...'

'And you,' I said, my voice quieter.

Xander looked up at me and our eyes met. His chest rose as

he took a deep breath.

'Do you miss performing in front of thousands?' I asked.

He stilled. 'Yes.' His eyebrows gathered in.

'Why did you stop?'

'I need to finish my medical degree, plus I want to continue with biomedical science.'

'Is that for you, or your father?'

Xander shifted on the tree branch. I was digging deeper in an area that hurt in his life. 'Medicine to please my father, biomedical science for me. I want to contribute to advances in modern medical science ... I want to develop treatments for diseases—if it's at all possible.'

'But it's not your passion.'

'I won't be able to dance forever. You know very well that one injury can end the life of a dancer. I need something else to become passionate about.'

I shook my head at him. 'Helping people ... you're too nice.'

'Insult or compliment?'

'Neither. Just a statement of admiration.'

He raised his eyebrows at me. 'Admiration?'

'Yes. Not gooey admiration, an intellectual admiration. I love a brilliant mind that has compassion for others.'

He breathed a sigh of relief.

'My opinion doesn't matter that much, Dr. Alexander Parker.'

'To me it does,' he said, holding my gaze.

I lowered my head. If he knew what I had done, my opinion wouldn't matter to him.

I looked up at the stars through the tree branches and swung my bare feet. 'I wonder what it's like being a star, emitting a bright light for all to see, all the time, with no darkness to be found within?'

'Boring for the star,' Xander said, surprising me, 'amazing for us to look up at and wonder.'

I looked at him. 'Boring? How?'

'The star can't see its own brilliance, its own illumination. Much like you.'

I breathed slowly. 'Are you saying I'm boring?'

'No. I'm saying you don't see the bright light you emit for all to see.'

It's because I'm dark inside ... so dark ... if you knew, you would run ...

I looked down at my hand and stretched it to push out my anxiety. Xander put his hand over mine. I had nothing to say to him. I wanted to go home now. He was making me feel uncomfortable. I wasn't who he thought I was. We needed a topic change.

'Would you rather be a moon or a star?' I asked.

He pressed his lips together. 'Hmmm ... the moon I think.'

'Why's that?'

'Because it dances around the earth, showing us an ever-changing profile and light ... sometimes hiding from us. It has control of something that is so much greater than itself—the tide ... and it has a dark side—one that no one can see. What about you?'

Xander had just partly described me. I danced around life, not wanting to participate fully, and changed how people perceived me with the mask I wore ... and I had a dark side, a very dark side. I was a moon walking on the earth ... incessantly hiding my dark side.

What would I rather be? 'A star, I think ... because it's mysterious. There's more to the star than we can see and understand. Perhaps it's not a star at all, but a planet that allows souls to walk on its sacred ground ... souls who give love and receive love, souls who have no darkness ... or evil, souls who resonate in harmony with the vibration of the universe and of our Creator and of eternal life.' I kept my eyes on the stars and the moon in wonder, until the clouds hid them, not wanting to share the glory of them anymore. Selfish.

A deep rumbling of thunder sounded in the distance. 'Trees are not the best place to be during a storm,' I said and looked at Xander.

'Unless you don't value your life,' he said, and raised an eyebrow at me. Did he know something I didn't want him to know? He started to climb down the tree, branch by branch, and I followed.

As I reached the lower section of the tree trunk, Xander put his hands on my waist like a danseur would. He helped me to a soft landing on the grass. I turned around and smiled at him.

'A smile of relief from climbing down the tree, or are you laughing at me, Andi?'

I shook my head. 'I'm laughing at me, Andy!'

'Do share ...'

'I had a vision of me in a white tutu and you as the prince, dressed in your ballet tights and a magnificent, grand coat.'

Xander tilted his head to the side a little. He placed his finger under my chin, lifting my face to his. When I looked up into his blue eyes, I felt their pull on me.

My whole life came to a point, a destination, right then. I think it had always been him, even before we met.

I placed my hand on the side of his face. His skin was warm, a slight stubble to the touch. My eyes wandered to his lips— his sensuous lips. I ran my thumb over them, wanting—no, needing him to kiss me for a moment in time, where he could ignite a spark of light in the darkness inside of me. Just for a moment in time where I could feel like a normal woman again. Not this broken, damaged, self-loathing one, with a crying soul.

I closed my eyes and his soft lips touched mine. Once. Twice. Caressing. Lingering. Sending a warmth through every cell of my body, awakening parts of me I had shut down three years ago.

And my tears fell. They trickled. Down the right side of my face, exposing me.

And I ran.

Across the field to the lights in the distance, with tears flowing and dripping from me. I wanted to run to the edge of the earth and step off into eternity, where the souls of love and light were. To that place where darkness was obliterated.

I heard Xander's voice behind me, calling, beseeching, getting closer. I turned to see how close he was, then stepped out onto the road where the lights were—and the sound of tires screeching. The smell of burning rubber. And the blast of a horn.

Once my heart started to beat again, I rushed to the door of a taxi, opened it and clambered inside.

'Go ... please ... just go!' I said through a broken voice. I looked out at Xander as he stopped on the roadside, holding my shoes, pinching the bridge of his nose.

'Are you okay, ma'am?' the driver asked.

'Yes. I just need to go home ...' I said, and looked down at my bare feet.

I should have worn my work boots ...

Chapter Thirty-Five

The painting before me wasn't working. Dr. Jones said that art was a healing outlet for me. But not today.

Damn you, Alexander! You can't have feelings for me. Ever. And I can't have feelings for you. Not me. The monster. Happiness couldn't dwell inside of me. Especially after—

The door burst open.

I turned and he stood there, holding my dance shoes.

His eyes were naked with emotion and he clenched his teeth. He was the color of light red, of sensitivity, of longing, of love, and my heart screamed.

'I kiss you, and you run?' His voice broke. His eyes moved to the ugly scar on my right cheek. The one I hid from others so carefully with impeccably applied make-up since that terrible day that I wished had never happened.

Xander swallowed hard and sucked in a deep breath. I then watched as his face contorted while his eyes followed my facial scar to my chest that ran down to my exposed nipple.

I pulled my tank shirt up and turned away from him, panicked and wide-eyed. My studio was supposed to be my safe place.

Damn you, Alexander!

I stilled as the soft patter of feet grew closer. Ballet feet. Ballet dancers walked differently to other people. The sound stopped, and I felt the heat from his body, and smelled a spicy blend of cedarwood and cocoa-vanilla scent. I wanted him to go away.

Far away.

He wrapped his arms around me.

I dropped my head forward and sobbed.

He turned me in his arms and I buried my face into his shoulder and cried harder. And I couldn't stop. Ugly, loud sobs. Ugly, like the darkness inside of me.

His arms tightened. Tighter than I thought possible without squeezing every living breath out of me. Without breaking me. Maybe he could push all my broken bits back together.

When I could cry no more, I took a step back from him. I kept the right side of my face turned away from him.

'Don't look at me!' I spat at him, filled with dread and shame. So much shame. So. Much. Shame. I held in a sob.

Xander placed a finger under my chin and turned my face towards his. I kept my eyes focussed on the floor. I couldn't bear to see his reaction to the scar on my face.

'Fucking bastard!' he said in a barely audible voice that was fuming with anger. 'Look at me, Yolande ...' His voice was gentle.

I gave a slight shake of my head. I couldn't look at him. I wasn't worthy. The strength I used every moment of every day to project a different me was gone. Empty.

Xander moved. He knelt in front of me and into my line of vision.

Damn you, Alexander!

He looked up at me and a tear rolled down his face. On that same side. That same place.

He reached over and grabbed a red oil pastel. He held it in front of me. 'Draw your scar on me,' he whispered.

I stiffened. 'I can't ... I can't do it. I'm not a monster like those two men!'

'Do it,' he said. This time his voice more forceful. He stood in front of me and looked down into my eyes.

He placed the red oil pastel into my hand.

I hesitated before I lifted it to his face. His perfect, beautiful face. I shook my head. 'I can't.'

Xander raised his eyebrows at me. 'You can.'

I pressed my lips into a hard line, then placed the tip of the oil pastel under his eyelashes and followed the line of his tear down his cheek and stopped at his jaw. I hung my arm by my side. Doing this to him hurt like hell.

'And the rest,' he said.

'The rest?'

'Whoever did this to you followed the trail of your tear, didn't he?'

I inhaled a shuddering breath at the memory.

Johnno looked down at the knife he held in his grubby hand and grinned. He turned it from side to side, the light reflecting off it, onto my face. My eyes burned. I didn't want to cry in front of these despicable excuses of human beings. I widened my eyes to contain my tears, but I was betrayed by one. I looked up at his face. His eyes followed my tear as it rolled down my cheek to my jawline, where it stopped.

I swallowed slowly as I felt the tear gaining volume and became too heavy to stop there. It dropped onto my chest and trickled down to my nipple.

'Who's the weak one now? You're crying, like a typical girl!' He moved the point of the blade to where the tear started on my cheekbone, just below my eye. The tip of the knife pierced my skin. I closed my eyes as I felt the sharp cutting of my flesh, with a searing pain that screamed at my core. With a slow, torturous speed, the tip of

the knife traced the path of my tear—down my cheek to my jawline, then onto my chest.

I held my breath as the knife went in a direct path, following the tear, to my nipple—piercing, cutting, tearing.

I swallowed hard, standing dead still. Everything inside me was trembling. I could feel blood running down my face, and dripping onto my chest, dribbling, running further down my naked body, pooling at my feet.

'Yes,' I said to answer Xander's question, my voice wavering and nausea rising.

Xander unbuttoned his shirt and dropped it onto the floor. 'Do it.'

I looked at his body of perfection. Of defined muscles born of ballet. Of muscles that made every girl and some guys swoon. I shook my head. I couldn't blemish his magnificence, his luminosity.

He raised an eyebrow at me. 'Do. It.' His voice cracked as he whispered.

I hesitated, then placed the point of the oil pastel onto his collarbone. I drew in a direct line down his chest. His muscular, unblemished chest. As I continued towards his nipple, he stopped breathing. Just like I had on that terrible day. I looked into his anguished eyes and kept drawing the scar in red, just like my blood on that day, that terrible day, and stopped at the areola. I dropped the oil pastel to the floor, emotionally exhausted. My arm fell beside me, lifeless.

Xander stumbled back from me, almost losing his balance, and lifted his chin. He fell to his knees with his hands behind his head and cried.

I watched him. I didn't know what to do. And then I held my hand out for him. The same hand that was covered in blood, holding on to Mia's on that terrible day. Xander placed his hand in mine and rose. Slowly, keeping eye contact with me.

'Do you want a glass of water?' I asked. I didn't know what else to say. I didn't realize drawing on him like that would cause such an intense reaction. Had I damaged him in some way? Did I take away some of his luminosity?

He shook his head and sat on my studio stool. 'Now make it beautiful ...' he said, his eyes holding mine.

'How?'

'With art ... like a tattoo ...'

I swallowed. Scars couldn't be beautiful. They were better hidden. If you turned it into a piece of art, people would ask questions about it. I could never make mine "beautiful".

But for his sake, I gathered a variety of colored oil pastels and started to create a tattoo of art on his glorious face, that beautiful face I so loved; born of light, not darkness.

I worked slowly, meticulously, creating a winding green vine with colored flowers, a teardrop, and an added heart. Each time I looked into Xander's eyes with caution, his pupils were large, drinking me in. He watched my every movement. And sometimes ... just sometimes, I allowed my eyes to stay in his for a little longer, so I could steal some of his courage, his light, his love, hoping it would make the darkness inside me tremble in fear and want to escape.

I stepped back from him when I had completed his scar art. It was beautiful. But only because he was beautiful to start with. He was a never-ending source of light that shone like the stars in the heavens.

'My turn,' he said.

'Your turn for what?' My chin trembled.

'To make your scars beautiful ...'

I burst out laughing. The task he had set himself was impossible.

'Sit,' he said. 'Please.'

I obeyed, grasping at the glimmer of hope that somehow my scars could be beautiful. I watched as his eyes wandered over my scars, from my bottom eyelashes to my jaw to my collar bone to my areola. He turned away from me and gathered some oil pastels, then faced me, connecting our eyes.

'Trust me?' he asked.

I frowned at him, trying to ignore the poison of anxiety that traveled through my veins.

I nodded. Slowly. Yes, I did trust him.

'Good,' he said. He looked deeply into my eyes again, like he was looking for the truth of my trust. He lifted his finger and placed it under my eyelashes, then traced my scar with the lightest touch. He followed it down my cheek to the bottom of my jaw, and let his finger drop onto my collarbone, and traced my scar, moving all the way to the areola.

He took his finger away, then repeated the action, this time with his lips, kissing my scar. I closed my eyes as a fire started deep within me, spreading quickly through my entire body. I focussed on the sensation he had awakened, and I yearned. I wanted to reach out to him and pull him inside of me. But I couldn't. If I did, all his light would vanish. And I needed his light like I needed the air to breathe.

I opened my eyes when I felt an oil pastel touch my skin. I watched Xander's face as he worked, his eyes connecting with mine every now and again.

He was gentle. And somehow, he filled every stroke of color with a love I could only imagine existed. Who was this beautiful man, and why had our paths crossed in such a profound way?

Xander stepped back from me. 'Aah—my masterpiece. So much better than yours!'

My body stiffened at the loss of contact with him, and my breath was taken from me. For a moment, I had to relearn how to breathe.

'Not!' I said, gathering my senses, and grabbed his hand and pulled him over to the mirror.

We stood, face to face, neither of us looking into the reflective surface.

'On the count of three, face the mirror with me,' I said.

Xander reached for my hand.

'One, two ... three.' I turned at the same time as Xander.

We looked at our own scar art, since we had already seen each other's.

I burst out laughing at Xander's wonky attempt.

Xander looked at me with an infectious smile. 'My work here is done!'

'Meaning?'

'You can now look at your scars and laugh! On the other hand, your artwork is intricate and ... stunning.' He leaned in closer to the mirror to look at my artistry.

'And covers your ugliness!' I said and waited for his reaction.

He looked at me with a serious look, then broke out in a wide smile. 'Ah ... the Yolande I adore is back.'

'Maybe,' I said.

He handed me his phone. 'I want a picture of me with my new tattoo!'

'Say cheese,' I said and captured the moment.

'Now one of you, and then us, together.'

I frowned. 'Only on my phone.' That way I had control of it.

'Agreed.'

Xander took photos on my phone, one of each of us by ourselves, then together, and finally, cheek to cheek. When he returned my phone to me our fingers touched. And that spark was there, the one that lit my entire being.

Xander gazed into my eyes, put his finger under my chin and moved his lips to mine, slowly.

He kissed me so gently, so carefully, it almost broke my heart.

I sagged against him and he pulled back, and dropped his forehead against mine.

'I can't be what you want me to be,' I said, trying to catch my breath.

'I can't be just friends with you,' Xander whispered. 'I've tried, but I want more.'

'I can't give you more.' My words hung heavily in the air.

'Love conquers, Yolande. Trust me. Let me in,' he said, his voice breaking.

I stepped back from him. 'I can't ... not yet.'

'Then I'll wait for you.'

'Xander—'

'The moment I saw you at Flowers for Fleur, I knew ... when you laughed at me—no girl had ever done that to me, and yet you—you made me feel nervous. I wanted you then. When your gram insisted that you tag along with her bicycle, my heart jumped with joy at the thought of spending time with you. You have no idea how much I enjoyed listening to you make up stories about what you did for a job. Your creative construing of your work was simply genius.'

I pushed my hand into a tray of blue paint, lifted it out and placed it onto Xander's chest, leaving a hand-print there, right over his heart.

He looked down at it and placed his hand over the wet paint, then pressed his hand to my left cheek. 'This is what I love about you—your spontaneity. I know no other girl who would climb a tree in her ball gown. You make moments into precious memories I never want to forget.'

'I think you have that the wrong way around, Xander—you, who decorated the hall with fairy lights—'

'For you ... because I wanted to impress you.'

'Consider me impressed. Who wouldn't be impressed by everything you do? Who wouldn't fall at your feet the moment you appeared?'

'You ...'

I gazed into his eyes. 'Xander ... you're reacting to our closeness while we were dancing, to the sexual tension of the dance—a common phenomenon between dance partners.' The words were a lie for me. I loved him. There was no doubt about the way I felt.

'No, I'm not, Yolande. I dance with women all the time and I've never wanted to kiss them. I've never wanted to spend every waking moment with them. I've never counted down the hours, the minutes until I saw them again.'

'It's the love potion of the music ...'

He took a step closer. 'No. When you left our dance school, I was shattered ... and then we met again, by accident or by fate. I don't know, but you're the one I've been waiting for.'

I took his hand in mine, threading our fingers. 'When you wake up in the morning and relive seeing my scars, you'll have second thoughts. You are perfection. And I am so far from it we may as well be living on different planets—'

'And still, I would find you—please, Yolande, it's not about physical beauty, it's about heart, mind and soul connection. Please ... be mine.'

I wanted to say yes. I so wanted to say yes. I shook my head. 'I can't ... yet.'

'Then I'll hold on to hope ...' He gazed deeply into my eyes, his brows furrowed. I had hurt him by rejecting him. I wanted to say I was sorry. But I couldn't. He was better off without me.

I picked up his shirt and threw it to him. 'I've got some art to do. It's for Gram.'

Xander looked deeply into my eyes and nodded, stepped forward and kissed my forehead, then left.

Chapter Thirty-Six

I sat on the regular chair with the imprint of my butt on it. The door opened with a slight squeak. Dr. Jones was dressed in a black jacket and long black pencil skirt with a white button-up blouse. Her deep red court shoes were stylish. Unlike my steel-capped safety boots ...

'Yolande.' Dr. Jones' voice was soothing, like the smell of freshly baked bread.

I nodded before I stood, then followed her into the room. Dr. Jones put a light hand on my shoulder.

'I'll lie on the couch today,' I said before she asked me the question. The couch was better when I didn't want to make eye contact with her.

I made myself comfortable and ran my hand over the soft fabric. Dr. Jones went to make of pot of tea. I heard the boiling water and the chink of the china teacups and saucers. I closed my eyes and knitted my fingers together before I placed them on my stomach. I needed to talk about Xander.

At the sound of approaching footsteps, I opened my eyes. Dr. Jones placed two teacups and saucers on the table. I reached over and picked one up. The warmth of the brew touched my lips when I sipped it and I relaxed a little. Aah ... tea. *Water is the mother of tea, a teapot its father, and fire the teacher:* a Chinese Proverb. Another tea saying. In Dr. Jones office. Every. Single. Time.

'What brings you here today, Andi?'

'Xander kissed me.'

'Tell me about Xander.'

I took a sip of my tea. 'He's a ballet dancer, a danseur, a ballerino, my ballroom dancing partner for one night, as you know. He's studying medicine. He's beautiful and he wants to be more than a friend with me.'

'Does that worry you?'

'Yes.'

'Why?'

'Because of my scars. Because of what happened ... you know ...'

'When people love, it's not love for the physical body, they love what's inside you, so your scars won't matter.'

'So they say. But when it comes to me, it's hard to believe.'

'Perhaps it's because of the trauma you suffered when you acquired the scars.'

I took a deep breath. The terrible day of the scars never got any easier.

'Are you scared of love, Yolande?'

I hesitated before I answered. 'Yes.'

'What about your parents and grandparents. Do you love them?'

'Yes, but it's like I was born loving them.'

'Not all families love. Some hate.'

'I know ... but my family is love.'

'So, it seems your fear about love is conditional on people outside your family. Is that correct?'

'Xander in particular.'

'Love comes by grace. It has its own will and timing. It can't be planned. It goes beyond the physical, Yolande. It is its own law. When you are treated with love, your heart can feel that love, and responds.'

Dr. Jones wrote some notes in her book. Seriously, it would be quicker for her to type on a laptop computer or a tablet.

'Have you spoken to Mia yet?'

I looked at the picture on the wall. It always came back to talking to Mia. Every. Single. Time. It was getting old. 'No.'

'In my experience, once you have spoken to her, you will feel a sense of relief, a sense of healing, a sense of closure, and will be able to overcome some of your obstacles. What are you scared of regarding a relationship with Xander?'

'I'm scared of getting hurt.'

'That's not uncommon.'

I almost rolled my eyes. Why did she not say, "that's common" or, "that's normal"?

'Relationships are about risk. Anyone who enters a relationship of any sort is taking a risk, whether it be a friendship relationship, work, teams, physical, or emotional relationship. What if you go out with Xander and it works well? What will you gain?'

'Someone I can trust. Someone I can love. Someone who will love me, unconditionally, as I would them.'

'And what will happen if it doesn't work out?'

'I'll have a broken heart, and will be by myself ...'

'A broken heart will mend, and you're already by yourself ... the way I see it, you have far more to gain, than to lose.'

I finished my cup of tea and put the teacup onto the saucer.

'Thanks, Dr. Jones. Our session was what I needed, as usual.' I stood, and so did Dr. Jones. We walked to her door together.

She leaned forward to open the door for me. 'You and Xander danced beautifully. Thank you for inviting me along to the competition. It was very romantic.'

I gave Dr. Jones a rare smile. 'It was way beyond everything I thought it would be.'

'I'm glad. Don't overthink, Yolande.'

'Hmmm, you know me too well ...'

Flowers for Fleur was busy when I walked through the front doors of the store. I should have been quicker at Dr. Jones's office. I looked to my right at Darcy. He was making coffee, but he looked up at me and gave me a quick nod. I looked straight ahead at Charlotte. She smiled at me and inclined her head to her right.

I looked to my left, and there stood Gram at the workbench of flower imagination. She was the color of pink, the type that kissed the ocean at dawn, filling you with love at the exquisite color palette that adorned the sky.

I smiled, walked over to her at once and hugged her, gently. 'Gram, it's so lovely to see you. Today is a great day!'

'Landi, darling! Today *is* a great day. I'm here. Please go to the cold room and collect some red roses in their bud form, twelve to be exact.'

'Sure. Anything else while I'm in there freezing?'

'No thanks.'

I placed the twelve red roses on the workbench for Gram.

'Oh ... love ... eternal. Your grandfather gave me twelve roses when we first started going out. They mean *be mine* ...'

Xander ... 'Gram, you're a hopeless romantic!'

'I know. That's how Flowers for Fleur came about.' She gathered the roses together and tied them with twine, then wrapped them in soft green translucent paper and finally in natural brown paper and tied a red bow around it. 'You danced wonderfully with Xander at the competition. It was so romantic.'

'You came?'

'Yes. We made it home just in time for my head to spin.'

'I'm sorry about your vertigo, Gram. But I'm glad you came to see me dance with Prince Siegfried.' We both giggled.

Gramps arrived then. He collected the flower orders and left.

I moved about the store with enthusiasm. Was it the thrill of dancing with Xander making me feel alive again? Was it that he had declared his hand to me? Or was it a combination of both? Perhaps it was because Gram was here in the store today, making the world seem right again.

At 2pm, I went outside to spritz the flower blooms with water. As I was rearranging some flowers there was a loud sound from inside, followed by running footsteps. I rushed through the doors to find Charlotte next to Gram and glass splintered on the floor. Charlotte was holding Gram's arm, blood dripping through her fingers. Blood dripping, like on that day ...

I sucked in a sharp breath through my closed teeth and tensed. My heart rate spiked as my head began to swirl. Blood. It's just blood. I visualized my seven pieces of artwork and calmed almost at once.

I ran to the first aid kit and grabbed a bandage and returned to Gram. 'Are you spinning?' I asked, taking over from Charlotte with Gram's arm.

'No. I just dropped to the ground, without warning.'

I assessed the cut she had sustained. It needed stitching. I bandaged it to stop the blood flow while Charlotte swept the glass from the floor.

I texted Gramps.

ME: *Gram's had an accident. No vertigo. Stitches needed.*

GRAMPS: *I'll be there soon.*

I helped Gram to her office and sat her in the wing chair.

'Hate is not a strong enough word for this damn disease.' Tears slid down her cheeks.

My heart cried for her. Life was so unfair.

As Gramps took Gram out of the store, she walked amongst the flowers: smelling, touching, crying.

I had to look away. It was excruciating to watch. I concentrated hard on holding in my need to cry uncontrollably.

I rode my bicycle home slowly after the closure of the store. My thoughts wandered to finding someone else in our family to take over the store in my place. I needed to go back to the Base and resume my engineering life. Flowers weren't me. Xander would have to understand.

If only Charlotte was family—she knew how to run the store. She knew everything about it to keep it going successfully. But, she wasn't family ...

How was I going to tell Gram and Gramps I was leaving, and Xander?

Chapter Thirty-Seven

After three days, I still couldn't find the right words to tell my grandparents about returning to the Base. Gram was not well. I would have to wait until this cluster of symptoms settled, and then I would tell them of my plans.

I texted Xander.

ME: *Thanks for the 12 red roses. They are divine.*

XANDER: *You're welcome. Missing you.*

ME: *Missing you too. Let's have the paper plane challenge soon.*

XANDER: *I would love that. Just deep in study at the moment.*

ME: *Okay. Tell me when you're free.*

XANDER: *I will. xx*

ME: *xx*

I would talk to Xander about leaving while we flew paper planes. He would have something to distract him from my words that would hurt him. He would have something to look at instead of me. And then I wouldn't have to see the pain in his eyes. I placed my hand over my heart where it ached.

Darcy walked over to me. He ran his hand through his hair and pulled his eyebrows together. 'Your grandfather called. He wants you to call him back. Immediately.'

'I will. Thanks, Darcy.' I wondered why Gramps didn't call me first.

I walked into the cold room amongst the flowers and dialed Grampapa's number. He picked up before the first ring even finished.

He started to speak. I froze at his words and ran from the cold room out to the store, my work boots slamming against the floorboards.

I dropped my phone. 'I've got to go, Darcy!'

I retrieved my bicycle from the office, wheeled it between the flower displays, out the front doors, mounted it and rode to the tallest building in Tarrin: the Crown of Tarrin.

The hotel elevator was taking too long to arrive, so I ran up fifteen flights of stairs and walked out on to the roof of the building, sucking in deep breaths.

I stopped when I saw Gram standing on the edge of the roof.

The skin on the back of my neck prickled and a shiver ran down my spine. She was no longer the color of pink. She was the color of black. Pitch black, with an electrical storm.

I took slow steps towards her. 'What are you doing, Gram?' I asked, keeping a gentle tone in my voice like jumping off a building was an ordinary everyday event. I ignored my heart beating double time.

'I want to end it!' she said, looking over the edge of Tarrin's only hotel.

'No. You can't. I love you, Gram! My heart will break!' My voice cracked while my thoughts scrambled to understand. But then I did. Perfectly. I too had wanted to escape the pain of this world after that terrible day of the scars; mentally and physically. But I'm so glad I didn't. There were beautiful things in my life now, and I was thankful to be here to experience them. Each day wasn't always perfect. But it was getting there.

'But it's my life, and I get to choose, Landi. I don't want to live this way anymore. I'm not living. I'm like a passenger trapped inside a vehicle on a cruel journey of which I have no choice and no control ... I'm done.'

'No, Gram! What about Gramps?' My voice was desperate. My chest tightened, and my limbs started to tremble.

'I'm right here, Yolande—it's what Gram wants.' He stepped out from the shadows.

I turned towards my grandfather's voice. His color was a swirling mass of dark gray mixed with black. He was betraying us all. And at that very moment, I hated him.

Gram sighed. I turned back to her. 'Vertigo from heights is nothing like the vertigo of Meniere's—the cruel and unforgiving Meniere's disease ... oh how I abhor it!' she said.

'What about the people below who will find you. They will be forever traumatized—that's not fair to them! You say you love us—but how can you do this to us?' I had found a sudden strength in my voice. The one that wanted to be heard.

Gram looked down towards the pavement far below, and the wind blew her hair. 'You say you love me—but why won't you let me choose?'

'You're not alone in this, Gram ... let me help you!'

Gram sobbed. 'I wanted to kill my Meniere's vertigo with height vertigo. It seemed fitting really ...'

I held out my right hand to Gram, my pulse thrumming all the way down to my fingertips. If she took it, I would hold it so tight that it would be impossible to ever let it go ... not like with Mla ... I was trembling.

Gram looked at my hand and let out a breath.

Panic seized me. I could hear my heartbeat thrashing in my ears. 'Please, Gram ... I need you,' I whispered. I stretched my hand desperately further towards her. 'Please, Gram. Hold my hand.' I held in my sob.

Gram's eyes softened as she looked at me, and placed her hand into mine. I swallowed hard, not feeling any relief from the panic inside me.

'Landi ... my life is nothing now. I can't work in my flower store. I can't drive. I can't walk without losing my balance. I can't socialize. I can't hear. I can't eat what I want ... I can't ride my bicycle. My independence has been stripped away. Every moment is lived in fear of a vertigo attack, even while I sleep. I will never hear silence, or peace and quiet again, with the five impossibly loud sounds of tinnitus, incessantly torturing me. Meniere's has taken everything from me ... *everything* ... except family!'

'Gram ... we can beat it, together!' I said, nodding my head. There was a pain in the back of my throat.

'There's no cure, Yolande. No. Cure!'

'There is—we'll find it. We'll fund research. We've already set up a Meniere's account at Flowers for Fleur, and we've been raising money. We'll employ doctors to find the cure. It's there. I know it is—waiting to cure everyone who has it—including you. Together, Gram, let's find the cure ... let's make a difference!' I was frantic.

Gram looked down again, and a moment of time felt like a thousand years. She looked at Gramps. 'I love you, forever and a day. Start singing, my love.'

My eyes darted over to Gramps. I had difficulty swallowing

and I started to shiver.

Gramps stepped forward and took Gram's other hand and kissed it. 'Fleur, my love,' Grampapa's voice fractured. 'I will love you until my dying breath ... I will grieve until we are together again.' He let go of Gram's hand and stepped back from her.

Nausea rose in my stomach. I placed my hand over my heart where it felt like it was bursting out of my chest. 'No, Gramps, no—no—no! Remember how you felt when you first met Gram?' My words were ridiculously fast.

'Landi,' Gram said with a haunting peacefulness. 'It's okay. You know how to run Flowers for Fleur. I've been training you for three months now. The business is left to you in the will.' I released a short quiet squeal. Gram had already given up.

'No! This—' I waved my hand over the building. 'This ... is not an option. What if, you're not allowed to take your own life, and you won't be singing with the angels ... ever?'

Gram looked at me, her eyes wide.

'There's treatments you haven't tested yet. Try the gentamicin, Gram. It will stop the vertigo attacks!'

'But it will destroy my balance on that side ...'

'You will learn to balance using your sight. The brain will relearn. And I'll be there with you, step by step ... please, Gram ... please,' I sobbed. 'I love you ... I couldn't bear it if you left—and it would be my fault because I didn't save you.' I let out a loud, sharp sob. I didn't want to cry, I had tried to be emotionally strong, but this was beyond heartbreaking.

Gram's eyes softened. 'Oh, my dear Yolande. I wish it was all so simple.' Her voice was gentle.

'Nothing good is simple, Gram. You told me yourself—remember—when I was little, trying to do ballet while learning my own version of rocket science—remember? There were cupcakes baking in the oven, Gramps was singing, and you and I were sipping on hot chocolate solving the world's, and my problems … remember?'

Gram gave a loving smile. 'How could I forget?' She stared at me for a moment. 'Yolande, what have you done?' Gram's voice was impossibly higher.

'What do you mean, Gram?' My eyes widened while my heart thudded in my chest.

'I found an escape—a way to escape from the Meniere's … when I fell into that memory, of that time we had together, it was just me and you, and no Meniere's. I was free, just for a moment.' Gram looked at me with a wide smile. She turned her body fully towards me. 'I want to explore that more … distraction over Meniere's … I think I can do it!'

'Yes, you can, Gram—we can!' I smiled back at her, my heart leaping with joy, but it vanished.

Gram wobbled on her feet—and slipped.

I fell forward at the tug of Gram's hand in mine. My shoulder seared with pain as I was reefed forward. But I held her hand tightly. I slid along the rooftop until I stopped at the raised ledge, where my knees hit and stopped me from going further, from free falling, with Gram.

I squeezed my eyes shut and held on to her hand impossibly tighter, and I would never let go … I would *never* let go. I didn't want to remember Gram as the color of broken, nor let her last breath be the color of broken.

Gram's scream pierced the air. 'Don't let go, Yolande!' she yelled.

'It's okay, Gram. I've got you!' I yelled.

I could hear Grampapa's desperate mumbled pleas beside me. Then he started singing, like a final good-bye.

'Stop singing, Gramps! Don't you dare utter another note!' I yelled, raging with anger. The pain in my hand and shoulder was horrendous, but I would *never* let go of Gram's hand.

I closed my eyes and groaned at the excruciating pain that

was ripping through me. *Please ... why wouldn't somebody help?*

I sent a silent prayer to heaven. The exact same prayer I had said on that terrible day of the scars with Mia.

When I opened my eyes, another hand reached down to Gram. It didn't belong to Gramps. But I knew those fingers ... those beautiful fingers; that lovely warm hand.

'It's okay, Gram. We're okay ... our rescuer is here.'

Gram let out a sob.

Xander pulled Gram and lifted her back onto the rooftop.

I fell onto my back and looked up into the sky. *Since when is the sky so blue?* My heart hammered against my chest and my shoulder throbbed, rhythmically.

I looked over at Gram. Dr. Alexander Parker was beside her, holding her hand, guiding her to breathe to calmness.

He was the color of bold blue: protection.

He looked over at me and I gave him a quick nod. I was okay, except for my shoulder. In fact, I was more than okay. My heart was bursting with love for the man I trusted with my life.

Earned, not given.

Chapter Thirty-Eight

Xander sat on the end of my hospital bed. 'How's the pain?'

'I'll cope.' I gave him a fake smile.

Xander gazed into my eyes and a sadness fell over his beautiful face. 'You could've died with your grandmother.'

'I had it sorted. I was anchored on the ledge.'

'And dislocated your shoulder and did major damage to muscle and ligaments that only surgery could fix!'

'Better that than the other alternative.' I shuddered.

'Absolutely.'

'Thanks for saving us. You placed yourself in a danger, too.'

'I had it sorted. I was anchored on the ledge,' he said, and raised an eyebrow at me.

'How's Gram?' I clenched my teeth together as a wave of pain hit me.

'She's had gentamicin injected into her middle ear in the hope that it stops the vertigo. There's other treatment options, but she chose to try the gentamicin. She's also having counseling, and has a support system in place. You're on her support team.'

'Good,' I said and pressed the button for a morphine fix. I

looked up at Xander, and sighed when the medication took effect. The last thing I saw was Xander's blue eyes gazing into mine, emitting that light I so wanted to sample.

'Are you sure you're ready to tell me what happened on that day?' Dr. Jones asked.

I was lying on the couch facing away from her. That way I wouldn't see her reaction to the story I was about to entrust to her. Not that she ever showed reactions to anything I said. But today, I needed to tell someone the entire story, not the censored, edited one that six other people knew, who reacted with a sense of terror—bulging eyes and a stiffened body, followed by tears and reaching out to hold me.

I sipped on the tea she had served me today. It was divine. I think she added a dose of courage to it. 'I'll never be ready. But keeping it inside is like being self-destructive.'

'Yolande, you can either tell the story in first person, or third, like you are detached from the situation and looking on. Which do you think you will use?'

'First person. I need to express what I was feeling through the entire event.'

'Good. When you're ready ...'

I took another sip of the tea and placed the cup back onto the saucer, the clink of the china sounding too loud. I lay back on the couch and placed my hands on my stomach, my fingers entwined, then knotting together. I looked up at the ceiling and watched the shadows of plants dance on the ceiling, like they were celebrating a moment of significance.

I took a deep, shaky breath.

'Mia was a party girl. She loved the music, the drinks, the laughter, the dancing ... she loved flirting with men, taking it as far as she could go without any intimacy. She's my best friend and I love her for eternity. I was always her anchor. When she went too far, riding on the moment, I would pull her back in, saving her from embarrassment, or regret.'

I took another sip of tea. Of courage.

'On that day we were at a party. A day party, which was unusual. Two men walked into the party room, unknown to the birthday boy. They were the color blue, a safe color. They were good looking men. Buffed and full of self-confidence. A magnet for Mia ... she found them at once and started flirting with them while I watched from the distance, unsure about their type, that intuition type of feeling. But Mia was having a ball.'

I cleared my throat.

'The one named Jack, put his arm around Mia's shoulders and led her outside. His mate, Johnno, followed. And so I followed from a safe distance behind. When Mia got into a car with them, I ran up to her and opened her door.

"Mia, I have something insane to show you!" I grabbed her hand to pull her out of the car, to stop her from making a mistake.

'But Johnno was behind me. I could smell the stench of the liquor he'd been drinking. He gave me a firm shove and I landed across Mia's lap in the back seat. I heard and felt the car door shut. And then another door closed. But by the time I had raised myself up, Jack was driving the car away from the party.

'"Where are we going?" I asked, taking note of the scenery around us, and looking for a moment of slow speed where Mia and I could jump out of the moving car. Their color was no longer blue. It had become red, bright red: danger.

"Up to the outlook to watch the sunset. It's amazing at this time of the year."

'My heart slowed down a little. There would be heaps of people at the outlook watching the view. It would be okay.

'But the outlook was different to the one I knew. Jack had

to follow a bumpy, rugged, off-road track to get there. When he stopped the engine, he turned to us. "This is the real party, girls!"

'Jack and Johnno got out of the car. They gripped our wrists and pulled us out of the back seat. They pushed us down onto the grass and laughed. I kept my eyes on them. We had to run.

'Jack pulled out a bag of white powder from his pocket and snorted it, then handed it to Johnno, who did the same. In an instant, their unlikeable demeanor became surly and repulsive ...'

I swallowed and shook my head. I couldn't do this. I couldn't say any more about the events out loud. It was like a black monster growing larger inside me with every word I spoke. And it scared me. I didn't want to unleash it. Not yet. Not today. I closed my eyes and brushed my shaking hand over my forehead and up into my hair.

'That's all I can tell you right now, Dr. Jones,' I lied. I wouldn't be telling her, or anyone the entire event that changed my life on that terrible day of the scars.

'Thank you for trusting me to share a part of your difficult story, Yolande. If you'd like to tell me more, I'm here when you are ready.'

I turned and faced her. 'I will. Thanks,' I said with a calm voice that betrayed the turmoil inside of me. I wanted to run out the door, and never return.

I stood and brushed my sweaty hands down my jeans.

Dr. Jones stood a moment after me. 'You need to talk to Mia.'

I nodded my head. If she had told me once, she had told me a thousand times. I took six long strides, and I was out of her office.

For good.

Chapter Thirty-Nine

'Flowers, tea, coffee or books?' The words rolled off my tongue with a melodic sound. It felt like the millionth time I had said it. It probably was. The couple who stood before me were the same color, purple—wisdom and spirituality.

'One of each, please.'

I beamed a megawatt smile at the couple before me. This was an insane moment! A quadfecta! I had never sold all four at once. UN-believable! I looked around to see if someone was playing a trick on me. Nope. Although I had my suspicions, and they rested with Darcy.

'What type of flowers would you like?'

'Star of Bethlehem if you have it. If not, irises and some peonies—hope and healing.'

I stilled for a moment and thought of Gram. Hope and healing. It's also what I needed too. 'I'm thinking of an outstanding bouquet that boasts of the secret language of flowers that will permeate the air with hope and healing for you. I need to go the workbench and put the collection of blooms together. Meanwhile, please go over to Darcy, our barista, and have a tea and coffee on the house. Tell Darcy that Andi sent you. The books are on the shelf to the left to the café.' I watched as they walked away, happy.

I opened Gram's order book and wrote down the flower recipe I was about to create. Heavy footsteps stopped before me.

'Flowers, tea, coffee, or books?' I asked without looking at the person, breaking my own rule.

'Thanks,' said a familiar voice. I looked up at Gramps. He was smiling at me. He was the color of yellow, with a new enthusiasm for life. 'How's your shoulder?'

'Better now, after six weeks ... more importantly, how's Gram?'

'She's so happy, Landi. She has more hope than she's ever had with this disease. Her ear has healed well after the injection of gentamicin, and she's been vertigo free for five weeks now. But it's still early days. We're taking one day at a time and capturing precious moments while we can.'

I smiled at Gramps and put my hand on his arm. 'It's good news then.' *It was Gram's answered prayer.*

'Yes. I can't thank you enough. What you have done for Gram ...' he shook his head, 'and me ... I still have my Fleur, my beautiful Fleur—' His eyes teared up.

'It's okay, Gramps. It's the way it should be. We're still together, and that's what counts.'

'Yes,' he said. 'It does.'

'When is Gram returning to her flowers?'

'Tomorrow.' He beamed a sunshiny smile at me. I hadn't seen that smile for a long time.

'Good. I can't wait,' I said. 'Now, Gramps, I hate to cut our conversation short, but I have flowers and customers to attend to. See you tomorrow, shall I?'

'Of course.'

I pulled out my phone.

ME: *Xander, will you do something for me?*

XANDER: *Anything.*

ME: *Will you drive me to Mia's. I need to talk to her.*

XANDER: *Sure.*

I sat on the steps of Flowers for Fleur, holding a large bouquet of pink roses, waiting. I had something I had to do, for me, and for Mia.

Xander stopped the car and walked around to the passenger door and opened it for me. I waved my free hand about at him, and he raised an eyebrow at me.

'Thanks for doing this,' I said while he drove.

He looked over at me for a moment. 'I'm yours, any time you want, or need.'

I placed my hand on his thigh and closed my eyes for a moment. I didn't want to visit her, but it had to be done.

I opened my eyes, and the split rail fence of Mr. Johnson's clover field came into view. The paddock was bursting with clover, more now than ever, much more than when Mia and I had stolen time there together.

'Stop here. There's something I need to do.'

Xander pulled the car over to the side of the road and I got out before he could open my door. I jogged across the road.

'Yolande?' he called after me.

I turned to him from across the road. 'Come with me,' I said, and ducked between the timber rails of the fence. I heard the car door close, and turned to see Xander jogging, before he jumped over the fence, one hand on the top wooden rail.

I stood before the field of clover, a mass of white flowers with green peeking through, and pink. I looked for a pathway between the bees that visited the clover flowers, buzzing around happily, unaware.

I took slow steps, avoiding the bees until I found a comfortable patch to lay on, stomach down amongst the clover. I watched as the bees flitted from flower to flower, a safe distance away.

'Do you have a death wish?' Xander said when he stopped before me, then rested on his stomach next to me after checking for the deadly bees.

Once upon a time, yes, but not now. 'No,' I said, and picked clover flowers with long stalks and started to split the stem and thread a new flower stem through it to make a garland of clover, like a crown.

'Mia and I used to come here and make princess crowns.' I looked up at Xander. He held a crooked smile on his face and my heart fluttered. I worked quickly with the flowers and completed the garland, then lifted it to place on top of Xander's head. I smiled at him.

'Does that make me a princess now?' he asked.

I laughed at his words. But not too loudly, lest Mr. Johnson hear and chase us out of his clover field in his bee-suit that made him look like an angry astronaut.

I placed my hand over the top of Xander's and threaded my fingers between his. 'Only if I can be the prince,' I said.

Xander smirked at me and raised his forearm so the back of my hand rested against his lips. His kiss, right there, right then, was the most perfect thing in the entire world, melting my insides, making me feel all gooey la-la.

He took the crown of clover off his head and placed it onto mine and paused for a moment. I wondered if something was amiss, like he had suddenly seen my darkness.

I swallowed as anxiety bubbled inside of me and took a deep breath. 'Is something wrong?' I asked, not wanting to hear his next words.

'Quite the opposite. It couldn't be more right,' he said, and kissed my forehead. When he opened his eyes, he was drinking me in, surrounding me with a light and love that I wanted to touch my soul. It took all my restraint not to reach out to him, to place my lips upon his. I stole my eyes from his and picked a clover flower and twirled it in my fingers.

'Do you want to know what happened to me—you know ... how the scars came to be?'

He put a finger under my chin and lifted my face to his, gazing deeply into my eyes, searching.

My eyes stung with unspilt tears. 'You know ... just you and me and the deadly bees,' I said to lighten the mood.

Xander rolled onto his back and looked up into the cloudless sky. He blinked.

I placed my hand over his heart. 'I think you want to know, but I'm scared that you'll hate me,' I whispered, my voice wavering.

His hand covered mine with the lightest touch. He turned his head, so our eyes connected and locked, the blue of his eyes reflecting the color of the sky, making them luminous, like his soul.

'I could never hate you. No story you could ever tell me will change how I feel about you. This beautiful woman beside me is the one I want to be with, regardless of her past.' He stopped talking for a moment and my stomached churned with anxiety. 'It's your story to tell, Yolande, or not. Whatever you're comfortable with. And whatever your choice, I will understand without question.'

I placed my head on his chest and listened to the beat of his heart. There would be a risk in telling him what had happened. If things went wrong in our relationship, I would always blame it on him knowing the story of that terrible day of the scars, and exposing him to the darkness inside me that I try to conceal. It would always be something that would come between us, if not in his eyes, always in mine.

I decided not to tell him. I wanted to leave it in the past. I wanted a clean slate, and someone to look at me as the new person I had become—the new me who had ultimately grown stronger through tragedy—grown more compassionate, with more love to give than I could ever imagine, because of him. I wanted to be able to give him more, untainted by my past.

'I'm ready to visit Mia now,' I said, and sat up.

I looked around and waited for a clear path between the bees before I stood, then took careful steps out of the clover field with my garland on my head like a crown, Xander right behind me.

I fussed about Mia's flowers and sat beside her.

I looked back at Xander. He was leaning against the oak tree, his hands behind his back, waiting for me. He had the patience of a saint.

I blew air between my lips.

'Hi, Mia. It's been a while since we chatted. Three years in fact ... I'm so sorry I couldn't hold your hand tighter that afternoon. I tried so hard, you know. I broke nine ribs on that hanging tree. But I got off lightly compared to you ...'

I lowered my head and started to cry, my shoulders moving in time with each heavy sob.

I looked up at the blue sky and closed my eyes and let the memory of that terrible day of the scars come. It had been shut inside me for what seemed like forever. I needed to release it.

'Mia, I have something insane to show you!' I grabbed her hand to pull her out of the car, to stop her from making a mistake.

But Johnno was behind me. I could smell the hard liquor he'd been drinking. He gave me a firm shove and I landed across Mia's lap in the back seat. The door shut behind me, and then another door closed. By the time I had raised myself up, Jack was driving the car away from the party.

'Where are we going?' I asked, taking note of the scenery around us, looking for a moment of slow speed where Mia and I could jump out of the car. Their color was no longer blue. It had become red, bright red: danger.

'Up to the outlook to watch the sunset. It's amazing at this time of the year. You girls will love it!'

My heart calmed little. There would be heaps of people at the outlook watching the view. It would be okay. We would be okay.

But the outlook was different to the one I knew. Jack followed a bumpy, rugged, off-road track to get there. When he stopped the engine, he turned to us. 'This is the real party, girls!'

Jack and Johnno got out of the car. They gripped our wrists and pulled us out of the back seat. Jack hit the left side of my face as he pushed me down onto the grass and laughed. I kept my eyes on them as I felt my cheek smarting.

We had to run.

I stood, then reached down for Mia's hand and pulled her up beside me.

Jack pulled out a bag of white powder from his pocket and snorted it, then handed it to Johnno, who did the same. In an instant, their unlikeable demeanor became surly and repulsive ...

'Jack, that white shit is great. Do you see what we have here? I smell something mighty pleasurable ... two of 'em!'

Jack laughed. 'Look at what we have here ... two chicks!'

I clenched my fist. Chicks is such a demeaning word.

'You know why women hate some men, don't you—' I started.

'No more, Andi,' Mia whispered.

'Not that I would call either of you a man! Your violence shouts

of your weakness,' I continued.

'Shut the fuck up, bitch!' The sharp bite of Jack's hand stung my already bruised cheek.

'Coward,' I spat.

'Andi, not a word more, you're making them angrier!" Mia said, her voice trembling.

'Girls ... we need you naked ... take off your clothes, or we'll cut them off!'

I looked at Mia, enraged, then turned back to them. I didn't want their filthy hands to touch me. If they cut my clothes from me, I wouldn't have any clothes to put back on. So, I started to undo my buttons, lulling them into a false sense of control, then started to run. Past the car and into the trees, my heart belting in my chest as I sucked in precious breaths. I lengthened my stride, fuelled by my adrenaline, then fell. I had been ankle tapped.

My wrist smarted as Johnno wrapped his fingers around it, then pulled me back to Jack.

'Chasing games are fun,' Jack said. 'Now be a good girl and take off your clothes like Mia.'

I scowled at him, then closed my eyes and did as he asked. I removed every stitch of my clothing until I was standing naked, beside Mia.

Jack laughed, then pushed Mia to the ground. He took a swig of vodka, then started to unbuckle his belt.

I turned my head away and tried to shut out Mia's desperate voice. 'No! Please ... don't. Stop! Leave me alone!'

Fury built inside me. I turned my eyes back to Jack. It was time to mess with his head to stop his violent violation.

He pushed his jeans down. No underwear. His cherished appendage popped up and bounced.

I giggled, while suppressing the need to vomit.

He looked at me and I giggled again. Get away, Mia, make your move, I mind communicated to her.

'What?' he said.

'I thought it would be bigger.'

He ran his hand along his length. 'Big enough for fucking.'

'Oh wait—is it getting smaller?' It wasn't, but planting the thought in his head might do the trick.

He took a step towards me.

I tilted my head to the side and pretended to study his penis. 'I'm pretty sure that alcohol you're drinking will cause erectile dysfunction.'

He looked at his drink.

'You know Mia has the clap, don't you?' I was lying, of course.

He looked at me as if he didn't know what I was talking about.

'You know … a sexually transmitted infection … genital herpes to be exact. You'll end up with painful blisters on your …' I twirled my finger in the air while looking at his penis, then pointed at it, '… your dick. And they'll recur for your entire life.'

I could see Mia inching backwards on the ground. Good girl.

The whack echoed when he slapped my face. Hard. My cheek stung before pain set in. I seethed inside.

Johnno looked down at the knife he held in his grubby hand and grinned. He turned it from side to side, the light reflecting off it, onto my face. My eyes burned. I didn't want to cry in front of these despicable human beings. I widened my eyes to contain my tears, but I was betrayed by one. I looked up at Johnno's face. His eyes followed my tear as it rolled down my cheek to my jawline, where it stopped.

I swallowed, slowly, as I felt the tear gaining volume and become too heavy to stop there. It dropped onto my chest and trickled down to my nipple.

'Who's the weak one now? You're crying, like a typical girl!' He moved the point of the blade to where the tear started on my cheekbone, just below my eye.

The point of the knife pierced my skin. I closed my eyes as I felt the sharp cutting of my flesh, with a searing pain that screamed at my core. With a slow, torturous speed, the tip of the knife traced the path of my tear—down my cheek to my jawline, then onto my chest. I held my breath as the knife followed my tear in a direct path to my nipple—piercing, cutting, tearing. He stopped at my areola.

I swallowed, hard, standing dead still. Everything inside me was trembling. I could feel blood running down my face, dripping, onto my chest, dribbling, gaining volume and running further down my naked body, pooling at my feet.

'Get on your knees. You will bow to me, slut,' Jack said.

'I bow to no human! Look up.' I tried to stop my shaking.

He looked up, then looked back at me and narrowed his eyes. 'Bitch. You'll die!'

Mia scrambled beside me. She threaded her fingers through mine. She was trembling, her breaths short and hard. I wanted to collapse on the ground, but I couldn't. I had to hold myself together. I didn't want the bastards to win.

Jack lifted his hand to my throat but stopped at the sound of a noise. I changed my grip with Mia, so it was tighter.

Car lights appeared, and Johnno pushed us.

Over the cliff edge.

They say time is constant. It never changes. But I swear when Mia and I were falling that time slowed down. Everything in my life flashed before my eyes, and I knew it would be the end. At least I was with my best friend ...

'Ugh!' I moaned, as my breath was punched out of me when I became wedged on a tree jutting out from the cliff face. I groaned when I felt a terrible, sharp pain, every time I inhaled the salty air. It was impossibly hard to breathe.

Mia's hand was still in mine. I could feel it. Gripping tightly. I looked down. Firstly, at the jagged rocks far below beside the sea, then at my hand holding on to Mia's. It was covered in roads of blood. My blood. Mia was dangling mid-air and our eyes connected. My chest constricted. The pain in my chest was unbearable and my shoulder was agony. I couldn't keep hold of her for much longer.

I watched as a drop of my blood dripped onto her face. Right there, in the middle of her forehead, like she was marked. Another drop of blood fell. She turned her head and it landed on her cheek. Like the kiss of death.

She turned her face back to mine. 'I'm terrified, Oliander,' Mia said, using my childhood nickname. Her voice was filled with terror.

'I've got you, Mamma Mia,' I replied with her nickname.

'Tell my parents I love them ... and my brother.'

'You tell them yourself, Mee. Hear those sirens?'

Mia's hand slipped a little more. A little closer to death.

There were shouts of voices from above and hope bloomed. Just a little longer and we'll be rescued. Just a little longer ...

I felt Mia's hand slip a fraction more. But it was more than enough. Her eyes widened in that exact split second and our hands parted.

'Miiiaaaaa!' I yelled as she fell. I squeezed my eyes shut as her scream pierced my ears. I couldn't bear to watch her hit the rocks below.

And then her scream stopped.

The silence of death.

Nausea made its ugly arrival and I vomited. Hard. I opened my eyes and Mia was there. On the rocks below. Her arm moved. She's alive?

I sobbed as I balanced on the hanging tree. I moved my hand that was holding Mia's. It was covered in blood. My blood. I watched as, drip by drip, it fell to the jagged rocks below.

Where were our rescuers?

A net fell beside me. And there was a man with safety gear, looking at me in my nakedness. I looked up at him and felt the blood dripping from my face.

He swallowed. Hard. He spoke to another man on the other side of me. But the words were a jumble as the sound of a helicopter hovered nearby.

I vomited, and my vision faded.

I wiped the tears from my face. 'It's your favorite type of day today, Mia. A blue sky with funny floaty clouds. It's the type of day where we would gather up our kites and go fly them at the park, seeing whose kite could touch the clouds first. Remember all the times our kites ended up in the trees and we would have to climb them to get our kites back. So much fun.' I smiled.

I looked over at Xander. 'I found someone who likes to climb trees as much as we did. You'd like him. He's a beautiful danseur. That beautiful danseur with the boy germs—do you remember him? You went gooey over him when we were eight and told me a story about the two of you, and I made a funny dark twist to your tale.'

I wiped more tears from my face. My scar would normally be visible now, but the surgery to make it invisible had been successful.

I took out my handkerchief and wiped Mia's headstone. It was shiny now. Like Mia's soul light. I placed the clover garland on the corner of it, then lay on my stomach on top of her grave. 'I love you so much it hurts. I miss you every single day. Sometimes I wish I had died with you.'

I breathed in the scent of the grass and the dirt.

'I have something to leave with you, Mia. I added sparkles to them because you would have said that the sparkles were ridiculous. But the sparkles remind me of you—your eyes would sparkle when you saw me, and when you thought of a new plan—a new adventure of mischief where we would get ourselves into a muddle and I would have to find the anti-muddle solution.'

I rolled onto my back and looked up at the sky. I thought I could hear her singing. I sat up and untied the laces to my steel-capped safety work boots. I took them off and placed them next to her headstone.

'I don't need these anymore. I figured they would keep you laughing, because I would wear them with every type of clothing. Everywhere. It was so uncouth! Sometimes I even wore them to bed, mud and all. Underneath them, a long time ago, I carved some pictures. On the right shoe is a flower garden with you and me sitting together—we're groovy stick people. You're sticking your tongue out at me.' I smiled. 'On the other right shoe— remember our joke—I carved your name backward with a heart, so everywhere I walked, I would leave your name, and you would never be forgotten. You'd be with me, always.'

I lay on my stomach on top of Mia's grave again and spread my arms wide, like I was hugging her.

My tears came, heavily. 'You know how we both wanted to be clean-skins—no tattoos—and made a pinky promise? Well, I broke our promise. I have a tattoo. I had to take my shirt and bra off to have it tattooed. The tattoo artist smiled when I exposed my chest to him! I have a heart over my heart, with your name in it ... I love you forever, Mia. Xander will probably get jealous of the tattoo if he ever sees me naked. He's under the tree watching us. He has the most beautiful soul, and a luminous heart. I'm totally in love with him but I haven't told him yet. I wanted to make sure that you liked him first.'

I stilled when a breeze came from nowhere, and upon it the scent of Mia's favorite perfume—J'adore by Dior—the lovely rose and jasmine notes. I smiled. 'I'll take that as a yes.'

I kissed my hand and blew it towards the sky to Mia. 'Make sure you're dancing with the angels up there. I'll come and join you one day, far in the future. I love you, Mia, forever and a day.'

I wiped my eyes and stood, took a deep breath then walked over to Xander with bare feet, the soft green grass caressing each of my steps. He wrapped his arms around me, being careful of my shoulder.

He kissed my forehead. 'Are you wearing perfume?'

'No,' I said. 'What do you smell?'

'Rose and something else.'

'Me too,' I said, and wiped away a tear, profoundly aware that I felt my own color shift.

I was no longer the color of broken—the color of crackled dark gray with an "a" with other colors that seeped out … drips of red for anger, specks of black for self-hate, blushes of pink for my love for Mia and my family, and explosions of turquoise that screamed at me to love myself.

I was now grey with an "e", where deep thought, philosophy and ponderings happened, and it would vanish without leaving a bitter aftertaste.

I smiled. My heart felt lighter. 'I'm ready to go.'

Chapter Forty

There was a note in the flowers of Gram's bicycle basket. I pulled it out and opened it.

Dear Yolande,

I found a tree you will adore.
Be waiting for me at 6pm.

Love Alexander ❀

I smiled and folded the note and pushed it into my pocket. I couldn't wait for 6pm.

I sat on the steps of Flowers for Fleur at 5.55 and waited.

On the dot of six, Xander arrived with perfect timing. He got out of his car and opened the door for me. I stood, and waved my hands about at him while I walked towards his car.

'I know. But I'm looking after you,' he said.

Xander stopped at the familiar hall where we used to practise our ballroom dancing. He held my hand and pulled me around to the yard behind the hall. He turned to me with a huge smile on his face as a tree came into view. A very large, old tree, with the best climbing branches I'd ever seen. Mia would have loved it.

Xander stopped before the tree. He gazed into my eyes and ran his fingers down my arm, leaving a trail of fire in its wake, before he squatted down and removed my shoes.

'You go first. I'm right behind you,' he said.

I looked up at the branches and climbed, giggling. When I found the perfect branch, I sat on it, swinging my legs.

Xander sat next to me, our thighs touching.

I inhaled his scent—a spicy blend of cedarwood and cocoa-vanilla, that reminded me of slumbering in a hammock on a hot summer day, and watermelon and iced tea. I drew in a calming breath. His presence was making me all gooey la-la.

'It's a beautiful tree,' I said.

'It depends,' he said.

'On what?' I asked.

He pulled my hand into his, and a heavenly tingle shot up my arm. 'On whether you're staying here or going back to the Base.'

I lifted my finger to his jawline and traced it. My heart thudded as the silence stretched between us. 'I've taken leave ... for a little while ... for Gram.'

Xander breathed deeply. 'I like that you've taken leave,' he said. He closed his eyes, and when he opened them, they were filled with light.

My breath hitched, and I was suddenly aware I had never felt like this; lit up, made new.

'I thought you would,' I whispered. He was turning my insides into all kinds of crazy.

He shifted his gaze from my eyes to my lips, and I was filled with nervous energy. I looked away and ran my fingers over the rough bark of the tree branch. I needed to change our focus before my desire intensified for him. 'What disease did you decide to study in biomedical science?' I asked.

'Meniere's. I'm going to be the one to find a cure!'

'Gram will love you then.' I leaned into him, enjoying the spark arcing between us, making my knees feel weak.

'I think she already does,' he said, his eyes connecting to mine.

'Somehow, I think she does too,' I said, bathing in the adoration I saw in his eyes. 'What about your dancing, Prince Siegfried?'

Xander's eyes twinkled and a captivating smile spread across his beautiful face. 'I'm not giving it up. I'll find a balance between dancing and research.'

My heart smiled, and the sunset seemed more spectacular than I had ever seen before. I cast my eyes to where heaven touched the earth, painting the sky with the glorious colors of scarlet, tangerine, dusty pink and violet. It was breathtakingly majestic, and filled with hope.

We sat in the tree in silence, our fingers entwined, then he tucked my hand between both of his, holding on as if I was someone to be adored and protected.

'The rain is coming. We should go,' Xander said. He climbed down the tree, branch by branch, and I followed.

As I approached the lower section of the tree trunk, Xander put his hands on my waist like a danseur would. He helped me to a soft landing on the grass and I turned and smiled at him.

He stilled and gazed into my eyes, and I became lost in the intense hypnotic love that swirled there. 'Will you be mine, now?' he asked, his voice wavering.

I exhaled a slow breath between my lips, trying to control the exhilarating, and terrifying feeling flashing through me like an electrical storm.

Xander tilted his head to the side a little, his eyes smoldering. 'I ... I—'

He placed his finger under my chin and lifted my face to his. I felt the pull of his blue eyes, his soul caressing mine. I placed my hand on the side of his face, his skin warm to the touch, and looked at his sensuous lips. I ran my thumb over them, needing him to kiss me.

I closed my eyes as his soft lips touched mine. Once. Twice. Caressing. Lingering. Sending a warmth through every cell of my body, awakening parts of me I now allowed to open. He pulled away slightly, his lips still touching, and I sagged against him, overcome with intoxicating pleasure that seeped into all those broken crevices inside me, healing.

Our lips parted. 'Please don't run from me this time,' he whispered. His gaze searched mine as if he was looking for something.

The first drops of rain began to fall as I pressed my hand to his chest, over his heart. His hand covered mine, and the gentleness of it took my breath away. His gaze shifted from my eyes to my lips, and back to my eyes, with a vulnerability that sent a ripple of pain through my chest.

His eyes softened with tenderness then, and I became completely lost in him, bathing in the love and light he offered me. He frowned. 'I love you, be mine ...' he said, his voice barely audible.

My breath caught, and tears stung my eyes. I had something to give him—my heart.

'Yes,' I whispered, profoundly aware of my beautiful new color shift, filled with calescent pink like in the center of a cherry blossom flower, reminding me of a cloudless, warm spring day, sitting under a Kawazuzakura cherry tree beside a peaceful blue lake, breathing in a hint of the floral, bittersweet aroma.

I gazed into his luminous blue eyes and breathed deeply, inhaling his scent of blended spicy cedarwood and cocoa-vanilla. Warmth rushed through me as his color shone brightly: indigo-blue, swirling with healing turquoise.

Xander brushed a ringlet of hair from my face, his brows creased with barely controlled emotion, then our eyes locked. I rose up onto my tiptoes, my lips close to his, and felt a sacred energy flowing between us as he moved his mouth to mine, his lips caressing with a tenderness that splintered everything, and changed everything as our souls touched.

I closed my eyes and bathed in the ecstasy of the sensual, unconditional love that bound our hearts, our minds, and our essence, while time stood still.

And in that moment I knew, that I, Yolande Lawrence-Harrison, was no longer the color of broken ...

Meniere's Disease

Prosper Menière (18 June 1799 – 7 February 1862) was a French doctor who first identified a medical condition combining vertigo, hearing loss and tinnitus, which is now known as Menière's disease. It's a disorder of the inner ear.

Very briefly, Meniere's disease causes episodes of:
- *vertigo* (episodes of feeling like the world is spinning)
- *tinnitus* - ranging from mild to severe.
- *a feeling of fullness* or pressure in the ear,
- *sudden falls* without loss of consciousness (*drop attacks*) may be experienced by some people, or a sensation of being pushed sharply to the floor from behind.
- *low-frequency hearing loss,* which usually fluctuates in the beginning stages and becomes more permanent in later stages, so that little or no hearing remains.
- a common and important symptom of MD is hypersensitivity to sounds, also known as *hyperacusis.*

Attacks may be characterized by periods of remission and exacerbation. After a severe attack, most people find that they are extremely exhausted and must sleep for several hours. People with Meniere's disease may suffer from psychological distress, high anxiety and depression.

It is important to note that many people suffering from MD lead productive, near-normal lives; others face greater challenges in coping.
There is no cure for Meniere's disease - yet. But with advances in medicine and research, there is always hope for a cure.

Further Information and Support

- *Brain Foundation Australia*
http://brainfoundation.org.au/disorders/menieres-disease
- *Meniere Society - UK*
www.menieres.org.uk
- *Vestibular Disorders Association - USA*
http://vestibular.org/menieres-disease

MEDICAL DISCLAIMER:
The information provided is designed to support, not replace, the relationship that exists between a patient and his/her existing health care professionals.

SUICIDE/CRISIS HELP: The events in this book are fictional. However, if you are feeling suicidal, visit **Suicide.org** for a list for worldwide numbers to call
http://www.suicide.org/international-suicide-hotlines.html
or **1-800-SUICIDE** or **1-800-784-2433**
Suicide is never the answer. Getting help is the answer. *Take my hand . . .*

Acknowledgements

This novel kept nudging me to write it for two years but I kept shutting it down because emotionally I wasn't ready to write it. Once I allowed myself to begin to engage with the characters in my mind and on paper, the story fell onto the pages. It's a story that had to be told, trying to give a true representation of what living with Meniere's disease is really like, warts and all—no sugar coating, no brushing over it, no minimizing the symptoms. If you have Meniere's disease, this book is to *honor* you, and your families, who can only look on as spectators of your life. I have written *The Color of Broken* with dedication, passion, and a deluge of tears.

My biggest thanks goes to my husband, for his forever support and understanding that writing is the only place where I can escape from my incurable disease.

Thank you to my three children, who have all at some time or another, stood beside my bed and held my hand for a little bit, while I suffered from the torturous violent vertigo. *Take my hand . . .*

A heartfelt thank you to my dear mum and dad, who always dropped everything the moment I went into a spinning session (I used to call it a SPAT – spinning attack), which was often, and would come to take care of my three kids, and me.

A huge thanks to my beta readers - Michelle Upton, Shez Kennington, Belinda Hind, Alice Wooley, David C. (psychiatric nurse) & Virve M. (psychologist). Your feedback was gold.

A massive thank you also to my editor ✤

And to you, the reader of this novel, thank you for choosing to read my fictional story. It means more to me than you can ever know! ✤ ✤ ✤

Finally, thank you to my Creator, for always carrying me through the terrifying storm, for giving me hope when it felt like there was none, and for giving me a Light to hold on to in the darkness so I could find my way back home.

The artwork of Yolande,
created in her studio haven, from *Chapter Nineteen*.

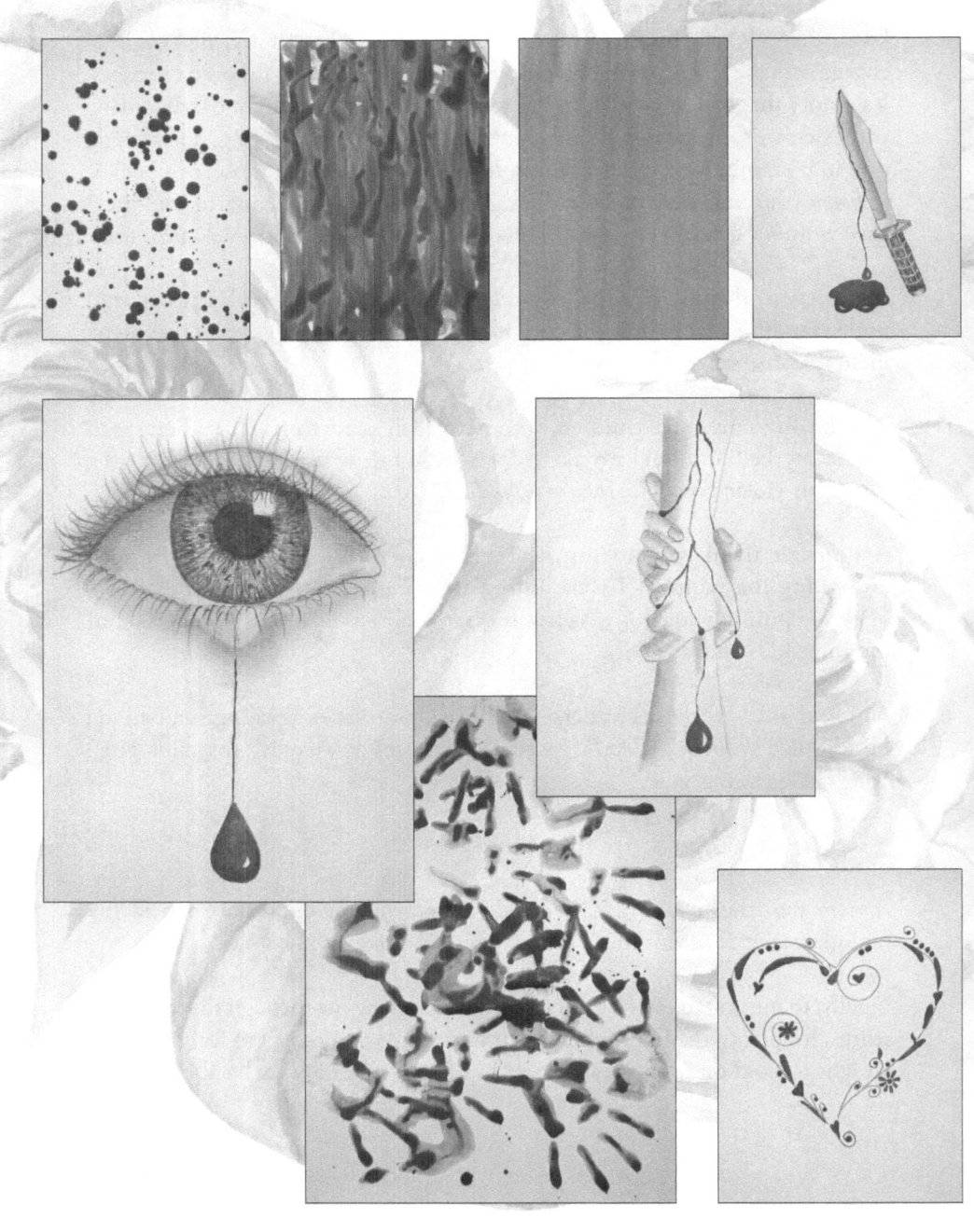

The sequel to *The Color of Broken*

All the Colours Above

Mirror. Mirror.
Two mirrors. Two of me.
Who am I?

INDIGO FEATHER DANUBE is a neuroscientist studying memories, how to access them, then remove them, *digitally*.

One day, her parents implore her to attend a reunion at the park of her youth, where TOBIAH BROOKS dares her to climb the Jacaranda tree of her childhood. But first, *she must remember who he is.*

They meet before sundown, with Indigo's intention to succeed at the dare, then leave. But his intention is to win her heart. Tobiah orchestrates a secret rendezvous at the Jacaranda tree on the luminous full moon, when it's light enough to see, but dark enough to cloak their presence. No one could possibly know they were there once a month. *Together. Alone.*

Every story has a beginning. At the beginning of Indigo and Tobiah's story, is a girl who meets a boy. A girl who wasn't in the habit of falling in love, until her heart bloomed like a thousand red roses with the scent of citrus, spice, and sweet fruit, surrounded by a dreamy and exhilarating melody of love. Until ... that day that can't be *undone*. On that day of the wish that can't be *unwished*. And that moment in time ... when she learned the *truth*.

Print book available at online bookstores
eBook available at Amazon

www.ingramcontent.com/pod-product-compliance
Lightning Source LLC
Chambersburg PA
CBHW060243030726
47493CB00025B/1594